THE LAST LETTER HOME

The Emigrant Novels

———————

Book I
THE EMIGRANTS
Utvandrarna

Book II
UNTO A GOOD LAND
Invandrarna

Book III
THE SETTLERS
Nybyggarna

Book IV
THE LAST LETTER HOME
Sista brevet till Sverige

THE EMIGRANT NOVELS
Book IV

THE LAST LETTER HOME

Vilhelm Moberg

Translated from the Swedish by Gustaf Lannestock
With a New Introduction by Roger McKnight

BOREALIS
BOOKS

The characters and situations in this work are wholly fictional;
they do not portray and are not intended to portray any actual persons.

Borealis Books is an imprint of the Minnesota Historical Society Press.
www.borealisbooks.org

The Minnesota Historical Society Press is a member of the
Association of American University Presses.

Manufactured in the United States of America

10 9 8 7

∞ The paper used in this publication meets the minimum requirements of the American
National Standard for Information Sciences—Permanence for Printed Library Materials,
ANSI Z39.48–1984.

International Standard Book Number
ISBN 13: 978-0-87351-322-7
ISBN 10: 0-87351-322-3

Library of Congress Cataloging-in-Publication Data
Moberg, Vilhelm, 1898–1973.
[Sista brevet till Sverige. English]
The last letter home / Vilhelm Moberg.
p. cm. — (The emigrant novels / Vilhelm Moberg ; bk. 4) (Borealis books)
ISBN 0-87351-322-3 (paper)
1. Swedish Americans—History—19th century—Fiction.
I. Title. II. Series: Moberg, Vilhelm, 1898–1973.
Romanen om utvandrarna. English ; bk. 4.
PT9875.M5S513 1995
839.73′72—dc20
95-15845

A note on the pronunciation of the Swedish names

å is pronounced like the *a* in *small* (see *Småland,* literally *Small Land*)

ä is pronounced like the *a* in *add*

ö is pronounced like the *ea* in *heard*

j is pronounced like *y*

CONTENTS

Introduction to the Emigrant Novels

Vilhelm Moberg: The Early Years

"HOT-TEMPERED, easily moved, and changeable" was how the Swedish novelist Vilhelm Moberg once described himself.[1] He might have added that in the first half of the twentieth century he was both the most widely admired and the most deeply distrusted of all Swedish authors. A man of humble origins but immense ambition and strong opinions, Moberg spent his entire literary life championing the rights of the common people. This tendency, combined with his volatile temperament, earned Moberg a deep, abiding respect from the general reading public while it created barriers for him among conservative critics, politicians, and religious leaders.

Moberg's biography has many elements of a rags-to-riches tale. He was born on August 28, 1898, in a small family cabin in southern Småland, historically one of the most impoverished areas of Sweden. The region had long been known as "darkest Småland" because of the people's conservative Lutheranism and reluctance to accept other religious views. During Moberg's childhood years, only one railroad station existed in the vicinity of his family home, and the horse was still the most common mode of transportation. Clothes were made locally and often paid for by barter.

Moberg's father was a career soldier who farmed a small plot of forest land. His mother, who lived into her nineties, cared for the family. Although Moberg in his later nonfictional works remembered this rustic setting as the spot "where I ran barefoot," his boyhood was one of hardship.[2] He received just five years of formal schooling and was the only boy in his family who survived to adulthood. Even in his fifties, Moberg recalled the frustration of trying to satisfy his hunger for learning in an environment where the teaching was poor and books scarce.

In his teens and early twenties, Moberg worked as a manual laborer, chiefly

1. Magnus von Platen, *Den unge Vilhelm Moberg. En levnadsteckning* (Stockholm: Bonniers, 1978), 310.
2. Vilhelm Moberg, "Där jag sprang barfota," *Berättelser ur min levnad* (Stockholm: Bonniers, 1968), 29–46.

among the lumberjacks and farm hands of Småland, and with great reluctance did his compulsory military service. His firsthand experiences from these years were later to serve as important motifs in his writings. Moberg left his parents' home in 1916 to attend adult continuing education school (*folkhögskola*) in Grimslöv. A nearly fatal bout of influenza brought his final attempt at formal schooling to an abrupt halt.

The enduring pattern of the aspiring writer's life emerged in the decade of the 1920s. He worked as a journalist for small-town newspapers in southern Sweden, met his future wife, and got his start as a novelist. This period began what his biographer Magnus von Platen has called "the gigantic day of work at the writing desk, which his life came to be."[3] Moberg was nothing if not indefatigable. In addition to the daily routine of writing news stories, setting type, and selling advertising space, he wrote several novels before having one accepted for publication.[4]

His literary breakthrough came in 1927 with *Raskens: en soldatfamiljs historia* (Raskens: the story of a soldier's family). This novel, set in rural Småland, established Moberg as a writer for and of the common people and solidified his place among the ranks of the renowned Swedish working-class novelists (*proletärförfattare*) of the 1920s and 1930s. These authors, including Jan Fridegård, Ivar Lo-Johansson, and Moa Martinsson, were the first in Swedish literature to describe the lives of the lower classes from the perspective of men and women who themselves had grown up among the working poor. Moberg's depictions of the customs and way of life in Småland constituted his major contribution to this group of writers. The local realism in his early fiction was the foundation on which his popularity in Sweden was built. It was not until the publication of his four great novels about Swedish emigration to Minnesota that his fame spread to other countries in Europe and across the Atlantic.

In 1929 Moberg moved north to Stockholm with his wife and family. Despite his restless spirit, he kept a permanent residence near that city until his death on August 8, 1973.

Moberg and Emigration

Since his childhood, America had been an ever-present reality for Moberg. Historically, this is not surprising. Of the 1.2 million emigrants who left Sweden for America between 1845 and 1930, more than three hundred thousand

---

3. Von Platen, *Den unge Vilhelm Moberg*, 9.
4. Moberg, "Från kolbitar till skrivmaskin," *Berättelser ur min levnad*, 119.

came from Småland. Moberg recalled the impact the waves of emigration had on him. In his collection of autobiographical essays, *Berättelser ur min levnad* (Tales of my life), he wrote that his mother and father came from families so poor that all their brothers and sisters emigrated to the United States, leaving only his parents to perpetuate their respective family lines in Sweden.[5] He claimed more relatives in America than in Sweden itself.

In his boyhood fancy, Moberg envisioned the word America as meaning "mer-rika" (more rich). The steady supply of America letters, the money orders in dollars, and the Swedish-American newspapers Moberg described as "invading" his boyhood home so sparked his imagination that at the age of eighteen he planned to emigrate himself, only to be stopped at the last moment, as he reported it, by his mother's and grandmother's laments that seeing a son off to America from the railway station was the same as attending the boy's funeral.[6]

Perhaps as a substitute for his blighted hopes, Moberg dreamed as early as the 1920s of erecting a literary monument to those of his family members who settled in the New World. This dream was not to be realized until the late 1940s. During the 1930s Moberg, long a staunch supporter of socialist reforms, attacked the ruling Social Democratic party for its perpetuation of the bureaucracy and for its support of the Swedish State Church. Later, when World War II broke out, he criticized the government in Stockholm for its failure to take a firm stand against Nazism. His bestselling novel *Rid i natt* (*Ride This Night*), although set in the seventeenth century, was read by many as a comment on the tyranny of the Nazi era.

Moberg's outspoken tendencies concerning national issues produced a two-fold personal effect. First, they guaranteed his disfavor among many influential public figures. Indeed Moberg remained embroiled in cultural debates on sensitive issues throughout the 1940s and early 1950s. He protested cases of blackmail and cover-ups in the Swedish police force and legal system and argued against the continued existence of the Swedish monarchy.

Second, his political involvement—in combination with limitations on travel during World War II—delayed until 1947 the time when he could begin writing on Swedish emigration. By then Moberg was almost fifty. He was celebrated in Sweden yet disillusioned with the country's leadership. Seen through the lens of his personal dissatisfaction and from the perspective of a war-torn Europe, the United States appeared to Moberg in the late 1940s as the world's

5. Moberg, "Romanen om utvandrarromanen." *Berättelser ur min levnad,* 292.
6. Moberg, "Romanen om utvandrarromanen," 293, 298.

last bastion of freedom and democracy. He seems to have felt a genuine desire to record the contribution made by Swedish emigrants to the country he thought was the world's only remaining hope. Looking back on this time in 1968, Moberg wrote: "I know that I have a genuine streak of stubbornness, a quality to be taken for better or worse. And I had made up my mind that I was going to cross the Atlantic Ocean in order to search out my unknown relations. For I could not get their destiny out of my mind. The older I became, the more it interested me."[7]

In 1945 Moberg began background study for what became the emigrant tetralogy and appears to have started actual work on the novels two years later.[8] The first volume *Utvandrarna* (*The Emigrants*) appeared in 1949, followed in 1952 by *Invandrarna* (*Unto a Good Land*). The final volumes *Nybyggarna* (*The Settlers*) and *Sista brevet till Sverige* (*The Last Letter Home*) were published in 1956 and 1959. The author often referred to these books as a single work, the Emigrant Novels (*Utvandrarromanen*), and insisted that they be read as a documentary novel.

To ensure the verisimilitude of his story, Moberg did extensive historical research in both Sweden and the United States. He studied county records in Småland and read many collections of letters that immigrants in America had sent to relatives in Sweden during the nineteenth century. His studies also included trips to the Maritime Museum in Gothenburg. This research gave him a record of living conditions in nineteenth-century Sweden and a feel for life aboard sailing vessels in the days when emigration had not yet become an industry backed by large steamship companies.

Some readers have felt that *The Emigrants* is the most successful of the four volumes largely because Moberg was writing about his home turf, the Smålandish countryside. No one can doubt that his novel gives an accurate and inspired account of the way the author's predecessors lived and saw the world. From a Minnesota point of view, the reader is reminded that this first volume carefully traces the customs of the Smålanders, who were the most numerous of the Swedish immigrants to this state and whose descendants still make up the largest number of Minnesota's ethnic Swedes.

---

7. Moberg, "Romanen om utvandrarromanen," 294. For similar comments in English, see: Moberg, "Why I Wrote the Novel About Swedish Emigrants," *Swedish Pioneer Historical Quarterly* 17 (Apr. 1966): 63.
8. Gunnar Eidevall, *Vilhelm Mobergs emigrantepos* (Stockholm: Norstedts, 1974), 19–20.

In order to build a historical framework in which his characters Karl Oskar and Kristina could move in the New World and especially in frontier Minnesota, Moberg embarked in 1948 on a study trip through the United States. An inexperienced traveler with little knowledge of English, he nevertheless gathered an impressive array of documentation that placed his immigrants in the mainstream of frontier experience.

Moberg carried out his studies in the archives of the Swedish-American museum in Philadelphia, among the Swedes of Minnesota, and through back issues of Swedish-American newspapers. His firsthand contacts with Swedish Americans in Chisago and Washington counties afforded him invaluable information on the lives of those people's immigrant forebears. *Unto a Good Land* places the immigrants on American soil. *The Settlers* and *The Last Letter Home* offer an accurate overview of pioneer life in Minnesota. These novels give details of a riverboat trip up the Mississippi River, the challenge of staking out a claim in the wilderness, the devastation of grasshopper plagues, the fear of Indians, the pace of life during the Civil War, and the difficulties faced by European immigrants in adjusting to the culture of the New World.

Moberg left nothing to chance in documenting the daily life and historical events of Minnesota from 1850 (when Karl Oskar and Kristina arrive in Minnesota) until 1890 (when Karl Oskar dies). The novelist's friends in Minnesota told of receiving letters from him inquiring about the nature of thunderstorms in the state, the cost of postage stamps in the nineteenth century, the number of daylight hours in summer, as well as distances between different parts of the state. Moberg even insisted that friends show him firsthand what animals strange to a Swede, such as crickets and skunks, looked like.[9] Indeed so insistent was Moberg that his fictional tale also be used as instructional history that he appended a bibliography of his sources to the Swedish edition of the Emigrant Novels. In this Borealis Books edition that bibliography is published for the first time in English.

On only one major historical point did Moberg allow the exigencies of plot construction to interfere with the dictates of historical accuracy. There are no known cases of a group of Swedish settlers journeying directly to and settling permanently in Minnesota prior to 1860. At midcentury the pattern of

9. For discussions of Moberg's research methods, see Philip Holmes, *Vilhelm Moberg* (Boston: Twayne, 1980), 110–32; Ingrid Johanson, "Vilhelm Moberg As We Knew Him," *Bulletin of the American Swedish Institute* (Minneapolis), no. 11 (1956); Bertil Hulenvik, *Utvandrarromanens källor: Förteckning över Vilhelm Mobergs samling av källmaterial,* ed. Ulf Beijbom (Växjö: House of Emigrants, 1972).

Swedish migration in the Midwest invariably included an initial stay of several years in Illinois or Iowa. Only after the immigrants had gotten their feet on the ground among fellow countrymen in those states did they venture up the Mississippi to more remote Minnesota. In taking Karl Oskar and his group straight from the East Coast to Minnesota, Moberg emphasized the true, hardy pioneer nature of his characters' journey.

Writing the Emigrant Novels

Like the fictional Karl Oskar, Moberg himself wanted to be the first on the scene. He saw himself as a literary discoverer and pioneer, a fact that presents some intriguing questions to American readers. Knowing something of Moberg's personal relationship with America can serve as a helpful guide in understanding some of the themes he developed in the Emigrant Novels.

"We're off to a good start," Moberg told reporters in Stockholm as he departed on his first trip to the United States in June 1948.[10] On that occasion, he entertained friends and journalists by playing the harmonica. For better or for worse, he was unable always to maintain such high spirits during the years after his arrival in America. Indeed his own meeting with America was one of joy mixed with bitter disappointment.

Moberg's period of legal residence in the United States lasted from 1948 to 1955. During that time he held two different immigrant visas and spoke repeatedly of settling permanently. As he told one Swedish reporter: "That which I find most attractive [in America] is the sense of freedom. It appears to me as if the authorities here have more respect for the individual than at home, and I like that."[11]

Gustaf Lannestock, Moberg's translator, wrote of the novelists's high hopes of gaining wealth and fame in the United States. Lannestock argued that Moberg in the late 1940s envisioned a promising future for himself as a writer and an adopted son of America until his aspirations were suddenly disappointed in the mid-1950s by a series of personal reverses, chiefly in disagreements with his American publishers, who Moberg felt had unjustifiably censored the Emigrant Novels.[12]

10. Don Josè [pseud.], "Vilhelm Mobergs amerikabagage nära att gå till Europahjälpen," *Svenska Dagbladet,* June 4, 1948, p. 11.

11. Sven Åhman, "Vilhelm Moberg ser på USA," *Nordstjernan,* May 26, 1949.

12. Gustaf Lannestock, *Vilhelm Moberg i Amerika* (Stockholm: Zindermans, 1977), 36. Much of our knowledge of Moberg's life in America is derived from the two men's correspondence and from this volume.

It now seems clear, however, that Moberg—to his own surprise—began experiencing mixed emotions about the New World as early as 1948. On one hand he admired the material success of Americans and appreciated the generosity of ordinary citizens. Especially appealing to him was the sense of independence and self-reliance exhibited by American workers. In America he found none of the obsequiousness toward the monied classes so common in Sweden. Here a man was judged "for what he can do."[13]

On the other hand some aspects of American life proved to be less agreeable. The oppressive summer heat, the perceived absence of a vital literary life among the common people, and the conservative religious politics of middle America were among Moberg's earliest complaints. By the beginning of the 1950s, his dissatisfaction extended to the political sphere. He was angered by the disruption caused by Senator Joseph McCarthy's hunt for Communists and responded with disgust when Charlie Chaplin was expelled from the country for his leftist sympathies. In an exasperating personal confrontation in 1955, the Internal Revenue Service in New York required Moberg to deposit nine thousand dollars as a lien against possible back taxes before he could return to Sweden for a visit.

Moberg's general views on the United States were crystallized in his attitudes toward two states: Minnesota and California. He returned to Minnesota several times after his initial 1948 visit. He found the people hard-working. Swedish farmers in Minnesota had opened up more land for cultivation in a hundred years than farmers in Sweden had managed since the Viking Age, Moberg stated with pride. The Swedish settlement areas and the Småland-like countryside around Lindstrom in central Chisago County appealed to him. Visits to Swedish cemeteries in Minnesota inspired some of his most poetic nonfictional accounts of America as he imagined the lives and deaths of his beloved Swedish farmers in fields far from home.

Everyday life in Minnesota proved to be more prosaic, however. Moberg lamented the drabness of the state's small towns, and the November chill

13. For works in English detailing Moberg's impressions of America, see Moberg, *The Unknown Swedes: A Book About Sweden and America, Past and Present*, ed. and trans. Roger McKnight (Carbondale: Southern Illinois University Press, 1988); McKnight, "The New Columbus: Vilhelm Moberg Confronts American Society," *Scandinavian Studies* 64 (Summer 1992): 356–88. Moberg expressed many of his opinions in letters to Lannestock; these letters are now in the House of Emigrants in Växjö, Sweden, and are referred to in "The New Columbus." See also Lannestock, *Vilhelm Moberg i Amerika* (in Swedish). My comments here and five paragraphs below are based on these works.

brought uncomfortable reminders of Sweden. Still, it was the intolerance and bigotry he found in the Lutheran churches of the Upper Midwest that provoked him most. In the long run, the climate of Minnesota, both meteorological and spiritual, proved to be too rigorous. The North Star State bore the unmistakable stamp, he wrote, of Calvin, Zwingli, and northern European puritanism.

If Moberg had a love affair with America, it was with California. Beginning in the autumn of 1948 he lived in Carmel, where one of his American aunts rented a house to him. In the sunshine there and in close proximity to John Steinbeck's Cannery Row, Moberg basked in what he called the joyous spirit of Petrarch and Bocaccio. Here he completed *The Emigrants* and began *Unto a Good Land*.

And it was here that he met Gustaf Lannestock, who became his translator. Lannestock was a native Swede who resided in Carmel, where he worked in real estate and collected rare books. They met by chance while walking on a California beach in the late 1940s. Moberg persuaded Lannestock to undertake the translation of the novels. Lannestock stayed with the translation project through the entire tetralogy. The friendship formed through this project lasted until Moberg's death.

Moberg was not to stay put, however. A case of wanderlust (which was to last seventeen years) had taken control of him, as he explained years later. He moved to Florida in 1953, then back to the Monterey–Carmel area, eventually to Laguna Beach in California, and even spent some time in Mexico, with short stops in New York interspersed. In 1955 he returned to Europe, bothered by the political and literary winds blowing in America and admitting his failure at adjusting to American culture. He completed the emigrant tetralogy in Europe.

Themes in the Emigrant Novels

Moberg had a strongly populist view of history and rejected the mythologizing "great man" approach so popular among Swedish historians and novelists before his time. He argued that older writers had praised the deeds of Swedish monarchs and statesmen in an effort to keep the commoners as loyal, unquestioning subjects of the ruling classes. This approach he described as historical casuistry and blamed it for creating feelings of "ultra-royalism," "ultra-patriotism," and "ultra-heroism."[14]

---

14. Moberg, *Min svenska historia* (Stockholm: Norstedts, 1971), 1:14.

In the process of emigration, Moberg saw a historical movement set in motion and sustained by daring commoners who acted without a significant portal figure as their leader. Emigration changed history, according to this argument, in that it deprived Sweden of a cheap labor supply and aided America in the building of a new society. On a material plane, America is the land where people of modest means but the right abilities can thrive. Karl Oskar is undistinguished as a leader of men. He is only "one emigrant among many emigrants," according to one critic.[15] Yet he is successful as a farmer in America because he possesses the proper practical skills. Karl Oskar is thwarted in Sweden but sees his hard work rewarded with ever-increasing affluence in Minnesota.

So interested was Moberg in this pioneering theme that he came to present his own actions in a similar, though more individualized, light. He wished to be viewed as the first in Sweden to practice the art of writing the documentary novel. Likewise, Moberg argued for his importance as the discoverer of the topic of Swedish emigration. Swedish scholars and writers before him had neglected the subject, he felt, because the movement revealed the Swedish government's lack of foresight in failing to prevent it.

Just as Karl Oskar stakes his claim in Chisago County four years before the first historical permanent settlement of Swedes there, so Moberg, by his own reckoning, turned virgin literary soil in depicting the lives of ordinary Swedish Americans in Minnesota. In this respect, Moberg's fertile creative imagination took control over his otherwise strong sense of realism. While no critics have questioned the historical accuracy of the Emigrant Novels, it is clear that other writers (both Swedish and American) had preceded Moberg in recording Swedish settlement patterns in the United States. In fact, Moberg listed names of some of those researchers in his own bibliography for the novels.

Still, Moberg's faithful depiction of the lives of humble people involved in a historic undertaking remains constant throughout the Emigrant Novels. This narrative consistency is one of the strengths of the series.

Reading the Emigrant Novels as a psycho-history of Moberg and his America is perhaps equally as instructive as searching for historical motifs. Scholars have often asked how Moberg's personal impressions of America after 1948 influenced the directions his epic narrative takes. It is tempting to view the storyline as leading in a linear fashion from poverty and oppression in the Old World to affluence and freedom in the New World. A more complex set of psychological variables can be seen to enter the novels, however.

15. Sigvard Mårtensson, *Vilhelm Moberg* (Stockholm: Bonniers, 1956), 202.

In this connection, the Swedish novelist Sven Delblanc has pointed out how the dictates of realism led Moberg to conclude that the basic human condition is constant regardless of time and country.[16] Likewise, Professor Rochelle Wright considered how Moberg—in spite of his early infatuation with America—often portrayed the new land as a "shadow kingdom," a land to which one's relatives disappeared, never to be heard from again. America was the great divider of families.[17]

Karl Oskar and Kristina illustrate this theme. While Karl Oskar believes in their future in America with almost total optimism, Kristina sees their emigration as the abandonment of age-old traditions and the loss of an ancient Swedish birthright. Moberg never allowed the reader to forget Kristina's homesickness for her native Småland.

Even Karl Oskar's material success is tainted. First, he never fully understands the emotional impact of his leaving his own aged parents in Sweden. By the same token, he is slow to grasp the irony of his statement to Kristina that his children one day will thank him for taking them to America, when in fact they grow up to marry into other ethnic groups and leave Karl Oskar behind much as he had left his own parents. Furthermore it is ironic that the period of Karl Oskar's rising prosperity on his Minnesota farm corresponds to the general time of Kristina's death. It is after Kristina's passing that Karl Oskar seals his fate by questioning God for the second time in his life.

In addition, it bears mentioning that a recurring motif in Moberg's nonfiction writings was his admiration for the spirit of enterprise he saw in Americans. Yet he was equally as shocked by what he perceived as their callous individualism and lack of sympathy for the less fortunate in society.[18] No character better embodies these traits than Karl Oskar, whose qualities of diligence and practicality are counterbalanced by his impatience with and lack of understanding for Robert, the incurable dreamer. Karl Oskar is also skeptical about Native Americans because he considers them lazy.

The Emigrant Novels should be seen, in short, in their full realistic light. They are stories of blighted hopes as much as of personal fulfillment. Of all Moberg's characters, only Ulrika and Jonas Petter gain a kind of lasting happiness. Most of the others (from Inga-Lena to Kristina) succumb soon after their

16. Sven Delblanc, "Den omöjliga flykten," *Bonniers litterära magasin* 42, no. 6 (Dec. 1973), 267.

17. Rochelle Wright, "Vilhelm Moberg's Image of America," (Ph.D. diss., University of Washington, 1975), 34–40.

18. McKnight, "The New Columbus," 384.

arrival here or long before their time. In the end, Karl Oskar remains, old and lonely, residing in Minnesota in body only.

Moberg saw at firsthand the difficulty of ever totally adapting to a new culture. He remained forever Swedish, perhaps despite himself. And in his novels he dramatized the problems of adaptation. Still, more than any other Swedish writer he succeeded in bridging the gap between the Old and New Worlds, between Sweden and Minnesota. The great resurgence of ethnic interest among Swedish Americans and their relatives in Sweden, which began in the 1950s and 1960s, was triggered largely by the Emigrant Novels.

Moberg strove to debunk the old heroic myths of Swedish history. But in his tales of the immigrants to Minnesota, he succeeded in his own right in creating a significant popular image. The figures of Karl Oskar and Kristina, the ultimate commonfolk, speak so powerfully to our imagination that they assume a dimension larger than life. Like many other contrasts in his life, this ironic twist would have hit home with Vilhelm Moberg and appealed to his literary sensibility.

Moberg's writing style has been a subject of discussion since the 1960s when critic Gunnar Brandell denied him a place among the great creative artists of modern Swedish literature. According to Brandell, Moberg wrote a solid everyday prose that did not adequately express shades of difference or depict characters in sufficient depth. Moberg lacked "lyrical resources," Brandell concluded.[19]

Since that time several writers have defended Moberg's writing style. Gunnar Heldén pointed out Moberg's strengths in dealing with three central motifs in classic lyricism: nature, love, and death.[20] Sven Delblanc described Moberg's prose style as *en poesi i sak,* that is, a style that pays steady attention to small details, thus creating a harmony and poetry of everyday life without reliance on the neat turning of phrases or on striking images.[21] Finally, Philip Holmes explained Moberg's use of alliteration, phrase-pairs, and repetition in his prose. These devices allowed Moberg to slow his narrative tempo and to strive "for clarity and fullness of expression."[22]

19. Gunnar Brandell, *Svensk Litteratur 1900–1950: Realism och Symbolism* (Stockholm: Förlaget Örnkrona, 1958), 261.
20. Gunnar Heldén, "Vilhelm Mobergs lyriska resurser," *Emigrationer: En bok till Vilhelm Moberg 20-8-1968* (Stockholm: Bonniers, 1968), 215–29.
21. Delblanc, "Den omöjliga flykten," 266.
22. Holmes, *Vilhelm Moberg,* 126.

Holmes described the Old Testament and the medieval Swedish laws as major influences on Moberg's writing style. Moberg strove in his prose to produce the thought patterns of rural people from the nineteenth century. Although unlettered, these people were confronted with and forced to sort out a new world of impressions and complicated emotions. Moberg's task was to give a realistic voice to his characters. His success in finding this voice speaks for his creativity.

Gustavus Adolphus College   ROGER McKNIGHT

Introduction to
The Last Letter Home

MOBERG ONCE estimated that he wrote three-quarters of the manuscript of the Emigrant Novels in California.[1] He wrote all of *Sista brevet till Sverige* in Europe, finishing it in Locarno, Switzerland, in 1959. The Swedish title means "The Last Letter to Sweden." In the 1961 American edition, the series was published as a trilogy, with *The Settlers* and *The Last Letter Home* presented as one volume. Lannestock explained: "Large parts of both books had been omitted; the publisher felt that they were of greater interest to European readers."[2] Later editions of the series presented the tetralogy as a whole, however, as does this Borealis Books edition.

Details of the difficulties between white settlers and the Ojibway and Dakota people (also known as the Chippewa and Sioux, respectively) form an important subplot in *The Last Letter Home.* Numerous first-person accounts by both white and Dakota people document the shock and cruelty of the Dakota War of 1862. Moberg had read sections of the journals of Swedish immigrant Andrew Peterson, which tell how Peterson and other Swedes fled with their families to an island in Lake Waconia during the war.[3] Moberg also read historical texts to learn about events and other aspects of those troubled times (see his bibliography, p. xxv). Historians now argue about the validity of some of those texts, and readers should not accept Moberg's use of historical sources uncritically.

Despite its relative briefness, the Dakota War of 1862 was a complicated series of events marked by acts of extreme brutality and exceptional humanity by different individuals on both sides of the conflict.[4] This is information of

1. Moberg, "Romanen om utvandrarromanen," 317.
2. Lannestock, *Vilhelm Moberg i Amerika,* 124.
3. Andrew Peterson and Family Papers, 1854–1931, Minnesota Historical Society, St. Paul, Minn.
4. Gary Clayton Anderson, *Kinsmen of Another Kind: Dakota-White Relations in the Upper*

which Moberg was well aware; therefore, in describing the Dakota War in *The Last Letter Home,* he was faced with the difficult task of joining his narrative of actual historical events to a description of his fictional immigrants' immediate experiences and emotions. For example, he incorporated into his novel the grisly accounts of mutilation of the bodies of whites by Dakota people. While some stories of this type may have a basis in fact, many others of questionable reliability were told by members of the military burial parties that reached the dead after several days. Exposure of the bodies to animals and August heat may have produced gruesome results that the whites were all too ready to blame on the Dakota.

Regardless of whether such stories were true or false, they were widely believed by whites in Minnesota in 1862. Moberg used them in his novel to heighten the sense of alarm felt by his fictional characters, whom he referred to as "the immigrated Europeans" (*de inflyttade européerna*). With limited access to factual reports in their own language,[5] such immigrant groups often saw the peoples and customs of the American frontier as strange and frightening. Their judgments were frequently based on rumors rather than on facts. This tendency may be seen as a case of one minority (the recent immigrants) being aroused against another (the Native Americans) by a lack of understanding that instilled suspicion and fear.

While some readers in the late twentieth century may find certain details in *The Last Letter Home* to be less than complimentary to Native Americans, it is interesting to note that in the late 1950s and early 1960s Moberg received numerous letters from American readers who protested that he had portrayed American Indians "as altogether too sympathetic and pleasant [a people]."[6] This reaction reflects the changing sensibilities and the tangled emotions of Moberg's readers and of his fictional characters alike. In short, Moberg felt the necessity to depict in certain of his Swedish figures an apprehension about

Mississippi Valley, 1650–1862 (Lincoln: University of Nebraska Press, 1984), 261–80. On the Dakota War of 1862, see also Kenneth Carley, *The Sioux Uprising of 1862* 2d ed. (St. Paul: Minnesota Historical Society, 1976); Anderson, *Little Crow, Spokesman for the Sioux* (St. Paul: Minnesota Historical Society Press, 1986); Anderson and Alan R. Woolworth, eds., *Through Dakota Eyes: Narrative Accounts of the Minnesota Indian War of 1862* (St. Paul: Minnesota Historical Society Press, 1988).

5. In the early 1860s, the only Swedish-language newspaper available on a regular basis to Swedes in Minnesota was *Hemlandet,* published in Chicago. *Hemlandet* contained little news from Minnesota, and those few items from this state it published appeared weeks or even months after the events described.

6. Moberg, "Romanen om utvandrarromanen," 330.

Native Americans. Since this perception was a historical fact among many immigrants, Moberg insisted that literary realism demanded that it be described as existing among various characters in the Emigrant Novels as well.

Readers wishing to assess Moberg's own personal sentiments on this issue should understand that he was indeed sympathetic to Native Americans. He had a great interest in the culture of American Indians and saw the loss of their lands as a calamity. In Moberg's own words, the white Americans' treatment of the Native Americans was "one of the most reprehensible deeds in world history." According to his own later writings, he felt he had written this same message into the Emigrant Novels. He wrote in 1968: "In my novels I laid the blame for the Indian uprising principally on the white man's hard and inhuman treatment of his red brother." Earlier American novels of the frontier had pictured Native Americans as bloodthirsty savages, Moberg wrote. He argued that he himself had gone against that tradition by portraying them as peace loving.[7]

Determining the true relationship between actual nineteenth-century Swedish immigrants and Ojibway and Dakota people in Minnesota is extremely difficult because there are so few accounts written on the topic from a Swedish perspective. One line of reasoning is that the two groups enjoyed good relations. In 1932, Andrew Porter of Chisago County reminisced that his Swedish parents traded food with Native Americans in the 1850s and remained on good terms with them even when wild and unfounded rumors about Indian atrocities spread throughout the area in the late summer of 1862. Porter commented: "These Indians were very friendly and they never did any harm to people or stock."[8] Likewise, Moberg himself talked with descendants of the first Swedish settlers around Chisago Lake. These people recalled their own parents' tales of friendly contacts with Indians, who were "peaceful and nice, *if they were left to live in peace.*"[9]

Other comments hint at less cordial contacts. In his work on the Indian leader Little Crow, historian Gary Clayton Anderson wrote: "Most newcomers were from Germany or Scandinavia and carried a cultural baggage into Minnesota that was of necessity thrifty, so they saw no reason to share resources with Indians."[10] There were instances of white settlers taking (and keeping for

7. Moberg, "Romanen om utvandrarromanen," 330–31.
8. Lloyd C. Hackl, *The Wooden Shoe People: An Illustrated History of the First Swedish Settlement in Minnesota* (Cambridge, Minn.: Adventure Publications, 1990), 37.
9. Moberg, "Romanen om utvandrarromanen," 331, author's italics.
10. Anderson, *Little Crow,* 130.

themselves) excessive amounts of fish and game in areas near Indian camps. This approach could have caused serious misunderstandings with the Dakota, who considered it "exceedingly uncivilized to hoard food."[11] During the Dakota War of 1862, furthermore, one of the more aggressive white citizen-soldier units guarding against Indian attacks was the Scandinavian Guards of Nicollet County.[12]

One writer has concentrated on the subject of Swedish immigrant-Native American relations as portrayed in the Emigrant Novels. The Swede Kent Adelmann wrote that, even though Moberg was sympathetic to Native Americans, he depicted them in the novels as seen through the eyes of Europeans. According to Adelmann, Moberg determined through his research how different Swedes understood the American Indian way of life. But because he was writing from the perspective of "immigrated Europeans," he could not picture a close relationship between settlers and native people.

Adelmann argued, furthermore, that Moberg's immigrant tale focused sharply on the concept of freedom. In America, Moberg's fictional Swedish settlers attained freedom from an oppressive European class system, but they did so at the expense of another people (Native Americans) who themselves were being oppressed in the social system of the United States. This situation, incidentally, gives to the novel an ironic touch that the practical-thinking Karl Oskar has difficulty understanding and accepting.

Native Americans did not have the opportunity to speak for themselves in the novels, Adelmann continued. Samuel Nöjd, a character Moberg generally portrayed as repulsive, defends the Native peoples against Karl Oskar, who argues that they are lazy. Meanwhile, the reader hears from the natives themselves only indirectly through a speech made by Dakota leader Red Iron, quoted in the novel. Adelmann's reasoning was that Moberg, although not Eurocentric in his intentions, was at critical moments in his novels unable to divorce himself from a Eurocentric narrative approach.[13]

Moberg returned to the journals of Andrew Peterson for information on the Swedes during the Civil War. Peterson wrote of his attempt to join the Union Army. He was turned down for medical reasons—his advanced age and a chronic back problem. Peterson had incurred his back injury while lifting stones on his farm and spent his declining years as a semi-invalid. Moberg used

11. Anderson, *Kinsmen of Another Kind*, 11.
12. Carley, *Sioux Uprising of 1862*, 49.
13. Kent Adelmann, *Vilhelm Mobergs utvandrarserie: en introduktion till "indianproblemet"* (Lund: Kent Adelmann, 1976).

a similar series of events involving Karl Oskar to show both the protagonist's part in the drama surrounding the Civil War and his advancing old age. Like Peterson, Karl Oskar attempts to pass a physical examination for the military. For the first time, however, Karl Oskar is forced to become a bystander. Then back troubles increasingly hobble him, and his sons take over the farm.

Although some readers prefer the storytelling qualities of *The Emigrants* over other sections of the Emigrant Novels, there is little in Moberg's corpus that exceeds the poetic nature of the final parts of *The Last Letter Home*. Here Moberg captured the feelings of homesickness, anger, regret, and lost love in one aging figure. Karl Oskar has changed from the forward-looking young man "K. O. Nilsson, Svensk" to the backward-peering "Charles O. Nelson, Swedish American."

In the end Kristina finds peace, while Karl Oskar is left to ponder the depth of his love for Kristina and to dream of home. His life is behind him. Upon Karl Oskar's death, Moberg established a final link between Minnesota and Sweden. Inspiration for this connecting device came to Moberg from a letter he found in Andrew Peterson's papers. After Peterson's death in Waconia, one of his neighbors wrote a letter to Peterson's relatives in Sweden. In order to include the letter in his novel, Moberg reworked and rewrote it, while at the same time retaining its authentic flavor. Moberg's version of the letter functions as the conclusion to *The Last Letter Home*. With it, the author invoked God's blessing on the native land of his Swedish immigrants.

R. McK.

Bibliography for the Emigrant Novels

Compiled by Vilhelm Moberg

Pehr Kalm: En resa i Norra Amerika. I-III. (1753-1761.)

Carl Aug. Gosselman: Resa i Norra Amerika. (Stockholm 1835.)

Hans Mattson: Minnen. (Chicago 1890.)

Johan Bolin: Beskrifning öfwer Nord-Amerikas Förenta Stater. (Wexiö 1853.)

Ole Rynning: Beretning om Amerika. (Kristiania 1838.)

Gustaf Unonius: Minnen från en sjuttonårig vistelse i Nordvestra Amerika. I-II. (Uppsala 1862.)

Emeroy Johnson: Early Life of Eric Norelius. 1833–1862. (Rock Island 1934.)

Oscar N. Olsson: The Augustana Lutheran Church in America. Pioneer Period 1846–1860. (Rock Island 1934.)

N. Lindgren: Handlingar rörande åkianismen. (Wexiö 1867.)

E. Herlenius: Åkianismens historia. (Stockholm 1902.)

———. Erik Janseismens historia. (Stockholm 1900.)

M. A. Mikkelsen: The Bishop Hill Colony. (Chicago 1892.)

George M. Stephenson: The Religious Aspects of Swedish Immigration. (Minneapolis 1932.)

L. Landgren: Om Sectväsendet. (Härnösand 1878.)

Joh. Schröder: Vägvisare för Emigranter. (Stockholm 1868.)

H. Hörner: Nyaste Handbok för Utvandrare. (Stockholm 1868.)

A. E. Strand: A History of the Swedish-Americans of Minnesota. I- III. (Chicago 1910.)

Theodore C. Blegen: Building Minnesota. (Minnesota Historical Society. 1938.)

———. Norwegian Migration to America. (Northfield 1940.)

———. Land of Their Choice. (Minneapolis 1955.)

Lawrence Guy Brown: Immigration. (New York 1933.)

W. J. Petersen: Steamboating on the Upper Mississippi. (Iowa City 1937.)

Herbert and Edward Quick: Mississippi Steamboating. (New York 1926.)

Joseph Henry Jackson: Forty-Niners. (Boston 1949.)

———. Gold Rush Album. (New York 1949.)

Henry K. Norton: The Story of California. (Chicago 1923.)

G. Catlin: Nord-Amerikas Indianer. övers. från eng. (Stockholm 1848.)

Colin F. MacDonald: The Sioux War of 1862.
I. V. D. Heard: The History of the Sioux War. (New York 1863.)
J. F. Rhodes: The History of the Civil War. (1917.)
C. Channing: A History of the United States I-VI. (1925.)
Edvard A. Steiner: On the Trail of the Immigrant. (New York 1906.)
Francis Parkman: The Oregon Trail. (New York 1950.)
Oscar Commetant: Tre år i Förenta Staterna. Iakttagelser och skildringar. (Stockholm
    1860.)
Clarence S. Peterson: St. Croix River Valley Territorial Pioneers. (Baltimore 1949.)
John R. Commons: Races and Immigrants in America. (New York 1907.)
A. W. Quirt: Tales of the Woods and Mines. (Waukesha 1941.)
The Frontier Holiday. A collection of writings by Minnesota Pioneers. (St. Paul 1948.)
Robert B. Thomas: The Old Farmers Almanac. First issued in 1792 for the Year 1793.
    (Boston 1954.)
Minnesota Farmers Diaries: William R. Brown 1845–1846.
————. Y. Jackson 1852–1863. (The Minnesota Historical Society. St. Paul 1939.)
Swedish-American Historical Bulletin. 1928–1939. (St. Paul.)
Year-Book of The Swedish Historical Society of America. 1909– 1910. 1923–1924. (Min-
    neapolis.)
G. N. Swahn: Svenskarna i Sioux City. Några blad ur deras historia. (Chicago 1912.)
Roger Burlingame: Machines That Built America. (New York 1953.)
Railway Information Series: A Chronology of American Railroads.
————. The Human Side of Railroading. (Washington 1949.)

Andrew Peterson: Dagbok åren 1854–1898. En svensk farmares levnadsbeskrivning. 16
    delar. (Manuskript i Minnesota Historical Library. St. Paul.)
Mina Anderson: En nybyggarhustrus minnen. (Manuskript tillh. förf.)
Alford Roos. Diary of my father Oscar Roos. (Manuskript d:o.)
Peter J. Aronson: En svensk utvandrares minnen. (Manuskript d:o.)
Charles C. Anderson: Levernesbeskrivning. (Manuskript d:o.)
Eric A. Nelson: My Pioneer Life. (Manuskript d:o.)

V. M.
Locarno, June 1, 1959.

Suggested Readings in English

Compiled by Roger McKnight

About Vilhelm Moberg:

Holmes, Philip. *Vilhelm Moberg*. Boston: Twayne, 1980.

McKnight, Roger, "The New Columbus: Vilhelm Moberg Confronts American Society," *Scandinavian Studies* 64 (Summer 1992):356–89.

Moberg, Vilhelm. *The Unknown Swedes: A Book About Swedes and America, Past and Present*. Carbondale: Southern Illinois University Press, 1988.

Thorstensson, Roland B. "Vilhelm Moberg as a Dramatist for the People." Ph.D. diss., University of Washington, 1974.

Wright, Rochelle. "Vilhelm Moberg's Image of America." Ph.D. diss., University of Washington 1975.

About Swedish Immigration:

Barton, H. Arnold. *A Folk Divided: Homeland Swedes and Swedish Americans, 1840–1940*. Carbondale: Southern Illinois University Press, 1994.

———, ed. *Letters from the Promised Land: Swedes in America, 1840–1914*. Minneapolis: University of Minnesota Press for the Swedish Pioneer Historical Society, 1975.

Beijbom, Ulf, ed. *Swedes in America: New Perspectives*. Växjö: Swedish Emigrant Institute, 1993.

Blanck, Dag and Harald Runblom, eds. *Swedish Life in American Cities*. Uppsala: Centre for Multiethnic Research, 1991.

Hasselmo, Nils. *Swedish America: An Introduction*. New York: Swedish Information Service, 1976.

Ljungmark, Lars. *Swedish Exodus*. Carbondale: Southern Illinois University Press, 1979.

Nordstrom, Byron, ed. *The Swedes in Minnesota*. Minneapolis: Denison, 1976.

THE COUNTRY THAT CHANGED THEM

THIS IS the last installment of a story about a group of people who left their homes in Ljuder parish, Sweden, and emigrated to North America.

These immigrants settled in the St. Croix Valley of Minnesota, in the land of the Chippewas and the Sioux. It was a wild-growing region, never before touched by ax or plow. When the settlers had built their abodes and secured their daily needs they began also to concern themselves with their spiritual requirements. According to their ability they organized for a life beyond their corporal needs: They built churches and schools, they employed ministers and teachers, they agreed upon laws for peaceful community life with equal rights for all. They elected councils to solve their quarrels and mete out justice among them. In their frontier world they had to start everything from the very beginning. They changed the land that had received them and created for themselves a new community.

The region these immigrants helped develop was admitted to the Union as the thirty-second state, and they themselves became citizens of the United States.

But this alone did not guarantee them peace and security in their new land. After ten years in the New World their existence was threatened to its very foundations. Within the Union such great antagonism had arisen between opposing factions that it resulted in a four-year, utterly bloody civil war. And while this was still going on, their own new, free state was shaken by another internal strife: The Indians who had been forced to vacate their ancestral hunting grounds by the ever-encroaching settlers started an uprising to drive them out and regain their land.

The gift of liberty so generously extended to the immigrants made great demands on the recipients: It saddled the settlers with responsibilities that had been unknown to them in their native country. The United States demanded of its citizens talents never needed in their homeland. In Sweden they had been subjects of temporal and spiritual authorities they themselves had not elected, and—like people not of age—they had had a government over them to decide what was best and most beneficial for them. Here in the New World they were citizens of age: They themselves elected their government, and they elected as their officials men who had their confidence and who would serve the people rather than hold them in obedience.

The ability wholly to govern themselves was exacted of the settlers. And the necessity to decide for themselves forced and stimulated them to new efforts and developed in them new strength. In exercising their newfound liberty the immigrants gained the experience which gave them the strength to build their new society.

Thus, in turn, the immigrant-citizens were changed by their new country. They changed the country and the United States of America changed them.

PART ONE

I

OLD ABE CALLS

—1—

IT WAS in the beginning of the age of the telegraph. This remarkable invention was in use everywhere in North America; in a few short minutes it could transfer important news from one end of the country to the other. The morning happenings in the South were known in every city and village of the North long before evening. The telegraph was a miracle not yet become commonplace.

What happened in South Carolina on the morning of Sunday, April 14, 1861, was known to every city dweller in Minnesota within a few hours; the news reached many of the smaller villages before the day was over; more remote settlers were perhaps not aware of it for still another day. It reached the people of Lake Chisago in the forenoon of Monday the fifteenth. This April day was never to be forgotten by any one of those who lived it.

It was the season of seeding. Karl Oskar Nilsson, owner of the first settlement at the lake, was harrowing his field for the spring wheat. For the first time he was driving his recently acquired team of horses. The weather was mild for that time of year, it had rained moderately, and the soil seemed ready after the stirring of the harrow pegs. The black earth was pregnant with growing and sufficiently dry after the rain not to clog his shoes. Pigeons, meadowlarks, and sparrows faithfully followed the team across the field and picked with eager beaks at worms and larvae exposed by the harrow. The horses pulled this heavy implement easily enough with such a brisk pace that the driver had difficulty in keeping up with them. Karl Oskar still dragged his left foot a little due to an old injury in his leg which always made itself known under stress.

He was pleased with his new team. There was a great difference between the lively, brisk horses and the dull, sluggish oxen. Now harrowing was easy. This afternoon he must sow his wheat, for tomorrow morning the Spring Court convened in Center City and he was to serve on the jury.

He had sent his oldest boy, Johan, on an errand to Klas Albert's store—Pers-

3

son's Store, as they called it in Center City—and now and then he glanced
down the road. Why was the boy so slow in returning? Finally he spied him
down by the old log cabin. As soon as Johan saw his father he began to run.
Karl Oskar reined in his team: Why suddenly this hurry?

Before the boy had gained the field he began shouting: From the son the
news reached the father: *War had broken out.*

Johan was excited and short of breath. In Center City he had read a poster
on the bulletin board of the parish meetinghouse. The Southern rebels had
stormed Fort Sumter and shot down the Union flag. The slave states had
begun warring against the North. A great many people had gathered at Persson's Store, all talking about the war. The boy of fifteen was proud to have carried this message; he panted for breath as he repeated it.

Karl Oskar let the team rest and sat down heavily on the harrow. To him the
news was not unexpected. He had long feared war would break out. It had
been an uneasy winter, full of anxiety and uncertainty. Now spring had come
and with it outbreak of war. And as war finally had come, at least he was relieved of the worry about its breaking out.

Last fall he had been one of those who helped elect Abraham Lincoln, himself a settler's son. The men of the ax and the plow had placed Abe in the President's chair: They trusted him. Karl Oskar had thought: Old Abe won't have a
war, if he can help it. He is sure to make peace with the slave states. He also
wants what is best for the South—the best of both North and South—they
must remain united. He wants the people of the New World to settle their dif-
ferences peacefully, not with bloodshed. In the Old World the English, French,
Russians, Austrians, and Turks had recently fought bloody battles. But over
there kings and warlords had always driven their people to death, and people
had meekly endured it. But Honest Abe—himself born in a settler's cabin—is
not going to ape leaders who have ruined the Old World.

But now the slave states had inveigled each other to attack the Union. The
flag had been shot down! What could the President do now? What must they
all do? The one attacked must defend himself.

Johan was standing beside the harrow, keyed up, waiting eagerly and with
apprehension: "Do you think, Father, the rebels are coming all the way up
here?"

No, his father didn't think so; the boy mustn't be afraid. The Southern
rebels would never come as far north as Minnesota. Long before they got
halfway they would be killed on the battlefields. And he told his boy to go on
home and finish cleaning out the sheep pen, a chore he had started in the

morning. He must tell Harald to help him, there was great hurry, the sheep manure was to be spread on the oat field before seeding.

Johan looked disappointed but obeyed reluctantly. He had expected his father to unharness the team and come home and forget about the sheep pen. He had in some way expected a reward for bringing the message of war. It was unfair, on a day like this, to have to shovel sheep dung.

A swarm of mosquitoes buzzed around the horses and bit them in the groins; the animals stamped with their hind legs, rattling the harnesses. Karl Oskar remained sitting, squinting at the sun, his thoughts disturbed, pondering. War! Never could a war have started at a more inopportune moment. But whatever happened, he must plant the spring wheat today. A new crop must grow; people would need bread next year also.

He resumed harrowing but row after row with each furrow he was pursued by the question: How many men in America must now leave their daily chores and go to war? He did not stop harrowing until the dinner hour. Kristina, his wife, had already set the table as he entered the kitchen, and he sat down to eat with his family.

Johan repeated to his mother and brothers and sisters what he had read on the poster in Center City. This last year in school he had learned English quite well and could read it almost fluently.

Kristina listened with great calm. A change had come over her these last years; nothing disturbed or frightened her.

"War is punishment for our sins," she said. "We can only ask God to have mercy on us."

Karl Oskar said, "Those armies of the South can do us no harm up here. They'll never get here!"

"I mean: May God have mercy on the people in the South and the people in the North!"

He protested that the rich slave owners in the South had started the war. They alone were to blame, and they alone ought to suffer. If one were attacked by a criminal must he suffer the same punishment as the attacker?

"Punishment belongs to God," explained Kristina. "A Christian is not allowed to go out and kill."

"Isn't he allowed to kill a murderer and criminal?"

"No. He mustn't kill any human being."

"But I've the right to defend myself. A murderer must blame himself if he gets killed!"

"If someone is killed, is it therefore necessary to kill others?" Kristina replied. "Can it help the dead one if other people die?"

Karl Oskar and Kristina had had many discussions about the South and the North and could not agree. Now he replied, as he had done many times before: If one couldn't defend oneself against an attacker, no person in the world could live in peace in his home. And the slave states had attacked because the presidential election last fall hadn't gone the way they wanted.

"They want to govern themselves, as we do," she said. "Why can't they?"

"It ruins the Union," he explained. "The rebels have broken the laws of the Union."

"But the people of the South don't like them. They don't want to obey the same laws as we. Why must they? Why must they be forced to obey?"

Karl Oskar could not make Kristina understand that the slave power in the South was criminal. Hadn't they not long ago read in their paper *Hemlandet* about the South's plan to murder President Abraham Lincoln, the most honest man in North America? The slave owners had conspired to prevent him from occupying his office. For a long time they had planned this deed, and hired the assassins. When Father Abe was to ride the steam wagon to the government house in Washington, the murderers were to turn over the wagon and crush him against the rails. Such was their intent; he was never to reach the presidential chair alive. Praise be God, the conspiracy was discovered in time, Abe was warned, and guards were posted along the whole line of the railroad and he arrived unharmed in Washington. This fully proved that the slave powers instigated murders. And murderers could not be endured in this country.

Kristina looked at him across the table: "And now they must go to war, the men . . . ?"

It was half a question, but he did not reply this time; he looked down at his plate.

She had something more to say to him but she couldn't quite get it out now—there was one more question she would have liked to ask him: Are you going?

The next morning, Tuesday, Karl Oskar drove single-horsed to Center City to do jury duty. He tied his horse and walked up the steps to the meeting-house, which also served as courthouse, where he met Mr. Thorn, the Chisago County sheriff, a tall, well-built man. The sheriff said there would be no sitting of the court today because war had broken out.

Mr. Thorn was a Scotchman. Karl Oskar knew him as an honest and capable person and he had helped elect him sheriff. In Sweden the farmers were never allowed to elect their sheriff; there they must accept whoever the Crown sent them, however badly he might treat them. A Crown sheriff in Sweden was a puffed-up, vain person, a magistrate wearing gold-plated buttons and uniform cap, who cursed and ruled. He threatened and frightened and no one dared do anything but obey. Mr. Thorn on the contrary was a helpful, kind man who neither ruled nor swore at people. And if he had done so he would not have lasted long in his office. There was a great difference between a sheriff in Sweden and a sheriff in America; here the settlers were his equals.

"Old Abe has called for troops," said Mr. Thorn.

He showed the Swedish settler a big placard nailed to the meetinghouse wall. Yesterday Abraham Lincoln, the President of the Union, had sent this proclamation to all the Northern states; this poster concerned each and every citizen.

Karl Oskar began to spell his way through the poster. He understood most of the English, and what he didn't understand the sheriff explained to him.

Southern rebels had conspired to get possession of fortresses and war matériel from the Union. The laws of the nation must be enforced and therefore the booty must be recaptured. Lincoln, in his capacity as President, urged all loyal citizens to hasten to the defense of the Union. He asked for 75,000 men to enlist immediately.

The tall Scotchman already knew Lincoln's proclamation by heart. He spoke with great feeling—those scoundrels in the slave states had besmirched the flag, they had shot at the thirty-two stars in the Union flag. The thirty-second and last star was that of Minnesota. These Southern bandits in shooting at their flag thus, had actually fired at the people of this very county; it was as if they had tried to murder him, Karl Oskar, his friends, and fellow settlers.

Mr. Thorn had his duties as sheriff and because of this, sadly enough, he was forced to stay at home. Otherwise he would already have hearkened to Old Abe's call and enlisted. As he said this he glanced at the Swede beside him in a way that could not be misunderstood.

Twice Karl Oskar read through the presidential proclamation very carefully while he barely listened to the sheriff. Mr. Thorn kept fingering his badge of office as he poured out his bitterness over the insult to the flag; such an insult could be washed off only in blood.

Karl Oskar untied the halter chain and harnessed his horse to the wagon. He made some purchases in Klas Albert's store where today the customers elbowed each other. Then he drove back home again; with no court he had nothing more to do in Center City.

And today he wished to be alone to gather his thoughts.

Twenty-two thousand Minnesotans had last fall voted for Old Abe to be President. He himself was one of them. Those 22,000 considered the settler-son Lincoln one of them, indeed, the foremost of them. He was wiser, more capable, and more honest than anyone else. A man's worth meant everything in the settlers' republic, and that was why the boy from the log cabin had risen to the highest office in North America. In Sweden it was only required that a man was born in the royal palace and slept in a golden cradle to reach the highest pinnacle in the nation; his ability counted for nothing.

And those who had chosen Honest Abe had confidence that he would preserve the Union.

But the President couldn't do it single-handedly. Now the Union was threatened and now the people of the North must gather round their elected leader. Today Old Abe called upon all loyal citizens: Help me save the Union!

Karl Oskar assured himself that he was a loyal citizen in the country that had received him and his family and opened a new home for them. The presidential proclamation was directed to him; he had read it carefully: The United States are threatened! You are one of those who elected me President! Now you must help me! Help me against the rebels! Help me save the Union! I have confidence in you: Come!

Old Abe was calling him. Being a citizen he was called on to shoulder his duties. For an honest man there could be only one reply to the call.

But as Karl Oskar approached his claim he looked over his land and the fields his hands had wrested from the wilderness and this acted as a serious reminder: here lay his earth waiting for the seed. Regardless of what happened his fields must be planted. This must not be put aside for anything; if a crop were to be harvested in the fall, seeds must be put in the earth in the spring. This rule of nature must not be altered even by a war. Therefore he must wait for a while yet. He was simply forced to wait. Sowing came first. People must have food next year also. Old Abe, born in a tiller's cabin, wouldn't he understand this?

—2—

MINNESOTA, THE youngest state of the Union, was the first to reply to the President's call: on the very day it arrived the Republican governor, Alexander

Ramsey, offered in a telegram to Lincoln the first regiment of volunteers. And the Minnesota settlers were proud that their state was first. They were seized by an immeasurable anger and bitterness over the insult to the flag at Fort Sumter and several thousand of them were at once ready to sacrifice their lives in battle. Volunteers streamed in in much greater numbers than anyone had counted on. One regiment after another was trained and equipped at Fort Snelling and readied for the war.

Old Abe had asked for 75,000 men. He received in reply a song from the mouths of all the people in the North:

> We are coming, Father Abraham,
> Six hundred thousand strong . . .

In *Hemlandet* Kristina read about this great joy over the war which had seized people's minds, and she was profoundly perplexed. She had thought that if people needn't go to war except of their own free will there wouldn't be any wars. But her thoughts and feelings had been entirely wrong. Up here in the North no one was forced to go; nothing happened to those who stayed home. Yet they took off, people rushed to the battlefields of their own free will. Of their own free will they went out to kill and be killed. Not only that, they were happy and joyous and exhilarated to be able to kill and be killed. They couldn't get away fast enough, these volunteers who in their eagerness stepped on each other's heels at the recruiting places; people were jubilant because they would have an opportunity to kill their neighbors.

The Lord's commandment was: You shall love your neighbor as you love yourself! But it seemed they hated those neighbors in the South since they were in such a hurry to kill them. This desire of man to kill his own kind must be a curse of the original sin, which would cling to him to the end of time. War was punishment, war was caused by the original sin.

It said in *Hemlandet* that God took part and fought in the Civil War; fortunately he had decided to be on the side of the North. Eight hundred rebels had for two whole days bombarded Fort Sumter which was defended by one hundred men, but not a single one of the defenders had been killed. Thousands of shots had been fired but not a single Union soldier had fallen—this was a miracle that had taken place in the fort. And this miracle proved that God fought on the side of the Union troops.

How could they print such rot! wondered Kristina. God must have created the Southerners as well as the Northerners and he couldn't be on either side in the war, for he couldn't fight against his own creation, his own handiwork. He could only be against the war itself.

Karl Oskar felt the Union must be kept intact whatever the cost. But she replied that if the people in the South didn't want to belong to the Union, why not let them go? Weren't they fighting for the right to govern themselves, the same as the people up here in the North? It was senseless; both sides fought for the same thing! Both sides wanted to rule themselves! Why fight over it?

They could easily have come to an understanding if they had said to each other: We will leave you in peace if you leave us in peace! In that way the people of the South as well as the people of the North would have saved their lives.

It wasn't that easy, explained Karl Oskar. For only through war could the enslavement of the Negroes be abolished. No, said Kristina, however deeply she felt for the black ones she could not believe that a mass slaughter of other people was the right way to help them. It could not be God's will that people killed each other by the thousands to liberate some from slavery. To keep your neighbor as a slave was a grave sin, to kill a neighbor was graver.

They could not agree. But the inhabitants of their new country had begun to shed each other's blood, and each new issue of the paper told about it. In the settlements they read only of the Civil War, but each paper printed a comforting assurance: The North was many times stronger than the South, therefore the North must win. The North would win the war before the summer was over.

They sowed their seed and the kernels sprouted and came up. They planted the potatoes in the furrows and the potatoes returned in rows of dark green stalks. Even in this war spring the black earth fruited with wheat, corn, rye, oats, and root crops. This year too the earth promised the nourishment that would sustain people's lives.

Summer came and it remained quiet and peaceful in the settlements round Lake Chisago. The thunder of the Civil War rumbled so far away it could not be heard up in Minnesota. Several regiments had left for the battlefields and more were prepared in great hurry. But the void after the soldiers left was not great enough to interfere with daily life; it went on without interruption, each one attending to his chores, no one disturbed in his daily work.

But the war did not go the way the papers had predicted. Everything happened except what was supposed to happen. The war went very badly for the North. Union troops lost one battle after another and were forced to one withdrawal after another. And Northern soldiers fell in unbelievable numbers, their bodies lay stacked in great piles on the battlefields. It was said they fought valiantly but had poor weapons: a soldier could consider himself lucky if he had been given a gun that was no more dangerous to him than to the enemy. Besides, the Union troops had incompetent generals. But the setbacks were not blamed on them as much as on the competent generals of the South.

And after Fort Sumter no more miracles took place to prove that God was fighting on the side of the North. The rebels had the upper hand from the beginning and kept it. Lincoln named a new general to have full command of the North's forces, but it didn't help, since the South hadn't fired any of theirs.

By the end of the summer, when the Union troops already should have won the war, they suffered a great defeat at Bull Run, Virginia. When the papers announced this severe defeat a shock of fear hit the people of the North: Suppose we lose the war?

It seemed the end of the fight was near, but a different end than the one so surely predicted in the spring.

In April Lincoln had asked for 75,000 men, and 600,000 had volunteered. All had been convinced that this great army would be sufficient to win the war. But the inexperienced volunteers had first to be trained and equipped and it was a long time before they could be used in the field. And then came the defeats—and now more soldiers were needed.

In August President Lincoln issued a new call: He asked for another 300,000 men. If this number had not volunteered before the first of October, conscription would be necessary.

This was alarming.

And one day, in the beginning of September, just after the new call had been issued, Karl Oskar Nilsson read in *Hemlandet* a summons to the Swedish settlers of Minnesota to form a company of their own:

This country has permitted us to settle here in peace, it has received us foreigners with friendship. We enjoy here the same rights, are protected by the same laws, as the natives. Swedes constitute the greatest numbers of foreigners in Minnesota—it is time for us to fight for our adopted land, for the Union!

I myself offer to go! Let's meet at Fort Snelling, where we ourselves will choose our officers!

A pox on him who says this is a war among Americans and doesn't concern us! This fight concerns us and our children!

We have sworn loyalty to this country!

This country is now in danger!

The appeal was dated, Red Wing, September 2, 1861, signed H. Mattson, "a countryman." Karl Oskar read it several times, and thought deeply about it.

It was high time . . . !

The following night he could not sleep a wink, and in the morning he said to his wife that he was going to Stillwater and sign his name on the volunteer list. He would report for the war.

II

I AM CONCERNED WITH
YOUR ETERNAL LIFE

—I—

KRISTINA was sewing on her new sewing machine in the living room. Her right hand controlled the balance wheel while her left fed it the cloth. The pedals moved rhythmically, she felt them as a pair of heavy iron soles. She sewed with foot power rather than hand power. This sewing machine, Karl Oskar's gift to her last Christmas, had already saved her many hours of sewing and basting with needle. American menfolk made many inventions that helped greatly. This machine was an expensive apparatus—it had cost twenty dollars—but with it she could sew ten times faster than by hand. It was a very clever invention: the sewing contraption had pedals and buzzing wheels, shuttle and spool, over-thread and under-thread. It was truly unbelievable that such a capable machine—made for women's use—would have been invented by a man.

She was sewing shirts for Karl Oskar from a roll of flannel she had bought at Klas Albert Persson's store. Flannel was the cloth used by Americans for strong everyday wear. Otherwise she bought cheap calico or the most inexpensive cotton but the latter came in only a few ugly patterns at Klas Albert's.

It was a warm day even though it was already in September. Kristina pedaled her machine with bare feet. In winter the iron felt cold against the soles of her feet, but in summer cool and pleasant. The wheel's buzzing turned into a noisy roar when she pedaled the machine at high speed.

Karl Oskar came in and sat down beside her. She slowed down her tramping and stopped the balance wheel, letting her hand rest on it as she turned to her husband.

She had seen in his face, earlier today, what he had to say. She had expected it for a long time. He had decided at last.

"I can't delay any longer! I must volunteer! Otherwise I'll be forced to . . . "

She was prepared and calm. Nor had he expected his wife to burst out crying.

She said quietly, "You're not forced yet."

"No—but I might be soon. They might start conscription the first of October."

She raised her voice. "Wait till then!"

"It's more decent to volunteer before they begin drafting. I'd be ashamed to be forced."

Kristina looked questioningly at him. She moved her bare feet from the pedals of the sewing machine and rested her hands on her knees. "You wish to go to war of your own free will, Karl Oskar?"

"I've fought it the whole summer. Now I must go."

As early as April Old Abe had called his loyal citizens. It was now September and at last he would answer: I'm coming! He said he had no wish to go out in any war if he could get out of it honorably. He could always find excuses and delays: Last spring the fields needed seeding, now in fall he could say he needed to harvest the crop. Still later he could use the threshing as an excuse not to volunteer. And during the winter there was timber to fell and saw for the new main house he intended to build. That would bring them to spring with the new planting and the same old excuses. In that way he could go on year after year.

Until the North had lost the war!

Of what use would it be then that he had stayed at home and tended to his chores? If the North lost, the slave powers could do what they wanted. The slave owners used their Negroes like cattle and they could use the people up here in the same way. Who could say that they would be allowed to keep their land and their home? Here they had been able to live and govern themselves because the United States was their protection and security. But would it remain so if the Union were broken?

Many had gone out in the war before him. He, as they, had believed it would be over in one summer, in which case it would have been unnecessary to volunteer. But now everyone realized that this misery would last long, and he could not expect others to jeopardize their lives and defend his wife, children, and home while he himself dodged. If a healthy man stayed home after this he must be a coward.

"But I don't know of anyone hereabouts who has gone," she said. "You'll be the only one from our settlement."

"The others are too old."

Danjel Andreasson and Jonas Petter were both near sixty; Petrus Olausson and Johan Kron were somewhat younger but both had reached fifty; Anders Månsson was a drunkard and useless for military service; Algot Svensson was about his own age, but last winter he had torn one of his eyes on a sharp branch and consequently was not able-bodied. The only one in their section who would have to go in a draft would be himself.

Kristina's fingers returned to the piece of cloth in the machine. Would she have to prepare Karl Oskar for war? Then she must hurry up and get these shirts ready for his rucksack.

The memory of an evening long ago in another country came to her. The children were asleep, it was silent in their house, the fire had burned down to glowing embers. Then he had suddenly begun to talk: He had decided they would emigrate to America.

For a long time she had been against it; she wanted to remain in her home community. To emigrate seemed to her as perilous as to go to war. Many had fallen on the emigrants' road. But he had thought through his decision carefully, and his will had prevailed. Now he wanted to go to war; this time too he had long pondered and weighed before he decided.

Kristina remained silent. Karl Oskar became uneasy. Had his decision hit her harder than he had expected? He added: It was not that he wished to participate in the singing of joyous war songs; it was not in happiness that he went, rather in deep sorrow. But he was forced to, he must not fail, his conscience bade him. If he threw off his duties on others, he would feel like a weakling, a clod.

"You mean you must enlist to set your conscience at rest?"

"Yes, to regain my peace of mind."

"But your conscience says you must not kill your neighbor. Don't you know the fifth commandment?"

"That commandment doesn't hold in war."

"The catechism doesn't say war is an exception?"

"One must defend oneself."

"The neighbor you'll kill says the same: I must defend myself!"

Karl Oskar moved closer to his wife and took hold of her hand: "Kristina, are you against it? Are you absolutely against it?"

"I only want you to wait till you're forced to go."

"But I'd rather go of my free will than be drafted."

"That's because of false pride. It's only vanity."

She pushed back her chair from the sewing machine. "Do you want to know why I'm against it?" It came almost as an outcry. "I don't want you to go out and kill people! I don't want your hands to kill anybody! I don't want your neighbor's blood on you! I don't want you to be guilty of people's lives! I don't want you to be a murderer, Karl Oskar!"

"Oh—in that way . . . " was his embarrassed reply.

"I don't want you to go into eternity with blood on you! That's why! It is your eternal life that is in question! If you take someone else's you lose your own! I don't want you to be lost forever! I am concerned with your eternal life!"

He sat quite dumbfounded for some minutes. This was not what he had expected to hear from his wife. He had thought she might say: You want to go to war before you are drafted? You want to leave your home of your own free will? Leave your wife and children, your fields and all you have built up here? Leave us alone with all the work to do here? You want to throw off everything on wife and children? Sacrifice your own life? How much do you really care for me when you are willing to make me a widow? How much do you feel for your children when you're willing to make them fatherless?

How can you? How can you risk your life in war before you're forced to? I pray you—stay at home! Stay and be my husband as long as this is allowed you! Remain here and be a father to your children as long as you can! Please, Karl Oskar, stay here!

Thus he had long in advance heard her persuade him, and that was why he had dreaded this moment. But now when it was here none of these words escaped her lips. She said nothing about herself or the children or the home. She only said: *I am thinking of your eternal salvation!*

As a citizen he had received a call from the nation's leader, a reminder of his duty. From his wife the husband and father now received another reminder, another call. But it did not concern this world, rather the eternal one.

— 2 —

KRISTINA had accepted her fate and made the best of her lot in life. Nothing could happen to her. That was why she didn't ask him to consider her. She was not afraid to be left alone. Here at home she and the children would have God's protection.

During this war summer she had often thought of her mother's mother, whom she remembered from her childhood home in Duvemåla where the old one had lived on her "reserved rights" for thirty years. She had been left a

widow while still a young woman. Toward the end of the last century the
Swedish king had made war against the Russian empress, to gain honor and
praise, and Grandfather had been forced to go to war. It was always the little
ones who must go out and kill each other so the big ones could get along. And
Grandfather never returned; he fell on the field of battle. His widow was left
alone with seven children on a small plot. She was thirty years of age. For
twenty years she slaved stubbornly, in great poverty, for her children. When
she was no longer able to work, the farm was sold and she moved into her "reserved room": Grandmother's reward in life was thirty years of loneliness in
this little hole of a room—a farm woman's life, not much noted or remarked
upon because it was the fate of thousands of other women as the result of war.

So it was with women and war; the men went out but the wives were left
home with children whom they alone must look after, feed, and foster. The
men went out to destroy life, the women stayed at home to preserve it. The
men must be alone, without their wives, the wives must be alone, without
their husbands. And yet God had created man and woman for each other's aid
and comfort.

So it had been of old, so it was still, and so it might remain. Kristina had already reconciled herself to the lone woman's lot in war-torn America.

—3—

Now KARL OSKAR replied to her: She had got it all wrong. He could not become guilty of blood—in the eyes of neither God nor man—if he killed enemies in the war. The guilt would lie with the slave powers who had started the
bloodshed. The North had done no injustice to the South. It was the South
who wanted to rule America with force, and that they mustn't allow or suffer.

Didn't she know how badly they used humans in the slave states? Whoever
taught a Negro to read must pay a fine of five hundred dollars for the first of-
fense, and if he were caught a second time five thousand dollars! And should a
person be caught a third time teaching a black person to read he would be
hanged! Down there they forced the Negroes to work in the infernal heat in
the cotton fields so they could sell the cotton cheap. If a Negro fled from the
slavery-whip he was pursued by starved bloodhounds and these beasts tore out
his entrails as soon as they caught up with him. Could any decent person be on
the side of the slave states?

Had they lived in the slave states, he would have been sent to war long ago;

all men between seventeen and fifty-five had been drafted. Had they lived in the South, it would soon be time for Johan to go. Here in Minnesota they were still free from the draft but by the first of next month it might begin. And he would feel ashamed and humiliated if he didn't volunteer before then. Old Abe must think he was a shirker if he must be forced to do his plain duty. Therefore he must volunteer of his own free will, but he did not do it out of false pride: He was forced to by his conscience. He must gain his peace of mind.

Tomorrow he would go to Stillwater and join the Swedish company with other men from the old country who wished to perform their duty to the new one. He had just read in the paper that there were many others who felt the way he did. He presumed that, like him, they wanted to get rid of the pain in their consciences.

"Well, I guess you must then," she said, as if talking to herself. "If you think you'll have peace in your soul afterward."

Karl Oskar was not very concerned as to whether or not he jeopardized his eternal life, she thought. She knew him; his mind could not be changed once it had been made up. It had never yet happened that he had changed a decision. Therefore there was nothing more to say.

Karl Oskar went out, and Kristina resumed her work, starting her sewing machine again. The pedals went up and down, the balance wheel whirled, the machine buzzed. If he was going to war she must finish his flannel shirts. And there were other garments he would need. Now she was in a hurry. Besides, she had other things to do than sit at the sewing machine. Yes, Karl Oskar's clothing must be the most important of her concerns for the moment.

It must always have been that way, about preparing the husband's clothing, when he was to go to war.

—4—

THE FOLLOWING EVENING Kristina was again at her sewing machine after supper. She was expecting Karl Oskar back from Stillwater, but he was late. The children had gotten hungry and so they had eaten their supper without the father at the table. What was left of the corn pancakes she had put into the Prairie Queen to keep warm for him.

It was already bedtime when Karl Oskar returned. The sewing machine kept buzzing and muffled her ear so she didn't hear him before he was inside the kitchen. She stopped the machine and went to take the plate with the pancakes from the oven; she poured milk into the pitcher and cut a few slices of bread. He threw his hat onto a peg and sat down silently at the table.

Karl Oskar seemed depressed and listless after his journey to Stillwater. Nor had he been especially happy when he left in the morning. But he had never been one of those who kept singing "We are coming, Father Abraham" even though he had a good voice, well noticed in church at the psalm singing. And by now that war song was sung mostly by those stay-at-homes who never had any intention of hearkening to Honest Abe's call.

Kristina wondered if perhaps he had changed his mind. Had he regretted his decision at the last moment? Maybe he had thought he wouldn't go out and seek death of his free will. Could it be that he didn't want to leave them all perhaps never to see them again? Maybe he had changed his mind and would wait until he was drafted for the human slaughter?

Something was wrong with him, that much she could see. But she would not ask. He must come out with it himself. Perhaps he had enlisted and now regretted it—when it was too late.

He mumbled something between swallows—the pancakes tasted awfully good; he had only had a sandwich in Stillwater, he was quite hungry.

He had stilled the worst of his hunger when he said, "Kristina do you want to know—I'm not going to war . . . "

"You're not! Didn't you enlist . . . ?"

"No."

"You changed your mind in the end? You'll wait till they take you?"

"No. I didn't change my mind."

"What happened . . . ?"

"They rejected me in Stillwater. I'm not up to it . . . "

"They rejected you!"

A powerful feeling of joy pierced Kristina's heart.

"I'm not good enough to go to war. Because of my leg. My lame shank . . . "

Karl Oskar pulled out his left leg from under the table, held it up for his wife to see. It seemed she had never seen her husband's left leg before. Meanwhile he sat and looked gloomily at the floor.

She had been wrong a moment ago; he had not regretted his decision. Instead he felt disappointed, ashamed. Yes, by jiminy, he was ashamed and gloomy because he had been rejected!

He bent down and felt the leg across the injured bone which he held pointed toward her.

"Some doctor had to examine me first, to see if I could do military service. The doctor rejected me, because of my leg . . . "

She was told how everything had happened. The recruiting office in Stillwater was housed in the old tailor's shop across from the bank, and Swedes and Norwegians who wanted to join the rifle company had to go there. It was called a rifle company because they were to use the new guns with rifles in them to make them shoot much faster than the old guns. An officer in gold-braided uniform with many stripes and tassels had received him and the other volunteers. His name was Captain Silversvärd; he was a Swedish nobleman who had emigrated and he spoke the mother tongue. So in the beginning it was quite like home there in the office. And that man, the captain, was quite a decent sort of fellow and treated them all as equals, since they were all in America where soldiers are free men who themselves select their company commanders. In Sweden a simple soldier had only one duty—to obey—but here he could help select his own officers. The captain had told him he would make a splendid soldier and warrior, so tall and strong as he was; most settlers were of course accustomed to heavy work and severe conditions. He had been a little embarrassed by this talk and had said that he thought his big nose might be in the way when he tried to find the sight to aim at the enemy.

He was promised thirty dollars recruit money the moment he was accepted. During his term of service he would receive fifteen dollars a month besides food and uniform. Old Abe was to his soldiers as a father to his children and saw to it that they received everything they needed, the Swedish captain had said. Karl Oskar would have nothing to worry about while he was in the war.

Then came the physical examination and he was shown to another room where a doctor took charge of him. He had to take off every thread of clothing from his body, standing there so naked in that room that he felt ashamed even though only the doctor and another man were in there. The doctor looked over every part of his body, listened to his chest when he breathed, peeked down his throat, felt him in the groin, as if he must be able between the legs also, or whatever it was for. Then the doctor went to a corner and whispered words he had to repeat and showed him a picture with terribly small letters he had to read. And the medical inspector said the same thing as the captain: He was a fine soldier. Lungs, heart, vision, and hearing were as good as they could be in a human being, each part of his body was in excellent condition, all his faculties perfect.

Finally he was asked to run across the floor, just to try the legs a little. He ran around, strutted about, and stretched out his legs and it did hurt a little in the left shank, as it always did when he moved it quickly. He always dragged that leg when he was tired. After a few turns the doctor asked him how long the leg had bothered him. He told the truth: He had injured it the first year he was in America and it had never healed properly.

He was told to run a few times more. Then the doctor said: "Sorry, your left leg is not good enough for a soldier." No one could go out in war with such a leg. He limped on it when he ran, and a soldier could not limp in any way, he must be able to run perfectly if need be. He should have taken care of his leg, attended to the injury while there still was time for it to heal right. Now it was grown together in such a way that he would have it as long as he lived.

Karl Oskar himself felt that his leg had improved this last year, he had never for a moment thought it would prevent him from enlisting. Nor did he think it would be so important for a soldier to be able to run fast. The most important thing, in his opinion, was to hold his post and not turn and run away from the enemy. And he had told the doctor as much; he knew he was no runner, but he didn't think the troops of the North would have to run away all the time. The doctor laughed and said, on the contrary, he was afraid Karl Oskar couldn't run fast enough to pursue the enemy.

Because of his left leg he had been rejected. The Swedish captain felt very sorry about it, and before Karl Oskar left, this nobleman made a speech and thanked him for having shown his loyalty as a citizen in honestly offering to do his duty to his adopted land. However, since he was a farmer he could still do great service to the Union. He could sow and harvest his crops and raise cattle; those who were in the war needed food, said the captain, probably to make him feel less bad because he had been rejected and was useless for military service.

Kristina pricked up her ears at the last words: Perhaps he needed to be consoled. She said, "Now you can stay home without anyone reproaching you. I hope your conscience is at rest."

But she had understood right along that he wasn't satisfied.

"It's galling to be a useless person," he said, "one who isn't quite worthy of full measure . . . "

Kristina exclaimed hotly, "Are you ashamed because you aren't worthy to slaughter people? That's the silliest thing I've heard in my whole life!"

"You don't quite understand this sort of thing, Kristina."

"Oh no! It's an awfully vain man who is ashamed because he can't go out and kill!"

"Well, I was a little disappointed and hurt when I was rejected as a useless weakling and not up to standard."

Kristina knew Karl Oskar had some great shortcomings, the shortcomings of all men. He suffered from pride and self-assurance, he thought he was good enough to do anything. This was the original sin in him. Deficient! Because he was rejected as a soldier! If she were a man she would be proud that she was found unsuitable to kill people!

She resumed: When cattle were chosen for slaughter, usually the injured or old or deformed came first, worn-out oxen or cows that gave little milk. But when they sent men to slaughter on the field of battle then they took the healthy and young and perfect first! Those best fitted to live were sent away to die!

Karl Oskar rose slowly from the table this evening. He set down his left foot heavily on the floor, as if he wanted to test it, to assure himself that the leg still was able to carry him. Then he shook his shoulders and threw out both his hands as if shaking off a burden of long standing: "Don't let's talk about it any more! You'll have me here at home now as long as the war lasts!"

If he had heard Kristina's prayer the evening before, he would have known who had prevented him from going to the Civil War where he might have lost his eternal life.

III

THE FIRST COMMANDMENT
FOR EMIGRANTS

Thou shalt not regret Thy emigration,
Thou shalt love America as Thy young
Bride and Sweden as Thine Old Mother.

—I—

IN THE EVENING Kristina dug around the Astrakhan apple tree under the east gable of the house. With her fingers she pulled out quickroot and other weeds, with the spade she piled a bank of black earth round the trunk. In this way her old father in Duvemåla had attended to the fruit trees in fall. This tree, grown from a seed from her parents' home in Sweden, was already taking on height and breadth. The sapling was now a young tree that had bloomed three springs. But as yet it had produced no fruit. Two springs in succession the blossoms had withered away from severe night frost. Last spring was warmer and the blooms remained, but at fruiting time the tree was covered with caterpillars which gnawed on the stems, and during a storm in June the unripe apples fell to the ground.

The seasons in America were unpredictable and unreasonable. Her Astrakhan tree had suffered badly from exposure so far each year. But the Sweden sapling was still in its early youth and it would surely bear fruit in another year.

The bank of topsoil was ready and Kristina straightened her back and rested her foot on the spade. She had not yet done the evening milking. Johan and Harald had driven the cows into the corral at the barn. Round and about lay the fields where the stubble left from harvested crops shone golden brown in the clear evening light. The sugar maples to the front of the house had changed the color of their leaves to deep yellow and the oaks beyond the field stood rust-red. Already in the mornings a sprinkle of frost, like drops of milk,

23

glittered on the grass. And gusts of wind had begun to feel chilly against the cheeks—the autumnal wind which harrowed the ground with rough strokes.

Soon winter would knock at the door, Kristina's twelfth winter in North America. She wondered if she would still be alive when the next snow melted and next spring arrived.

Since her miscarriage two and a half years ago she had not enjoyed the same health and strength as before. However little she worked she felt tired and her limbs weak. Her body strength simply would not return. After her childbeds she had quickly recuperated, but perhaps it was harder for a woman to bear a stillborn child than a living one. She suffered also in her soul: the sorrow that she—in bearing a lifeless offspring—had brought death into the world.

From time to time she was bothered with pain in her lower abdomen. The pain might disappear for a few days but it always came back. She wondered if this had anything to do with her great fatigue. Every evening when she went to bed she feared she might be unable to rise next morning. And how she would have liked to stay in bed in the morning! She felt as if she had only just tasted the rest, barely sipped of the refreshment. She would have liked to stay in bed for weeks and months and only enjoy herself. Perhaps this tiredness would remain in her body as long as life itself remained.

But death did not frighten her any more. The day before Robert walked into the forest and lay down to die at the side of a brook he had pointed out to her how he had reconciled himself to leaving this world: He had stopped complaining to the Lord about life and death and was satisfied with man's lot in life: Believe me, Kristina, Death can bring nothing evil to me—I am untouchable! Now she herself had gained the same conviction: She had conquered the worldly; death could not reach her soul. Why should she fear death which could take nothing from her except this earth, which everyone must lose?

She had over the years harbored longings for earthly things and tried to be satisfied with this world. It bothered her that life offered so much of goodness and beauty which others enjoyed but which she never would have an opportunity to partake of. She suffered because the lot of the emigrant had fallen on her. Year after year she suffered here in America from the thought that never would she return to the land of her childhood and youth. A homeland had once been given to her—she had lost it, and she could never have a new one. Her mind would never be at peace because of her longing for home. She lived as an unhappy and strayed creature and was afraid she might be lost to eternity. Until God rough-handedly showed her the right way and she accepted her lot; until she got rid of her worldly inclination and opened her mind to the thoughts of eternity. Only then did she know that her soul-suffering and inner disturbance were not caused by her inability to liberate herself from the old homeland, but rather that she was unable to give up this world.

The emigration was not her unlucky fate. How could a move on this earth affect a person? What did it matter if she lived her fleeting days in one place on the globe or another? Why was she concerned about dying in one spot or another? In the New World or in the Old? In Sweden or North America? She had her permanent home in a land she could never lose.

There was only one move now that meant anything to Kristina: her soul's liberation from the body, the move from one life to another, from temporal life to eternity. From this belief sprang her understanding of her life on earth.

And once she had reconciled herself to her fate no more uneasiness disturbed her. Nothing that happened in this world worried or frightened her. But for her husband who shared her life and for the children she had borne into this world she harbored love's anxiety. She had entrusted them to the Creator: Give me strength to endure a few years more! Don't make my children motherless as yet!

Every evening Kristina thanked God that she had been granted another day with Karl Oskar and her children.

—2—

ANOTHER DAY was counted out of her life. She leaned the spade against the house and went into the kitchen for her milkpans.

Karl Oskar had driven to Taylors Falls today and was not yet back. She wondered why he was late. She had sent him on an errand to Anders Månsson's since he anyway was so close.

As Kristina sat on her milking stool in the stable, her thoughts wandered to Anders Månsson, who had come here before them and had housed them in his cabin during their first months in the Territory. He had been struck by the same misfortune as she—homesickness. But he had sought other aid than she: He tried to drink away his regret over his emigration. He ruined himself and his possessions with the American brännvin. She had heard that he had been forced to sell his last cow, and she felt sorry for Fina-Kajsa and her son that they had now no milk. Her thoughts went to the day when Anders Månsson had lent them the milch-cow Lady during their first winter in the wilderness. The milk had helped her save the lives of her children that winter. Now they themselves had a cow that had just calved and today she had sent milk and some biestings-pudding to the Månssons with Karl Oskar.

Before she was through with the milking she heard the sound of a spring wagon as it stopped before the stable door: Karl Oskar was back. A few moments later he came into the stable.

She noticed at once that his expression was not his usual one. He was tense; his lips were contracted, and his eyes under the wrinkled brows were severe.

Did he bring a message of accident or misfortune?

"Has anything happened?"

"Don't be upset. Nothing has happened to me, but when I came to Anders Månsson's this morning . . . "

During the last days Fina-Kajsa and her son had often been in Kristina's thoughts. Perhaps it had meant something?

She received the answer as she now heard what Karl Oskar had to relate.

ANDERS MÅNSSON's place had seemed completely desolate and deserted when he had arrived there. Not a living soul was in sight outside. The fields were neglected; a rusty plow lay in one field but no fall plowing had been started, some scythes had been left in the grass, the barn door hung askew on one hinge, and by the wall stood the old ox cart—the screech-wagon—with broken wheels. In the potato field were still the frozen, black stalks—the potatoes had not yet been picked in spite of the night frost.

The cabin door was bolted from the inside. Karl Oskar banged at it but no one opened. Not a sound inside. He tried to peek through the window but the curtains were drawn.

He could not discover a sign of life at this place and he got a feeling that something was wrong.

Looking again toward the potato field he noticed something unusual. In among the blackened stalks lay some sort of bundle, a gray pile, it looked like. He thought he recognized pieces of clothing and went over to investigate.

It was old Fina-Kajsa, stretched out on her back in a furrow. She had the hoe beside her. She lay as immobile and still as the earth under her body; her eyes were half-open and stared at the sky. There was something final and finished about the old woman's position, something fulfilled and irrevocable. Karl Oskar guessed at the first glance how things stood.

As far as he could see Fina-Kajsa was dead. No one except a dead person could lie so peacefully in a furrow in a field. The old one had been hoeing up potatoes and it seemed natural that one laboring in the earth should assume this position at the last. Fina-Kajsa wore her dark gray shawl, the same color as the earth she rested on. Her body lay there like a hummock in the ground, as if it already were part of the soil.

At her head stood a basket, the bottom barely covered with a few great, oblong, reddish tubers, the best kind of America's potatoes. Her hands still held on to the handle of the hoe. The old hands seemed only sinews and bone under the skin, almost bare bones, and the fingers branched out like thin, peeled twigs. Fina-Kajsa had been miserably lean and scraggly the last years—now she seemed small as a child. Her body seemed mainly a pile of clothing, a heap of bundled-together rags. Her mouth was open, a toothless hole. The caved-in face was brown and scabby but the whites of her eyes shone like white daisies in withered grass in early spring. In those eyes life had remained longest.

The furrow the old one had begun to pick was long, stretching from one end of the field to the other. She had hoed only a few yards when she fell; before her lay much unfinished labor, perhaps she had mumbled to herself before she fell, chewing on her disappointment: She was never to see the great farm and the handsome buildings her son had painted in his letters from North America.

Fina-Kajsa had been hoeing in long, forceful strides. Karl Oskar could see her work here on the field, he could hear her voice mumbling: Hoe on, hoe on! The furrow is long! The field is big! *Ackanamej!* America is a big country! I'll never get there! Hoe on, Fina-Kajsa, old woman! *Ackanamej! Ackanamej!*

The farm woman from Öland, Sweden, had hoed her last in life. The furrows had been long, the field large, and in her basket were only a few potatoes at the bottom. Yet, even after death she had not let go of the hoe.

Karl Oskar remained standing there with the milk pail and the pudding from Kristina. Too late; now the gift could be used at her funeral.

But where was Fina-Kajsa's son? At the German Fischer's inn in Taylors Falls? Or did he lie dead drunk in his bed? Where to look for a son who let his worn-out, aged mother pick potatoes alone while he himself—well, where did he keep himself?

As if in reply a noise was heard from the log cabin. The heavy door opened slowly inward and Anders Månsson stepped out on the stoop. Karl Oskar's banging a few moments ago must have awakened him. He did not look toward the potato field, but went to the corner to let his water.

Karl Oskar hurried toward him.

Fina-Kajsa's son was bareheaded, his hair stood up straight as nails from the top of his skull, his cheeks were covered with a matted red beard. He was already stooping like a broken man. He peered at the caller with blood-shot, watery eyes as he greeted him.

"How goes it, Nilsson?"

Perhaps it seemed unusual to be lying inside in the middle of forenoon, a sunny, beautiful weekday, and he added apologetically, ashamed: "I was just resting a moment."

He was still walking half in his sleep, it seemed.

Karl Oskar had no time for greeting. He said tartly, "Your mother lies in the potato field—she's dead!"

Anders Månsson slowly opened his mouth, looking at his countryman as if he had not understood.

Karl Oskar took him by the arm and together they walked to the field. The son looked in silence at his mother lying so still on her back, her fingers clutching the hoe handle. Openmouthed he beheld the picture before him. Then he rubbed his running eyes and scratched his wild beard. After staring a few moments at the old body in the black-gray shawl he turned questioningly to his countryman beside him, as if Karl Oskar must explain this sight to him—as if he himself understood nothing.

Karl Oskar took him by the shoulder and shook him—wasn't he awake yet? He stank of whiskey, his head was still in a drunken stupor.

"Are you still drunk? Can't you talk?"

Anders Månsson had lost his power of speech at the sight of the dead one in the furrow. It was incredible to him that his mother could have laid herself down in this way out in the field, could remain lying so quietly in the same position regardless of how long he looked at her.

Karl Oskar felt sorry for him but couldn't help showing his impatience: "You must know your own mother!"

At last a word came from Anders Månsson's gaping mouth: " . . . Mother . . . oh yes, yes . . . Mother . . . "

Karl Oskar thought Fina-Kajsa had been dead for several hours, probably since early morning. And he also assumed that her son had been dead drunk since last evening and only now had awakened.

Now he stood here irresolutely and stared at his mother, and it looked as if he could stand like that indefinitely without any intention of doing anything with her lifeless body. Could he possibly have in mind to let her have her grave here in the potato field furrow?

"Help me, Månsson. We must carry her inside . . . "

Karl Oskar loosened the hoe from the dead one's grip. Anders Månsson bent down and took hold of her legs; his hands shook like those of a very old man. Together they carried her toward the cabin. Fina-Kajsa was not heavy, she was not a burden for one man alone, much less for two, but Karl Oskar felt that the son ought to help carry his mother home.

They placed Fina-Kajsa on her bed, and Karl Oskar pulled a blanket over the corpse.

He saw a whiskey keg beside the son's bed, a five-gallon one from Fischer's inn; Anders Månsson fed his drunkenness as long as the whiskey lasted. Karl Oskar would have liked to give the drunkard a good talking to: While drinking in bed he had let his mother work herself to death. But what use would there be in reproach? The dead body on the other bed was reproach enough.

In his soul Anders Månsson was a decent person, and now he had double sorrow: his regret over what he had done to his mother.

The two settlers went outside and sat down on the stoop. Karl Oskar said he would help as much as he could with the funeral. On his way home he would stop by at Jonas Petter's and tell Swedish Anna to come and wash the body and dress it for the coffin. The Irish carpenter in Taylors Falls was sure to make the coffin.

"Thanks, Nilsson. You're good to me . . . "

Karl Oskar replied that Anders Månsson had helped him greatly that first year they were out here; he was glad if he could help in return. Fina-Kajsa's son breathed heavily and his voice was hoarse; he coughed hollowly, as if his cough came from a deep hole, an empty space in his chest, a hollow, vaulted cellar.

"I don't feel well. I've spoiled my health here in Minnesota."

His power of speech was returning. He felt his head; returning also was the hangover.

"Life out here is hard on one's health; not all can take it . . . "

"But you must stop drinking, Månsson! You'll wreck your life and everything . . . "

"You mean I've wrecked my mother . . . ?"

"You're killing yourself as well! Stop your drinking!"

"Oh . . . oh . . . oh . . . ha . . . ha . . . "

It rattled down in his throat, it almost sounded like an eerie, echoing laughter. Stupefied, Karl Oskar looked at him.

But Anders Månsson was not laughing. There was some irritation in his throat; he coughed—he emitted a sound that was neither cry nor laugh, only an outcry from a man in hopeless despair:

"Stop drinking! What the hell! That's easy, ya betcha!"

"What's the matter? Are you still drunk?"

"You said to stop drinking . . . as if it were that easy! Like stopping your job or something. Just quit! It isn't that easy, Nilsson. You don't understand my trouble! Not one little part of it!"

"Have you tried to stop?"

"Every second day for ten years!"

"Why can't you stop?"

"Why!?"

"Yes, tell me . . . "

"Why . . . ? Because . . . because I'm afraid . . . "

"What are you afraid of?"

"Nilsson, you can't . . . "

He stopped. He seemed to have lost his speech again. He looked through the open door into the cabin. He could see the foot end of the bed, he could see a pair of feet in dirty white, worn-out woolen socks, a pair of old feet which today had tramped the earth for the last time.

He leaned over with both hands to his face. His body began to shake.

"What are you afraid of, Månsson?"

He did not reply, only mumbled again: "Mother!"

Karl Oskar waited. Fina-Kajsa's son must have time to gather his senses. Unprepared, he had seen his mother lying dead in the field—that was about as much as a man could take, even when he was well.

After a moment Anders Månsson began to talk again. He lowered his voice and looked about as if afraid some outsider were listening:

"I'll tell you, Nilsson . . . "

"What are you afraid of?"

"The madhouse . . . "

"The madhouse . . . ?"

"Yes—do you understand, Nilsson . . . ?"

"No, Månsson, I don't understand at all."

But in the next moment he understood. Fina-Kajsa's son was talking about the insane asylum.

"That place—you know. Can you understand my trouble now?"

Anders Månsson crouched and looked about as if danger lurked, as if something were round the corner of the house that he didn't want to see, as if the madhouse were quite close, on his own ground. Yes, wasn't it back there, beyond the field? He had seen it many times, it came closer each time he looked at it. Next time it might be right here, in his own field, opening its doors for him.

"The madhouse . . . "

Right here at his doorstep! Cozy and nice! Come right in, Anders Månsson! The doors are wide open! This is your home! Come in!

Fina-Kajsa's son saw things that weren't there, and Karl Oskar had received an answer to his question.

—4—

ANDERS MÅNSSON had once confided in Kristina that when he came to the Territory there were hardly any people there except Indians. For months on end he had no living soul to speak to; he could not have felt more alone and lost if he had been the only human being in the world. The loneliness made him long for the homeland. Perhaps he could have gathered together enough money for a return ticket but he felt ashamed to go back as poor and empty-handed as he had been when he left. Everyone would call him a failure. And when he left for America he had been so proud and uppity that he had called Sweden a shit-country, and said that he would rather be eaten by carrion than be buried there. He had emigrated with the thought of never returning, and if he went back he would have to suffer for his pride; he would have to eat every word he had uttered about the old country. He was ashamed to go back. Then he had written his parents a letter of lies: He liked it in America, all went well with him, he had a fine farm. They could come and live with him in their old age—he invited them because he was sure they would never come. But one day his mother had arrived and surprised him, and she had asked, where were his fine mansion and his vast fields he had written about? She would never believe he had lied so cruelly to her. As the years went by she became a little peculiar—at the end she thought her son was hiding his fine farm somewhere deep in the forest. And she kept asking, "Anders, where is your American estate?"

And while longing for Sweden Anders Månsson had begun to drink; he kept thinking about what he had done and worried about it, but once having changed countries he could never change back. Thus he had become the eternal whiskey-thirster.

Today Karl Oskar viewed one countryman's plight. But he could neither advise nor help.

He said, "Whiskey is a poor comforter, Månsson."

"Better a false than none . . . "

"But afterward you lie sick in your bed . . . "

Fina-Kajsa's son took a firm hold of Karl Oskar's sleeve, his eyes wild: "Yes, yes! And the worst is to wake up. It feels like my head were boiling in a caldron, a slow boil . . . Then I get scared to death! That's when I see the madhouse! *The madhouse!* Then there's only one help . . . one help . . . "

What did it help to warn or advise here? No outsider could lessen a burden or ache in someone else's body or soul. Anders Månsson fled from his torture to whiskey; he woke up with the same plague and fled again. He was in a vicious circle, he had walled himself in in a prison and each time he escaped he locked himself in more securely.

Fina-Kajsa's son turned about and looked inside the cabin. He could see two old feet in a pair of old socks, worn and muddy from the potato field. And by and by his eyes began to run, tears streamed down his cheeks and watered his matted beard—he was able to cry.

" . . . Mother . . . "

Karl Oskar had nothing more to say. He knew of no way in which to help the man beside him who kept crying—a man who had locked himself in and every day kept walling up the door to his prison.

—5—

THE SWEDISH PARISH in Chisago County had lost its oldest member: Fina-Kajsa Andersdotter had been seventy-seven years old.

She was buried under the silver maples, on the beautiful promontory beside the lake that had been set aside for burial ground. All the surviving members of that group of immigrants she had come with to the Territory in 1850 followed her to the grave. There were, besides her son, thirteen people, adults and children, who stood by and watched as the earth was shoveled onto her coffin. Only two of the original group were missing: Arvid Pettersson, who lay in an unknown grave, and Robert Nilsson, who had come to this plot before her.

The mortality rate had until now been low in the parish, as most of the immigrants were people in their best years. Only some twenty graves had been dug in the new cemetery, and many of these held children of a year or less. Old age would not for many years become an important cause of death among the immigrants of the St. Croix Valley.

A few weeks after Fina-Kajsa's funeral Jonas Petter came to Karl Oskar's and said that Anders Månsson had disappeared. People looking for him had found his cabin unlocked and deserted. He had not been seen in Taylors Falls for some time, not even at Fischer's inn, where he used to go daily. The German had begun to wonder why his whiskey customer did not show.

His gun was still hanging on its peg in the cabin; he was not out hunting. But some accident could have happened to him in the wilderness, some stray Indian might have murdered him, or he might have done himself some harm. Perhaps he had left because he couldn't endure living alone after his mother's death. But in that case, since he was a good old hunter, he ought to have taken his gun with him.

Jonas Petter wanted Karl Oskar to join him in a posse to look for their missing countryman. Danjel Andreasson and his son Sven would also come, and a few American settlers, old hunting friends of Månsson who wished to participate.

All told there were about a dozen men in the posse to look for the missing man. They searched the forest near his claim but found no sign of him. The posse stayed in the wilderness several days without discovering any clues to explain his disappearance. The men dragged the little pond near his cabin but caught only the half-rotten carcass of a drowned elk calf and an old canoe of the kind the Indians used.

Finally the posse gave up. They knew as little when they stopped as when they had begun. What had happened to Anders Månsson? Was he alive or dead?

The mystery was solved some time later.

A boy from Franconia was fishing at the rapids below Taylors Falls when he noticed a hat that had stuck between two stones in the St. Croix River. The boy fished up the hat with his hook. It looked as if it had been long in the water. And in the hat was a clue to its owner: two big letters printed on the sweatband in red ink, now somewhat blurred but still quite legible: A. M. And there was no doubt to whose head this hat had belonged, since Mr. Fischer in Taylors Falls recognized it as belonging to Anders Månsson. He had once forgotten it at the inn.

All thought that Fina-Kajsa's son had himself jumped into the stream. He could possibly have fallen in while fishing, but he never fished in the St. Croix River, and he could have had no other errand to the rapids.

His body was never found. Undoubtedly it had floated a long way from the place where his hat was stuck between the stones. During the fall rains the strong current might carry a corpse with it to the still greater stream, the Mississippi, which then would take charge and carry it to the big sea.

Anders Månsson had been the first Swedish settler in the St. Croix Valley, but no grave opened for him under the silver maples in the settlers' cemetery. He himself undertook the one emigration that remained for him.

One single decision had decided his life, the great decision to emigrate, the irrevocable, the irreversible. To him had been put a strong command which he was unable to follow, the first commandment in the emigrant's catechism: *Thou shalt not regret Thy emigration!*

IV

THE SETTLERS' HOLY DAYS

—I—

THAT AUTUMN Karl Oskar cleared and plowed the last of the meadow that had originally stretched from the forest down to the lake. Thus he had turned into a tilled field the entire slope which had at first attracted him and made him select this lakeside for his farm. He had now broken more than thirty acres and no more meadow ground for tilling was available on his claim. And Kristina thought they now had enough without further clearing.

But Karl Oskar liked to sit at the gable window and look out at the oak stand on the out-jutting tongue of land to the east of the house; those mighty, high-breasted oaks with their enormous crowns grew in topsoil at least three feet deep, a ground that was as fertile as his fields. The grove back there called for a tiller as it were; it would add fifteen acres to his field!

Up to now the tiller of these shores by the Indian lake had only needed to put the plow into the ground and turn the turf. It was easy enough to break new fields on even meadowland, it was something else to tackle a heavy oak forest. But those great trees—a mixture of white oak and red oak—kept challenging him: Try to make a field here if you can! Our roots are thick and strong and go deep into the ground—try to pull us from our hold! Here your strength won't suffice! Come and try!

This oak grove had trees that were four to six feet in diameter. The felling alone would be an immense labor. And afterward the greatest hindrance would remain: the stumps. How could he get rid of them? He pondered this problem at great length. Oak stumps in America were as much of an obstacle to a tiller as stones in Sweden.

How could Karl Oskar conquer these mighty oaks, so securely rooted in the deep soil? Well, his sons were growing up, and becoming stronger; he must wait with this new ground breaking until they could help him. As soon as Johan and Harald could do a full-grown man's work, they would tackle the oak grove; then the strength of the tiller would be measured against the oaks.

35

He was also planning for his new buildings. But with the Civil War came dear times. Prices on implements made of iron and steel rose quickly. Everything he needed to buy for his house building grew more expensive. He must wait awhile. He had hauled thick oak logs to the steam mill in Center City, where they had been sawed into planks and boards for the new house; he had a tall pile of timber already. And this year he planned to cut sills and foundation logs.

But the war delayed all activity, all building in this part of the country. There must be an end to destruction and ruination before new undertakings could be started; one could not build a new house while the old was still burning.

—2—

A MILE AND A HALF from their farm stood their church, a modest building of rough timbers, deep in the forest. But the church pointed a little wooden spire toward Heaven, indicating it was a God's house, a Lord's temple. The Swedish immigrants had sacrificed many days of labor on their church, they had gone in debt for it and had not yet been able fully to pay for it.

Karl Oskar and Kristina went to the timber church every Sunday unless blizzards or other bad weather prevented them. Once in a great while they would stay at home out of pure tiredness and celebrate their day of rest in the home. But the distance between the church and their home was not so great that they could not hear the ringing of the bell which had been hung last year. The bell had cost all of ninety dollars and was paid for by the "nuisance tax"— fines levied against parish members who in one way or another had misbehaved during the service. Petrus Olausson himself, the church warden, had suggested this tax, and he was greatly lauded for it when at last it bought the church a bell. To the poor parish, barely able to support a pastor, ninety dollars was a great sum. First and always, it was cash that the settlers lacked.

Kristina could again hear the ringing of a church bell. On days when a favorable wind carried the sound it seemed quite close to her. But to Kristina's ears the new bell did not have the thunderous, sacred tones of a real church bell. As a child home in Ljuder, when she heard the bells she would shudder deep in her heart: The sound came from the heavens, like the thunder of the doomsday trumpet. The ringing from on high called to communion or service. But the settlers' bell here in America had an entirely different tone. It almost sounded like a dinner bell on a farm, calling to an ordinary meal; it was better suited to a weekday than a Sunday. The bell did have a light, quite beautiful tone, but it jingled rather than rang. The sound was pleasing to Kristina's ears but found no response in her soul.

To her the church bells of Ljuder signified weddings and funerals, people's union in life and their departure from it, the move into a new home and the move to eternity. On Sundays the bells from the parish church hurled a mighty command to the inhabitants: It was the Sabbath, they must go to church to confess and shed the burden of sins accumulated through the working week, cleanse body and soul. At the first sound of the bell on Sunday morning her father used to say: Now I hear it is Sunday! I feel it is a holy day! Time to wash and change shirts! Those bells instilled piety in the minds of the listeners.

To Sunday belonged also organ music and the singing of psalms. For many years the Chisago people had held their services and sung their hymns without an organ, even though the service sounded empty without the musical instrument—God's house was a poorhouse. Then last year they had gone into debt to put in an organ that cost a hundred and sixty dollars. Karl Oskar had voted against this purchase, for he felt they couldn't yet afford it. And when the organ was installed he did not like the sound of it: It must not be a first-class instrument with a sound that was harsh and screeched in his ears and thundered like the roaring of an ox. It could also be that he didn't understand organ music.

Kristina had never missed the organ at the services; if the words of the psalms came from a heart in need of God they would reach him without the aid of an organ. She could feel reverence in her heart without the help of steeple, bell, organ, or other worldly instruments.

—3—

THE Chisago Lake parish had engaged a new pastor who arrived in October. His name, Johannes Stenius, sounded like a good minister's name and he was a real minister directly from Sweden. There was a dearth of educated preachers, and for several years the Swedes in the St. Croix Valley had borrowed pastors from other parishes. They were now well pleased to have their own shepherd, ordained in their homeland. Rumors had already reached them that Pastor Stenius was a capable preacher of God's Word, stringently adhering to the pure Lutheran religion.

At the first wedding the new pastor was to perform in the settlers' church, the bridegroom was related to Kristina—Danjel's oldest son Sven, her blood cousin.

Sven Danjelsson was to marry Ragnhild Säter, a young Norwegian girl who had recently come to the St. Croix Valley. Women invariably married shortly after their arrival, usually within a month. In this woman-empty land they had only to choose among the many men who showed up as suitors. And the men had indeed flocked around Ragnhild, who was an unusually attractive girl, and who had refused many before she decided to exchange her Norwegian name for a Swedish one and become Mrs. Danjelsson. Sven had staked a claim and built himself a cabin at Acton in Meeker County, at its western border where land still was plentiful and easy to clear. After the wedding, Danjel's son and daughter-in-law would live in their new home in Meeker.

Karl Oskar and Kristina were invited to the wedding feast, which was given by Danjel Andreasson, as the bride's parents were living in her old home in Norway. A heavy rain fell as they started out for the church in the morning. Kristina took the opportunity to use her new umbrella which Karl Oskar recently had bought for her. It was a fine gift, made of dark blue silk. For the first time in her life she was using an umbrella. In Sweden only upper-class wives had this kind of protection against rain; it was an object for show-off and vanity, not suitable for simple farm folk. Therefore Kristina almost felt like a noble lady today as she mounted the spring wagon and put up her umbrella. But here in America all women used many decorations and ornaments which in Sweden were reserved for upper-class wives. Even settler wives wore rosettes and bows and lace and other glitter on their clothes, and flowers and feathers on top of their heads. Moreover, an umbrella was not only an ornament, it was a protection against rain as well.

And it did rain this day! It literally poured from early morning till late at night on Sven's and Ragnhild's wedding day. But rain was a good omen since it promised great riches for the bridal couple.

To the parishioners this wedding in their church was a denial of the common statement that Swedes and Norwegians could not get along in America.

After the ritual Pastor Stenius spoke to the young couple of the appalling increase of evil in the world at this time and warned them against religious seducers and wrong preachers who might seek to lead them astray from their mother church. He also warned against the greatest sins of the day: whoring, drinking, and dancing. The pleasure of dancing was invented by the old creeping Snake; in halls of music and dance the virtue of women met its defeat. Finally, the pastor condemned the excesses of female dress which in these latter days stimulated men's carnal desires and increased the number of whoring men.

It was not a great company that afterward gathered for the wedding feast at Danjel Andreasson's farm, and the groom's father had invited only those countrymen who had come with him from the old parish. He had once paid for the journey of Ulrika of Västergöhl, now the wife of Baptist minister Henry O. Jackson. She had not come to the church—she would not enter Lutheran churches—but she joined the guests at the wedding reception.

Kristina was shy when she met people who spoke only English, which thus put her outside the company. She had been in America almost twelve years now but could hardly speak a word of the language, although she was a citizen of this country. She had gone through the years as if deaf and dumb, as far as the language was concerned. Often she had met Americans who seemed kind and helpful but because of the language barrier she had been unable to enjoy their company. She was beginning to regret that she hadn't started to learn English from the very first day out here. But she still shuddered at the sound of this tongue, so unseemly and twisted. In trying to use one single word she felt she would sprain her tongue. She was told to bite off her words and put her tongue against her teeth. But this only made a hissing and gurgling sound.

Here at the wedding feast in Danjel's house, however, Kristina need not feel apart from the company. But she confided to Ulrika: Each kind of animal had been given only one sound—the dogs in America had the same bark as dogs in Sweden—why had the Creator then given people different tongues so they couldn't understand each other?

"Punishment for their sins! Because they built the Tower of Babel, you know!" informed Ulrika.

Mrs. Henry O. Jackson was not of the opinion that an immigrant could learn English in school and then speak it fluently. The language must come to one's tongue of its own free will, of its own whim and fancy, on the spur of the moment.

"I myself, I speak English from inspiration!"

"Well, that's why you spoke it from the beginning, I guess. So your husband-to-be could understand you?"

"Yes, of course. Henry and I understood each other that way from the very beginning."

Ulrika considered the day when she was married to Pastor Jackson as the greatest happening of her life. Kristina knew she celebrated that day each year;

each fourth of May she put on her old bridal gown and the pastor donned his cutaway.

The two women had withdrawn from the other guests and were sitting in a corner of the room. It was only seldom they had the opportunity to speak to each other in confidence.

Ulrika had mentioned her husband's name, then she sighed and became silent. She seemed depressed. It was not the first time Kristina had been surprised at her behavior when her marriage to Jackson was spoken of. He was such a patient and good-hearted man, but there must be something here that wasn't quite right as it should be. Had something happened between the couple lately? It sounded as if Ulrika was burdened by something unsaid—why did she always sigh like that at her husband's name?

"Henry is very good to me, very good," she said. "But a woman can be happy in one way and unhappy in another."

"Unhappy in another? What do you mean?" Kristina's eyes were wide open.

Ulrika looked about and continued in a low voice: "We're at a wedding today, that's why my thoughts go in that other way. I'll tell you, but it must stay between us of course."

She pulled out her handkerchief, blew her nose thoroughly, and leaned intimately toward Kristina. Henry and she didn't fit together in bed any more. She had hoped for a long time that it could be worked out, so they would fit, but as they had shared the marital bed now for ten years, she knew there was no hope of improvement. Henry didn't handle a woman the right way at the very moment when it counted. She didn't want to blame him in the least for this, because he hadn't been trained with women from his youth, and when he got a wife—at a ripe age—he was too old to train. And perhaps a man's way in bed was something he was born with, something that came naturally, if bedplay were to be excellent.

Ulrika looked toward the upper end of the table; there on the bench, in today's seat of honor, sat the young bridal couple. Her eyes lingered a moment on the young Norwegian girl, whose cheeks were rosy-red with health and from blushing, whose eyes, glitteringly clear, never for a moment left the groom.

Ulrika sighed again in envy and desire: "You see, Kristina, in my marriage I don't get that bodily bliss a woman craves. The great temptations of my old body have come over me. Desire for sins of the flesh. I have eyed other men . . . "

Kristina grew disturbed at Ulrika's confidence: "What *are* you talking about?! You mean that you—the wife of Pastor Jackson . . . ?"

"Yes, it's true—I've been tempted to whoring."

Kristina made a sudden motion with her hand, as if to silence her. But Ulrika went right on.

"I had to tell you. It happened last summer. A Norwegian tempted me so I had to . . . You know him, Sigurd Thomassen . . . "

"The shoemaker in Stillwater? The one who always complains because he doesn't have a woman?"

"Exactly! It was he!"

Kristina remembered the man from Ulrika's great Christmas party when he had tried to become intimate with her: "I'm a kind man, I don't wish to do anything wrong with any woman . . . "

"Did the Norwegian tempt you to adultery?"

"He wanted the same thing as I."

And Ulrika's ample bosom rose with her deep breathing; in this woman-empty America Thomassen was far from the only one who had tried to seduce her. She had met men who had both the inclination, the lust, and the fresh approach. But the Norwegian was the only one whom she herself had been tempted to satisfy, because he had a gentle heart—he was a good man who had lived single for many years, poor devil. She had many times allowed him to take her around the waist and pat her—oh, quite innocently! But his eyes had always told her what he wanted.

Then it had happened, one time last summer. She had left a pair of shoes to be resoled, and late one evening she had gone to Sigurd Thomassen's house to pick them up. He offered to make coffee for her and she thanked him and stayed. They were alone, he had set the table in his bedroom, and while they drank their coffee he complained of how many years it had been since a woman had comforted him in bed. He was pining and yearning, he was almost at his wit's end. And then she began to wish sometime she could give him this enjoyment he had so long gone without.

Sometime—and when would be better than at this very moment?

At first she hadn't thought anything of it that they sat alone in his bedroom; when she came to fetch her shoes she had only innocent thoughts. But by and by the other thoughts came over her. Sigurd's bedroom was so small, his bed so large; they could barely move in there without touching the bed. And without realizing how it happened she was suddenly on his bed, while he patted and petted her—they were acting like young lovers. Then the thought came to her: What Henry didn't have the power to give her, the Norwegian might. A man who had lived single for so long must have saved much for a woman.

He was ready to turn her over in his bed, and she was ready to be turned over; she could not resist a man's hands as they stroked her loins and hips, and she grew utterly faint and helpless. At last she herself turned over on her back.

That was how far it had gone, so close to adultery was she: She herself had turned over.

Then rescue came. At the very last second help had come.

She had not noticed that Sigurd had locked the door when she came in, and this was not the act of a gentleman. Now suddenly someone was knocking to get in. He had already begun to undress and didn't wish to go and open the door. But the bangings were insistent and at last he had to go; two little children had brought a pair of their father's boots to be resoled. As Sigurd took the boots she could hear the voices of the children and couldn't resist opening the door just a little to peek at them. There stood two cute little girls with flaxen braids and rosy cheeks and eyes as blue as heaven itself. And as she looked at them she understood at once.

They were a couple of angels who had knocked on the shoemaker's door to save her in the moment of her temptation. It was so late in the evening—why would the parents have sent their kids on an errand at this time? It was God himself who had sent them. God's angels had come to save her.

And as she looked at them she received the strength to resist the desire that was burning her flesh. Her eyes were opened, and in fright she realized how close to the abyss she was. Only in the very last second had the Lord remembered her.

As soon as the children were gone she picked up her newly soled shoes and left. Sigurd didn't want any pay for repairing the shoes but she forced the money on him—he mustn't get the idea that he could pinch her for pay! She had long ago been redeemed from that sort of life! But she had told him that she forgave him for tempting her so much; he couldn't help it, she thought, because the evil one used men as his tools when he led women astray.

"I did no whoring," Ulrika ended her tale, "but it was pretty close!"

At first Kristina had listened shocked, then she was moved; no woman except Ulrika would have confided in her thus.

"God did indeed save you!"

"Not even a twice-baptized person can help it if she is assailed by temptations. I was overcome by lust, but it was only a sin of weakness—the sins God forgives most easily!"

Kristina understood that even a married woman might have her weak moments, with the flesh eager to gain the upper hand, but it surprised her that

Ulrika for one second could feel tempted by Sigurd Thomassen. She remembered well that when he had approached her he exuded such a strong smell of shoemaker that that alone would be sufficient for a woman to resist him. That rancid, pungent odor of tanned leather her nose could not take; the man who exuded it became repulsive to her. Perhaps Ulrika's weakness could be explained by the life she had led in the old country.

Jonas Petter approached them and asked if they had been watching the newly married couple. He had never seen such a well-made bridal pair, he beamed; that girl from Norway was truly a virgin, a delicious fruit to feast his eyes on! A womanly delight for a man! A fragrance of new-baked bread! Danjel's boy was indeed fortune's favorite prince! To lie under the bridal blanket with this fresh, untouched maiden! A king or an emperor could dream of no greater delights than those Sven would experience with Ragnhild!

Ulrika replied that yes, she could understand how his mouth watered, she could see Jonas Petter drool, the old whore-buck, as his eyes devoured the sweet kid he himself couldn't mount! With old goats the lust grew greater as the strength diminished! She felt indeed sorry for him, poor wretch!

Jonas Petter was hurt and mumbled to himself; since food was being served, he walked toward the table, where Karl Oskar already had a chair next to the bridal couple.

Sven had been fourteen years of age when he came with his father to the St. Croix Valley; now he was twenty-five. He was a capable, industrious young man, who had inherited his father's weak and brooding nature. He had grown into a handsome youth, no disgrace to his beautiful bride.

Jonas Petter kept his eyes on the bride as he spoke to the groom: "You've taken land in Meeker—that's where the Sioux are; they're bad."

"If you don't disturb them they won't annoy the whites," said Sven.

"But that tribe has always been warlike and treacherous."

"In the old days."

"I've heard you can never trust them. If I had been in your shoes, Sven, I would have taken a claim closer by. There's still plenty of land hereabouts."

If Jonas Petter had been in Sven's shoes—you could see from his eyes on Ragnhild what he wanted; the groom knew him well and tried to hide his smile.

Karl Oskar said he had heard from Mr. Thorn, the sheriff, that some of the Sioux to the west were becoming unmanageable because they hadn't yet received their pay from the government agent; they had been promised money for the land they gave up. The sheriff thought the slave owners in the South were behind it; they were said to have smuggled rifles to them.

Jonas Petter sat down beside the bride, as close as he could get: "The traders are skinning and cheating the redskins. It's easy to cheat the Indians, they can't read and don't understand numbers."

"That's true," affirmed Sven Danjelsson, in a reproachful voice. "It's always rascals and knaves who are sent out to deal with the Indians."

"They should send you instead," said Karl Oskar.

"I'm going to make friends with the Indians back there," said Sven. "That's the right way for a settler to behave!"

Karl Oskar reminisced. Almost every year they had had some scare-rumor about the Indians being on the warpath, but every time it had been a false alarm. And by now they were probably so weakened that they would be unable to do any harm to the whites.

The bride pointed to her father-in-law, who stood at the other end of the table. She asked the guests not to say anything to Danjel about the wild Sioux in Meeker County; now that she and Sven were moving there Danjel might unnecessarily worry himself sick about them.

"I'll keep my trap shut! Anything Ragnhild asks me I'll do!" said Jonas Petter. "Even if she asked me to walk on my hands!"

Sitting there at the bride's side his thoughts had wandered far away from Indian rumors: He had a story to tell, well suited for a wedding. It was about a farmer and a soldier, a rich farmer in Ljuder who hired the village soldier to make an heir for him and offered his bed for the purpose. He had started this story on many occasions, but always someone had said it didn't fit just now, and he had been silenced. But today, at this wedding, it seemed most proper.

Jonas Petter had made the roses bloom still redder on the cheeks of the girl-bride. Perhaps that was what he wanted. He began: "Once long ago . . . "

At that moment the host asked to be heard at the other end of the table: Before the guests sat down to enjoy God's many gifts he wanted to read a prayer.

The settlers were enjoying a wedding feast, yet at this moment Jonas Petter's story was less suitable than ever.

—4—

KARL OSKAR and Kristina remained in the bridal house for a while after the other guests had departed. Kristina wanted to talk with Danjel alone.

During their spiritual conversations she would confide implicitly in her uncle. He told her what God's will was, and gave her advice when she was in doubt. She regretted that she had not spoken to him before she had committed her grave sin of praying to God not to create any more life in her body. Only afterward had she mentioned that prayer to him.

Now Danjel looked at his sister's daughter and said with concern: "You look so pale and thin, dear Kristina. Life is hard on you, isn't it?"

"The same as always, but I'm not as able as before . . . "

"You look sickly—is your mind at ease?"

"I'm at peace, Uncle. I feel God has taken charge of me."

"Then there are no troubles left for you."

Danjel Andreasson had aged noticeably during the last years. His beard and hair had turned ice-gray, his cheeks had become sunken, and all his teeth had fallen out. But deep under his bristling brows shone the mild, good eyes which glorified his face. He had been banished from his mother country because of his religious beliefs, but instead he had seen the Land of Canaan, and he never neglected to thank God for his exile from Sweden.

Kristina said she wanted to pray to God that she might live a few years yet, until the children had grown up some. She had a demanding need to confide all her wishes to her Creator.

"He already knows them all," smiled Danjel, as if forgiving a child's fancy.

"Is it wrong to pray for it, Uncle?"

"I don't think you will anger God with that prayer. He is patient with us. But the soul he has given you he will take back whenever it suits him. Your hour of death is already decided."

Kristina wanted a special piece of advice today; it concerned Karl Oskar. What could be done with him? He went with her to the Lord's table in church, he read his confession. But in between he always forgot his prayers. It was as if he didn't want any help from God. He trusted only in himself, and knew no help in this world except his own strength and his own mind. He thought he could get along by himself. But he must be a grave sinner in his self-reliance; Karl Oskar's great fault was his conceit. And she worried lest he be lost in eternity. What should she do?

"You must pray to God for him," said the uncle. "That is all you can do."

"He's so stubborn and won't change."

"You must wait till his hour comes. Then Karl Oskar will realize that he can no longer help himself. If not before, when his strength is gone and old age frightens him."

Danjel also wanted his sister's daughter to keep something important in her mind. It was good that she had peace in her soul. But she must be careful not to fall into the fallacy of believing that she once and for all was guaranteed eternal life. That life she must still earn every day of her earthly life. He himself had once been tempted to self-righteousness, and he had received his punishment. No one must consider himself as God's chosen; He treats all his created lives alike.

To do good and trust to the Almighty's mercy—that was the only salvation for a human being here on earth.

Once more Kristina had had the experience that she and Uncle Danjel were united in some marvelous way, they belonged together: They had both given up this life for another. They had gone through the world—they lived for another world, for one their eyes could not see.

V

THE TOMAHAWKS ARE BEING SHARPENED

—1—

THE WINTER of 1861–62—their twelfth in North America—was the most severe Karl Oskar and Kristina had experienced.

Heavy snowfalls began early and by November high drifts had accumulated which remained throughout the winter. The cold sharpened its edge every day—the frost penetrated into the houses and painted its white nap on the walls. If they had still been living in their old log cabin they would have been unable to exist through this cruel winter. Even in this house—so well built and with good fireplaces—they had great trouble keeping warm. They might let the fires burn till late in the evening, yet when they awakened in the morning all the heat was gone. The first chore was to fire the stove and warm their house again.

It seemed as if Karl Oskar and the boys cut wood and carried it inside all day long. And outside the walls of the house the bitter cold lurked. As soon as anyone stuck his nose outside the door he was assailed by stinging bites. The cold was a persistent pursuer who bit into any unprotected part of the body. The skin on one's cheeks felt as if covered by a crust. They protected their hands with great woolen mittens, the thickest Kristina could knit, but even with these the fingers grew numb, clumsy, and stiff as wooden sticks.

They must constantly be on guard against frostbite; in this winter weather a limb could be frozen in a few moments, especially those of sensitive children. Dan and Ulrika attended school in the newly built meetinghouse in Center City, but during the coldest days they were kept at home. However much Kristina bundled them up it was never sufficient to keep them warm. If they should get behind in their lessons they might catch up later, but frozen ears, hands, and feet could never be replaced.

47

They spent most of the winter inside; only chores in the stable, tending the animals, and other necessary errands, brought them outside.

Tree-felling in the forest usually warmed the man who handled the ax, but this winter Karl Oskar had to interrupt his timber cutting for buildings because one of his legs turned numb during the work; the injury to his left leg became worse in this merciless cold. After a day of much walking his swollen shank ached and felt sore during the night, and his limp was more pronounced than before. Apparently he was stuck with this limp for the rest of his life, so he might as well learn to get along with it. The price he had paid for his life that time when he escaped the robbers who had coaxed him onto their wagon must be paid in installments during many years of pain and lameness.

Before he went to bed in the evenings, Kristina would rub his sore leg with camphor-brännvin which somewhat eased the gnawing ache. And each time she poured the fluid on his limb she comforted him about the injury: If he hadn't had this old injury he might already have lost his life in the war between the states. She herself was grateful:

"I can thank your bad shank I'm not a widow."

"Are you so pleased to be married to a lame man?"

"Better a lame man than a dead one!"

The sharp smell tickled Kristina's nostrils as she poured the camphor-brännvin into her hand and rubbed the swollen lower calf of his leg. She recognized God's meaning and purpose in everything that happened to them; God had lamed Karl Oskar's leg to save him from the human slaughter on the battlefield.

"I am still sound in life itself, of course," he said. "But I feel older every day."

He stopped, embarrassed that he had spoken in a mixture of English and Swedish; Kristina poked fun at his attempts at English and had asked him to use his mother tongue when he spoke with her.

This settler couple at Chisago Lake were still far from old age, if they counted the years. Karl Oskar was thirty-nine, Kristina thirty-seven. They were between youth and old age, they had used only half of life's measure granted a human being according to David's words in Holy Writ. But it was not the measure of a person's years that told if he was old or young, it was what he had gone through in his life. Karl Oskar and Kristina were old before their time, badly bruised by years of hard labor, marked by heavy chores. Minnesota's violent changes in weather—the summers' intense heat, the winters' severe cold—showed its effect in their bodies. Their limbs and joints had stiffened, their backs and shoulders bent. They were a toiling couple, moving heavily and sluggishly when they still ought to have used the uncumbered, light steps of youth.

If one counted the number of heavy work days that had filled their lives Karl Oskar and Kristina were already old people.

—2—

LUCKY HE who was warm inside four walls this winter. But there were people in their part of the world who had no timbered walls to protect them against the merciless cold. Kristina could not get her thoughts off the Indians who always—summer and winter alike—lived in wretched huts. A few animal skins and blankets spread over twisted, bent saplings—this was their house. Pelts and woven materials were their only protection; the wind must blow at full hurricane strength through the walls and roofs of the Indians' huts. Karl Oskar surmised the redskins must have been created different from the whites; perhaps their blood contained some warming fluid that protected them against freezing to death. But Kristina felt it was a miracle that they could survive Minnesota's winters year after year.

Besides, the Indians were always exposed to hunger in wintertime; the hunting season was over and the ground was covered with snow so deep it was almost impossible to snare game. The ice on the lakes lay so thick they could not catch fish. Perhaps they had saved a little from last summer's corn—"lazy man's corn"—which their women grew in small plots. In the fall they gathered wild rice along the lakeshores, but they were so lackadaisical that the rice often was frozen before they got to it. They would also eat roots and ferns and evil lizards and critters white people wouldn't taste. The savages were not squeamish. But it certainly couldn't be true that they fried rattlesnakes and considered them delicacies.

The hunger among the Indians this winter was gruesomely described to Kristina one evening when Samuel Nöjd, the old hunter, came around looking for pelts.

Nöjd had lived among the Indians and knew them better than any of the settlers in the valley. At one time he had had a Sioux girl living with him—he maintained he had saved her from starving to death—but she had gone back to her own people. At present he lived alone in his log cabin in Taylors Falls with twelve dogs and twelve cats. The dogs he used for hunting but the cats he kept to lick his plates and pots; the cats in the house, he insisted, did the same service as a woman—they washed the dishes.

Kristina felt sorry for Samuel Nöjd because he was an unbeliever and blasphemer. He was also dirty, with an evil smell, and full of vermin, but she could not feel aversion to him because of this—she had no right to detest any human being, however strangely he was created. But as he now came into their kitchen and sat down on the sofa bench she was afraid a few lice might stray from the old trapper. American lice were much more ravenous and vicious in their bites than their Swedish counterparts, and unbelievably tenacious of life, almost impossible to exterminate. Neither the brass comb nor boiling soap lye helped against American vermin.

Dan and Ulrika came in and stood beside the old man who sat on the bench; he always told them strange stories. Kristina thought, now the children would surely pick up some lice, and a louse became a grandmother in one night; tomorrow they would have grandchildren in the house from Nöjd's vermin.

The trapper had recently returned from a trip out West where the Sioux were in winter quarters. This year, he said, the hunger among them was worse than ever: The Sioux were eating their own children.

Kristina winced: "What in all the world are you saying, Nöjd?"

"I'm just telling you that there are Indians who eat their own offspring because they don't have anything else to sustain life."

As the old man didn't think she believed him he hastened to assure her. He had with his own eyes, which now rested on them, seen in Meeker County, near Acton, a pile of children's bones gnawed clean. He had inspected the heap very closely; there were skulls and thighbones and shanks, of people, fresh bones of devoured Indian children. There wasn't the smallest scrap of flesh left. And he had met soldiers who were stationed at the Indian post at Red Wood who had confirmed that this winter the Indians were eating their own.

They had told him about an Indian woman who had gone so crazy from hunger she had cut up her fourteen-year-old son when her husband was away. She had made the boy go to sleep with his head on her knees and then she had cut his throat and drunk his blood. Later she had sliced her son's body and cooked the pieces. The neighbors could smell the wonderful meat in her pot and wondered what it was. To keep them from telling her husband she shared the meal with them. The woman and her guests had eaten the boy in one meal; he was so little and skinny that was all there was of him. When her husband came back he missed his son and asked for him. The wife was evasive and wouldn't tell him but he found the bare bones and then she was forced to confess her deed. The husband instantly killed his wife with his tomahawk.

"You're scaring us to death, Nöjd!" exclaimed Kristina in horror.

Karl Oskar told the children to leave the kitchen and they obeyed reluctantly.

"It must be stories you carry around," he said. He looked at Kristina, as much as to say: Don't believe all you hear from Nöjd.

But the old hunter assured them that he had told only the truth about the devastating starvation among the Indians. Ever since so many of the buffalo had been shot the Sioux had suffered from hunger, but never had their misery been so horrible as this winter. He himself could take almost anything, but this was too much for him. The soldiers at Red Wood hated to be on guard duty at the supply house which was filled with food, while Indians, fainting from hunger, swarmed about outside. No food was permitted to be distributed without cash, and the redskins had no cash because they hadn't been paid what the government owed them. The food in the supply house was rightly theirs, but they were not allowed to eat it!

Kristina said that the whites, who were Christian people and knew what was right, must accumulate a heavy burden before God when they treated the Indians so meanly. Petrus Olausson used to say that the redskins were under God's curse and would be exterminated because they wouldn't turn to Christianity of their own will. But she couldn't believe that savages who didn't know the gospel could be under the Lord's curse. "If any are to be punished it should be the Christians!"

And Samuel Nöjd laughed derisively. The whites had brought the Indians cholera, smallpox, and venereal diseases; if they also came with Christianity the Indians must think it was some new deviltry. No wonder they were suspicious and resisted! At least the Church might have saved them from the missionaries who plagued them with the catechism; Christians ought to show their neighbors some mercy. Worst of all, of course, were those damned French trappers—they even used captured Indians as food for their dogs! Those confounded hunters thought this the easiest way to carry dog food with them!

"I shudder in my heart!" said Kristina, as she poured the evening porridge. "Those poor hungry wild ones! How can they stand it?"

"What can they do?" asked the trapper. "They must choose: Starve, or kill others!"

"What others? Who?"

"Try to guess!" And Samuel Nöjd winked secretively. He looked toward

Karl Oskar, who had gone to a corner as far away as possible so as not to have to listen to their guest's stories.

Who were the others the Indians might kill? After that question there was a moment's depressing silence. Kristina put an extra plate on the table; she intended to ask Nöjd to eat supper with them.

When the trapper told the story of the dog food, Karl Oskar had remembered some unfinished business he had with him; it had happened a few times that dogs had killed sheep that belonged to him. Last fall he had found two of his yearling ewes killed back at the Indian cliff, their throats slit open. And just about that time Johan had seen some of Nöjd's dogs near the path along the lake. There was no doubt they were Nöjd's, as no one else in the vicinity had dogs of that kind.

Nöjd mostly bought raccoon, mink, and muskrat pelts, but a few times they had also sold him calf and sheepskins.

"If you're out to buy pelts today I can sell you a couple of sheepskins," said Karl Oskar slowly.

"All right."

"But I want thirty dollars apiece!"

Nöjd laughed his derisive laugh again; he thought Karl Oskar was joking. "Thirty dollars apiece! Kiss my ass!"

"But those skins are from the two ewes your dogs killed last fall!"

The old hunter jumped up as if something had stuck him in his behind. "That's a lie! A hell of a lie!" he shouted.

"They were your dogs, Nöjd!"

"My dogs don't kill tame animals! That's a lie! A goddamn lie!"

"Our boy saw the bitches—why do you deny it?"

"No son of a bitch saw my dogs! Never!"

Nöjd's face took on a savage look; he roared and stomped about. Kristina grew frightened and tried to restrain Karl Oskar. But he took the trapper's American swearing calmly. "I have proof; you let your dogs run on my property!"

"Your property!" Nöjd spit sneeringly on the floor. "Your property as much as mine, Nilsson!"

"What was that you said?" Karl Oskar's voice had suddenly changed. "Isn't this my land? What are you talking about, old-timer?"

"All this land was stolen from the Indians!"

"I haven't stolen my land; I've paid the government a dollar twenty-five an acre for it."

"Yes, but you have bought stolen property, and cheap at that! You know it as well as I do! Better talk soft about *your* land, Nilsson! And I'll let my dogs run where they please!"

Karl Oskar rose. He took a few long, decided steps toward his guest as if he were going to throw himself on him:

"You say I've bought stolen property . . . you old . . . "

He fisted his hands and opened them again, the muscles around his mouth grew taut, his face tense, his eyes contracted and seemed to withdraw into his head. Kristina knew the sign; she rushed between the two inflamed men.

"You have accused me of dishonest dealings!" stuttered the settler.

At the sight of Karl Oskar's changed face the trapper drew back a step and lowered his voice:

"No! No! Your dealings are honorable, all right—according to the laws of the whites—their own laws—after the theft. There isn't an acre of land in America that hasn't been stolen or cheated from the Indians."

Kristina whispered to her husband: He mustn't pay any heed to Samuel Nöjd's talk. But their guest went on: What was the price promised to the Indians when they were forced to give up their land to Swedes and other whites? How much had the government paid for the whole Mississippi Valley? Ten dollars for twenty thousand acres! One two-hundredth of a cent per acre! Could one two-hundredth of a cent be called payment? For the most fertile land in the whole world? It was a thief's price, that's what it was! And that's why they could sell cheap to him, Nilsson! And even this trifle hadn't yet been paid to the Indians! The only thing left for them was starvation!

The trapper picked up his hat and hurried toward the door, spitting angrily: "Keep your sheepskins, Nilsson! Kiss my ass!" He stopped at the door and added that the whites had stolen all of America, yet they kept proclaiming in every church: Thou shalt not steal!

Their guest disappeared and Kristina said: "His eyes turned awful! He has lived so long among the wild ones we mustn't pay any attention to him."

Karl Oskar took a few deep breaths; his anger was soon over: "You're right; it was silly of me to get excited."

"And I thought of treating him to supper!"

She removed one plate from the table. But Karl Oskar could not forget what Samuel Nöjd had said: "He accused me of taking part in thievery!"

"Forget it! You know yourself you haven't stolen anything in America!"

"Only weeds grew here when I came! What grows here now? Crops to nourish us as well as others! I didn't get anything for nothing. I earned my land when I cleared it and broke it!"

Karl Oskar Nilsson mumbled the last sentence to himself several times as he sat down to supper. Kristina said nothing. After all, there was some truth in Samuel Nöjd's words, and she realized that that truth remained with Karl Oskar and disturbed him; they were intruders in this country. Other people had been driven away to make room for their home.

—3—

ON THE WEST SHORE of Lake Chisago rose the tall, red sand cliff which looked strikingly like an Indian's head; forehead, eyes, mouth, chin were those of an Indian. The cliff rose like an immense fortress against the sky and threw a deep, broad shadow over the ground and water near it. The Indian head was brown in summer and white in winter, but at all seasons it remained the same good guidepost for those who were not familiar with the paths of this valley.

This winter the Indian's head was covered with a deep layer of snow which glittered and sparkled in the sunlight; it sparkled as if covered with precious stones. But the sand-brown forehead was bared, and the Indian's deep, black cave-eyes looked down on the white intruders' houses along the shores.

When the Chisago people happened to look at the cliff formation they were apt to say: The Indian up there, he is looking at us! He's watching us! Who knows when . . . ?

The sight of the Indian head caused them an indefinable apprehension. He had watched here when the lake was still known as Ki-Chi-Saga, he remained when the lake's name was changed to Chisago. The Indian was made of stone. He could not be chased away. He remained rooted. He would not move—here he would for all time raise his head over the country.

It was the winter of the great Indian famine. At Chisago Lake no one knew what was happening out west where the numerous Sioux had their camp:

The tomahawks were taken out, the war axes were being sharpened. No tribe among the brown hunter people had such beautiful tomahawks as the Sioux. They were painted red and had a big black star on either side of the edge of the blade. The black star was an ancient sign, looked upon with reverence by each warrior who carried a tomahawk. It must always be present on a Sioux war ax. Warriors and hunters of the Sioux tribe had once been marked with this sign by the Great Father who had given them the land. They had kept it

on their weapons through thousands of years. The sign was their belief in victory. The sign was a promise: The ax with this sign was sure death to the
enemy.

This winter the Sioux axes were being sharpened on a grindstone that gave
the sharpest edge to war weapons. Out west, beyond the tall sand cliff, behind
the Indian's powerful back, there it took place:

The tomahawks were being sharpened.

VI

KRISTINA DESERTS HER
MILKING STOOL

— I —

DURING the cold season, Kristina's only chore outside her house was the milking. They now had eight cows, and this winter seven gave milk. She sat out in the stable one hour in the morning and one hour in the evening. Karl Oskar tried to help her but his fingers were clumsy and awkward in handling the cow teats. One must learn milking in childhood. Marta was now going on fifteen and had begun with the easy milking cows; the girl was both willing and handy.

The milking was more trying this winter because of the intense cold. Before Kristina walked out to the stable she bundled on all her woolen and heavy garments. In these she moved with difficulty, and she looked like a walking bundle of clothes. But however many garments she wore, she began to feel the chill after sitting for a while on the milking stool. Her limbs felt cold, her arms and legs grew stiff, the fingers around the udder rigid. She would cup her hands and blow in them to warm them with her own breath. And during the milking her cold body unconsciously sought the warmth in the animals; she pressed against the cow's furred body, her head leaned against the belly as against a soft pillow. She sought protection against the winter's bite in the warm closeness of living creatures; she felt safety in touching the animal. And the cow ate her mash in the bucket as she stood there calmly with her hind legs spread; she showed confidence in the milkmaid whose head leaned against her side.

Kristina had a good hand with animals and was friendly with her cows. As soon as she appeared in the stable door they would turn their heads toward her and low their welcome. They knew they would get corn mash in their buckets; they were accustomed to her closeness twice a day; twice a day they felt her hands as her fingers squeezed milk from their teats. And on her arrival they greeted her with the only sound they were able to utter. To the milker her cows were not soulless creatures; she felt their confidence in her as a helpless child to its mother. And she felt they wished to show her their gratefulness for looking after them. In the cows' eyes she read a pained, sad consciousness of the muteness which was their lot. They wished to tell her something but they were unable to do so.

During their first winter in Minnesota a cow had saved the lives of the children with her milk; Kristina showed her gratitude for this to all members of their kind.

During this cold winter Kristina often felt an ache in her lower abdomen. And one evening, milking her cows in the stable, it came upon her. She had only one cow left to milk. She had been sitting so long on the milking stool that her legs were stiff and her fingers lame and awkward. If she could only have used her woolen mittens, she thought. Now only the Princess was left but the Princess was the most difficult of the seven, for she wouldn't give her milk willingly. Kristina had to press as hard as she could and pull the teats with all her might before any milk ran into her pail. She always left the hard-milking Princess until the last.

She was moving her stool to the last cow for this evening. She rose with the stool in her hand. Then she felt such a sudden heavy pain that her body bent forward. Without her knowing how it had happened she was on the stable floor.

The pain was intense, cutting like a knife through her body. She was sitting on the floor, with the stool in one hand and the pail in the other, and was unable to rise. She remained there, staring in disbelief before her, as if she had done something unreasonable and foolish. The cow she had just finished milking turned its head and looked at her in surprise, as if asking: What's the matter with you? Haven't you finished with me? Why do you sit on the floor?

The sharp pain in her abdomen eased but left a fretting itching sensation. It was her old ailment. Then she suddenly felt moist between her legs. Something warm streamed down the inside of her thighs, toward her knees. The fluid kept coming: From inside her body, something pleasantly lukewarm flowed over her cold skin.

Kristina knew what it was. She recognized the tepid, sticky substance that flowed down her legs. She had had this same experience once before on a spring day when she was beating wash down at the lake. She need not lift her skirt to look. She was sure: red runnels down the inside of her thighs and legs. The red flow had come over her again at the moment she rose from the milking stool.

It was Kristina's own blood that warmed her cold, stiff limbs. But what did it mean? She didn't know. She only knew that she must get away from here, she must leave the stool and the milk pail.

She tried to raise herself but her legs shook under her, and only at the third attempt did she manage. She was standing straight now and moved one foot with the utmost effort. She took a few steps toward the door. There she sank down to the floor for the second time.

She remembered that Karl Oskar was currying the horses and she called to him. She called several times before he heard.

He rushed up to her: "What's the matter? Have you hurt yourself? You look pale!"

"I think I'm bleeding . . . "

He shot hurried questions at her but she only asked him to help her inside.

The wife put her arms around the husband's neck and he carried her inside the house. Before she lay down on her bed she removed her skirts. The children grew frightened at the sight of her bloody legs. Karl Oskar found some towel rags and dried her. The blood stuck to her skin so that she felt horribly gory, as she did when cleaning up a carcass after slaughter. She tied broad strips of rags around her as a bandage, but the blood kept on trickling. The flow stopped only after it had drenched a second bandage.

Each word from Karl Oskar was blurted out in apprehension. He wanted to send for Manda Svensson, the neighbor's wife, who knew something about ailments. Perhaps she could staunch blood? But Kristina said that she was not with child, and so she needed no helping woman. This was not a childbed, not a miscarriage. Therefore it could not be very dangerous; the bleeding would soon be over.

But her assurance did not calm Karl Oskar; rather it increased his anxiety. If the bleeding had been caused by a miscarriage he could have understood it. Then it would have been something natural. But such was not the case and he had to ask: What could this mean?

Kristina had never mentioned to him the pain in her lower abdomen she had felt for so long.

—2—

NEXT MORNING Kristina's bleeding had entirely stopped. She had been lying on her back as still as she could the whole night. But she was very weak and stayed in bed.

"You're limp because you've lost blood," said Karl Oskar.

He sent Johan to summon Manda Svensson and it didn't take long before their neighbor woman was sitting at Kristina's bedside. She was eager to help, for it was in her nature to take charge and decide for others. In her own home she ruled her submissive husband. Manda was the farmer's daughter who had married the hired hand. The couple could never become equal, as she had refused to give up the upper hand she had had over her husband from the beginning. Ever since they had come to America she had remained the boss who decided and her husband remained her hired hand.

When Manda heard that it was not a miscarriage that had forced Kristina to take to her bed, she said, "I believe you must be bleeding from pure weakness. That's a common female trouble. It could also be bleeding sickness."

Kristina must drink a concoction of healing herbs, insisted the neighbor's wife. She would have liked to prepare such a concoction but the herbs she needed grew only in Sweden, and she dared not pick and cook from those which grew here in America. She might get hold of poisonous plants. Once she had picked some unfamiliar berries and had vomited them up again; ever after she had been scared of American plants.

She advised Kristina to lie quite still with heated caldron lids on her stomach, night and day. If she had evil fluids in her body they would thus dry up and disappear.

Kristina listened to her neighbor with half an ear. She was not worried about herself. If the Creator wished to take her away from this world, what did it concern her what sickness hastened her departure?

Her weakness forced her to stay in bed. Meanwhile, Karl Oskar was filled with concern for his wife. He prepared nourishing food for the sick one, skimmed the cream off the milk and gave it to her, killed hens that weren't laying and boiled chicken soup for her, and prepared egg dishes of various kinds. He thought good food would put her on her feet again. But her strength came back very slowly.

The inside chores she had planned this winter remained undone. She had intended to put up the loom and do some weaving; the wool needed carding and spinning after the sheepshearing of last summer; she had wanted to make clothes for the children on her new sewing machine. Before, it would have bothered her that nothing could be done, but now she no longer was disturbed by neglect of worldly concerns. Why should woolen yarn and looms and clothes disturb the peace in her soul? Why should she be concerned for her daily needs which she soon would discard?

But there were chores in the house that must be attended to, and Karl Oskar and Marta assumed them in her place. They helped each other as best they could. From her bed she gave her husband and daughter instructions: how the milking must be done, how much skimmed milk to save for the calves, how to preserve the cream for butter. And they came to her and asked about the cooking: how long they must fire the oven before baking, when to put in the cornbread, how much time was required for the yellow peas, how to handle the pans on the Prairie Queen to keep the food from sticking to the bottom.

From a man never trained for women's chores there was nothing to expect, and less from a girl not yet fifteen. Kristina praised her successors when they succeeded and scolded them when they failed. However carefully she told them what to do they still made mistakes. There were accidents and failures. Some chores were well performed, others were done in a slovenly way or entirely wrong. And she could see it so clearly; as yet there was no one to take her place—in this house she was still irreplaceable.

She felt no concern for herself. She had peace. Karl Oskar tried to cure her with cream, chicken soup, and egg dishes, Manda Svensson with heated kettle lids. But she had only one she trusted, one who could give her back her health. Her close and loved ones needed her and she felt that God for their sake would let her remain in this world a little longer.

—3—

TOWARD THE END of January Kristina had regained so much of her strength that she could get up for short intervals and resume some of the easier chores. The merciless cold had eased a little and she didn't feel chilled so quickly.

Ulrika Jackson came one day to their house with a belated Christmas present for little Ulrika: She had knitted a woolen blouse for her goddaughter. She had planned to come during the holidays but had not dared because of the bitter cold.

At once she noticed Kristina's pale, gaunt face—Ulrika had not heard about her illness.

"You don't rest long enough between childbeds!" she said.

No one could believe that Ulrika herself had borne seven children—four in Sweden and three in America. She was twelve years older than Kristina, yet she looked the younger of the two. Soon to be fifty years old, the former Ulrika of Västergöhl appeared to be in the prime of her life. Time had left her clear, healthy complexion intact, uncorroded. Lately her limbs had somewhat fattened and she had put on weight around the waist, but the change was becoming to her. Her step was as quick as ever, and men still let their eyes rest on her.

"You're lucky, Ulrika, you have been given such good health," sighed Kristina. "When I look in the mirror an old hag looks back at me!"

Why hadn't the Lord created the white women like the squaws, wondered Mrs. Jackson. When an Indian woman rode through the forest and felt her hour was near, she jumped off her horse only long enough to bear her child. Then she put it in a bag on her back, jumped back up again on the horse, and rode on as if nothing had happened. A squaw birth took about as much time as a visit to the privy.

"We get labor pains because of the original sin," said Kristina. "Perhaps the heathen women don't have the original sin."

But God had chosen woman as the tool for his creation when he trusted her to bear children into the world and she must be worthy of God's trust. Kristina herself would always gratefully accept the new lives he wished to grant her. She knew now why a pregnant woman was called blessed.

The Lord had given to women the honor of bearing children because he put women above men, explained Ulrika. The great mistake with men had already occurred at the Creation: God had finished with all the wild beasts and had some stuff left over when he began to make Adam. In fact, he made man from that stuff. That was how some of the qualities of the beasts had got into men. It explained the similarity between men and the bucks in the animal world.

But fortunately there were also men who understood that a woman was made of nobler material than they themselves and didn't use her for their carnal lust in bed only. They knew she too needed joy and satisfaction.

"Are men really so different in that respect?" wondered Kristina.

"A hell of a lot different in bed, I should say! Didn't you know that?"

"No, I didn't. I've never had anyone except Karl Oskar."

"I see," nodded Ulrika. "No other man has ever got near you."

Kristina laughed: "What can I say when I can't compare Karl Oskar with anyone else!"

"But he is a first-class man in bed, isn't he?"

"I guess he is the best one I've had!"

Kristina laughed, but Mrs. Jackson, who once had been Ulrika of Västergöhl, was deeply thoughtful as she dispersed the knowledge of an experienced woman:

"I guess your husband is all right in that respect. It shows on a woman if her man is capable in that way. It shows on you that Karl Oskar can take care of you, for you look satisfied, your disposition is peaceful and even."

"Karl Oskar and I have always got along."

"Just what I thought! You're happy in that way, Kristina!"

Mrs. Jackson's bosom rose and fell in a deep sigh, and Kristina remembered Ulrika's confidence at the wedding of Danjel's son last fall.

The two women broke off their conversation as Karl Oskar entered the room. He was carrying an armful of firewood which he stacked against the fireplace, he then began to make a fire.

When the flames had a good start Ulrika removed her shoes and put her feet on the hearth. Her toes were cold and stiff after the journey from Stillwater, for she had traveled in a sled that had no heated stones to warm the feet.

It was an un-Christian winter this year, said Karl Oskar. Happily it was a little milder now, and Kristina wanted to resume her milking chores, but she was still so weak from her sickness he wouldn't allow her to leave the house.

Kristina told of the great flow of blood that had come from her one evening while she was milking.

"That sounds bad!" said Ulrika.

"But I didn't lose a life—it was not a miscarriage."

Kristina continued: She had had smaller bleedings before, but she had thought they were her periods coming at an unexpected time and had paid no attention to them. She had also had pains low down in her abdomen. She still had these—they came and went.

Karl Oskar looked up, startled: "What's that you say? You've never mentioned that to me!"

"I didn't think it was worth mentioning."

"How long have you suffered with it?"

"This last year."

"This whole year?" He looked in consternation at his wife. "Why haven't you told me?"

"I didn't think much of it."

"If you ache inside, then something is wrong."

"Karl Oskar is right!" interrupted Ulrika. "You shouldn't have kept it to yourself!"

"Well, maybe not. But you can't go around and complain every time you feel a little pain."

"But it's not right to have a sickness and not seek a remedy against it!"

"Not right?" Kristina looked at her. "You mean I have sinned with it?"

"Yes, you have, because God wants people to take care of their health."

Both Karl Oskar and Ulrika reproached her for having kept her sickness secret. Then all three of them were silent for a few minutes. The only sound was the crackling of the fire as great flames enveloped the dry wood. Karl Oskar kept stroking his thighs in great concern. A spark from the fire hit his cheek and left a red mark but he didn't seem aware of it.

He only felt this: Something must be done immediately about Kristina.

Ulrika said, "You must get your wife to a doctor, Karl Oskar!"

"That was my first thought when I heard what she said a while ago."

"It might be something dangerous in the womb!"

"It'll pass," said Kristina. "I don't think I need a doctor."

Ulrika took her hand imploringly: "You've lost a lot of blood! It can't go on like this! You'll ruin yourself! You must see a medical man!"

Kristina had never in her life been to a doctor. She had heard that doctors treated people horribly, using evil instruments when they looked for ailments in the body. And now her sickness was in a part of the body which a woman would be embarrassed to bare.

Karl Oskar asked Ulrika: There were doctors in St. Paul and Stillwater— where should he take Kristina?

"We have a new one in Stillwater, Dr. Farnley. I've gone to this medical man myself!"

"Is he better than the old one?"

"Much better!"

Cristoffer Caldwell, the old doctor in Stillwater, was also a carpenter and blacksmith, Ulrika said. Caldwell made sturdy tables and benches and no one could shoe a horse better than he. But he was not the right man to handle sick people, for his hands were big and rough and he had some ailment of his own that could only be cured with whiskey. Dr. Caldwell was really a drunkard and he stank of liquor yards away. But Farnley, the new one, was no self-made doctor like Caldwell. He had gone through certified schools and had big thick books piled up along the walls of his room. She had gone to him last spring when she scalded her right knee while cooking syrup. He had been so gentle with her—he had put ointment on her wound and bandaged it as carefully as if he had been swaddling a newborn babe. He didn't have those sledgehammer hands like Caldwell, his hands were soft and clean, he didn't use them to sharpen scythes and shoe horses. She had never imagined a strong, husky man could handle a woman's sore knee so carefully and tenderly. And because the new doctor was so tender—and for no other reason—she had gone to him many more times than she really needed to and let him rebandage her knee.

"You must take Kristina to Dr. Farnley," concluded Ulrika. "I'll go with her and interpret for her!"

Karl Oskar replied that there would be no delay in that journey. As soon as he put the new iron runners on his sled they would drive to Stillwater.

"But I don't want to go to any doctor!" said Kristina with determination, and stood up. She went to the kitchen to put on their dinner, and Ulrika assured Karl Oskar that she would speak to his wife when they were alone and make her go to Farnley.

A while later, when the two women were alone in the kitchen, Ulrika said, "There's something wrong with you, Kristina. But Dr. Farnley is good—he'll find out what's the matter."

"I know you want the best for me, but I don't think . . . "

"You might wreck yourself, it might be your life . . . "

Kristina looked up: "Over my life and death only God has power."

The words came out evenly and calmly. By them all her actions could be understood.

"But if the Lord blesses the doctor's hands then he can cure you."

"Don't you think God can cure me himself if he wishes?" smiled Kristina. "He doesn't need the aid of a doctor!"

"The doctor is God's tool!"

"The Almighty needs no tools. He has created my body and he can make it well also."

"But your mind is a gift of God—you must use your mind so you don't ruin your health."

"It's already been decided how long I am to live."

Now Ulrika must play her last card: If Kristina didn't care about herself and her own good, it was her duty to think of Karl Oskar and the children. They needed her and she must take care of her health for their sake. She must go to the doctor for their sake, since they couldn't do without her.

To this Kristina did not reply at once. She thought for a few moments. But even before she answered Ulrika knew that she had at last found the right means to persuade Kristina.

"Yes, I'll do it." Her voice was low. "Because Karl Oskar wants me to . . . "

"I thought you would."

"Will you go with me to the doctor?"

"Of course I will! I'll do all the talking for you!"

Kristina could not describe her illness to the American doctor but Ulrika would do it for her. And she must also interpret what the doctor said after he had examined her.

Kristina felt ill at ease: What would the doctor do to find out how things were with her?

"One has to undress, I guess, when he does it? Down to the shift? The thought repels me."

"You needn't be afraid of Dr. Farnley—he'll examine you carefully!"

"But a strange man—and feel my body down there . . . "

Ulrika laughed: "You have had so many kids! And you're as embarrassed as a little girl!"

"It seems disgusting. I can't help it."

"Don't worry! Dr. Farnley is kind and friendly!"

But whatever Ulrika said she could not reconcile Kristina to the thought that she must undress in front of a strange man and that this stranger's hands might touch her sexual parts. She felt as if she were going to participate in something indecent.

—4—

ONE DAY, when the weather was a little milder and the sledding good, Karl Oskar and Kristina drove to Stillwater. For the first time in her life she was to see a doctor.

It was a strange journey for her; she felt almost as she had at the time of her emigration; she accompanied her husband, but she did so without conviction and half in regret.

VII

HAS GOD INFLICTED
THIS UPON US?

— 1 —

KARL OSKAR NILSSON sat on the sofa in Pastor Jackson's living room in Stillwater. The sofa was soft and well padded, but he moved back and forth and couldn't find a comfortable spot. He stretched out his legs and pulled them back, he turned and shifted, looked out the window and changed his position every second minute. He was alone in the house, waiting for Ulrika and Kristina, who had gone to see Dr. Farnley.

He had intended to go with them to the doctor's house, which was only a few blocks from the pastor's, but Ulrika had said that he might as well stay at home and look after their house, as Henry was away preaching and the children were in school. She spoke English better than he, and she would be a good interpreter for Kristina and the doctor.

As they left Ulrika turned in the doorway and said, "You can be sure of one thing, Karl Oskar—Dr. Farnley will find out what's wrong!"

What would the doctor have to say?

Karl Oskar had killed the waiting time by inspecting the furniture in the room as minutely as if he had been an appraiser. He had looked at the pictures on the walls, of miraculous happenings from the Bible. He had leafed through the pastor's books on a shelf and he had found English words he didn't understand. Several times he had paced the room, lengthways and crossways, but time still dragged. The hands of the clock seemed glued in their position.

Walking to the doctor's should take no more than ten minutes, both ways. And the longest Kristina need stay with him might be an hour. They had had plenty of time; they should have been back by now.

He could think of nothing to do except sit and stare in front of him. For a long time he stared at the strange reproduction of Ulrika and Pastor Jackson as bride and groom which hung above the sofa.

It was not a painting made with a brush. Ulrika and Jackson were not painted, they were printed onto the paper. They had been impressed on the paper the way they were at that particular moment. They were accurately alive, made by a photographing apparatus. It seemed like the work of a magician, this exact replica of them. Karl Oskar had read about this new invention in the paper and he knew that it could catch all kinds of things, living or dead. The sight of something, anything, need not disappear but could be preserved to look at forever. The Jacksons could look at themselves the way they were on the day of their wedding. Indeed, discoveries and inventions were manifold these days!

And the same thing could be done with a house: the outside, its appearance, could be imprinted on a paper, never to be obliterated, and the paper could be framed like a painting and sent from America to Sweden.

The bridal couple above the sofa gave Karl Oskar an idea: He would have a man with an apparatus come to their place and make a reproduction of their house which he could send to his mother and sister in Sweden. His relatives in the Old World could then with their own eyes see his house in the New World! That would be something for them to look at!

For the present he was stacking up timber for a new house and he would wait with the photographing until it was built. It would be the fourth house he and Kristina had lived in since they moved to America. The first was a wretched twig hut with the wind howling through it until they shook with cold in the nights. But the next house he would build—that would be something to look at! That would be a house of the best kind! How many times hadn't he told Kristina: Wait till you see our next house! Only with the new house would he consider his farm complete. It would, as it were, crown his life's work. And when it was ready he would have it impressed on a paper and sent to Sweden.

The clock on the wall struck three. He had been sitting here waiting almost two hours. Why did it take so long? They should be through at Dr. Farnley's by now.

And what would the doctor have to say?

It was so late in the afternoon they ought to be starting homeward by now. He had his team hitched to the sleigh, the horses were young and eager and could indeed run, and the sledding was good with the new runners, but he didn't wish to drive the whole way after dark. The new road from Stillwater to Center City was two miles shorter than the old and they should be home before bedtime. Johan and Marta would have to do the stable chores alone tonight, but there must be a first time when they took care of the cattle by themselves. Children must learn to take over chores from their parents.

But now he couldn't stand it any longer, not to know. Why not walk over to the doctor's and wait outside there instead?

Just as Karl Oskar was putting on his overcoat, ready to leave, he heard women's voices outside: Kristina and Ulrika were stamping off the snow on the stoop. He opened the door for them.

"You must have been waiting for us, Karl Oskar," began Ulrika. "It did take us a long time."

She explained the delay: There had been so many sick people waiting to see Dr. Farnley today, and while they were there a couple of men came in with a litter carrying another man who had been hurt; he was with the lumber company sawmill, his nose had been torn off by a scantling which the blade had thrown into his face. The poor man's whole face was nothing but a bloody mess, like a meatball mixture. The injured man had to be attended to first, and the doctor scraped away what was left of his nose; he cried like a stuck pig under the knife and no one could wonder at that. He was a young, healthy specimen of manhood—too bad his face was ruined. It wouldn't be easy for him to live without a nose. Because of this accident they had had to wait a long time.

"It seemed long, didn't it?" Kristina had removed her woolen mittens and was blowing into her hands.

What *had* the doctor said?

The question was bursting inside Karl Oskar; he felt they ought to be able to hear it without his asking. Ulrika kept feeling sorry for the noseless mill worker, which was her right, but this concerned the person who was closest to him.

What was the matter with Kristina? He tried to interpret her looks, but she seemed as calm and unperturbed now as she had when they left; he could learn nothing from her face.

Ulrika put a wide kitchen apron over her dress: "I'll get dinner going; you must be hungry, Karl Oskar."

What did he care about food and drink! It was not thirst or hunger that plagued him. His tongue felt dry and his lips stiff but these were caused by something else. He sputtered out:

"What did the doctor say?"

"We have plenty of time to talk about that. Kristina has had her examination all right."

"I am not mortally sick—I have no illness," said his wife quietly.

"No illness? It is in some other way . . . ?"

"Farnley was careful and particular and examined your wife for the longest time," said Mrs. Jackson. "And I had a long talk with the doctor afterward."

Kristina turned to Ulrika: "You promised to explain to Karl Oskar."

"Sure, my dear. I'll do as we agreed, I'll speak to Karl Oskar alone."

"Alone!" There was a shock in his looks.

"Right you are! Come out in the kitchen with me!"

This sounded like an order and for a moment he wondered if Ulrika was pulling his leg: "Are you . . . are you serious . . . ?"

Ulrika grabbed Karl Oskar firmly by the arm and pulled him with her into the kitchen. He followed her like a foolish schoolchild who must be alone with the teacher to taste the rod.

Ulrika started to make a fire in the stove; she picked up some kindling and pushed it down through a slit in the masonry.

"What is it? Something secret? What did the doctor say?"

"He said I should speak to you, Mr. Nilsson!"

"With me? I'm not sick!"

"No, but it is your wife who must get well!"

"What is it really? Nothing deadly, I hope?"

"That depends on you!"

"On me . . . ? Have I caused it . . . ?"

"It depends on you if your wife shall live or die!"

The floor under Karl Oskar's feet rocked violently. He closed his eyes. When he opened them again the walls and ceiling also rocked. His head buzzed with dizziness. He closed his eyes again.

From somewhere far away he heard a voice:

" . . . or die . . . ?"

"Yes, Mr. Nilsson!"

"You frighten me, Ulrika."

"Dr. Farnley said I should frighten the hell out of you. And I prefer to do it when we are alone."

Mrs. Jackson found the match box on the stove shelf, scratched a match against the dry wood, and held the flame to the kindling; a lively fire began to sparkle.

"Kristina is torn to pieces inside, she's sick because of her last miscarriage and the childbeds before. She can't take any more!" She threw a quick glance toward the living room door. "Not a single time! Next childbed will be Kristina's death!"

The words were said, said to him, and his ears had heard them. Just six words he was to hear many times afterward, the same words, however he twisted and changed them. When he heard them now, for the first time, the full impact did not hit him; he was so shocked he could only close his eyes and feel dizzy.

"Now you've heard it! Now you know!"

Ulrika pulled out a kitchen chair for Karl Oskar. "Sit down! I'll explain everything to you. The doctor said to tell you all!"

She had a fire going in the stove and she blew at it to make a draft; between puffs she talked in broken sentences:

After Dr. Farnley had been alone with Kristina for half an hour and examined her thoroughly, he called in Ulrika. Farnley had found injuries in Kristina's womb; a membrane in there was torn and wounded. The blood had come from the womb and this was easy to understand when one knew there were open sores in there. But the injuries could be healed and then the bleedings would stop. Farnley had given Kristina two kinds of medicine to take three times daily, and she must eat well and not do any heavy chores.

But first and foremost the doctor had ordered her to bring an urgent message to Mrs. Nilsson's husband: If he wished to keep his wife alive he must stay away from her from now on. He must never again make her pregnant.

Mrs. Jackson's face stiffened. She leaned toward Karl Oskar, her voice severe:

"Farnley said, word for word: Next childbed will be her death! Now you've heard it in English!"

Karl Oskar Nilsson had received the report in clear words, in two languages. He had heard it in their old mother tongue, and in their new. In Swedish and English he had been told: *Next childbed will be Kristina's death.*

"I've told Kristina, of course, but she doesn't think of herself. But she asked me to tell you about it."

Karl Oskar stood with bent head, his ears buzzed, his cheeks burned, there was a weight across his chest. He stood close to Ulrika, he could hear every word she said, understood every one of them. But his mind would not follow, it had stopped with those six words, and it was those he heard all the time, drowning out all other sounds in the world.

"Your wife will get well again if you take good care of her. Be kind to Kristina, don't ever make her pregnant again."

Karl Oskar was beginning to feel insulted. Who was this woman to warn him how to take care of his wife? What did she think of him! Why did he keep listening to her admonitions? Why wasn't he angry? Why didn't he speak up to her? Why couldn't he answer Ulrika in one single word? But he only stood quietly and chewed and stared.

"I'm sorry for you, Karl Oskar. Because from now on you must lie in the ox pen!"

Couldn't that woman there shut her trap! But of course, it was Ulrika of Västergöhl, and no one as yet had made her shut up. Perhaps not even an earthquake would do it. Maybe God on doomsday might.

Karl Oskar had lost his power of speech. He tried to moisten his lips with his tongue, but his tongue was as dry as his lips. At last, with great effort, he managed to stutter forth a few words—he thanked Ulrika for her help at the doctor's.

That was all he managed; and what more could he say?

What does a man say at the moment when he is forever banished from his wife?

—2—

A LUMBERJACK from Center City was to ride back with them on their sleigh, so Karl Oskar and Kristina could not talk about Dr. Farnley on the way home. No words on the subject passed between them until they were ready to go to bed that evening. Since they had moved into the new house, they had each occupied a bed in the large room, while the children slept in the gable room and the kitchen. Tonight the children were asleep and the house had grown silent.

Karl Oskar began, "How was it at the doctor's?"

Kristina was unbuttoning her blouse; she swallowed a little. "It was horrible and repulsive."

"Did he hurt you . . . ?"

"The doctor was very gentle, but I guess he had to hurt me. Oh, I was so embarrassed I had to force myself . . . No one lets himself be treated that way for the fun of it! Don't ask me to talk about it!"

"You needn't, Kristina . . . "

He went on: Perhaps he had worried as much as she about this trip to the doctor. He had been afraid it might be some incurable disease. Now he felt relieved, for hadn't the doctor told Ulrika that the bleedings and the pain might be relieved? If they followed the doctor's instructions, she might regain her health and strength.

"Didn't Ulrika tell you everything?"

"Yes, yes of course . . . "

"Then you know: I'm no good any more. I'm a useless woman."

"But you'll get your health back—that's the only thing that matters."

"But I'm no use to you, Karl Oskar. I'm discarded . . . " Her voice thickened in a cry.

"You heard me—only one thing matters . . . "

"I'm a useless woman, you've no wife any longer, Karl Oskar."

She sat down heavily on her bed; her body trembled and slumped down. The tears came. She threw herself on her stomach and hid her face.

For many years Karl Oskar had not seen his wife cry. In every situation she had remained calm and controlled. But today, at the doctor's, she had experienced something entirely new. Tonight her strength had deserted her.

"You must be terribly tired, I'm sure . . . "

He sat down beside her on the bed and put his arm around her shoulder. Her crying was muffled, almost soundless. She tried to choke back her tears but they flowed evenly, quietly.

He said nothing; it would do no good just now, this he understood. But all the time he kept his arm on her shoulder; she must know he was there with her, ready to help.

Kristina's hand sought his. Silent, they knew each other's thoughts. So it had been many times. Perhaps they understood each other best in silence. In speech they had difficulty in finding words, in speech they never came close enough. But in a moment like this there was no need for words; between them was nothing left that words could explain.

In moments when there was nothing to say they came closest to each other. Then they felt most strongly what they meant to each other.

At last she made a decisive motion and sat up. Her tears had stopped. "I ought to feel ashamed—old woman that I am! I shouldn't be a crybaby any more!"

"There's no shame in tears if one needs them."

She looked at him with wide, glazed eyes where the tears quivered. "I'm so sad about my uselessness—that's why I cried."

"You shouldn't reproach yourself. No one is to blame. No one can help it."

"There must never be another time . . . we must never . . . that's why we must . . . "

"I know," he interrupted, and looked away. "Ulrika has made it quite clear to me."

"The doctor forbids us to be together . . . we must stay away from each other . . . Did you hear that, Karl Oskar?"

"Yes, I heard it . . . "

"What do you think . . . ?"

What could he say? Need he say anything? She knew so well what he thought.

Those six words were still buzzing in his head. He turned them over, back and forth, changed them:

Next childbirth will be Kristina's death.

It didn't help; however much he turned and changed, the word *death* was always there.

Therefore you must never touch her again. She cannot stand to be pregnant again. Next time it will be her death.

They had always had it good together, he and she. When he had his wife it was his greatest bliss in life. During the day he would go about in expectant joy at the thought of evening and their own moment. So it had been for him ever since in his youth they had found each other. And he knew she felt the same. There were wives who didn't care, who would just as soon have their men stay away from them. Kristina was not one of them. She too had her joy in their being together. She had said as much many times: He mustn't think that she liked it less than he. And lately she had said it more often than before. She was a shy woman, but when they were together her shyness disappeared. It might happen she was the first to express the wish: Tonight! He was her husband, it was God's intent that in lust also they should give each other joy.

Their moments together confirmed to her that they desired each other as much as in youth, that they were still in love.

But from now on it would be forbidden to them to be together. She had asked him what he thought of it and he hadn't answered, for he felt she knew. No words were needed in this matter.

"Karl Oskar—I'm thinking about something . . . "

"Yes . . . "

"Do you believe the Lord God has inflicted this upon us?"

Her question surprised him. He himself would never have thought of it. "What do you think?"

"I doubt it. We only know what the doctor in Stillwater said. Why would God begrudge us being together?"

"But we must follow what the doctor said . . . "

"He is only a human being like the rest of us."

"We must obey him anyway."

"But how can he know if I can stand a childbed or not? Someone else is the all-knowing."

Karl Oskar rose slowly from his wife's bed: "We must do only one thing: See to it that you get well and strong again! And now we must go to bed, tonight as always."

So at last they went to rest in their house, in the same room, in separate beds, at opposite sides of the room.

During their marriage of almost twenty years they had shared the day's labor and the night's rest. From this day on they were banished from each other during the night; their living together as man and woman was finished.

—3—

A settler wife's evening prayer:

. . . dear God and Creator! Tonight as all nights I surrender to your mercy before I go to sleep. I've been to a medical man today and sought aid for my pain, but you must not think that I trust him more than you, my Lord. He is only a frail human, like myself, and he can do nothing if he doesn't get his knowledge from the Almighty. You alone rule! If you bless the doctor's medicine then only will it heal me.

You mustn't think, dear God, that his words frightened me in any way. Who knows if I ever will be strong enough to bear another child? You are the only one to know if the next childbed will be my death or not. I'll come to my end when it's your will that I shall.

You know how much Karl Oskar and I have loved each other since youth. You know we have been together in sickness and lust. Can it be your will that we must not know each other from now on? Not be together as married people after this? Can you mean that we must stay apart all the time we have left?

Dear God! You know that we, according to your commandments, have kept our conjugal promises and through all the years lived harmoniously and in compassion. My husband has never desired anyone else and I just as little. Karl Oskar has never looked at another woman and I never at a man. Therefore, forgive us if we feel that we should be together as before during the time we have left together here in this world.

Is it only a human whim that we must live apart? I ask your opinion. You will let me know what the actual truth is. If this is a trial from you, then I'll accept it in humility. I'm only a simple, unschooled woman, but I seek your hand when I'm in doubt and need your advice.

And I pray you, dear God, as always: The children, especially Frank and Ulrika, are so tender still; don't make my little ones motherless before they have grown bigger.

Bless and keep all of us who sleep in our beds this night in the whole wide world! Amen!

VIII

THE LETTER FROM SWEDEN

Åkerby, Ljuder Parish,
February 19, Anno 1862.

Dear Brother Karl Oskar Nilsson,

Health and Blessing

I will sit down and write a few Lines to tell you that our Mother is dead, which happened the 3rd inst. She left this Life and entered Eternity at half past seven in the Evening of said date. The years of her Life were 67, 2 Months and a few Days. Our Mother's death-suffering was short, as She came to her End by a sudden Stroke. The day before we had found her on the Ground, her senses gone; she remained unconscious until She died the following Evening.

A few days before Christmas our Mother received the Money you had sent her in a draft of Five dollars. We got the money at the Bank in Växjö, it amounted to 18 riksdaler Swedish money. Mother asked to thank you heartily. The last Time I spoke to her before she died she told me not to forget to Write to you in North America and thank you for the great Christmas Gift. Our Mother was buried the 9th inst. we had a quiet Funeral. Auction and Settlement we have also had after her, everything belonging to the Estate carefully noted down as it was at the Hour of Death. The papers will go to Court and then we two surviving heirs will divide the Balance. Your share will be sent to you.

Both our beloved Parents are now gone from Time. It is not in our Power to stop the Guest called death. When a relative lies on Bier we may mirror Ourselves each time and see what shall happen to us.

Forgive my poor writing, I can not put my thoughts on Paper. But we hope to hear from you and forget not your Sister in Sweden. We are only the two of us left now. We had once a happy childhood home and we must not forget each other in this Life.

Best Wishes Brother,
Written Down by your devoted Sister
Lydia Karlsson.

The Astrakhan Apples Are Ripe

IX

THE RIVER OR THE FONT?

— I —

The Swedish immigrants in the St. Croix Valley had become divided in religious matters. In recent years Baptist and Methodist congregations had been established, and many other sects were proselytizing among the Lutherans. Most numerous were the Baptists, whose revivalist Fredrik Nilsson was very active among his countrymen. The Lutheran ministers considered him the most dangerous sectarian in Minnesota.

Fredrik Nilsson had been a seaman and had sailed the seven seas. Already in 1851 he had been exiled from Sweden for preaching immersion. He had sought asylum in North America and settled in Waconia in Carver County, where he had founded a Baptist congregation and built a church. From there he spread the new teaching to other Swedish settlements. His countrymen were disturbed to hear that he had been banished from Sweden because of his faith, and this made it easier for him to gain converts. Nilsson came to St. Paul to preach and on one single day he baptized thirty-seven Swedes in the Mississippi River. Then he traveled to Taylors Falls and preached, founded a Baptist congregation, and immersed twenty-two persons in the St. Croix River.

But when it was rumored that Fredrik Nilsson would come and preach to the Lutherans at Chisago Lake, their pastor issued an order from the pulpit: No home must be opened to this uncouth, unschooled sailor who was not ordained as a church official! No member of their parish must open his house to this false teacher who was trying to gain a foothold in their community!

Johannes Stenius, the new pastor, was more rigid against sectarians than had been his predecessors. He considered it a shepherd's first duty to fight irreligion and guard his entrusted flock against dispersal. In almost every sermon, he warned his listeners against the lost souls who were allowed to roam this country at will. He bitterly deplored the lawmakers of North America who, with entirely wrong ideas concerning spiritual freedom, had failed to safeguard the only true and right religion, the Lutheran. In Sweden Lutheranism was pro-

79

tected by the police authorities, but in America it was completely unguarded, so that simple and uneducated people were an easy prey. In Sweden false prophets were exiled or jailed on bread and water, but here they were honored and considered more important than those consecrated by God to preach his Holy Word.

This dart thus hurled against the Baptist preacher Fredrik Nilsson by the Lutheran minister had a result quite contrary to the one intended. At least ten different people offered him a room in which to preach. And he came to Center City and preached from Luke 2:7: " . . . because there was no room for them in the inn . . . " After the sermon a Baptist congregation was established among the Chisago people and twenty-four were baptized in the waters of the lake.

Great excitement followed in the Lutheran congregation; some twenty members, after hearing Nilsson preach, left the church and were baptized, and others wavered in their Lutheran faith. Women especially were open to the former sailor's preaching. And Pastor Stenius issued still stronger warnings from his pulpit: His flock must consider its eternal welfare and not be blinded by the Baptist will-o'-the-wisp; women, with their inherited ignorance, were more easily a prey to this convert-maker. Each time a woman was led astray, Pastor Stenius could hear the angels cry in heaven and the devils roar with joyous laughter in hell.

Then, in one sermon, he issued a stern order to all married men to watch their wives and prevent them from being ensnared in sectarianism. This irritated many of the women: How much must they take from the pulpit? Great disputes started in the congregation. Karl Oskar Nilsson spoke out to their new pastor: He had recently come from Sweden and they realized he did not understand the temper among the settlers; here in America they no longer obeyed orders from the clergy. The pastor had no authority over them; he was their servant. He did not decide what they should do, he was not their master, it wasn't like the old country. They had no wish for a new church power, they were glad to be rid of the old.

Pastor Stenius replied haughtily that he was not employed as the congregation's servant; in his office he obeyed only God.

A few settlers were angered because the pastor had called them Sabbath breakers when they harvested their crop on a Sunday. No sensible person could harbor such exaggerated ideas about God's protection that they could leave their dry crops in the fields when they saw rain coming. They appreciated the pastor's zeal, but the shepherd's care must not force them to lose their livelihood. Even in good things, many felt, their new pastor overdid it.

The congregation was now threatened with a serious disruption. And some said the pastor himself had caused this.

—2—

AFTER THE VISIT to Dr. Farnley in Stillwater Karl Oskar saw to it that Kristina followed the doctor's orders. She took her medicine, avoided the heaviest chores, and lay down to rest for a time each day. Already after a few weeks she began to feel stronger. The bleedings diminished and soon stopped entirely, while her appetite and strength returned. And when the sun again began to feel warm after the coldest winter they had ever experienced, she quickened for every day. Never had she been so glad to hear the first dripping from the eaves, never had she felt such joy at seeing the first blades of grass sprouting, never had a spring brought her such fresh renewal.

One day in Easter week when she was busy with spring cleaning, Manda Svensson came to call.

Kristina had not seen their neighbor woman for many weeks and had wondered about this.

Manda had completely changed. Her eyes were wild and roaming and her mind disturbed: "I don't know what to do! Can you help me, Kristina?"

Manda had helped them many times during the winter. Today she herself needed help.

"What in all the world . . . ? What is the matter?"

"Trouble in my soul."

"In your soul . . . ?"

Kristina stopped still with the broom in her hand. Manda had always been neat and clean, but today she looked dirty and sloppy, her hair hung in strings down her cheeks.

"Kristina!" It came like a wail. "I doubt the Lutherans have got it right. If I should die I'm afraid I'll be lost."

Now Kristina could guess what had happened; her neighbor had listened to Fredrik Nilsson, who said that a person must experience a new baptism in order to earn salvation. And Manda had felt that every word he said was true and right. Immersion seemed to her the only, the glorious, the true religion. She had started to doubt and worry. Should she leave their church and be baptized? For several weeks she had been unable to sleep nights, she only turned and twisted and suffered.

"What does Algot think?"

"He doesn't want to go through another baptism. He wants to remain a Lutheran."

"That isn't good. A couple should not separate in religion."

"Exactly what Algot says! I want to become a Baptist and he wants to remain a Lutheran. Who must give in?" And she looked expectantly, questioningly at Kristina.

"Have you talked to our pastor?"

"Yes, but he only condemns me. He calls Nilsson a false prophet, a seducer who should be put in jail. But he is really a martyr, like St. Stephen."

What Kristina heard depressed her. Must difference in religion now part married couples also, whom God had joined together?

"Pastor Stenius doesn't leave us in peace a moment, he wants so to baptize our little son."

Algot and Manda had a boy about six months old. He should have been christened long ago but it had been delayed because of the intense cold when babies couldn't be taken outside. And since the mother had begun to doubt the Lutheran tenets, she didn't want her son baptized in that faith. But Pastor Stenius gave her no peace. She actually had to hide the child from him.

"You mean he wants to christen him by force?" asked Kristina in surprise.

"The pastor says it is his duty to christen the child. He would rather see a mother throw her offspring right into a fire than leave it to the Anabaptists."

"But he can't christen him against the will of the parents?"

"It's his duty as pastor, he says."

And Manda told how Pastor Stenius, the day before, in the company of Mr. and Mrs. Olausson had come to their house; empowered by his office he was going to baptize their heathen child. Olausson and his wife, known as upright Christians, were to be the witnesses. Algot was out in the forest and she was alone at home. The pastor walked out into the kitchen and took down her fine soup tureen from its shelf, the one with blue flowers and leaves. Then he had ordered her to put on a kettle of pure water and when it was lukewarm pour it into the soup bowl which he wanted to use as a font. The Olaussons aided the minister and tried to frighten her: God's doom would be upon her if the child were lost because she refused to have it baptized.

But she didn't put on any water, nor did she swaddle the little one in christening-veil—she refused to hand him over for baptism.

She had been so upset she didn't know what to do, but when Mrs. Olausson poured the water into the tureen and Pastor Stenius opened his book, she had picked up her lastborn from his crib, wrapped a shawl around him, and run outside. She had run as fast as she could, a long way into the forest. There she had hidden in some bushes for a whole hour while the child cried to high heaven. At last she discovered why he hollered so—he was covered with ants and his whole body was red. Then she had gone home to put something on to ease the itch, and by that time the uninvited guests had left.

But now she was afraid they might come back sometime when she was out, and Algot would let them baptize the boy in the Lutheran religion.

"But they can't do it by force," Kristina comforted the worried mother. "Not here in America."

"The minister says I've forgotten my duties, and he must christen the child because God has ordered him to."

"In the old country they could do as they pleased, they were that mighty, but not here."

Kristina recalled that the minister at home in Ljuder had forcibly christened one of the Akians' children many years ago. It was her Uncle Danjel's father in Kärragärde who had thus been baptized while the parents were away. The minister had feared the Akians would themselves christen the child and he had wanted to save the newborn from the sectarians. The parents had been in the field haying and had left the boy at home with an old feeble-minded woman. The minister knew this and had used the opportunity. The Akians had been greatly incensed, but the minister had only replied: While the negligent parents harvested fodder for the cattle—which seemed to them more valuable than their child's salvation—he had harvested a soul for God's kingdom.

"But I don't believe a forced baptism is holy and just," said Kristina. "I think the pastor should leave the child alone until you and Algot agree about the christening."

Manda Svensson rocked her body back and forth on the chair, her eyes red, her mind befuddled.

"But I'm worrying about my own salvation." She wailed like a child. "Lutheran sermons don't comfort my soul any longer. What shall I do?"

Kristina had not been ordained, she was no pastor—how could she help another person in spiritual trouble? But she could not let her neighbor leave without some comfort; she would tell her what she herself believed, she would share her own convictions:

There were said to be more than a hundred religions in America. But there was only one God. In her heart she felt there could only be one. Yes, she was absolutely sure of it! Those hundred religions could therefore be nothing but people's inventions which God didn't pay any attention to. God could never have meant that the teachings of the Prince of Peace should cause strife and disunity and quarrels among people. And he surely did not intend that ministers should start fighting about a human soul as soon as it was born into the world. The ministers were wrong in fighting with each other for innocent babes in their cradles.

Nor did she believe a person's eternal salvation depended on membership in one congregation or another. Each one must seek God until he or she found him, and then she would know what was right; then she need no longer worry about eternity.

If Manda now let them pour water on her in a new baptism, then her husband would suffer from this; even though they were husband and wife they would have to go to different churches on Sunday. This would hurt both Algot and herself. She would be doing something wrong; she would not be obeying God's will.

Kristina's honest advice to her neighbor was this: She must wait with her baptism until Algot no longer objected.

Manda had listened eagerly and when she left she said she would deeply ponder the advice given her. She understood that Kristina herself had peace and joy in her soul, and only such a person could help another human being.

Some time later the news spread that Algot and Manda Svensson had baptized their son in the Lutheran faith. They had made a bargain: The wife let the husband baptize their child in the old faith, the husband let the wife be baptized in the new.

—3—

THE SETTLERS were living through a time of spiritual confusion. The hundred religions that were preached in North America caused Kristina great wonderment. She could not understand what separated the churches and the sects from one another. There were sects and offsprings of sects. Ulrika had said there were eight different kinds of Baptists alone in America. And there was the Institution of the Lutherans, the Immersion of the Baptists, and the Fulfillment Teaching of the Methodists. All kinds of teachings were preached, faith teachings, salvation teachings, eternity teachings, grace teachings. Who could keep them all in his head and explain them all? When Kristina read in

Hemlandet about Congregationalists, Wesleyans, Unitarians, Episcopalians, it sounded to her like so many tribes of wild heathens.

And in this country Messiahs arose anew every year. Last year alone fourteen persons each insisted they were the returning Christ who had come to America. Several of them were put in insane asylums. There was indeed a confusion in faith and baptism: I would rather see a mother throw her child into the fire than . . .

The Lutherans baptized in a font, the Baptists in the river—but could it really make a great deal of difference?

River or font? Christening water should be clear, pure, and unsullied, because it must blot out sins, but could it make any difference if it came from a well or a river?

One Sunday last spring Kristina had been invited to Stillwater to see the great baptismal festival of Ulrika's brethren. The Baptists had their place of immersion some distance outside town in the St. Croix River. That Sunday there were eighteen converts to be received into the congregation and enjoy the rebirth of a baptismal bath. Kristina was permitted to view the consecration from the shore.

A great many people were gathered and those who were to be baptized were standing apart near a huge boulder on the shore, separated from those who already were members of the congregation. They were all dressed in wide, white shirts that covered their bodies from neck to heel; converts' clothes were white as angels' wings. Men and women were dressed alike, but bearded faces and short hair indicated who the men were. In the group of the converts Kristina noticed women older than herself, and one old man with a gray beard covering his shirt front, perhaps seventy years, yet here he was to be reborn like a child in the river water.

It was a warm Sunday with the water calm under the tall trees at the edge of the river; it was almost like a lake. In a rowboat, half pulled up on the shore, stood Ulrika's husband, the congregation's minister, Pastor Henry O. Jackson. His head was bare and he wore a black coat which hung to his knees. He had preached in barns and sawmills, in cabins and sheds—today the rowboat was his pulpit.

The pastor began to sing a hymn and the people on shore joined in. Ulrika had sung this song for Kristina and she recognized some of the words:

> Down to the sacred wave
> The Lord of Life was led;

And he who came our souls to save
In Jordan bowed his head.

He taught the solemn way;
He fixed the Holy rite;
He bade his ransomed ones obey,
And keep the path of Light.

The human voices rose powerfully under the clear sky; there was an eagerness and life in the Baptists' singing that Kristina had never heard in a Lutheran church. The hymn about the Lord of Life echoed against the cliffs, rose heavenward, away from this fleeting world. It rose on the comforting assurance of another world that had no end. The congregation was filled with joy that eighteen people were to be reborn through baptism, their souls to enter the Kingdom of God.

Then the pastor in the boat began to speak to the white-garbed group on the shore.

Suddenly it seemed to Kristina that she had seen this before; her ears had heard this voice, her eyes had seen this gathering: a man in a boat, preaching to people in white garments on a shore! There had been men in long beards listening to the Word, standing quite still, as still as the cliff on which their feet rested. And on the riverbank rose high, brown hills. A wilderness land; she recognized it all! Where had she experienced this? Was it the memory of a picture that came to her mind? Only in *one* book could she have seen such a picture. Or was it an impression of something she had read in this book that changed into a vision: *"The people of the land were baptized by him in the river, and they confessed their sins."*

A man spoke from a boat to the people on the shore. But it was another river, another shore, another time. The river's name was Jordan, and it had happened many years ago.

Who was the man there in the boat? Who was it that spoke? He used English but she understood all he said, for it wasn't the words she heard, it was the voice that uttered the words. She recognized it so well, the voice that once had welcomed them on the shores of this very river. The man in that boat had met them when they arrived, had brought them to his house and given them food. He had sheltered her and her children when they were without house and home. Will no one help us? they had asked. This man had answered them. Who was he? Who was the man in the boat on the river Jordan preaching love and mercy to the people on shore?

Was it Christ himself she beheld?

Kristina put her hand to her head, feeling dizzy. Was she dreaming? Was she forgetting that she was among sectarians? That she was viewing the great Baptist festival? For a moment she had forgotten that these people were said to teach a false religion; she had felt uplifted in her soul by their singing of a joyous hymn. Yet had the pastor of her own church been here today he would have shed tears of sorrow over these lost souls who were gathered here.

Now she saw the man in the black frock coat leave the boat and wade out into the river. He waded fully clothed, his long coattails dragging in the water behind him. He walked resolutely forward, now the water reached to his knees but he walked on. When the water reached to his waist he stopped and turned toward the shore and said something. He was calling a name.

Pastor Henry O. Jackson had commenced to distribute the sacrament of baptism to the white group on the shore; he called the first by name.

The oldest among them was to go first. The old man with the gray beard heard his name and waded slowly toward the pastor. He moved clumsily, awkwardly, he was not accustomed to walking in water; he stumbled, almost fell over some stones in the river bottom. The water splashed around his legs, his white garments were getting soaked.

But out there in the river stood the black-coated man who stretched his hand toward the man in the white shirt. Pastor Jackson received the old one, took a sturdy hold of his neck with his left hand and laid his right against the man's chest. For a few moments both stood still. Then the pastor's hands became active: He pressed the old one's head and chest under water. The white-garbed one had vanished; the pastor stood alone in the river.

Kristina held her breath, moved her hand quickly to her mouth; she had almost cried out: He'll drown!

She waited, perhaps only a few seconds, but the waiting was tantalizing. Pastor Jackson read something, probably the baptismal prayer, then the gray beard popped up out of the water, the hair well slicked down over the skull. Water dripped from his forehead and neck after the immersion. The pastor let go his grip and the old one stumbled as if ready to fall. Pastor Jackson steadied him by his shoulders. Finally he laid his hands on the old man's chest, probably to bless him.

The old man had experienced his rebirth and began to wade back to the shore, splashing the water with his legs in his insecure, unsteady walk. Water fell in large drops from his beard, ran in runnels from his hair. He coughed, spitted, and cleared his throat; water had gotten into his mouth and nose. The

white shroud clung to his body as he stepped ashore and was met by fellow be-
lievers who took him by the hands and led him to their flock. The congregation
greeted their new member in a communal outcry, hands were raised over his
head—the brethren also wished to call down the Lord's blessings upon him.

  . . . and as He rose from the waters, lo, then were the heavens opened . . .

The immersion went on, Pastor Jackson calling for one proselyte convert
after another. And each in turn hearkened to his call and waded out in the river
and was immersed with his whole body. All were baptized in the stream—in
the name of the Father and the Son and the Holy Ghost, like unto a rebirth, a
new body.

The eighteenth and last was a tender girl with heavy golden hair falling far
down her back. Her head was dipped and when it came up again tufts of hair
stuck round her head—it seemed evil, hairy water snakes had stuck to her
down there and clung to her.

The girl almost fell on her face as she walked back to the shore; she had
stumbled on something. The pastor grabbed her under the arms, lifted her up,
and led her ashore. Trembling, the girl huddled in her soaked, tight-clinging
dress. Only a short time before had the ice broken up on the river, the last floes
were barely melted. It hurt Kristina to see the poor girl so cold after the
immersion—she walked like a dizzy person.

After the sacrament in the river the newborn were given warm milk and
cake at the pastor's home. Ulrika told Kristina that the converts needed a hot
drink after their soaking or they might catch cold. She herself had been taken
with a terrible influenza when her husband gave her the immersion sacrament
in the St. Croix River in the spring of 1851; that whole summer she had gone
with a dripping nose, blowing it and blowing until she almost blew the tip of it
away.

In the evening Pastor Jackson caught a ride on a settler wagon to Marine,
where he would hold a supper meeting. When Ulrika was alone with her guest
in the living room she wondered what Kristina thought of the baptismal celebration.

"I wouldn't want to be dipped down like that!"

"Why not?"

"Terrible to be pushed under!"

It had hurt Kristina to see the participants get water in their mouth, nose
and ears, and see them stumble like dizzy people after the baptism. In her catechism she had learned that it was not the power of the water—water was something external. And the amount of water at a baptism could not have anything

to do with the sacrament. She herself had been baptized in a font. Weren't a few handfuls of water sufficient for the entrance into God's kingdom? Why did they need a whole river?

Mrs. Jackson explained that every part of the old body, with real sin and original sin—the whole sin-carcass—must be immersed, washed, in order for it to be a real baptism. The Lutherans only splashed a few drops over the head, just fooling around. The Lutherans called themselves baptized but all their carnal lusts remained with them.

"Why do they put on white shirts?" wondered Kristina.

"Before the converts step into the water they dress in the clothes of the new body. The Lutherans wear their same old sin rags throughout life!"

Ulrika had been saved from Lutheranism's false teachings. She had never wanted to be a Lutheran in the first place; she had been told that she had fought when baptized as a child, crying so loudly the whole time that not one of the minister's words was heard, and flailing her arms against the book. Only since she came to America and met Henry had she learned that the Baptists were the true followers of Christ, the only ones who lived like the Saviour himself when he walked on earth. The first Christian congregation was a Baptist congregation.

"St. John is called John the Baptist in English! He was the first Baptist!"

"Is that really the truth?" said Kristina.

"Of course! I didn't know myself before I learned English that John was the first Baptist. Our religion is named after him. It says in the Bible that John baptized Jesus in the river Jordan!"

"Yes, I know that."

"The Saviour was thirty years old. Jesus was a grown man when he let John baptize him."

"I guess he never was baptized as a child."

"Of course not! God wanted his son to be a Baptist!"

What Kristina heard was fresh news to her, but she wasn't quite convinced.

"But you can read in the Bible that Jesus let himself be baptized when grown. That proves he was a Baptist!" Ulrika decided.

"You mean that John handled Jesus in the same way as Jackson handled the people today? Did he dip him under the water, big as he was?"

"Of course he did!"

"It sounds unreasonable."

"Take a peek in Holy Writ! If it isn't in the Lutheran Bible those devils must have hidden it. The same as they concealed from the Swedes that John was called the Baptist."

Ulrika had often explained to Kristina the great difference between Lutherans and Baptists: The Lutherans used their religion for Sundays only, the Baptists used theirs every day of the week. Consequently Ulrika and those of her faith were like the first Christians.

A silence ensued, then Kristina said: "You mean I'm wrong in my faith?"

Ulrika patted her feelingly on the arm and spoke like a mother to a dear, lost child: "You're baptized in the wrong religion, Kristina, but you can't help it. The Lord will have mercy on you because you're a good person!"

Ulrika continued to explain the tenets of the Baptists, especially those concerning immersion. Kristina listened, her thoughts deep within her. She put questions to herself and she received answers.

What did she know and believe for sure? That she was one life among the others of the Creation, that she belonged to the Creator and was lost without him. Once she had felt as if God didn't exist, but he had given her proof which would last for the rest of her life. And if she hadn't had God to trust in since coming to America, her despair would have wrecked her and she couldn't have survived to this day.

But did she know anything more for sure? She couldn't tell which was right: to be baptized as a child or as a grown person; to splash the head or immerse the body; to be baptized in a font or in a river stream.

River or font? Was she baptized wrongly or rightly? She didn't know. But she didn't care, it couldn't hurt her soul in eternity whichever way.

Whatever was right, Kristina would remain with her baptism and her God to the end of her days.

X

THE ASTRAKHAN
APPLE TREE BLOOMS

—I—

THERE WERE no frosty nights this spring; even, suitable warmth prevailed while the earth was being prepared for seeding, and afterward mild, slow rains fell. All the grasses, herbs, and plants—cultivated and wild—shot up in a few days and grew in such lushness and abundance as the settlers had never before seen. The colder the winter the milder the spring. When they bored the sugar maples the sap flowed more plentifully than ever; the more severe the winter cold the greater the flow of nourishing fluid in the trees. The weather gave promise of blessed crops next fall.

And the Astrakhan apple tree at the gable blossomed for the fourth time.

For three consecutive springs the blooms on the tree had frozen. This year they remained their full time, this year the apple tree would bear fruit for the first time.

A sapling had grown up from seeds that had come from Kristina's parental home, Duvemåla in Sweden, and now the sapling had grown into a tree. Kristina had worried lest the young roots freeze and die in the cold Minnesota winters. During the cold season the naked, icy branches poked up through the snowdrift against the wall as if reaching for help. But each year anew the large, rough, hairy leaves decked it in green.

And now Kristina's tree had reached its fruiting age. Never before had it displayed so many blossoms. The white-pink flowers hung in clusters, and unharmed by frost or wind they lived their lives to fullness. Then the branches shed their flower clusters and the fruiting began. As the mild spring days passed, the limbs became covered with tiny green nuts; by summer the tiny apples crowded each other for space. The swelling of the fruit could be noticed from day to day; within a few summer weeks they would grow into large, juicy apples.

The Swedish tree bore a noble fruit; Kristina's mouth watered as she thought of the fresh taste only Astrakhan apples offered. In this taste her childhood memories lay embedded: In the mornings when she picked the fallen fruit she would split an apple by squeezing it in her hand; then she would count the seed compartments: each apple had five, always five. The fragrance of the fresh fruit filled her nostrils like morning's own breath. She would bite into the apple, bite through its transparent skin to which the dew still clung, and moistened her lips.

Here the Astrakhan apples were said to ripen in August. This autumn Kristina's own children would for the first time taste the fruit of a noble tree from the country where their mother had grown up. She pointed to the green, unripe fruit; soon they could eat the kind of apples she had eaten at home. How delicious they were! But they must not touch them until the apples were ripe!

Kristina would be able to show her children how she had transplanted part of her childhood from the Old Country to the New.

—2—

FROM THE WORLD outside their home came further evil tidings. The Civil War—predicted to last only a summer—had gone on through the whole winter, and this spring it took on still greater proportions in combat and bitterness. During the first year the North and the South had fought each other to train, as it were, but during the second year the soldiers were experienced and knew how to handle their weapons. Consequently the war grew bloodier.

The long-awaited successes of the North were not yet apparent, but the adversities were smaller than during the first year. The great trouble was that the Southern generals remained as clever as before while the Northern commanders were as incapable as ever. Karl Oskar had subscribed to the *Minnesota Pioneer,* printed in St. Paul, and he tried to follow the war in English. His two oldest sons, who read the language well, were very helpful to him. The news was seldom encouraging. But he still trusted fully the country's leader whom he had helped elect: Old Abe would put everything in order! Lincoln would save the Union! Sometimes, however, he wondered if he trusted so much in the President because he wished to rely on his own ability to select the man.

They had not yet heard anything about the threatened draft. The North still had as many volunteers as they could train and equip. The number of soldiers increased on both sides.

The Civil War grew by and by to be the greatest war in the world to date.

The war was remarkable in another way also, if not inexplicable. Peoples who had warred against each other in the Old World fought side by side in the New World. English and Irish, Germans and French, Austrians and Italians all fought in the Northern army for the preservation of the Union. Immigrants from different nations in the Old World went of their own free will to jeopardize their lives for the right to remain one single nation in the New World.

When Karl Oskar read about this in the *Minnesota Pioneer* he wondered why these people hadn't been able to live in peace in their homelands when they could be friends and fight side by side in America.

But the rumblings of war to the south were now part of their daily life and did not cause much concern among the Minnesota settlers. In New Duvemåla life went on without disturbing events. With the arrival of spring Kristina felt almost as well as before, indeed, she considered herself fully recuperated. With the help of Marta, whose handiness daily increased, Kristina had now resumed her chores. All seemed well in their house.

During the days the man and wife labored industriously, as they had done during their twenty years of marriage. But during the nights a change had taken place in their lives; during the nights Karl Oskar had no wife and Kristina no husband.

They enjoyed their rest in the same room, at opposite sides of the room, in different beds. The distance was not great from bed to bed, there were no miles between them, only six or seven easy paces. But there might as well have been a road a thousand miles long: the great ocean they once crossed could not have separated them more completely.

Six words continued to echo deep in Karl Oskar's ears: *Next childbed will be her death.*

A great denial had been laid upon him. He went without one joy he had shared with his wife during all their years. It was something essential for a healthy man—the way he felt it. A sudden interruption had taken place in a habit of many years. Now when he lay down on his bed in the evening he was assailed by the demands of his unsatisfied body. He felt his sex as a burden, it annoyed and irritated him. It took longer for him to go to sleep, and he slept restlessly and in fits.

How far away from a man is the woman he must never approach?

He noticed that his wife also lay awake long after going to bed. He could hear her stir in her bed, move and turn. And he need not guess how she felt.

Sometimes they would talk for a while from their separate beds across the room before they wished each other goodnight. They spoke of the work they had done today, what they would do tomorrow—about anything except that which filled their thoughts: They were not allowed to sleep together.

Both missed deeply the bodily contact they had shared for twenty years. After being together and having satisfied their desires, often the moments of their deepest confidences arose when they could say things otherwise suppressed through embarrassment. Then they opened to each other all that otherwise was locked in. They spoke of the life they had shared, in the Old World and in the New, they spoke of death which awaited them sometime, death which would separate them. And they talked of eternity which had no end. Then Kristina would speak of her soul's conviction: Death would not separate them forever, only for a short time. They would meet again. They would meet in the life that would last—eternity.

The meeting of their bodies had for them become the moments of intimacy which opened their souls to each other.

Month after month Karl Oskar endured his denial. But the longer he was denied the more he suffered from his denial. The longer his body was denied what it craved, the more often it craved it. His thoughts were busy with just the things they were not allowed to be busy with. A remembrance of lust and joy in days gone by increased the present lack of it. The good moments he had shared with Kristina excited and stimulated him. In his dreams he was with her again as before—he awakened in terror: What had he done to her . . . ? What had he done?

Next childbed . . . Six words hummed in his ears as a warning bell, a threatening reminder to be on guard night and day.

—3—

DURING the Whitsuntide holidays Ulrika came for a visit and could both see and hear that Kristina had regained her health. She could see new clothes the settler wife had sewn for the children on her new sewing machine; a carpet loom was put up and the carpets were expected to be ready for Midsummer. And Kristina showed her the tree at the east gable wall: The Swedish tree would bear apples for the first time this summer! She could see the apples grow in size from day to day! And she promised Ulrika a bushelful next fall.

It was Ulrika who had carried the doctor's order to Karl Oskar concerning his wife, and that was three months ago. They had not seen her since. Now

Ulrika's eyes seemed to say that she felt sorry for him, and this made him feel uncomfortable.

Ulrika knew. She had shared in something that ought to have stayed between him and Kristina. She was sharing the secrets of a married couple, and this was wrong. No third person should have knowledge of this. The Baptist minister's wife was Kristina's good friend, but he himself had not entirely accepted her. He supposed this had to do with his knowledge of her Swedish activities as parish whore which he couldn't forget. He didn't fully trust Ulrika of Västergöhl, formerly known as the Glad One. She was a talkative woman, she did not willingly keep quiet. If it had been up to him she would not have been in on the secret.

On her way home Mrs. Jackson had to make a call in Center City, and Karl Oskar drove her there. They were alone on the wagon.

She said, "I'm glad Kristina is well again."

"Yes, I am too."

"You can thank the Lord for that!" Ulrika turned and searched the driver's face. "But you! You've lost weight, Karl Oskar!"

"I lose a little every year. It's the heat here in Minnesota."

"You needn't blame the heat! Not to me! I know what it is! I know what you need!"

He did not reply. He jerked the reins and urged the horses on; damn that Ulrika must know!

"I want to tell you, Karl Oskar; I feel sorry for you!"

"You needn't!" His reply was short.

"You have to lie in that ox pen! How you must suffer during the nights! You get hotter that way, of course!"

In one way Mrs. Henry O. Jackson was still Ulrika of Västergöhl, thought Karl Oskar. She could spew forth almost anything. At times she still talked like the parish whore, especially when she talked to men. He disliked women who talked that way.

"Poor you! You must go without and suffer! Nothing else left for you, because you care for Kristina!"

"A wife isn't for bedplay only!"

"But a healthy man needs a woman! It must be hard on you! Don't pretend to me!"

He had some crushing words on the tip of his tongue but he bit them off. And he decided that he would not reply to her any more.

Ulrika continued to describe the tortures a healthy man must endure when he was denied a woman, but from now on only her voice was heard on the wagon; the driver sat completely silent. Why, she wondered, did he keep so silent?

Yes, Ulrika wondered about Karl Oskar. Old as he was she had been able to embarrass him. He was a father many times over but as shy as an untried youth. Here he sat beside her now, embarrassed and blushing like a little boy who had just messed in his pants and didn't dare tell anybody. But there was something attractive about strong, rough men who could feel embarrassed as Karl Oskar did. They were like little boys who needed a woman's hand to help unbutton the fly. And it was such boy-men women liked to help if they had an opportunity. Now she felt sorry for Karl Oskar because he couldn't find help with some woman.

Karl Oskar reined the horses to a stop in front of Persson's Store. He was going to make some purchases from Klas Albert, and his woman rider had errands elsewhere. With a sigh of relief he saw Mrs. Henry O. Jackson get off his wagon.

—4—

IT WAS AN EVENING in May; Karl Oskar had gone to bed and said goodnight to his wife. As long as day lighted him he had remained in the field preparing it for the corn. With some satisfaction he stretched his tired limbs in the bed. He was waiting for sleep. Crickets chirruped in the grass and trees outside—those screech-hoppers kept on without end in the spring nights, like an eternally buzzing spinning wheel.

But above this familiar, persistent noise from outside he heard a padding sound here in the room: steps of bare feet across the floor. Quickly he lifted his head from the pillow.

Kristina stood at his bed. White linen against the dark of the room— Kristina stood there in her shift.

He thought she had already gone to sleep.

"You're up?!"

"Yes."

"Are you sick, Kristina?"

"No."

"What is it then? Something wrong?"

"Don't worry—nothing is wrong with me."

"But what do you want?"

"I'm coming back to you."

"What did you say?"

"I want to be your wife again . . . "

In a sudden motion he sat up in his bed: "You want to . . . ? What *are* you saying?!"

"You heard me. I think we should sleep together again. Here I am . . . "

For more than three months they had kept apart. Tonight she had unexpectedly come to his bed, saying: Here I am!

He bent forward, trying to look his wife in the face for an explanation, but it was too dark.

"I've come back to you, Karl Oskar. Don't you want me?"

"Are you walking in your sleep, Kristina?"

"I'm awake!"

"Is your head all right?"

"Don't worry—I'm all right . . . "

Her voice seemed all right; she spoke slowly, calmly—she was not sick, she wasn't out of her head, she wasn't walking in her sleep, she was fully awake. Her mind was all right and she came to him and wanted to be his wife again.

He was stunned; in his confusion he stuttered: "You . . . you, you don't . . . you don't know what you're doing! You forget yourself!"

"I'm not forgetting myself. I've thought it over, really."

"But you know as well as I—it mustn't happen!"

"Karl Oskar—it can't go on like this any longer between us two. It's unbearable. You haven't complained, but I know how you suffer . . . "

She sat down next to him on the bed. He felt her warm breath on his ear; he took her around the waist, his hands trembling.

What was the matter with Kristina? What had come over her? Was she feverish? He stroked her cheek but it felt cool, her forehead, but it wasn't fever-hot. She was herself in all ways, and her senses and thoughts were clear. Yet she had walked the road between their beds which they were not allowed to walk—she had traversed the distance that had separated them for three months.

"Don't worry!" Her voice was confident, sure. "I know what I'm doing."

"But *next time*!" he cried out. "There must not be a next time for you! Don't you remember what the doctor said!"

"I don't believe in what the doctor said—he's not omnipotent."

"But something was injured and that he must know . . . "

"I am not afraid."

"But your life—we can't take a chance . . . "

"The Almighty alone rules over my life."

"It's dangerous—how dare you . . . "

"It is simple—I don't pay any attention to the doctor. I trust in God."

Her mouth was near his ear; she whispered: He asked how she dare? Must she no longer believe she was under the Almighty's protection? Must she now doubt God who had seen them unharmed through all the dangers and vicissitudes of their emigration? Must she think that God would not look after her through one more childbed?

And it was not God who had forbidden them to live together. On the contrary, it was his will that married people should have each other. And God must know they loved each other. It was a human order that kept them apart—why must they obey humans? Didn't they dare trust in the Creator's wisdom?

Karl Oskar had been told. Now he knew why she had come to him. But he was not at ease, he must think, he must use common sense. It was true that at their emigration he had exposed his wife and children to great dangers to life and limb. But that time, as always, it had been his responsibility. And he had thought it over thoroughly before reaching the final decision.

Kristina trusted God in his heaven more than the doctor in Stillwater. But Karl Oskar trusted more in the doctor than in God.

"You must understand." His speech was thick, his throat felt too narrow to let air through. "Kristina! I don't dare!"

"Don't dare? Why?"

"I must think of you. Even if you don't . . . "

"I'm not afraid . . . "

"It could be fatal!"

"We're all well. Thanks to whom? What do you think?"

Who was Kristina's helper? Where was her confidence? Her strength and security? Who had given her the courage to come to him tonight?

She had no fear, and therefore she was stronger than he. Her courage could not be defeated in a few groping words: It might be fatal! And he had dared assume responsibility before, many times—why didn't he dare now?

The crickets were still screeching unceasingly outside the window; those invisible critters were noisier than anything else in the spring night. Inside the house all was silent except for a man and a wife who spoke in whispers. Even if someone had stood beside the bed he would not have heard what they said.

His hand stroked her neck. His hands knew her body.

She said: "I trust in the Creator. It is his will if I live, it's his will if I die . . . "

"But must I let you dare . . . your life . . . "

"Whatever you and I do—he will do with me what he wants."

In his mind Karl Oskar was still resisting: Use your common sense! But he was dazed by the demanding force in his body—a force that had already surrendered him to his wife in the moment when she stood at his bedside and said: I'm back with you!

She remained with him, and he yielded his body.

XI

KRISTINA IS NOT AFRAID

— I —

ALONG THE SHORES of Lake Chisago runs a path that has been trod by Indians and deer; here the Indians hunted the deer as the animals sought their way to the lake to drink of its water.

The path goes in sharp twists and bends around fallen tree trunks, leaves the lakeshore at moors and bogs where the ground sinks under foot, penetrates deep brambles and bushes, turns sharply away from holes, steep cliffs, and ravines, disappears in the undergrowth with its thorny, pricking spikes. Winding, wriggling its way, it never leaves the shore; as the wanderer least expects it he is met by the glittering water before him and his path lightens.

This path is without beginning or end, for it runs around the whole Indian lake Ki-Chi-Saga with its hundreds of inlets and bays and points and promontories, islands, and islets. Of old it was tramped only by the deer and the hunter people's light feet, shod in the skin of the deer. Now the redskins are seldom seen on the road they themselves trampled out through the wilderness. It is used by another people, who have come from far away, of another hue: The whites now wear away the bared roots with their heavy footgear, wooden shoes, iron-shod boots, crunching, crushing heels. These people also break their own roads through the forest, straight roads, cutting through the grave mounds of the Indians. These people are in a hurry and cannot waste their time on the meandering Indian paths.

On an evening in June, one of the immigrant women walks on this path. It is near sunset yet she walks slowly. Her steps are short, perhaps tired. She doesn't tramp heavily on the Indian path and she is in no hurry.

Kristina is out in the forest, looking for a cow, Jenny, named after a Swedish singer with this name who has recently been to America, and about whom *Hemlandet* has had much to report. Jenny did not come home with the other cows this evening; she is ready to calve almost any day now, and that is why Kristina was concerned when she was missing this evening. Once before Jenny has had her calf out in the woods; Johan and Harald had found her then, far out in a bog, and had managed to get the cow home with the calf uninjured. Perhaps Jenny was repeating her forest calving. Or had she been caught between some boulders, unable to free herself? All this wilderness is full of crevices and holes where grazing cattle might easily break their legs.

Kristina stops now and then, calls the name of the lost cow, calls until she is hoarse, but the only replies are her own calls, echoing back from the tree trunks. The cows know their milkmaid's voice and will answer with a soft lowing when she calls them. She stops short on the path, listens intently, but no sound from Jenny reaches her ears.

It is already growing dark among the trees. Should she turn back without having fulfilled her errand? No, she must look a little bit farther. She is not afraid of losing her way after dark, for she knows the lake path well—she has only to follow it back the same way she came.

In a clearing where grow tall, lush raspberry bushes she stops to eat of the berries. The wild raspberries are already ripe, although it is only June. She crouches near one bush and enjoys the sweet fruit. She loves to go out in the woods in summertime to pick all the wild, edible berries that grow here. To her it is a means of liberation and of being alone, a welcome change in the monotony of daily chores. And in fall she likes to pick cranberries that abound on the tussocks in low-lying places. But no lingonberries grow here, as in Sweden; instead of lingonberries she preserves the somewhat sourer cranberries; in fact, they do have a taste of sweetness if picked after the frost has set in.

Darkness falls, yet she is not aware of it. Kristina will never cease to be surprised at the urgency of the twilight in America; it rushes by. Tonight it seems to last only five short minutes.

In her childhood in Sweden she had been afraid of the dark. This feeling had remained with her through youth, and she had been terribly afraid of the dark during the first years after their arrival here. Then a change had taken place; the fear of the dark left her. She does not know when this happened. It was only thus: One evening she noticed her fear was gone. From then on it made no difference to her if it was day or night. It might be daylight, or dark, in the place she happened to be, but which ever it was—she was not afraid. However great the difference between day and night she did not feel it. And now it is this way: Be she outside or in a house, it doesn't matter. She walks as calmly through a dark night as through the bright morning, because she feels herself within the same safe protection, the same secure home, in the dark of night as in the light of day. She knows nothing evil can happen to her. She cannot understand how darkness and night could have frightened her so before. On the contrary, it now seems to her she is best protected when veiled in darkness. It envelops her, hides her, follows her to guard her welfare, just as it must comfort the many of God's creatures that hide in brambles and bushes from enemies and pursuers.

But she can no longer search for her cow Jenny; it is too late now. She must return home. First thing in the morning they will send the boys out to look for the animal; Johan and Harald enjoy hikes in the forest, they have just begun to hunt, they know the places where a cow might hide. Or perhaps Karl Oskar had better go with them, in case the cow is caught somewhere.

Kristina turns homeward on the path. But the fatigue after her day's many chores falls upon her like a burden, and she sits down to rest on an upthrust root. Weakness still comes over her at times, and against this neither rest nor peace helps. And her thoughts have dwelled upon this: Is there any permanent cure against fatigue other than death?

Is there anything sweeter than to awaken in the morning completely rested?

She sits, surrounded by darkness, on the old tree trunk. She is alone in the wild woods, completely defenseless against anyone wishing to harm her. But she is not afraid. She feels as secure and protected as a child who has climbed up on its mother's knee.

Nor is she alone. This is a moment of meditation for her, a moment to think over what has just happened to her. For something has happened: She is pregnant again. She has just become sure: God has created a new life in her.

The last time this happened she had sinned gravely, and he chastised her and took back his creation. This time she has received assurance that she is again worthy. She enjoys God's confidence again. She has received his grace; he trusts her.

The curse has been removed from Kristina and she is again a blessed woman.

One night last month Karl Oskar and Kristina had again become husband and wife, and immediately this had taken place, it must have occurred as soon as it could. It was understandable that it should happen at their first, intense being together. After all, it was as if they had been married for a second time. And these last weeks they had lived like a newly wedded couple, who had long suffered in their impatient expectancy. It is a blissful time that has been granted them. And it began just as spring broke. Her Astrakhan tree was in full bloom then and this seemed to her a good omen.

Kristina is not afraid; all will be well.

As yet only a few days have passed since she learned for sure what had taken place. While she was still uncertain she had not wished to tell Karl Oskar, but now she must no longer delay. She knows in advance how he will take it: *It is he who is afraid!* She has noticed how worried he has been ever since they started to be together again. She knows him so well, she knows his reactions to one thing or another. In his eyes she has all the time read his anxiety: What have I done? What have I exposed you to? What will happen? When will it happen?

Now it has happened, and he must be told at once. Karl Oskar, who is so afraid of this next childbed—how sorry she feels for him. Now he will be terribly scared, and this she must prevent.

He believes blindly in the Stillwater doctor, that's why he is concerned about her. He'll be worried to death now if she doesn't give him courage. Men can't stand as much as women. They are more easily frightened by what they fear might happen. She must calm him; all will come out well.

While Kristina sits on the tree trunk this evening in the forest, it comes clearly to her—all that she must say to Karl Oskar: Listen to me now! I have news! I'm pregnant again! You expected it, you know that—you expected it and you were afraid of it! You haven't said anything but I've seen how scared you've been. But now you must stop! Now you needn't fear, because it's already happened. It's nothing to worry about—everything will be all right as before. I've been with child eight times and all has come out well in the end. Why not this time? Believe me, Karl Oskar, it will!

I have figured out the time—February. Yes, sometime in February, because it happened in May, the very first time, I'm sure. And no wonder—or what do you think, Karl Oskar?

But now you mustn't worry about it while I have my time of waiting. Please, Karl Oskar, I beg you—don't worry the least little bit during this time! Don't feel you've done something wrong! It's no sin to be with your wife, it's no evil thing to make her pregnant! Your mind must be at rest; you must have the same confidence as I. Why won't you?

Now you hear what I say, Karl Oskar: Forget what the doctor said! Don't think about it any more. It only makes you unhappy. Forget it! Cheer up!

All will be well with me when my time comes. Eight times I've gone through it successfully. Who has helped me those times? Who do you think? He will help me this time also! You must know I'm in good hands!

So she will speak to Karl Oskar. But what will he answer?

Kristina remains seated on the fallen tree and forgets time. The evening wears on. She begins to feel a chill on her bare legs; some nights in June are chilly. She pulls her skirt around her knees; now she must go home. She hadn't meant to sit here and rest such a long time. But her mind had been full of her new pregnancy and her worries about Karl Oskar. Now she knows what to say, how to weigh her words when she speaks to him.

She rises and continues homeward on the path. Now it is as dark as it can be in the forest. She can hardly see where to put her foot down. Twigs brush her in the face as she walks, she bends down to avoid them; she must walk slowly in this darkness. But she has tramped this path hundreds of times during the years they have lived here; she knows where it bends and turns, she will not lose it. But she must take slow steps or she might hurt herself against trees or roots.

Still, her foot stumbles and she almost falls.

She regains her balance and is ready to go on when a tall apparition takes shape through the dark. Someone is coming toward her on the path, someone who tramps heavily, in solid, booted feet. A large man takes shape a few feet in front of her.

And Kristina suddenly pulls back a few steps in front of her. Suddenly a weight has fallen on her heart. What is this? Who is this walking on the path?

She takes a few steps backward, her hands on her throat as if in protection. She is utterly still.

The apparition has stopped in front of her.

"I hope I didn't scare you?"

"Karl Oskar!"

"You're late—I was getting worried."

"It turned dark so quickly . . . "

"Well, yes, that's what I thought. That's why I came . . . "

"Have I been looking for the cow so long that you had to look for me!"

"Did you find the cow?"

"No, I didn't. She might be stuck somewhere . . . "

Karl Oskar and Kristina resume their homeward walk on the path. They walk side by side, but the path is so narrow they find it difficult to walk beside each other; at times he must go ahead a bit, then wait for her when the path broadens.

And now as they walk together here in the dark forest she feels the moment has come to tell him:

She tells him what has happened to her, she tells him everything she has thought of while sitting on the tree trunk, she says all in a few minutes, all she has intended to tell him.

Kristina wishes to share with her husband her own unwavering confidence and conviction:

She will survive her ninth childbed.

—2—

A settler wife's evening prayer:

. . . yes, dear God . . . it was terrible . . . worse than I had ever feared . . . He was frightened beyond reason. Never have I seen him so frightened as tonight . . . never! I couldn't help no matter what I said. Therefore I wish to pray to you, dear God—help me! Help me reassure Karl Oskar! Help me remove the anxiety from him! For he cannot carry on like this all the time till February . . .

I myself . . . I know not what to do any more . . . but I trust in you, dear God. You are the only one who can remove the fear from my husband. Don't let Karl Oskar worry! Tell him there's no danger! Now he only says everything is his fault, his responsibility. But you—you know all, you know how it happened . . .

Myself . . . I'll do all I can to help him in this. But I'm so tired, dear God, you know how tired I am . . .

XII

AND A NEW CIVIL WAR
BROKE OUT

The Cause:

According to the Mendota Agreement the government was to pay the Sioux in western Minnesota the sum of $70,000 in gold during 1861. By the beginning of 1862 this debt had not been paid. Meanwhile, famine raged among the Indians and their situation was greatly worsened by the intensely cold winter. Their spokesmen several times dunned the government agents for money but were sent away empty-handed. While the Sioux waited in vain for their money, disturbance arose in their camp. Red Iron, a prominent Sioux chief, had met with Alexander Ramsey, governor of Minnesota, for negotiations which took place at Mankato in October 1861.

Red Chief Speaks to White Chief at Mankato:

Man does not own the earth. What he does not own he cannot sell. What no one can sell no one can buy. Your people, White Chief, therefore cannot buy the earth. All objects you can move from one place to another may be bought. A horse, a bow, a buffalo hide you can buy. But the land you cannot pick up and move from one place to another.

My people do not own this land and therefore we cannot sell it to your people. We have only granted your people the right to use this ground and live on it. All the gold and silver you might offer us—be it even enough to fill our valleys to the very brim—would not buy from us the beautiful hunting grounds the Great Father gave to our forefathers. We will not give up the graves of our fathers for all the money in the world.

My people have been forced to let your people use this land. Your chiefs have given us paper with written promises of sufficient gold to sustain our lives. We have waited for many moons in our camps but this gold has not arrived. We are still waiting.

Your people are rich, my people are poor. Your people have fine buildings, my people live in poor wigwams. Your fires are warm, our fires are not able to keep out the cold. The white children are strong and well fed, our children are weak and starved. Your people have food in great plenty, my people are sick from hunger. Your storehouses are filled, my people have no storehouses. Deer and elk will soon be gone, the fish in our lakes disappear. Soon the snow will fall over the ground and hunting will be over. Soon ice will cover the waters and we will not be able to catch the fish. How then will my people live?

We cannot survive in this country without food. Without food we shall perish. As deer in the forest and fish in the lakes diminish and disappear, so our people will disappear and die.

We have surrendered our hunting grounds and our fathers' graves. Soon there will be no place in this land where we can bury our dead. We have no land left for our graves. Your people have taken our land and will not give space even for our dead bodies.

Our Great Father will see his children die in the land he has given them to possess. We will only leave our bones, to whiten aboveground. When our bones have turned to dust there will be nothing more left of our people. Your people alone will possess that beautiful land our Great Father once gave his children.

Thus spake Red Chief to White Chief at Mankato.

The Start:

On August 18, 1862, there arrived for the government agent at Fort Ridgely the $70,000 in gold which was overdue the Sioux tribes of western Minnesota.

It was exactly one day too late. The day before, the Indians had begun to exact their claim in settlers' blood.

—1—

IT BEGAN on Sunday, August 17, on Sven Danjelsson's homestead near Acton in Meeker County.

Sven had staked out his claim of 160 acres close to a small reedy lake a mile from Acton, and even before his marriage he had built a log cabin and cleared a few acres. After their wedding the previous autumn, Sven and Ragnhild had moved to the claim and lived there during the winter. In the spring they had done their first sowing and planting, and their first crops were now ready to be harvested.

Danjel Andreasson and his son Olof, who was three years younger than

Sven, had early in spring promised to help the young couple with their first crop. Ragnhild was expecting a child and did not feel strong. On Friday evening, the fifteenth, Danjel and Olof arrived at the new clearing near Acton. Sven was pleased with the prospect of help from his father and brother; now his young wife need not overwork herself during the harvest, so close before her delivery; Ragnhild was in the last month of her pregnancy.

On Saturday Sven started to mow his rye, his father bound the sheaves after him, and his brother put them in shocks. Before evening the field was finished, but Danjel and Olof would remain over Sunday to help with the wheat during the following week.

During Sunday forenoon a Swedish neighbor came to visit the family. His name was Ivar Eriksson, a young man about Sven's age. He brought with him his two children, a boy four years old and a girl of three. Ivar and Sven had helped each other with work and were good friends.

The neighbor and his children stayed for Sunday dinner with the Danjelsson family. It was a humid summer day. At table the men talked about the crops and the intense heat; it was now about as warm as it ever was in Minnesota in August—how long would the heat wave last? This weather suited the settlers until the crops were in, even though they perspired greatly in their work in the fields.

Dinner over and Danjel having read the prayer of thanks, the men sought shade outside to enjoy their rest. The coolest place was at the back of the log house. Ragnhild remained inside to wash the dishes, and the neighbor children stayed in with her to play on the floor.

The four men stretched out in the grass against the wall.

During dinner Ivar Eriksson had happened to mention that some Indians had been seen near Acton yesterday, but he thought this was of no particular significance since the redskins frequently appeared in groups nowadays. Some of the Sioux had camped in Meeker before and had always been friendly; they had disturbed neither him nor any other settler in the vicinity. However, someone who had seen the Indians yesterday insisted their faces were painted red, whatever that might mean.

Sven Danjelsson had replied that sometimes the Indians painted their faces just for the fun of it, to be dressed up like. They enjoyed everything that glittered and shone, they would deck themselves out in anything they might lay hands on, they were like children in that respect. If one of them found a colorful rooster feather he would immediately put it in his hair. To look really festive they would rub their hair with bear fat until it seemed they had been ducked in a kettle of grease.

Ragnhild told about several squaws who had come to the house during the winter, their poor children blue in the face from cold; she had given them whatever clothing she could spare. Sven said she had given them more than she could spare, she had coughed the whole winter because she was dressed too lightly.

Pleasantly sated, the men were dozing at the wall. Half asleep they noticed some Indians approach the house from the forest.

Sven Danjelsson arose to meet the callers—six Sioux. Their faces were not painted; he did not suspect any treachery. It did surprise him, though, that all six carried new guns; he had not seen Indians with guns before. He recognized two of the men, who had often come to the cabin to beg for food. They had always been given something and they had always appeared friendly. They spoke a little English, a few words for food, and their request had always been the same: They were hungry, could they have some potatoes today?

It was the same today. Sven replied that he would go and pick some potatoes for them; usually they ate the tubers raw.

He picked up a basket and went toward the potato field, about two hundred yards from the house. The other three men had remained in the shade of the house, but as the Indians now approached, they rose and watched their movements with some concern.

The savages split up into two groups: Three men walked into the cabin while three snooped around the outhouses, apparently looking for food. They caught sight of the small chicken house which Sven had hammered together; inside a setting hen was on her eggs. Startled by their approach the hen rose with a cackle from her nest and ran away. The Indians threw themselves over the nest, grabbed the eggs, and seemed to swallow them, shell and all. Not one single egg was left. The yolks were running down their chins.

Sven Danjelsson had just reached the potato field when he heard the cackle of the frightened hen. He turned and saw the visitors plunder the nest. He had promised them potatoes—why must they now steal from him? Enraged, he shouted to them to leave his property alone. Didn't they understand that this was a setting hen, ready to hatch chickens! They must . . .

These were the settler's last words in life. Still chewing on the eggshells, one of the Indians lifted his gun, aimed, and fired. The shot hit Sven in the chest. He dropped the basket, fell face forward across a potato furrow and lay still among the broken stalks.

Sven Danjelsson died instantly.

From the cabin wall his father and brother had been calling to him about the plunder of the nest, and Ivar Eriksson had run toward the chicken coop, threatening the robbers. At that moment the first shot cracked, and Danjel Andreasson saw his oldest son drop to the ground.

Until then he had irresolutely watched the Indians' doings; now he ran to the potato field, Danjel was hastening to his fallen son as fast as his stiff old legs could carry him.

He reached only halfway: The Indians at the coop aimed two shots at him; the first wounded him in the arm, the second hit him in the back and killed him.

Danjel Andreasson survived his son by only a few moments.

Ivar Eriksson was going after the egg thieves and intended to give them a good talking to, but when they started to use their guns he stopped and looked about; what must he do now? Within the span of the same minute he saw father and son fall from the Indians' bullets and remain lying where they had fallen. What could he do? He was unarmed—all three Indians had guns. If he wished to save his life, there remained for him nothing but flight. But his children—they were inside the cabin.

He turned and rushed toward the house.

The Indians, however, had their eyes on him and fired several shots. Eriksson was hit in the shoulders and neck, and fell a few paces from the corner of the cabin. His wounds bled copiously but he remained conscious.

While this took place outside, three of the Sioux were inside the cabin of the young couple. They walked into the kitchen before any shots had been fired outside, and the young wife, busy at her dishes, had no suspicion of treachery. Ragnhild recoiled a little at the vile smell of their dirty bodies but she was not afraid of them. They asked for some milk. Many times before Indians had asked for milk, it was a drink new to them and they liked it.

The wife went to the cupboard for her earthen crock where she kept the morning milk. The uninvited guests drank in turn from the crock and soon emptied it. She hoped they would leave when they had quenched their thirst.

Just as they handed her the empty crock, the first shot was heard from outside. The young woman cried out in fright and rushed to the window; she had heard the shot that robbed her husband of his life out in the field. As Ragnhild peered through the window, the Indian who had first drunk of her milk lifted his tomahawk and struck her in the head from behind. She sank down to the kitchen floor, lifeless.

Ragnhild Danjelsson followed her husband in death as quickly as Danjel Andreasson had followed his son.

The Indians threw the empty milk crock to the floor, scattering the pieces against the walls. Then they pulled out their scalping knives and cut open the body of the pregnant woman; they pulled the child from her womb and hung it on the fireplace hook.

They were looking for edible things in the cabin. In the next room they came across the Eriksson children, the four-year-old boy and the three-year-old girl, who were playing on the floor. They grabbed the children by the legs and flung them against the wall, crushing their skulls. With their knives they deftly cut the bodies into many pieces.

They stayed in the log house and ate all the food they could lay hands on.

Meanwhile, the three Indians outside had scalped their white victims. But one of them was still alive: Ivar Eriksson, who had fallen near the house, was still conscious. A bullet had entered his neck and come out through his throat. He tried to stop the profuse bleeding by pulling up grass and pushing it into the bullet hole. As the Indians came by and noticed their victim was still alive, they cut his throat from ear to ear.

Ivar Eriksson had used snuff ardently and when his body later was found it was revealed that the Indians had allowed themselves a joke with the snuffbox they had found in his pocket. His thumb and right index finger, which he used while taking snuff, had been cut off and put in the snuffbox. The savages knew that the finger, the thumb, the snuff, and the box belonged together, and they wanted to gather all the pieces in one place.

The Indians had now fulfilled their mission to the Sven Danjelsson cabin: Here were no more whites alive. They set off for the next white homestead.

But it so happened that one life had escaped them. Olof, Danjel's younger son, had seen his brother and father hit by Indian bullets and fall. He had realized they were dead and had run for his life toward the forest. He was a good runner and managed to hide behind trees before the Indians were aware of it.

But he was afraid the savages would find him in the forest, where he knew of no sure hiding place. Unnoticed he made his way down to the little lake; he waded out into the water until he was in up to his neck. Here he meant to hide. He covered his head with the broad leaves of water lilies that floated on the surface. If he could keep this position, his head hidden by the leaves, no Indian eyes from shore would spy him, however sharp they were. The question was: Could he endure remaining in this place? His mouth was just above the surface, permitting him easy breathing, and the thick leaves protected him against the burning sun, but the water was slimy with silt, hungry mosquitoes swarmed about his head, and leeches crept and crawled onto his body. And his legs felt weaker as they sank into the mire.

But Olof Danjelsson endured, and remained in his hiding place throughout the rest of the day, this whole, long Sunday afternoon. As soon as it grew dark he crept out of the water. He dared not go to his brother's cabin—the Indians might have remained there after the attack. Following unfamiliar paths through the woods he managed to get away from Acton.

After a half night of wandering in the dark he reached a shanty beside Norway Lake, where a Norwegian trapper lived. The shanty's owner was horrified when he saw the youth come through his door; mud and slime on his face and clothing had dried in cakes until he looked like a black apparition. The trapper must be forgiven if he thought the devil in person was calling on him in his shanty this night.

That was how Danjel's younger son saved his life.

But it was a long time before the sole survivor of the Indian attack was able to relate what he had experienced this Sunday and make known that the Sioux uprising had begun.

—2—

FROM THIS SUNDAY, August 17, 1862, the young state of Minnesota had its own civil war.

A setting hen's nest was robbed by hungry Indians—and the owner became the first victim. The great Sioux uprising was started by people who long had gone hungry, and hunger was its cause.

The Call to Alarm:

> All through the gloom and the light
> The fate of a thousand Minnesotans was
> Riding that night.
>
> > (Freely after Longfellow)

—1—

ON THE NIGHT of the eighteenth of August an Indian alarm was issued from Fort Ridgely. It was carried by a common soldier, William J. Sturgis, Company B, of the Fifth Minnesota Regiment.

On Monday, the eighteenth, Fort Ridgely had been completely surrounded by Indian warriors, but toward midnight Sturgis, aided by the intense darkness, managed to slip out from the fort with his horse. He rode eastward, down the Minnesota Valley. To the right he had the river to guide him. His way led through the most beautiful regions of Indian country; here stretched great lush leafy forests, here lay broad meadows, rich valleys—a region of fertility and growth. On recently broken clearings the crops stood yellow and ripe. The valley at this time of year flaunted its great abundance. Private William J. Sturgis rode through a good and fruitful land, wherein people of many nations had built for themselves new homes and found sure sustenance.

But he carried a message of death and fire, of cruelty and blood. The sky behind him was streaked with flames that lighted the sultry August night: Fires were rampant; flames rose from settlers' houses, from immigrants' homes.

William J. Sturgis was only nineteen years old and he had enlisted as a private only a few months earlier. Yesterday morning he had for the first time participated in the duty that primarily is the soldier's: To take enemy life and defend your own. His company had been sent out from the fort against the rebelling Sioux—Chief Shakopee's band had begun to murder, plunder, and burn down settlers' houses near and far. At the bend of the river near Red Wood Ferry the forty-five soldiers had been caught unaware by Chief Shakopee. So sudden had been the surprise that he had seen his captain as well as many of his fellow soldiers fall, victims of Indian bullets. William was one of eight survivors of the group who had been able to return to the fort by fleeing along little-known forest roads.

In the evening he was ordered by his superior, Lieutenant Thomas P. Gere, to ride as courier to Governor Ramsey in St. Paul. The state's highest official must be notified of yesterday's happenings.

The Sioux had during the summer gathered in Meeker and Renville counties and were now on the warpath under their chief, Little Crow. On Monday they had attacked the Lower Sioux Agency at Red Wood. This attack had come without warning and the whites were wholly unprepared for it. The attack was successful in every way; by evening all the whites in Red Wood had been killed, all the houses burned down. The Agency was a smoking pile of embers.

After Chief Shakopee's victory over Company B the Sioux warriors had surrounded the two forts on the Minnesota River—Fort Ridgely and New Ulm, the two defense posts for the Minnesota Valley. For Fort Ridgely's defense there were now only twenty-nine soldiers under the command of Lieutenant

Gere; the lieutenant was twenty-three years old. As commanding officer—after the captain had been killed—he now sent his courier to the governor with a report of the attack and with an urgent request for aid.

Relief immediately! Those were the most important words in the message young William was carrying to Minnesota's capital.

Lieutenant Gere had supplied his courier with the fleetest horse available at the fort, and William pushed the animal to its utmost. For long stretches he galloped through the roadless country, along unfamiliar paths, often hindered and delayed by ravines, fallen giant trees, unexpected precipices. He was often forced to detour and urged his horse ever harder to regain the lost time. His ride with its perils seemed the ride of an insane man, but it was undertaken by a cool, courageous person, to save human lives.

Behind the rider the sky was fire-red; he rode to get help and to warn those who could help themselves—those who still might flee.

The settlers had been busy with harvesting, and they slept soundly in their beds, worn out from the work in the fields. They slept peacefully in their ignorance but were rudely wrested from the sweetness of sleep by thundering horse's hoofs, a rider outside the house who banged against the door, calling with all the strength of his lungs: The Sioux are on the warpath! They are murdering all whites—men, women, and children! They're burning houses, plundering, ravishing the whole country! They're coming this way—hurry! Send women and children away! Hide if you can—in the woods, in cellars, in caves, in haystacks! Shakopee's band is coming this way! Hurry! Hide from the Sioux!

Startled out of their sleep and still dazed, people stuck their heads out through the door, but the rider was already gone, on his way to another house. What was it he had called? Could they believe him? But it was not a dream—everyone in the house had heard the call: The Sioux are on the warpath!

Some believed the message, others did not. But as they looked toward the west and saw the sky yellow-red in flames, then they knew. Indeed, the rider had said: They're burning everything.

Young William knew what he was doing, he knew whereof he spoke, knew the danger he warned against. But how many would have believed him if he had had the time to relate all he had seen and experienced in the regions where Chief Shakopee and his band had ravaged yesterday and the day before? Most would probably say: Such things could not happen! But none would ever see what he had seen, to none could he lend his eyes; the horror of it was still with him.

Shakopee and his band had left their camp at Lake Kandiyohi and spread out along the left shores of the river. This feared Sioux chieftain had gathered more scalps than any other of their chiefs, and yesterday William had encountered him, between Red Wood and Fort Ridgely, where he and his warriors swung their tomahawks in bloody battle.

William J. Sturgis was young, his mind was impressionable, he had seen something that again and again would return to his inner eye, until his eyes lost their light in death.

A settler is leaning backward against the picket fence enclosing his field. He might be resting thus after his harvest work. But he is nailed to the pickets by spears that have been stabbed through his groin. The grass at his feet is as red as roses in bloom. The man is screaming with all his might. His eye sockets are empty, the bloody globes lie in the gore on the ground. As William pulls out the spears the man suddenly becomes silent. He falls forward along his fence; he is dead.

Private Sturgis is fleeing to the fort and hides in the tall grass. He stumbles over a dead woman, her body cut open, her innards removed. Instead of intestines he sees parts of a cut-up child. A pregnant woman has had her child returned to her body, after death.

A dead boy about six or seven years old lies a few paces away from her. The little forehead is crushed, the nose cut off. The right hand still clutches a knife he must have used to defend himself.

Two settlers lie naked in their wheat field, their torn clothing some distance away. Both lie on their backs, their scythes beside them; they were surprised in their harvesting and lie now among sheaves they'll never gather. Their heads are crushed to a pulp—Chief Shakopee's warriors prefer to use their tomahawks and do not waste bullets unnecessarily. Each of the harvesters' bodies had a red blotch in the crotch: Their male organs have been cut off and stuck in their mouths.

Outside a shanty sits an old man, his back leaning against the door; he looks comfortable, as if enjoying his afternoon siesta. But he cannot be awakened, he has been scalped, and both arms have been cut off and laid in a cross before the dead. He sits as if he were dreaming pleasant dreams beside his lost limbs.

Face down, across the threshold, lies a man's naked body. On a hook above the door hang the man's testicles.

The heat is intense, the smell of decaying flesh follows, pursues William; this odor will soon contaminate the air in all this region.

Crushed, shot, scalped, maimed—the entire way from Red Wood Ferry to Fort Ridgely he had seen only one living individual. From inside a hollow oak came a pitiful complaint as from a hurt animal. It was a child's cry. He went over to the oak: A little girl crept out of a hole in the trunk. She whined, wept with dry eyes, hiccupped for breath, stammered, but could not reply to his questions. She seemed to have lost her power of speech through fear. He spoke reassuringly to her for a while, and then she began to tell her story.

Her father and mother had been in the field, she alone inside with her older sister. Then some strangers came, they had feathers in their hair, and their faces were painted red. Four of them. They had tied the hands of her sister, torn off her clothes, and laid her on her back on the floor. Then each man in turn had lain down on her stomach and laughed terribly. But her sister only cried and asked them to stop. She herself had at first hidden behind a bed but when one of the redskins looked at her, she had jumped out through the window and run through the bushes until she found the oak with the hole in it. She had stayed in this hiding place the whole night and hardly dared move, she was so afraid the Indians who had treated her sister so badly would find her.

In the whole region—from Red Wood to the fort—he had found only a single human being alive, a ten-year-old girl, saved in a hollow oak.

He took the girl with him to the fort, and when they were almost there they met a woman with wild eyes and flying hair who kept screaming: Where is the haystack? Where are my children? The woman seemed to have lost her mind, but by and by he managed to calm her and learned that she had hidden her children in a haystack when she heard the Indians were coming; one child was only six months old. She herself had hidden in a well and thus saved her life. But when she crawled up again she couldn't find the haystack where she had hidden the children. There were so many haystacks and she had looked in every one without finding the little ones. She had forgotten to observe which stack she hid them in; she had been so excited, she had pushed them into the first one she saw.

Perhaps the Indians had found her children and killed them?

Where is the haystack? Where are my children?

Private William had left the mother without being able to help her. But her screams he would hear forever.

He had seen it all, with these very eyes which now tried to penetrate the darkness as he rode toward St. Paul. He felt those sights would be with him always, he could never shake them off, they proved to him man's powerlessness when such forces were let loose.

Private William J. Sturgis rode through Minnesota and spread his alarm through its settlements, shouted to the mothers: Hide your children! Hide them in haystacks and hollow trees!

He knew the danger he was warning them against.

—2—

AT THREE O'CLOCK in the morning Sturgis reached St. Peter, where he changed horses. And twelve hours later, at three o'clock on Tuesday afternoon, he rode into Fort Snelling, where he at once delivered his message to Governor Alexander Ramsey.

Through a country primarily without roads, the courier from Fort Ridgely had covered a distance of 120 miles in fifteen hours. He had made the fastest ride known to anyone in Minnesota.

Private William J. Sturgis, one of the eight survivors of the Red Wood Ferry massacre, was himself granted a long life. Fate allowed him to see a new century—he died in 1907, on his farm near the Rocky Mountains. During the many years after it happened, he had had the opportunity to tell his neighbors, over and over again, about his fast ride from beleaguered Fort Ridgely to St. Paul on August 19, 1862. It was his life's great accomplishment: He had warned the people about the Sioux uprising and in so doing saved thousands of lives.

Because of his ride Private Sturgis has found a place in the history of Minnesota.

The Panic:

—1—

ABOVE THE SHORES of Lake Chisago the sandstone Indian head rose like a guardtower over the St. Croix Valley. A wreath of greenish bushes decorated the Indian head this summer as in other summers. His broad stone forehead was turned toward the east, and from his elevated position his black cave eyes surveyed the land the white intruders had taken from his kinfolk. The stone Indian at Lake Ki-Chi-Saga had watched as the whites came in endless droves to build their houses on his people's hunting grounds, he watched them open roads through his forefathers' graves, watched them change the beautiful, good land between the rivers. The intruders had spread, until those born in these regions had to withdraw. All around the great water where he had seen hundreds of campfires, lit by his people, the stone Indian could now see only a lamplight here and there.

The proud, free hunter people were being degraded to beggars. "As the white man comes the Indian must go."

The settlers around Lake Chisago were aware of this sandstone cliff, the Indian head, and to them it was a monument to the natives' savagery and unfetteredness. They saw before them a constant reminder of the people who before them had possessed this valley. Now they had become masters of this land, but back there the Indian still stretched his defiant neck against the sky and threw his dark shadow over the lake's water. The stone Indian seemed to them an ever remaining threat. There he stood and there he would remain. The high sand cliff was a fortress no one could conquer. It would never fall. The redskins could be conquered, obliterated, but this cliff could not be moved or obliterated: The Indians could be banished—but not *The Indian!*

The stone Indian would remain long after those now living—the final victor.

— 2 —

WHEN NEWS of the great Sioux rising to the west reached the St. Croix Valley, panic spread among the people.

Ever since their arrival the immigrants had feared the country's old inhabitants. To the settlers the Indians were a wild, savage people, and they looked upon them as treacherous, unreliable, and cruel. Yet the Chippewa of the St. Croix Valley had been peaceful, and hardly anything could be remembered that indicated cruelty and bloodthirstiness in the redskins. But as long as the Indians remained they would be a constant cause of apprehension among the whites; their camps in the vicinity of white settlements were always felt as a danger: No one knew what they might have in mind or when they might attack. Time and time again rumors of uprising spread: The Indians were on the warpath! Each time fright seized the settlers. Through repeated false alarms the Indian fear was sustained over the years.

During those few days in August the Indian scare spread rapidly across the St. Croix Valley. All the old fear that had accumulated in their minds rose to the surface; they remembered all the old stories of Indian cruelty in war, the way of all savages, merciless, relentless warfare. They killed everyone, regardless of sex or age, they spared not even the unborn children in the mothers' wombs. They treated human beings in the same way they treated fallen prey during a hunt—as carcasses to slaughter.

Under the settlers' fear lay a feeling of guilt, more or less conscious; they felt there was an unsettled matter between them and the country's former owners: The Indians wanted to rid themselves of the whites. This they must count on and fear: One day the redskins would try to exact their revenge on them, and exact it in blood.

That day had come.

Indian panic spread through the St. Croix Valley. The people were drawn from their daily chores by a new urgent concern: their own lives. They knew they were all intended as slaughter-prey for Little Crow and Chief Shakopee's warriors.

The Sioux war cry, which was aimed at every white inhabitant of Minnesota, echoed over the valley in those days. People feared to repeat five words which were soon known to everyone—the flaming red letters in the sky, as it were:

Every white man must die!

And during these days of panic something strange happened: The tall cliff at Chisago Lake grew in height. The formation assumed greater proportions and threw its shadow ever wider. The stone Indian straightened his rebellious and proud neck and held his green-wreathed head higher in the sky. The unusually brilliant sun gave to the forehead a red glow which no one had seen before.

And people turned to the cliff and said: Look! The Indian is coming to life! He has war paint on his face! Look!

The Indian at Lake Chisago waited in stony immobility. From the west they would come, there behind his mighty back, there they were in motion; his kinfolk were approaching.

The hunter people had arisen to drive out the intruders and take back their own land.

XIII

EVERY WHITE MAN MUST DIE!

—1—

ON THE AFTERNOON of Wednesday, August 20, Karl Oskar Nilsson was busy shocking wheat on his last clearing. With an iron bar he made a hole in the ground, pushed a pole into it, and leaned eight sheaves against the pole; then he hung four more crossways on the pole as a "hat." Each hat-sheaf he bent against his knee before he hung it so that heads and roots of the four top sheaves pointed downward and made a protecting roof in case of rainy weather. The wheat was tall enough to make stately shocks in straight rows, like a long line of soldiers in the field.

In the past wheat had been cheap, as low as forty cents a bushel, but during the war it had constantly risen in price until it now brought a whole dollar a bushel. That was why he had planted three quarters of his field with this grain last spring. And all his wheat had now ripened at one time and must be cut and harvested as soon as possible while the favorable weather lasted. This year they had a great harvest rush at his farm.

But today, as Karl Oskar raised shock after shock, his thoughts were not with the labor of his hands; instead they were inside the house where his wife was lying in bed.

Kristina had taken sick last night. She had been seized with pain in her lower abdomen, and a flow of blood. These were the signs of a miscarriage, and he had sent Johan with the team to Stillwater to fetch Dr. Farnley. If for some reason the doctor was unable to come with him, Johan was to fetch Miss Skalrud, the Norwegian midwife.

In the morning Manda Svensson had come to see Kristina and she had confirmed their suspicion; it was a miscarriage. It happened at the beginning of the fourth month.

Now Marta was at home and looked after her mother, who had a high fever with spells of dizziness and great fatigue. Marta would call her father if he were needed.

Karl Oskar put up one shock-post after another but worked as if he neither heard nor saw anything. He counted the sheaves wrong, he put seven around the pole and five on the hat, one too many on top and one too few at the bottom. At one point he put thirteen sheaves in one shock. It had never happened to him before that he couldn't count to twelve at shocking time.

Kristina was in bed.

Johan could not be back from Stillwater with Dr. Farnley or Miss Skalrud before evening at the earliest, even if he drove the team at bolting speed. Karl Oskar had urged him to drive as fast as the wagon and harnesses would permit. But even if nothing delayed him, the entire day would be required for the round trip.

Meanwhile, Karl Oskar would shock the wheat they had cut so far. He would work as long as daylight permitted him, as long as his eyes could distinguish between the top and bottom of the sheaves.

The tiller's hands picked up the sheaves by the straw bands, one after the other. But today he did not notice how full were the heads, how heavy; nor did it gladden his heart. He was not conscious of what he was handling. Eight sheaves against the post, four to the hat—he was not capable of this simple counting. Instead he was counting a few words, and they were old words: A half year ago he had heard them for the first time, that threatening reminder.

Next . . . Next time . . . Even if he looked about while working he was not aware of what happened around him.

He had not seen the man down on the road who now came running rapidly across his field. He had not heard the heavy, noisy boot-steps behind him.

"Nilsson!"

Only when his name was called did Karl Oskar turn around.

It was Petrus Olausson. He was no daily caller at this farm. Their neighbor had not come to see them for several years, because they had refused to close their door to the wife of Baptist minister Jackson.

But today he must have an urgent errand, since he came in such a rush. He was a heavy man, yet he was running; he was bareheaded, and he had no time for a greeting. He puffed and sputtered as he blurted out:

"The Indians! They're coming!"

Olausson had stopped a few paces from Karl Oskar, panting for breath. His face was shiny with perspiration, he dried his forehead with both his hands. You could both see and hear that he had been running a long distance.

The words stuck in his throat:

"A horrible Indian outbreak! They're murdering the settlers . . . !"

At first Karl Oskar was more aware of his neighbor's behavior than of his words. He knew the church warden as a calm and placid man. Never before had he seen this easygoing farmer run. But here was his neighbor, agitated, distraught, running like one pursued.

"They've warned us from Fort Snelling . . . ! The redskins are after blood . . . ! They're killing every settler they get near . . . !"

Olausson caught his breath and began to speak more coherently. When he was in Center City this morning, a man rode in from Fort Snelling with the Indian alarm; the Sioux to the west were on the warpath along the Minnesota River and had attacked all the settlements in their path. They had murdered every white and burned down every house. Fort Ridgely and New Ulm, which protected the Minnesota Valley, were surrounded by the red savages. People were fleeing toward St. Peter and Mankato, leaving behind a blood-red sky from burning settlements.

The commander at Fort Snelling had sent couriers in all directions to warn the settlers about the Indian danger.

"I've run from house to house . . . !"

Petrus Olausson's shiny, hairless head glittered as wet and red as his face. His eyes were wild, his mouth trembled, his voice was now low and thick, now loud and piping.

Karl Oskar understood that this time it was no false alarm. When the Fort Snelling commandant himself had sent riding messengers to the settlers the information must be correct.

He mumbled: "Indian trouble on top of everything . . . ?"

The red murderers had used the right moment, said Petrus Olausson. These treacherous savages waited till the whites were busy with their own war. Five thousand Minnesotans were gone, and the redskins must have figured that with all ablebodied men away there were now only children and old men left behind on the farms.

"We are not entirely without manpower," observed Karl Oskar.

"But the redskins don't fight like humans! They're pure beasts!"

Karl Oskar stood weighing the iron bar in his hand, looking at his neighbor who had brought him the message. Olausson's feet tramped about in the stubble, his frightened eyes flew in all directions, and he could not say a single word calmly or clearly.

Karl Oskar saw before him a man who feared for his life.

Petrus Olausson had been proven right and now he wanted to remind you of it. He had always said they should drive the heathen pack away from

Minnesota, for the Indians had always been and remained beasts whom no one could convert. The Lutherans had sent many missionaries among them, and they had collected money for catechisms to distribute among them so that they might at least learn God's commandments. He himself had collected money for the books, sent whole wagon loads of Luther's catechism in strong leather bindings to them. To what use? How had it helped? Now people could see for themselves; the red bandits thanked their givers by murdering them! The whites had offered the redskins Christ's gospel; the redskins had answered their benefactors with tomahawks! They replied by crushing the skulls of the noble Christians who wanted to save them from heathen darkness!

When the whites had moved into the Indian country they had only followed the one path indicated by God! It was his wish that different people should succeed each other on the face of the earth. The Indians—like once the Canaanites—were under God's doom. It was the Almighty's will that these heathens should be obliterated from the earth, and a Christian no longer need feel sorry for them. President Lincoln was entirely too kind and compassionate with this beastly pack in allowing them to remain within the borders of the United States. There was only one way in which to treat the savages—get them out of Minnesota! This had always been Olausson's opinion, and now everyone could see that he had been right!

Leaning on his iron bar, Karl Oskar Nilsson listened to his neighbor's rancorous outburst against the Indians. He had indeed heard before that the redskins did not conduct their wars in a Christian or Lutheran manner but stuck to their Indian and heathen ways. In war they did not follow any rules, they only killed. And the savages acted as savages always had, he thought.

He wanted to know how close the Sioux were: "They haven't got to St. Peter and Mankato yet, did you say?"

"They might be here any moment! We don't have any soldiers left to stop those bandits!"

"What about the settlers? Can't we do anything?"

"We live too far apart. No time to get together."

"What's your idea—to run away?"

"Of course! Flee as fast as you can, Nilsson!"

"Take off to the wilds, you mean . . . ?"

"Yes! And let your cattle loose in the forest!"

Karl Oskar turned his head slowly and looked out over his fields with the still uncut, ripe wheat: "You mean leave . . . ?" Then he looked toward the house: "Leave . . . everything . . . ?"

"It's the only thing we can do!" And Petrus Olausson held both his hands over his red, bald head, as if defending himself against the sharp scalping knives: "We must leave at once and hide from the Sioux murderers!"

Karl Oskar was a little surprised at this great fear that had come over their pious parish warden: "Don't you have any trust in God's help, Olausson . . . ?"

"The Lord helps only those who help themselves!"

"No one else . . . ?"

"No! Not a one! Remember that!"

"Well, that's what I've always thought. It depends on oneself . . . "

"We must warn all the settlers hereabouts . . . I'll see to it that we ring the church bell!"

"So we must leave our homes and run . . . ?"

Karl Oskar looked again toward the house up there in the shade under the tall sugar maples. At the east gable he could see the Astrakhan tree, its limbs bent by the heavy fruit. The apples glittered in the sun. This year the Sweden-tree bore for the first time.

"It isn't so easy for me to leave . . . " Karl Oskar took a deep breath and added: "Kristina is in bed."

In the last words he had explained his plight to his neighbor. What he had said ought to be sufficient.

But it seemed Olausson hadn't heard. His ears were closed to everything except the Indian scare: "I'm in a hurry! I must be off and tell the other neighbors! And get the church bell going."

And he was gone on the moment. He vanished along the path that led to Algot Svensson's.

Karl Oskar remained standing beside a shock he had not yet completed—the hat-sheaves were still lacking. He leaned against the iron bar and tramped on the wheatheads without noticing. Desert his home? Run away and leave all they owned?

For twelve years they had lived here. They were citizens, they had paid for their land and had the papers to prove it. They had tilled fields that gave good crops, they had built houses—a home. After twelve years of hard work they were getting along well and had enough for all their needs. Everything was in order. Here on the shores of Chisago Lake the immigrants had founded their own little community where they lived in peace and comfort. It had been a long time since he carried his gun with him while working in field or forest. They had never been bothered by the redskins.

Karl Oskar Nilsson had never believed anything other than that he would remain undisturbed on his farm for the rest of his life.

Here he had only used the tools of peaceful work. He had carried his ax for cutting and clearing; he had timbered up a home for himself and his own. Back there stood the house, serene and farmer-secure, with its new-painted walls and splendid shake roof. How many days' labor hadn't he put into it? How many trees hadn't he felled for the walls? How many rafters and scantlings hadn't he dressed? In great concern he had chinked his house, put on the roof, hewed the floorboards, built the fireplaces, finished the rooms. Twelve years of labor all this had cost him.

It was his home in this world. He had built it with his own hands and paid for it with his sweat. This farm was his by the tiller's right.

And would all he had built up suddenly be destroyed, all he had done be undone? His home no longer his, not theirs who lived here? Their home in ruins, surrendered to savages and fire? They themselves fleeing to the wilderness, without a roof or a place to live?

To flee from their home: From one day to the next they would change from secure property owners to paupers, from settled homesteaders to vagabonds. After twelve years they would be thrust back to their situation on arrival. After twelve years they would change into impoverished immigrants, walking on foot through the wilderness from Stillwater to Taylors Falls, each night making their beds on leaves and twigs under the bare sky. Again they would be poor people who carried all they owned with them, all their possessions in their arms. From one day to the next they would lose fields and cattle, house and home.

So insecure and unsure was the pioneer's right to the soil, so little rooted was he in his new state of Minnesota, so loose his settling in North America—so hazardous was the settler's life.

—2—

KARL OSKAR slowly opened the door to the big room and walked on tiptoe across the floor; perhaps she was asleep? Marta had said that Mother dozed for moments but was awake most of the time. She often asked for water, and had also asked what time of day it was.

Kristina lay motionless on her back, her eyes open. The color of her face had changed; now her cheeks were light red and her eyes had the warm glitter of fever.

"Johan should be here with the doctor soon . . . "

"Don't worry, Karl Oskar. I'll get well."

Her voice was clear. She asked for water, her fever-thirst could not be quenched. He picked up the pitcher on the table beside her bed and filled it from the pail in the kitchen. He held his wife's head in one hand as he lifted the water glass to her mouth. The sick one drank in long swallows.

She had not taken any food today as yet, and he asked if she would like anything to eat. No, she felt as full as if she had come from a feast. And her lips formed a smile as she said it.

His face was rigid with suppressed anxiety.

"I've had a new lost journey. Too bad. I was sure I would be allowed to keep it this time."

Kristina had for a second time borne death.

"Don't think about that. As long as you get well again . . . "

"I'll get well again. I know."

She wanted to say something more between two short breaths but she was interrupted by a sound from outside. A bell was chiming. The gable window stood open; today the wind was favorable and carried the sound of the little church bell strong and clear.

Kristina lifted her head from the pillow and listened. "Is that the church bell? In the middle of the week?"

"It sounds like it."

"Why?"

"I wonder."

Olausson had said they would ring the bell, to warn the settlers.

Karl Oskar said, "Perhaps they're ringing for someone . . . someone who is . . . " One word was missing in that sentence, but he could not let it across his lips.

The ringing of the bell from the settlers' wood church went on. It was a holiday sound and it was disturbing because it was heard on a weekday.

"Don't worry," said Kristina. "Remember what I told you."

"I remember. I know."

But what did he know? What could he be sure of?

God ruled their lives and everything on earth. But Karl Oskar was not sure a person could trust God. He could not believe as his wife did. Kristina had given herself into the Lord's hands. Was she right in doing so?

They would now be finding out. Soon they would know: Was God to be trusted?

—3—

JUST AS TWILIGHT began to fall Johan returned from Stillwater. And Karl Oskar choked as he looked at the wagon; the boy was alone. He must have driven at bolting speed. The team was in a cloud of perspiration. The driver had not spared the animals. Johan jumped off the wagon and explained that Dr. Farnley had not been at home. A sign on the door announced that he had gone to Wisconsin for an indefinite stay. An old man next door had said that Farnley had taken off because there was an alarm about the Indians. Many frightened people in Stillwater had today crossed the St. Croix into Wisconsin. Miss Skalrud too was not at home. Johan had gone to Pastor Jackson's house to ask about her, but no one there knew where she was. Perhaps she had run away with the others. He had talked to a servant girl who said that Mr. and Mrs. Jackson were in Chicago for a Baptist congress.

Then Johan had gone to the other doctor, Cristoffer Caldwell, the one who called himself *Physician and Housebuilder, Carpenter & Blacksmith,* according to the sign on his door. But Caldwell was as plump as a fatted pig and could hardly walk. He had said he wasn't well himself and was not able to go on long journeys to sick people in the wilderness. But if Johan would tell him what ailed the sick one he would send medicine. And Johan had explained about his mother as best he could. Dr. Caldwell had mixed a bottle of medicine which cost four dollars. He said himself it was rather expensive but it always healed the sick. With this medicine he had got many settler wives on their feet after miscarriages and childbed fever. He assured Johan it would help Mrs. Nilsson. And the doctor was drinking from a whiskey bottle all the time he mixed the medicine! Perhaps he used whiskey for his own ailment?

All Johan had brought with him from Stillwater was a fat-bellied flask which contained a brown-yellow syrupy fluid. That flask was now the only help they had but Johan explained that the doctor had said it was a sure remedy against childbed fever.

Karl Oskar poured a tablespoon of Dr. Caldwell's medicine for his wife. It was strong; one could smell it a long way off. It looked like syrup as it flowed into the spoon. He coaxed the sick one to swallow all of it.

"What a nasty taste," she said with a grimace. For a moment it seemed as if she would throw up the medicine.

"It chokes me!"

"Try to keep it down, dear!"

He gave her a lump of sugar to take away the nasty taste.

He had a lot of trouble because of her, she said. But she didn't feel any pain any more; she was only tired and wanted to sleep. She would like so to get her fill of sleep for once.

—4—

MARTA had done the milking and prepared the supper, and Karl Oskar sat down to table with his six children, four sons and two daughters. Each one had his given place at the table. The father had the oldest son on his right and the oldest daughter on his left. The two smallest, Frank and Ulrika, still ate standing up.

Johan and Marta, the two oldest, understood and knew what had happened to Mother. They also remembered it had happened once before. Johan was tensely serious and silent, while Marta had cried several times today. But none of the children could understand what was the matter with Father. Since early in the morning he had hardly spoken to any one of them and did not reply when spoken to. At table he ate only a couple of slices of bread and drank a little milk. When he rose from supper he told the children to be quiet when they moved around the house so they wouldn't waken Mother in case she slept.

Frank and Ulrika had recently begun the fall term in the Center City school and after supper they read their lessons, competing with each other in their reading. Frank had a piece containing one- and two-syllable words to memorize and Ulrika a piece with several longer words.

Frank read his piece carelessly and with great speed.

"Lords without virtue are like lanterns without light. A wound never heals well enough to hide the scar. Poor and rich are alike to death. If you want the kernel you must crush the nut. Better bow than hit your head on the door lintel. Mistakes of others make no law. Trust in God makes the nation safe. Better a good death than an evil life."

The boy babbled on so loudly that the father had to admonish him; he went outside and sat on the stoop to read.

But Ulrika obeyed her father and read slowly and in a low voice. She was two years older than her brother and had been given a little more difficult lesson.

"For all the good my parents have given me I have not been able to give them any good in return. Nor have they done this to reap payment for their concern. They ask nothing from me except that I be a good child. This is their greatest joy and reward. I will love them with all my heart; I will constantly show them my gratitude. May I never sadden them with recalcitrance and disobedience. When they grow old I will take care of them in their old age."

The monotonous voices of the children reading their lessons was the only sound heard in the house.

The children went to bed, but Karl Oskar did not undress this evening; he would stay up. He sat down beside Kristina's bed where she lay in a deep fever-doze. As soon as she woke up she asked for water, and he also gave her the brown-yellow medicine, forcing the spoon between her lips. She swallowed only reluctantly. Later in the night she grew delirious and talked of high billows she was afraid of, as if she were on a ship sailing across the ocean.

The bell-ringing in the church tower continued intermittently until late at night. Kristina no longer heard it and had stopped asking what it meant. And Karl Oskar himself listened to the sound without realizing that it was an alarm bell. For long periods he forgot what the ringing meant. Everything he had heard today about approaching, bloodthirsty Indian hordes was suppressed in his mind by what was happening in his own house. What was going on in this room occupied him and ruled him.

Here he watched over Kristina.

—5—

It was Wednesday, August 20.

On the evening of this day Chief Shakopee and his warriors danced a war dance around their campfires on the shore of Lake Kandiyohi. Sunday, Monday, Tuesday, Wednesday—for four days the Sioux war had gone on, for four days the redskins had had uninterrupted success, and they were celebrating the victories of these four days. The shouts of jubilation from Shakopee's warriors echoed over the water, and the flames from the victory fires lit up the August night.

But neither the tall flames nor the loud shouts nor the great commotion could frighten any white person in the vicinity where the Indians had ravaged the settlers' homes; no sound, no noise is strong enough to frighten the dead.

During the victory celebration at Lake Kandiyohi, Chief Shakopee made a statement that was widely spread, a Sioux warrior's proud assertion: Shakopee was asked why he moved his right arm so clumsily and stiffly while dancing.

He replied that today his tomahawk had crushed so many white skulls that his right arm felt lame.

While Karl Oskar Nilsson shocked wheat on his field this Wednesday, four hundred other tillers in Minnesota had paid for their land with their lives. That was the price for the land the previous owners meted out to each white man.

XIV

WHILE KARL OSKAR KEPT
NIGHT WATCH

—1—

TWELVE SHEAVES to a shock—eight around the post and four for the hat—eight and four, shock after shock. His hands obeyed and picked up the sheaves and put them in place and bent them for the hat. But the wheat field was broad and the sheaves lay close and the heat sucked the strength from his limbs. It was the hottest August they had experienced out here.

Karl Oskar started with the shocking at six o'clock to take advantage of the morning coolness. But already after one hour the sun was burning so intensely that perspiration ran over his brows and smarted like salt in his eyes. Regularly he made a visit to the water crock which he had put in the shade of a linden at the edge of the field.

The church bell began to ring again on Thursday morning. In clear weather the little church spire was visible from this slope. Calm as it was now, the sound came clear.

Two men emerged from the forest carrying guns and rucksacks. Karl Oskar recognized them as his neighbors, Jonas Petter and Algot Svensson.

They cut across the field and approached him. He need not ask the men their errand or why they were out so early.

Jonas Petter said, "The settlers have been called—we must all go and fight the Indians."

Jonas Petter had put on some weight these last years and walked rather heavily. "I never thought I'd have to go out to war at sixty years of age!"

Algot Svensson said, "I'd hoped I would never have to go . . . "

A red flame glowed in Algot's left eye, which had been torn to pieces by a branch when he was clearing his claim. "But it can't be helped," he said. "A one-eyed man might do some good."

"It'll help you aim!" said Jonas Petter. "Now you won't have to close that eye!"

"How near are they?" asked Karl Oskar.

"No one seems to know for sure," said Jonas Petter, and shouldered his gun.

He went on: Last night the sheriff had called a meeting in Center City, and he and Algot had been there. During the meeting two men had arrived who had walked all the way from Carver County. They said all the settlers in Carver had fled to the forest, leaving cattle and everything behind. People in Hennepin and Nicollet had fled to St. Paul and Fort Snelling. The men had also said that great hordes of fugitives from out west were heading in this direction. Thousands had gathered in St. Peter and Mankato, completely destitute. They camped in the streets and slaughtered oxen or whatever animals they could lay hands on. All roads from the Minnesota Valley were crowded with wagons and cattle.

They had been told at the meeting that Governor Ramsey had sent Colonel Sibley, the ex-governor, against the Indians, leading the soldiers from Fort Snelling. But unfortunately the good soldiers were already in the South, fighting in the Civil War, and only four companies of new volunteers had been available at Fort Snelling. Of these a few hundred men had been sent to relieve Fort Ridgely and New Ulm, which were surrounded by the Sioux. There was a rumor that Little Crow had gathered several thousand redskins and that all of them had guns. If the forts fell, the road would be open to St. Paul, but Colonel Sibley was organizing the defense for all of Minnesota and if he had time he would stop them.

At the meeting last night the Chisago settlers had decided to evacuate the women and children and organize all the men. Across from Nordberg's Island, at the narrow passage between the shore and cliffs just west of the church, they would gather and build a defense wall. The sheriff would get ammunition and guns from the governor, he thought. The men were to meet at the pass and start digging in the morning.

"I can't go with you," said Karl Oskar. "Kristina is sick in bed—she had another miscarriage . . . "

Algot asked how she was getting along and Karl Oskar said there was no change since yesterday.

"Well, of course you can't leave her," said Jonas Petter. He had shared many dangers with his fellow emigrant from Ljuder and knew Karl Oskar was not trying to get out of defending his family and home. With his wife seriously ill he had just cause.

"You've never shit in your pants from fear, Karl Oskar. But Olausson has already run away with his wife and children. They took off to some island."

"He shouldn't have rushed about and scared people the way he did. People'll lose their sense in fright," said Karl Oskar.

"Who doesn't love his own family!" said Algot.

"The redskins are awfully cruel," said Jonas Petter. "I want to kill at least one before they cut me up like a pig."

Jonas Petter was going to the Norwegian gunsmith in Center City to have the mechanism of his old Swedish muzzle loader fixed. It was still a good gun; he could fell a deer seventy paces away, and an Indian couldn't have a thicker hide than a buck.

"I wonder what Colonel Sibley is up to," said Algot.

"If anyone can stop the redskins he can," said Karl Oskar.

Colonel Henry Sibley had lived among the Sioux for long periods as a government agent. During that time he must have learned some of their tricks, he ought to know their kind of warfare. At the first gubernatorial election his opponents had claimed that Sibley had fathered a number of children with squaws, but the Republicans had never proved this. Nor would it detract from his military qualifications if true.

"Well, then he'll fight his own brats," said Jonas Petter. He took out his snuffbox and loaded his nose, puffed and dried from the perspiration. A hell of a heat! he thought. It melted the lead in his fly buttons so he couldn't keep his horn in.

"If you stay here you must at least get your children to a safe place," said Algot.

"You think it's that bad?"

Yes, continued Algot Svensson, he and his neighbor, Johan Kron, were sending their wives and children to Cedar Island. Of all the many islands in the lake this one offered the best protection. Cedar Island was covered with impenetrable thickets and heavy woods, and gunshots couldn't reach it from either shore. Karl Oskar's children could join the group when they rowed them over.

Jonas Petter added that he had heard last night that Colonel Sibley, who lived in Mendota, had already on Tuesday sent his family to Fort Snelling. This more than anything else had frightened people in St. Paul.

Now Karl Oskar grew concerned; the former governor did not consider his family safe in Mendota! The officer in charge must know what he was doing.

He made a quick decision: "Yes, the children must get away! You take them with yours, Algot!"

As the men were leaving, Karl Oskar remembered that Danjel Andreasson had gone to see his son in Acton to help him with the harvest. He called after his neighbors: "Are they back at Danjel's?"

"No, they're with Sven in Meeker."

"They must be in the midst of it!"

Jonas Petter stopped still; it struck him that Danjel and his sons and daughter-in-law were indeed in Meeker County, the very place where the Indians had started the uprising.

"You're right, Karl Oskar. I wonder how they'll manage . . . "

Jonas Petter's face had stiffened. Slowly he folded his hands: "O Lord God! O Lord, save Danjel and his . . . "

Jonas Petter was not a pious man; he seldom prayed. But now he was standing with folded hands. And it was not for himself that he called on the Lord God. He prayed a warm, fervent prayer for some people who had been his neighbors, people whom he had been close to for many years, people he wanted to see live, whom he wanted to be with again.

—2—

Music from a black organ:

But today was Thursday, August 21, and the people Jonas Petter prayed for were no longer to be found among the living. They were on one of the hundreds of farms where already all life was extinguished.

This Thursday had been preceded by a Sunday. During their dinner rest on the Sabbath they had been caught unaware. While resting in the shade behind the cabin their minutes ran out and they entered another rest which no one could disturb.

Four days had now gone by, and Danjel Andreasson and his eldest son remained in a field, undisturbed in their new rest. It would be another two days before the soldiers found their bodies.

Only a few paces separated the bodies of father and son. The father was running these paces when he fell. He had seen his son fall and was hurrying to his aid. Thus his life was crowned by his death. The God Danjel confessed sacrificed his only son for humanity's salvation. Danjel sacrificed himself, his own life, for his eldest son.

But he was an earthly being, he was made of earth, he belonged to the soil of the field that was now his bed. His body was rotting on the ground near his son with whom he had shared the moment of death. Under the hot sun baking the field, their bodies soon were transformed and returned to their home in the earth.

Coming from far away they had sought a new home in a new country, and here they had found their permanent home: They had returned to man's sure and everlasting abode.

Their resting place in the field, from early morning till late night, was marked by a thick swarm of big, black, fat flies. An uncountable number of these winged creatures held a wake over the dead settlers. A black cloud of the air's buzzing life hovered over their corpses. The flies kept the wake faithfully, untiringly. They gathered and formed their dark cloud around the bier as soon as the sun began to shine over the field in the morning, and they did not part when twilight fell in the evening. During the night the swarm disappeared, it was invisible to the eye, but its sound told of its presence.

Uninterrupted, through day and night, the buzzing, whirring sound of the flies continued. From the black swarm over the field it rose like the surging peal of an organ; a monotonous playing as from eternity's depth, it strained on through day and night. A buzzing, whirring psalm was sung over the unburied corpses. From the swarm of small, whirring lives organ music was played over humans who had returned to the dust.

Play, black organ, play over this field, and over the other hundreds where the tiller has come home. Play over these dead, sing the whirring psalm for those who here enjoy rest in the earth! Play and whir through day and night, strike up a hymn for a funeral aboveground for these tillers who here have settled for eternity!

On a hundred settlements all life had ceased; this black cloud was the wakers' organ.

And the black organ hummed, it whirred, it buzzed its psalm over Danjel Andreasson and his son, and for all those who had fallen back upon the earth that owned their bodies.

On this day the black organ played at seven hundred funerals in the settlers' country. It would play at other places, still waiting.

—3—

ON ONE of the oldest farms only the husband and wife were left behind. Their children had been evacuated with their neighbors, who had left their homes and sought safety.

The wife lay sick and the husband sat beside her bed. He watched over her through day and night. While she slept he had sent away the children and he worried lest she should ask for them when she woke up. But only once did she wonder why she didn't see them or hear their voices. He told her the boys were busy with the harvest and the girls were picking berries in the forest. The wife did not seem to suspect the husband was lying to her.

The sick one was not able to take any food, but as she suffered from fever-thirst she drank a great deal of water. From a bottle on the table beside the bed, the husband poured a yellow-brown, syrupy fluid into a spoon and gave it to the wife, who swallowed reluctantly.

On this farm quiet and inactivity reigned. No chores were performed; neither inside nor outside was there any sound of activity. No children ran about and played and laughed. The cattle had been let out into the forest, and in the evening the cows came to the gate and waited for their milkmaid. But she did not come to meet them with her pail and stool, she did not sit down to lean her head against their sides. In her place a man attempted to relieve their swollen udders with his rough, clumsy fingers which squeezed the teats awkwardly. In the fields the crops were left overripe and the heads grew heavier and bent lower each day. No scythe was touched, no straw cut, no sheaves bound, no shocks built, no ricks brought the crops to the barn. No one called any longer from the stoop, announcing mealtime, no one went to and from his work, no one went to rest or rose from his bed.

The place seemed desolate, deserted. But a man and a wife remained. She lay in her bed inside the house and seldom made any sound, he moved cautiously when he approached or left her. He went in and out of the house without her noticing. He answered her when she spoke but did not speak to her if she lay with her eyes closed.

During the last days he had not noticed any change in her. She herself had said she knew she would pull through.

Thus a husband kept watch over his wife. Only for the shortest moments did he leave his chair at her bed and stroll outside. Under the clear sky a serene peace reigned over his land these days. There lay his farm with all the crops, trees, fruit, grass—surrendered to itself. Under the flaming sun the earth enjoyed a long, lazy dinner rest. His claim sloped toward the shore, and it seemed as undisturbed and peaceful as the day he had discovered it, resting here and waiting for him since the day of Creation.

When he stepped outside he looked and always peered in the same direction: to the west, where there rose a sandstone cliff which had the appearance of a man's head, but a hundred thousand times larger. There rose a high cliff wall, glittering red in the sunshine—a wall of threat and danger. The Indian head!

All his life until now he had followed this command: You must always help yourself! Always use your common sense and your strength! In every situation you must only trust your own ability. Never give up in danger! Never think there is no use going on! Always try once more! Never lose heart and say, there is nothing more I can do.

But these days he no longer made decisions as to what happened around him. What happened decided over him. He kept watch on the chair beside his wife's bed, he walked outside and looked to the west.

And what he did did not help him any more.

—4—

NO MORE REPORTS about the Indian danger arrived. But Karl Oskar no longer kept track of the days. It had been in the early morning on Wednesday that Kristina took sick, and after that he didn't count the days. With his whittling knife and a stick he started a new calendar: He cut a notch in the stick every evening—one more day. He cut the first notch on the evening the children had been sent to Cedar Island.

There were three notches now, and it was morning again. He was dozing on his watcher's chair; fatigue had closed his eyes. He woke up startled by a noise outside.

No one had come to his house these three days. Now someone was knocking on the gable window. He rose and rubbed his smarting eyes. His face was pale gray in the dawn light.

Algot Svensson was outside, his gun under his arm and a good-sized food sack on his back. His torn eye shone dark red like a ripe cherry.

"It's you, Algot! I thought maybe the redskins had come . . . "

"We're building at the wall, back by the church. I'm only going home to do the milking."

"Have you heard from the island?"

"I rowed over last night—all is well there. The kids are well and seem to enjoy it."

"How near are the Indians?"

"Don't know. Haven't seen them hereabouts yet."

About a hundred of the settlers were gathered back at Nordberg's Island, said Algot. They were digging an entrenchment, and a small cannon had been sent with some men from Fort Snelling. A few more days of preparations and he felt sure they would be able to hold back the redskins at the church. Pastor Stenius himself was helping them, digging like a real farmer, he was so anxious to save the church from the savages' violation.

But the men were uneasy about their families and farms; the crops were overripe, cows unmilked, calves and smaller animals unfed, and the loose cattle broke into the fields and did damage. This couldn't go on very long. As far as Algot could learn every farm hereabouts was deserted.

He was going home to look after his animals and then he would take some food and other things to the people on Cedar Island. They had told him last night they had eaten all the potatoes and meat they had with them and had no milk for the children. The boys were chasing and catching rabbits but they had no salt. They had also caught some fish, but they were bothered terribly by mosquitoes and ants.

Algot said he would come back and pick up whatever Karl Oskar might wish to send over to the children, but he didn't think they were suffering.

The neighbor left, and when Karl Oskar came in again Kristina had awakened. She was talking to herself, her eyes on the ceiling boards as if she were addressing them. He asked if there was anything she wanted but she replied in disjointed, incomprehensible words.

From his wife's speech Karl Oskar understood that she no longer recognized him.

ANOTHER DAY passed with the sun shining unchangeably in a high, cloudless sky. From morning to night Ki-Chi-Saga's surface glittered in its immobile smoothness. The leafy trees along the shores dipped their boughs in the lake's water. In the reeds the young ducklings tried their wings, not yet quite ready for the long flight. No activities at the farms now disturbed the large flocks. Brave birds from the forest came and perched on the apple tree at the east gable, now tempting with fruit.

Karl Oskar cut a new notch in his time-counting stick.

Every evening after dark he saw fires in the forest, especially on a tongue of land in the lake to the east. But they didn't disturb him; they were the settlers' campfires across from Nordberg's Island where the entrenchment was being built. The fires burned the night through and their glare was reassuring. The Indian watch was in order and ready. The tillers had gathered to defend their labor; the Chisago people would not be taken unaware.

The night fires in the forest were reminders of danger and war. But in daytime nothing could be seen that heralded imminent threat.

Cedar Island was not visible from this shore, but he could see smoke from the other islands where people from other farms had gone for protection. In the old days these islands had been camping places for the Indians during their hunts. During their first years at Ki-Chi-Saga he had often in the gathering dusk seen the hunting people's tall flames and heard their eerie cries, so unlike those of ordinary human beings. What they then saw and heard had frightened the newly arrived immigrants, and when the Indians had their powwows, the settlers had stayed away from their fields so as not to divulge their presence. Now the whites had fled their new homes and sought safety in the redskins' old camping grounds.

The whole section was now empty of people. But one morning a rider from the legislature in St. Paul came by and asked the way to Taylors Falls. He had no special news about the Sioux uprising, which had happened so unexpectedly, but he felt sure Colonel Sibley would choke it. Several thousand settlers from the counties around St. Paul had also gathered and been armed.

The rider spoke of the prices on Indian scalps: Tuesday, last week, twenty dollars had been paid for a redskin scalp in St. Paul, but by Thursday the price had risen to fifty dollars, and by Saturday to a hundred. With each new report of the Sioux cruelty to the whites the value of their scalps rose. The man from the legislature thought the price of redskin scalps would reach two hundred dollars before the end of the war.

Karl Oskar pondered the remarkable in this: Only when dead was a red man valued highly. Before the uprising no white would have offered a tenth as much for a living Indian.

The days which he marked on his stick slid away from him in a strange drowsiness. He sat watch by his wife night and day, he dozed for short intervals sitting on the chair. Daylight and darkness followed each other, but day and night mingled in one endless, monotonous, unchangeable day. Time did not move forward one second. It had stopped still for him. Yet when he picked up the knife to whittle a new notch he knew another day had again passed.

He worked his way forward on the stick to Tuesday, August 26. And still Kristina did not recognize him.

—6—

KARL OSKAR lived his present life in the events closest to him. Therefore, he didn't know afterward on which of his watch-days the report finally came—the message that the Indian uprising had been put down.

A couple of settlers on their way back to their deserted farms told him about it. He thought he knew them, but later he couldn't recall their names or where they lived. They said that Colonel Sibley had come in time to relieve Fort Ridgely and New Ulm, and since the Sioux couldn't storm those portals to the Minnesota Valley they would not be able to reach the St. Croix Valley. The settlers could now return to their chores. All the refugees on the Chisago Lake islands could return to their homes.

Karl Oskar seemed rather surprised at the men's tale; he listened to their report as if it didn't concern him, as if the Indian fright in some way had not pertained to him. The panic was over? The redskins were stopped! All could return home? But he was already home. He had been in his house all the time. He was on his farm, he need not return.

He was the only settler in the St. Croix Valley who had remained in his house during the Indian panic those August days. He had kept watch over his wife as long as her life lasted.

XV

THE ASTRAKHAN APPLES ARE RIPE

—I—

THE SUN had just risen; it shone through the gable window and slowly searched its way to the bed where Kristina lay. She had opened her eyes. On her forehead near the hairline drops of perspiration glittered; her complexion was refreshed and rosy. Her cheeks blossomed: A young girl's coloring had returned to her after twenty years.

A moment before she had complained faintly in her sleep. Karl Oskar had picked up a towel and gently dried her moist forehead. When he bent over her, he saw in her eyes that she recognized him. For the first time in three days she knew him again.

Her voice was so low he had to make an effort to catch the words.

"Is it already morning?"

"Yea—but pretty early."

"So quiet—the others aren't up yet?"

"No . . ."

"The children . . . all of them are asleep . . . ?"

"I think so."

"Only you up . . . already?"

"I have not been in bed."

"You've watched over me?"

"Yes . . ."

"How kind of you. I must have slept long . . ."

"You have slept a long while."

"I dreamed I was swinging . . . you remember the ox thong I used to put up in the barn at home . . ."

The blanket on Kristina's chest rose and fell in rapid, short movements. Her breathing had been quicker and panting these last days.

"I was at home in the barn, swinging and carrying on . . ."

"Can I give you something?"

"Only a mouthful of water. I'm thirsty."

He held the pitcher to her mouth and she tried to lift her head but it sank down on the pillow again. His left hand steadied her at the back of her head.

She drank slowly, swallow after swallow.

"I can't swallow very well . . . "

A few big drops escaped and ran slowly down her chin; the sun glittered in them. When his hand touched her he felt the glow of fever that burned in her body.

"Thanks, dear Karl Oskar . . . "

She made a motion with her shoulders as if wishing to sit up.

"Better lie down, dear . . . "

"But I'm not sick. Only mightily tired . . . "

"You must rest, you aren't strong yet . . . "

The silence inside was unbroken again, but down in the chicken pen the rooster started his shrill morning crowing. Something dark fluttered past the gable window, wings flapped; a bird had just lighted in the apple tree. The boughs of the Astrakhan tree were loaded down with fruit as big as newborn babies' heads. Against the dark green leaves the apples shimmered golden-red.

The sun moved and spread its golden squares over Kristina's blanket. By and by it reached a bottle and a spoon on the table beside the bed. The bottle was empty. It had contained the medicine for childbirth fever.

Every time Karl Oskar moved on his chair he was conscious of a fatigue from his long lack of sleep which threatened to close his eyes.

Suddenly Kristina put out her hand and fumbled for support.

"I'm falling! Hold onto me!"

"Don't be afraid—you're safe in your bed."

But her fingers clasped his anxiously.

"The thong! The swing! I'm falling out!"

"It's all right. Nothing to be afraid of . . . "

"Karl Oskar! Please . . . hold me . . . hold . . . !"

She tried to raise herself in the bed. He took her by the shoulders, helped her to lie down again, and comforted her.

—2—

ONCE AGAIN Kristina is thrown by the swing she has made of the ox thong in the barn at home in Duvemåla.

She swings from floor to ceiling, from ceiling to floor again. She rides up and down in the thong, she feels dizzy and cries out in fear and joy. She is playful and giddy and happy, like other young girls. She skips lightly on her feet, she plays and carries on and enjoys herself while youth is still in her body. Soon enough she will grow old and heavy on her feet, and then she can no longer ride a swing.

But she is thrown high, so high—far, far away from her father's barn. Frightened to the bottom of her heart she looks about and does not recognize her surroundings. She is not swinging in the ox thong any more, she is on a ship, sailing on a great water, and on that ship she is thrown up and down through the air. She is on an ocean with high waves, and the waves lift her heavenward and lower her into the depths. She flies through the air, she is flung into the black abyss, she is dizzy again and cries out. But she is entirely alone out on the sea, no one hears her cries, no one answers her, no one comes to help her.

Where is Karl Oskar? Why doesn't he hear? Why doesn't he come and help her away from here? What's she doing here on a ship anyway? Why did she go to the sea?

It was Karl Oskar who wanted it. She must go with him, he didn't give up until she promised. She didn't want to, but a wife must do what her husband wants.

The swing slows down, and she gets off again. She is a wife, a mother, a woman who bears children. She has returned from her journey. She is already old. Karl Oskar and she have been married for many years, and she is a tired and aged woman. She'll never be able to swing in the barn again. She has been through many childbeds, she has borne living children and dead. Once she carried a child without life in it which Karl Oskar buried somewhere out in the woods, she doesn't know where.

But now once more she must go through it, one childbed more, but only one more. She will survive her tenth childbed. And then . . . !

Then—oh, then she'll rest, rest till she gets rid of her immense tiredness. To lie still, sleep! To sink down in wonderful, sweet sleep! If she only could rest all she wished, then she would get well again. Then she would pull through. There is no cure for her other than this: sleep, sleep!

—3—

FOR A LONG TIME she had been in a coma but kept her hand about his fingers. He had been sitting without making any motion. Consciousness left her one

moment and came back the next, but for three days it had not been with her
long enough for him to talk to her as he had wished. There was something very
important he wanted to tell his wife, something he wanted to ask her. During
all the time he had been watching at her bed he had had the words on his
tongue, in his thoughts he had spoken them innumerable times, mumbled
them to himself, whispered them, stammered them:

Don't die and leave me! Stay with me yet!

It was she herself he wanted to ask. Unlike Kristina he could not ask another
One.

Beads of perspiration appeared on her fever-sick forehead, and he dried
them as lightly, as gently as he could. But she felt his touch and opened her
eyes. She spoke as if short of breath:

"You're here, Karl Oskar . . . ?"

"I guess I woke you."

"I fainted away. Did I cry some . . . ?"

"Not a sound."

"I have no pain any more."

"But you're weak."

"I'll pull through. All I need is enough sleep."

"I hope you're right."

"Don't worry! But you must need some sleep yourself, Karl Oskar!"

"Forget about me!"

"You're black under the eyes. You've been up watching me. You've worn
yourself out!"

"It's nothing."

She was short of breath from her effort to speak. The movements under the
blanket increased.

When her fast breathing subsided somewhat, she resumed:

"I am really better!"

"Truly, Kristina?"

"Yes. You needn't watch over me any more. Tonight you can sleep."

Karl Oskar blinked as if he had something in his eyes. He swallowed hard a
few times as he looked intently at his wife in the bed.

"Remember: Tonight you can sleep!"

The noise of fluttering wings was heard again from the apple tree outside
the window. Karl Oskar looked out. A bird was sitting on a branch, pecking at
an apple. The Astrakhan apples were soft and juicy, and the birds went after
them greedily.

Often this summer Kristina had felt the apples with her fingers and wondered: When will they be ripe? If the birds now were after them they must be ready to eat.

Karl Oskar rose and went out. He walked to the tree and from one of the lowest branches he picked a large, beautiful apple. He could feel it was soft, it must be ripe. It was still moist from the morning dew; through the skin he could see the juicy meat.

He went inside and put the big apple on the blanket before Kristina. "Look—your Astrakhans are ripe!"

Her fever-inflamed eyes looked at the fruit; they stared at it as if she hadn't understood what he meant.

"You must taste our first apple, Kristina!"

He put it in her hand and she held it.

"It's the first from your tree, Kristina!"

The sick woman did not understand; she couldn't grasp that she held an apple in her hand. She moved it slowly toward her mouth, as if curious as to what she held in her fingers. Her lips touched the clear, dew-washed fruit. The transparent skin was like the tender skin of a small child.

She did not bite into the apple, but only caressed it with her lips.

"Aren't you able to taste it?"

"Yes, yes. It feels soft . . . "

"It's ripe and juicy."

"It smells good." She stared at the apple in her hand.

"Can't you take one bite?" He added, encouragingly, "Astrakhans have a fresh taste."

Kristina moved the apple toward her teeth and bit off a very small piece. The juice moistened the corners of her mouth.

"Where did you get it, Karl Oskar . . . ?"

"From your tree out there, of course! The first one picked from that tree!"

Kristina did not swallow the piece she had bit off. She still looked in wonder at the fruit.

"I guess you aren't strong enough to eat it?"

"Oh yes, I'll eat it . . . "

At last she seemed to understand: "Now I can see—it's an Astrakhan . . . !"

And her voice vibrated at the discovery she had made.

"I recognize it now! It tastes like our apples! Our apples at home!"

Again she moved it to her mouth. But her teeth did not bite into it again, only her lips parted.

Suddenly the mouth grew stiff, the lower jaw stopped in an attempted motion. The eyelids twitched and the whites became enlarged. Her breath was drawn out while the voice grew even weaker. "I recognize it . . . our Astrakhans are ripe . . . "

Then there came only a soft sigh as she breathed out:

"Our apples are ripe. I'm home . . . "

There was a spasm in her arms, then they lay still and the hand's hold on the fruit loosened. The big apple rolled slowly down the slope of the blanket and fell with a thud on the floor near the bed.

Karl Oskar bent down and picked it up; he put it back in his wife's open hand.

But this time she did not take it, her fingers did not grasp it, her hand did not close around it. Kristina's hand lay still and open on the blanket, and the apple fell for a second time to the floor.

Karl Oskar looked at it and rose with a start. He bent over his wife and saw the blanket over her chest rise slowly and sink down just as slowly. Then it did not rise again. The movement was not repeated.

"Kristina!" he cried out. *"Stay with . . . !"*

Karl Oskar stood bent over his wife. Her eyes were half-open, and the whites glittered in their rigidity. The blanket over her chest did not rise again. No movement was visible in her—in her eyes, in her chest, in her limbs, nowhere in her body. The light in her eyes was extinguished and no breath flowed from her mouth.

In one corner of her mouth the little apple bite remained.

Karl Oskar stood as rigid as stone for a long time, staring into her unseeing eyes, listening for her lost breath. Only this moment she had tasted an apple— it was incomprehensible to him that she no longer saw him and that her breath didn't come back.

XVI

THE THIRD COFFIN

In the old log cabin where the family had lived during their first years as settlers there now shone a night light. This cabin had been built to serve as a home but after the completion of the new house it had been used as a workshop. A large carpenter's bench stood against one wall. Now a man stood at the bench and worked in the light of a candle lantern which hung from a beam in the ceiling; he was making a coffin for his wife.

To him fell a task which could not be delayed and which he must complete during the night. Hurriedly, untiring, his plane moved over the wood, as he smoothed boards that had been cut from oak timber. But the boards had been intended for another use. They had been sawed and stacked for the building of a house. They were meant for a new main house that he would build, but now they must be used for another purpose. The oak boards would not form the walls of a house where he and his wife would live out their lives. Of the boards he built instead her home after death.

Earlier he had built houses and homes for himself and his wife for life's time which in fleeting years would pass by, but the room he now built was for the time of death, which had no end. In this house she would stay.

Many times he had said to her: Next time I build . . .

That time had come. But now he built only for her.

The plane moved its even path back and forth over the board and spewed out long shavings which coiled like white snakes on the floor. The light from the candle in the lantern above the carpenter's head fell in a circle over the bench and lit him in his work with its fluttering rays. Round about him in the cabin were dim shadows. On the walls skins of animals had been nailed up to dry; shrouds that had belonged to four-legged beings hung there, limbs outstretched, as if crucified.

The plane dug and bit with its sharp iron tooth and tore shavings from the board. The shavings gathered in piles, coiled around his wrists, and rustled under his feet. The oak board was prime timber, hard under the plane, first class. It was white oak—no timber existed that lasted longer, no wood was better suited to wall a permanent resting place.

Twice before in his life the man at the workbench had made coffins. The first he had made in his homeland for a daughter who from hunger had eaten herself to death. That time he had stood out in a woodshed and worked. That time he was still a beginner in the carpenter's handicraft, his hands unused to plane and hammer, and he had had poor lumber for the coffin: only old boards, knotty and badly sawed, cracked and warped. He had chosen and discarded—very little had been needed for the girl's coffin. She had died early in life, when she was only four years old. It had not required many boards to enclose that little body. But he had sought out the clear and knot-free ones, he had chosen the finest planks he could find.

It had been difficult for him that time, for his plane was dull and unsharpened, the hammerhead flew off, refusing to stay on its handle, and it had been his first coffin, his journeyman effort.

(The carpenter's questions: This daughter was very dear to me, but before she was four years old she was taken from me and died in terrible pain. She died before she had had time to commit any crimes. Did God wish thereby to punish *me* for *my* transgressions? But one hears only of a God who is good and just. Can he who is good and just punish the innocent for the deeds of the guilty? Does he let my children inherit my sins? I have never wondered over this before, but now I do: Is our God good and just?)

The first coffin he made was just big enough so that he could carry it alone when his daughter's body was placed in it. He had carried it in his arms to the grave.

That was a father's labor for his child.

The second coffin he had made many years later, in another country. He had made it in the very place where he now stood, in this workshop, at this bench. That work was done one summer when haying had just started and he had been rushed to do it during a few humid nights.

They had found his dead brother's body in the forest. He had returned from the gold-land with a deadly sickness in his body which they had known nothing about. They had thought he was telling them lies and wanted to cheat them with his false riches, but he himself had been the victim of a cheater.

(The carpenter's thoughts: We came from the same womb and you were my only brother, but we became strangers to each other. You lied and told tales until I couldn't believe anything you said. But now I know that you yourself believed in the value of the money you wanted to give us. You brought us a gift, you wanted to share your abundance with your brother. But I could not trust you, and the hand I offered at parting was hard and fisted and hit you in the face.

You said you forgave me. And now here at the bench I say my real goodbye to you: I prepare your last home. The same hand that hit you is now hammering together the walls that will forever be yours. The same hand that hurt you is now trying to make you a good resting place. Here you will lie protected from all that pursued you. And I will put the lid over a brother who was a riddle to me.)

That had been the carpenter's second coffin. By then he was experienced and could handle his tools, and the coffin had been a fine piece of work.

It had been a brother's labor for a brother.

Again the years had run by, and now he stood here once more, in the same workshop, at the same bench, and performed the same labor he had completed twice before in his life. Now he was making a coffin for the woman who had been his wife, who had been his helpmeet, who had borne his children. Almost twenty years they had lived together. They had shared their home, their bread, and their bed. Twice, on two different continents, they had set up house together. Through all the years she had shared with him the day's labor and the night's rest.

She had said: I have One I can put my trust in! There is One who will pull me through! Therefore you must not worry! You must have the same confidence as I! And I have surrendered to his hands! I'll pull through! All will be well with me!

She had said this to him on the path along the lake one evening in June. Now August counted its last days, and of his wife was left him only her lifeless body.

(The carpenter had received his answer: She trusted in God, but he tricked her. She was a credulous child who surrendered to her Father in heaven. But the Father failed her. He let her die. Now I know what happens to one who trusts in God Almighty. If she hadn't done so, she would be alive. She was taken from me and the children because she trusted in the Lord.

Now I know: God is nothing for a human being to put trust in.)

The carpenter stood in the night at his bench and worked in the feeble, fluttering light from a stable lantern. The plane moved evenly back and forth over the wood. It rasped and cut, its iron tooth scraped shavings from the oak plank. The shavings fell in coils from the bench and gathered around the carpenter's feet. Above his plane the lantern swung slowly back and forth, setting in motion shadows on the walls where the pelts were nailed up; the crucified stood guard around the bench, saluting the carpenter with their extended, securely nailed limbs.

Again the carpenter was busy at his work. It was his third coffin.

It was a husband's labor for his wife.

XVII

SONG UNDER THIRTY-EIGHT
GALLOWS

Fort Ridgely and New Ulm were relieved during the last days of August; the two portals to the Minnesota Valley remained closed to the Sioux. Little Crow was finally defeated at Wood Lake on September 23. His warriors were scattered and disarmed later in the fall.

The Sioux uprising in Minnesota was the bloodiest Indian war in North America. More than a thousand white settlers were killed, a region two hundred by one hundred miles was ravaged and deserted, and thirty thousand people were homeless.

Many thousand Sioux were taken prisoner and a military court sentenced 303 of them to hanging. Abraham Lincoln reprieved 265 of these. The remaining 38 were hung at Mankato on December 26, 1862.

—I—

In October 1861, at Mankato, the Sioux chief Red Iron had pleaded his people's situation to Governor Ramsey, and in the same spot, a little over a year later, the final reckoning took place between Indians and whites in Minnesota.

A large warehouse was used as an Indian prison and to the stone floor of this building thirty-eight Sioux warriors were chained, awaiting their death sentence. When the date finally was set they asked to be permitted to dance their death dance in the prison yard the day before the hanging. This was refused them.

Early in the morning on December 26, fifteen hundred soldiers were called to stand guard around the prison yard where the hanging would take place. An enormous gallows had been erected: a circular iron ring from which thirty-eight ropes dangled.

It was a cold winter morning with a biting norther sweeping from the prairies across the prison yard. The prisoners were brought out in a group, their hands tied behind their backs. Not one of them uttered a defiant word. As soon as they were in the yard they saw before them the large gallows with the ropes swaying in the wind. Then a stir went through the group: They began to sing, all at one time. They were singing their death song in unison.

An eerie, penetrating sound came from the condemned prisoners' throats; it sounded like a prolonged *ij*: ijiji—ijiji—ijiji. One single syllable of complaint, the eternal, sad ijiji—ijiji—ijiji—ijiji. The Indians were singing their death song. It came from thirty-eight human throats, it was thirty-eight human beings' final utterance: ijiji—ijiji—ijiji.

The prisoners approached the great gallows—the iron ring with the thirty-eight swinging ropes—and they sang uninterruptedly as they walked, they sang the whole way. They sang as they climbed the scaffold, they sang as they stood under the ropes, they continued to sing as the ropes were placed around their necks. They sang in their lives' last moment.

At a given sign thirty-eight people dangled together from their ropes, a circular gallows of kicking, wriggling bodies. Then the song died, and after a few minutes the ropes hung straight with their catch and did not sway any longer in the wind.

It was a cold winter morning with a biting norther. The song of the thirty-eight under the gallows ropes at Mankato was the death song of the Minnesota Indians. Thus ended their last attempt to drive out the intruders and take back their land.

—2—

THE INDIANS had been put down, but *The Indian* remained.

At the shore of Ki-Chi-Saga the hunter people's watchtower of stone, the Indian head, still stood. The fall storms had been hard on him, tearing the green leaves from his summer-wreathed forehead. Bare, black branches sprouted from the skull and pointed heavenward, the red glow on his forehead was gone, and the cave-eyes had blackened and seemed to have withdrawn deeper into the cliff. And during the winter following the Sioux uprising, immense blocks fell from the Indian's eyes to lie at the base of the cliff.

The Indian was mourning. He was mourning his people's decline. From his elevated position he looked out over the hunting grounds his kinfolk never more were to use, the clear lakes that never more would carry their canoes, he saw the islands and shores where their campfires never more would be lit.

Above Ki-Chi-Saga's water the Indian rose, rigid and silent in his sorrow, the prisoner chained in stone. He did not weep human tears, it was not water that flowed from his eyes, it was not drops of an evanescent fluid. He shed tears of stone—indestructible, eternal as the cliff itself. In these was his complaint—his sorrow over his people's destruction, their decay and death. A new race had come to take the place of the vanquished.

Thus one people obliterates another from the face of the earth, and the earth sucks the blood of the dead, and turns green and blossoms as before for the living.

The Indian head still stands, green-wreathed in summer, bare and naked in winter. From his eyes still fall the boulders that gather at his feet. In his eternal petrification the Indian to this day mourns his dead.

XVIII

ONE MAN DID NOT WISH
TO SUBMIT

—I—

THE UNFORGETTABLE YEAR of the Sioux uprising came to its close and another began its cycle.

In the oldest homestead on Chisago Lake, they were one less in the family; there was no longer a wife or mother. The survivors tried to divide the chores of the dead one among them, but all the things she alone knew how to do remained undone. They were, and remained, one less in the house, a wife and a mother.

Better news came from the world outside. For two years only defeats for the North in the Civil War had been reported, but now they could read in the papers of victories for the Union soldiers. Already in the spring the news was good, and at haying time—in the beginning of July—a still greater victory was announced. It had taken place in Pennsylvania, near a town called Gettysburg. The battle was the most important in the whole Civil War, said the papers, predicting that the rebels would give up before the year was out. Earlier in the year President Lincoln had proclaimed all Negroes free from slavery.

But the rebels were not defeated, they won new victories, and at the end of this year also the war was still on. Now the North needed soldiers to replace those who had fallen, and at last conscription was resorted to.

To Karl Oskar Nilsson the conscription brought no change. Once rejected he need not go, nor need he send a man in his place, as many ablebodied men did.

The North still had plenty of men to fill the vacancies left by the dead, but in the South the manpower was running low, and that was why no one up north any longer feared the war would be lost.

There were settlers at Chisago Lake who would just as soon see the human slaughter go on forever. During the Civil War the merchants made good

profits. Klas Albert, Karl Oskar's neighbor in Sweden, bragged that he had sold
an old inventory at unexpectedly high prices. He could never have disposed of
it except for the Civil War. Karl Oskar told him he ought to go to the war himself since he was strong and ablebodied and a bachelor besides. But Klas Albert
replied that no one in his right mind would go to war unless he were forced,
and he was still of sound mind. And when conscription was put in effect he
hired his clerk to do the service for him.

The Swedish church warden's Klas Albert had, in a short time, prospered
out here and was now Mr. C. A. Persson, owner of the biggest store in Center
City. All day long customers thronged to his counter and money rolled in as
fast as he could handle it. He had found an occupation that suited him, and in
the right country. None of the emigrants from Ljuder was as successful as
Mr. Persson.

Karl Oskar was prejudiced against all merchants and did not like Klas Albert
too much. He felt he grew rich on his fellow immigrants. Whether he bought
or sold, he always managed it to his own advantage, and if the farmers hadn't
brought forth from the earth the things he bought and sold he would have had
nothing to profit from.

—2—

THE EARLIEST SETTLER at Chisago Lake changed to a remarkable degree after
his wife's death. He had always preferred to keep silent rather than speak unnecessarily and now he grew ever stingier with his words. At home, he divided
the chores among his children and explained how to perform them, praised
them when something was well done, scolded them when they were careless or
negligent. Aside from this he seldom spoke. And even outside the home he became known as sparing of words. He would have less and less to do with people, he resigned from all his activities for the county and the parish. From now
on he would not be a spokesman for others, only attend to his own business.
He stopped going to parish meetings, and the Chisago people wondered and
talked as Karl Oskar Nilsson never went to church after his wife's death.

The widower lived almost like a hermit, he closed himself off from the
world outside his home and more and more turned inward. He faced each day
in turn; he was able to endure his life only one day at a time.

Only each day in turn could he face the loss of Kristina.

The first weeks after her death he thought each morning as he awoke: I must live this day without her. And tomorrow I must live through the day without her. The same the day after tomorrow. So it shall be for me during all my remaining days. During all the time allotted me in life I will be without her.

It was every morning's reminder. And each day in turn was more than enough. Maybe he could manage one day? Maybe he could manage his whole life if he divided it into the small parts of single days. At first it had seemed, as it came over him in the morning, that he could not endure this heavy loss, and he began saying to himself each morning: This day I am without her. But only today. He pushed away the following day and the next day, and the next day, and all the following days, to let them take care of themselves. They had not yet come, and perhaps they never would come.

His days without Kristina gathered into weeks, months, and years. He could already say: Last year when I lost my wife. Soon he could say: The year before last, when I lost my wife. And eventually it would be: The year I lost my wife, that was long, long ago. And by then the loss of her would be gone, with his own life.

So Karl Oskar divided his sorrow into days and thought that in so doing it would be easier for him to bear.

In the evening he might stop on the path from the stable to the main house, as if waiting for her. Here she would be coming with her milk pails, one in each hand, and he must help her carry them. He would always help her when he was about. Can I give you a hand, Kristina? She would reply: So kind of you, Karl Oskar! Now she no longer came along the path as she used to, and he stood there desolate. Didn't he know it? Would he never understand it? There were no more pails to be carried for Kristina. He had no wife. He had raised a cross over her in the cemetery.

On warm summer evenings he would tend the beds under the window, weed the peas and the beans and water them, and it sometimes happened that he caught himself listening through the open window: Wasn't that Kristina's sewing machine in there? No. Now there was no whir from the balance wheel, no noise from the pedals under her feet. And her loom stood silent. She used to sing while weaving, she wanted to muffle the loom's noise, she said. But he liked the sound of the loom coming from inside the house, and he would stand there and listen for the shuttle.

And so each time Karl Oskar found himself equally disappointed when he compared the past and the present: Kristina's sewing machine had been put aside in a corner and emitted no sound, and from the loom *her* shuttle would never sing again.

In such moments he spoke aloud to Kristina: If I had followed my common sense you would still be with me! If you hadn't trusted in God you'd still be alive!

But she had said a few words which he remembered and would keep well during his remaining years. They had once been uttered by her lips, they were heard by his ears, he would keep them well. It was her answer to him: Don't worry about me, Karl Oskar. *I'm in good keeping.*

—3—

IT WAS Whitsuntide Eve and the house was being cleaned for the holiday. Karl Oskar was on his knees on an old sack scrubbing the stoop floor. He dipped the brush into the hot soap lye and scrubbed the planks with all his might, he scratched, he scrubbed, he rubbed. But whatever he did he couldn't get the floor as clean and white as he knew it should be. The dirt seemed to be glued between the boards; it must be poor soap, he thought. When they first came out here he had made the soap himself, from ashes and pork fat. But Kristina had complained that it didn't remove the dirt entirely. When she washed linen she refused to use his homemade soap and bought some from Klas Albert.

Well, the stoop floor would have to be good enough the way it was. Many other things had to be good enough nowadays, even if they weren't as they were before.

"My goodness, Karl Oskar! Are you scrubbing the floor!"

He recognized the voice, it was a woman's. She stood behind him on the stoop, dressed in an ample coat and wide hat. The scrubbing brush had made such noise he hadn't heard her coming.

"Ulrika . . . !"

"Good for you! Cleaning your house yourself!"

He moved his hand to his left leg, sore from lying on the boards, and rose slowly with the brush in his hand. The scrub water dripped from his wet knees.

He was a little embarrassed and it annoyed him.

"Now you're a real American, Karl Oskar!"

"I wanted to help Marta tidy up a little. But I don't care for housework."

"I bet you don't!"

And Mrs. Henry O. Jackson laughed the loud laughter of the Glad One: "You aren't ashamed of it?"

"Ashamed of woman-work? That's only in Sweden."

"You bet! Not Svenske any more!"

Ulrika knew that even while Kristina was alive he had started to help with milking and dishwashing, but so much had remained in him of the Swedish attitude that he had refused to scrub floors. Now she saw that this Swedish defect had left him.

"At last you're a real American!"

"Shall I bow at the praise . . . "

"The best praise I can give a man!"

"But I'm not good at scrubbing . . . " He pushed the pail aside. "Nothing is in order with us . . . But come in, Ulrika! Long time since you were here."

"I wanted to see my goddaughter on her birthday. Couldn't make it, though."

They went inside and sat down in the big room. Karl Oskar called Marta and told her to prepare something for their guest. But Ulrika explained that she was in a great hurry; she must get home and help Henry prepare for the Baptist love feast which they would celebrate tomorrow with the breaking of bread. She had been to St. Paul, to her eldest daughter's wedding. Elin had married none less than the chief of police of St. Paul. Her daughter was now in safe hands, and she hoped she could trust the police in America. Elin had worked in his house as a maid, and then a year ago his wife had died, and less than two months later the widower had proposed to her.

"Your girl has done well," said Karl Oskar.

Elin had a strong will, explained the mother. From the very first day in America she had shown she wanted to get ahead. Even that winter when they lived with Danjel in his old log cabin, the girl sat up half the nights and learned the American names for knives, forks, plates, spoons, and everything about the house. She wanted to be a maidservant. But when she got her first job with Mr. Hanley in Stillwater she still didn't know the names of the days. She dressed for church on Friday, and did housecleaning on Sunday, and sent out the wash on the wrong day. The girl had started from the beginning and worked her way up. And since the day before yesterday Elin was Mrs. William A. Aldridge, and she needn't be ashamed of that name in St. Paul.

"Well, well," said Karl Oskar. "So you've been to a wedding. Last time you were in this house . . . "

He stopped short and looked aside.

Ulrika had not been to see them for almost two years; the last time had been at Kristina's funeral. During his wife's last illness Mrs. Jackson and her husband had been in Chicago but they had returned in time for the burial. And not until after Kristina's funeral had Ulrika heard that she had died from a miscarriage.

"Yes, last time I was here there was mourning in this house."

A silence ensued for a moment. It was difficult for either one of them to continue. Dr. Farnley's strong admonition had never been referred to between them after Kristina's death. Ulrika was not one to reproach a wretched man, but sooner or later she aimed to let him know what she thought.

"I feel sorry for you, Karl Oskar. It's hard to live single."

"What you must go through, you manage . . . "

"I guess you keep thinking about it?"

"Thinking about what?"

"What you did. Causing it yourself."

Karl Oskar raised his head with a sudden jerk.

"You didn't take care of Kristina. You got her with child again. That's why you're single and alone!"

His face had turned deep red. He swallowed and swallowed but said nothing.

"You were warned!" she continued. "The doctor's report was delivered to you: She cannot survive another childbed! But you exposed Kristina to that danger."

He stared straight at her but let her go on.

"I never blame you for Kristina's death. I know you couldn't help it. You couldn't control yourself any longer, of course. You have a man's need. You were weak and sinned in weakness. But those sins are the smallest . . . "

"You think . . . " His voice was thick and he swallowed hard. "You think . . . I myself killed Kristina . . . "

"I'm not calling you a wife-killer! You did it out of weakness. Your kind of body isn't built to stay away from your wife. It's excusable. I don't blame you for it!"

"You're wrong! You're very wrong!"

"It hurts to talk about it, of course. I shouldn't have started. You've lost your wife and can't get her back. What's the use of talking about it. I must hurry!"

She rose to leave.

"Yes, we must talk about it! Sit down, Ulrika! Sit down!"

Suddenly Karl Oskar had become quick in his movements; he pushed the chair toward Mrs. Jackson again.

"You're wrong, exactly wrong! But I'll tell you! Just sit down!"

"All right, I will—if you yourself want to talk about it."

Ulrika sat down again and listened intently for a few minutes while Karl Oskar Nilsson spoke. She learned that she had been wrong. She learned that he had obeyed the doctor for three months, and that he had intended to keep on obeying. But one evening Kristina had come to him and said that she didn't believe God had burdened them with this. She trusted more in God than in the doctor in Stillwater. That was how it had happened.

"It was Kristina who wanted it!"

"She did? Poor dear child!"

Ulrika was deeply moved by what she had heard, tears quivered in her eyes and her voice vibrated:

"The dear child! She trusted her God! Good, honest Kristina!"

She could not remember when she had last wept. She pulled a handkerchief from her skirt pocket and dried her eyes.

"But I'm not trying to blame it on Kristina—I should have had better sense."

"No one can hold it against you, of course."

"I should have known better. It'll always be on my conscience."

"You only committed a sin of weakness. The Lord is eager to forgive sins of weakness. God will forgive you, I know it! You can be sure of it, Karl Oskar!"

"God . . . forgive . . . me . . . !"

Karl Oskar Nilsson jumped up so suddenly that his chair turned over and was thrown against the wall. His big nose shot out as if it had been a weapon to use against Ulrika, his eyes glittered and his mouth worked. His last word was a roar, and Ulrika shot up from her chair as fast as he.

"Shall *I* ask God for forgiveness? Because he took Kristina from me?"

"What's come over you, man?"

She had never seen such an explosion of anger in Karl Oskar. Ulrika had never let men frighten her, but now she was as frightened as a woman of her sort could be.

"Are you going crazy? I don't recognize you!"

"You said God will forgive me! It's he who ought to ask my forgiveness! For he tricked Kristina!"

"God tricked . . . ? You *are* crazy, man!"

"Kristina lost her life because she trusted in God. He tricked her!"

"You blaspheme, poor man! You curse the High One!"

"She died and left me alone! God is to blame!"

"Have you lost your mind, Karl Oskar?"

"No—now I've got it back again. But I had lost it that time. And now I only listen to my own common sense . . . "

"You talk as if you were out of your mind."

"No! I'll never forgive God for cheating Kristina! Never, as long as I live!"

"But when you die—do you mean to die and not be reconciled to your God?"

He stood with his back to her and did not reply; he had turned toward the wall.

Ulrika had heard him blaspheme and she was frightened. How could a wretched, helpless human being get the notion to turn against the Almighty? Either she had never known who Karl Oskar was or he had changed after losing his wife.

"God will find you too, Nilsson! God will bend you!"

He had suddenly become so alien to her that she used his surname.

He still kept his silence, with his back to her, staring before him as if he had suddenly discovered something remarkable on the bare wall. Ulrika felt perplexed; what had happened to Kristina's widower? Perhaps he mourned her so inconsolably that she must overlook his behavior. He was a bereft man, a suffering man. Above all, she must console him. It was comforting he needed.

Mrs. Jackson laid her hand on his shoulder, her voice sweet and pleading: "God has taken Kristina home to him. She is in heaven now, as you surely know . . . "

"She didn't want to die . . . " he stuttered forth. "She wanted to stay with me and the children."

"It must be a comfort to you that she's in eternal bliss."

"But she wanted to be here with us—she said so many times: I don't want to die yet!"

When Karl Oskar didn't show any joy because Kristina was happy in her eternal home in heaven, Ulrika no longer knew what comfort to offer him.

But she went on: He was the most ungrateful person she had ever known. How much didn't he have to thank God for? All had gone well for him—he was well-to-do and needn't worry about earthly things. Kristina had borne him many children, all well shaped and healthy. Many parents were given blind, deformed, or feeble-minded offspring. He himself was still in good health and had his strength. The Lord had until now helped him through all life's vicissitudes. How many times might he not have perished? Indeed, God had held his protecting hand over him! Instead of blaspheming the Almighty he ought to thank and praise him! He ought to go down on his knees, as he had just done while scrubbing the stoop, and thank God in humble submission!

She talked, but no one listened to her. Karl Oskar didn't hear her. He only stared at the wall. What in the world did he see there? Nothing but the paper—old pink roses, faded, spotted. He stared at the empty wall. He stared as if he saw a vision, as if his ears were plugged up; he stared at nothing.

How could one talk sense to a person who acted like that? Staring at a wall he had seen every day for many years! There was nothing to be done with Karl Oskar; she could do nothing but feel sorry for him. He did not move, he did not hear—it seemed he would remain in that position and stare at the old, spotted, faded wallpaper forever. Yet, perhaps he saw something in the emptiness.

Ulrika silently opened the door and walked out onto the stoop and away.

In this house she left behind today a man who did not wish to submit—a man who hated his God.

XIX

THE LETTER TO SWEDEN

New Duvemåla Settlement at Center City Post
Offis, April 23, 1865.

Dear Sister Lydia Karlsson,

May all be well with you is my daily Wish.

You write at long Intervals but you shall not think I have forgotten my only Sister. I have been sitting a few Evenings now and writing a letter to You.

First I want to tell you that the War is over and the Enemy beaten. The hard-necked Rebels are giving up everywhere. On the Battle Fields all is Stillness and Silence, all soldiers are going back to their homes. 100,000 Dollars has been promised to the one who can catch President Jefferson of the South. Much destruction has taken place but the Union between the States is safe for time to come.

Great Joy was spread here because of all the good News but like turning a Hand it became Sorrow instead. Our greatly beloved President Abraham Lincoln fell from a murderer's Bullet the 14 April. It happened in the evening when he had gone to view a Theatre in Washington, the message flew like a bolt of lightning over the whole land by the Telegraph. That moment I shall never forget.

I was in Stellwater with a load of potatoes that day. In all places of labor the tools were laid down and each one went to his home. Stores and Houses were draped in black, and many flags on half mast to show the sorrow. Much Lamentation was heard in the streets. Old men cried like Babies.

For here nothing is like in Sweden, people are not ordered to Mourn when the Head of the Nation passes but all happens of free Will. Our President was called the country's Father and we mourn him like a Father in the Flesh. He fought for the Right of the Poor, He made the Black free from Slavery, unchained their chains. The People had entrusted their government to Him. His portrait hangs in many houses for all to see. A man worthy of Honor is honored in Our Republic.

Father Abe's murderer is Taken, shot through the head, for he did not wish

163

to be taken in Life. Old Honest Abe will be brought to his home village in Springfield and will be buried there. His Corpse will be brought 1,300 miles and People will meet up and gather along the Whole way to say Farewell.

This might be of small interest to My sister in Sweden, but it has just happened and my mind is full of it. The Indian savages in Minnesota made an uproar and started a cruel war. But afterwards the Indians were told to keep 20 miles away from any house or white settlement. Now we are safe from the reds.

I want to tell you about my family now since Kristina left us. Her death I have not gotten over and don't think I will in Life. But otherwise all is well with us, I have had good luck in worldy matters, I have now 3 horses and one colt and 10 cows not counting young ones. Last year I fatted 18 Pigs. I sold most of the Pork, but since the war, prices are low. 20 acres of my claim still lies in wilderness but my Sons will help me break it. My six children are all well and full of Life. My oldest daughter takes care of my house, she is 18. And my good boys will be of great help. The youngest goes to school and is learning English fast.

After the end of the war the Country is improving. They are building one railroad after another through Minnesota and we can all ride the Steam Wagon. Good times are promised to us by our Government.

The Astrakhan tree from Kristina's home bears every fall. You can see it to the right in the Portrait I send of our House, taken by a photographing man from Stellwater. Now you can see how we live, they take portraits much like the object here in America.

My hope is that my thoughts which I have tried to put on Paper will find you and Yours at good health. Hope you don't forget to write and let me know about My beloved Sister.

Your Devoted Brother
Karl Oskar Nilsson.

PART THREE

XX

THE FIRST CHILD TO LEAVE
THE HOUSE

—I—

IT WAS Mr. C. A. Persson who had persuaded Karl Oskar to buy it. The storekeeper ordered all kinds of new inventions and displayed them in his shop, and one after another he palmed them off on the settlers. But this one appeared to be a most useful invention. Klas Albert promised to assemble it himself and show how to use it. He brought it one dark fall evening and everyone gathered around the rectangular wooden box.

Karl Oskar wanted to surprise his children and had not mentioned the purchase to them. He acted as if he didn't know what was in the box.

Mr. Persson broke open the box and displayed an object, the like of which had never been seen before in this house—a brass stand, a foot and a half high, which the storekeeper placed on the table. It stood there quite firmly on its solid, round base.

Marta had already guessed that Father had bought some useful kitchen utensil but she could not figure out what this brass stand could be used for. She could neither cut nor cook with it. It seemed to have no purpose. But it was beautiful, with its greenish tint, perhaps it was meant as a table decoration.

"What kind of knickknack have you brought, Klas Albert?" she asked.

"Wait till I'm ready—then you'll see something!"

And from the box the Center City merchant drew out several more strange objects: a porcelain globe, a glass pipe a foot long, and at last a kind of flask filled with a transparent fluid. Each object was exceedingly fragile and Klas Albert was most careful in handling them. His audience, standing in a circle around him, realized that the pieces must in some way be put together.

"Wait till I'm ready! Then you'll understand!"

Mr. Persson opened a lid over an enlargement at the upper end of the brass stand, and into this hole he poured the white fluid from the flask. Then he slowly turned a screw fastened to the stand. No one could guess the purpose of this screw. But it appeared that something was going to happen. And so it did.

Klas Albert struck a match and held it over the brass stand. A flame leaped up from its upper end—the brass stand was burning!

The circle of spectators broke apart; they all stepped back. What was this? Everyone in this house had been instructed to handle fire most carefully; Father had told them to stamp out any flame or spark outside the fireplace. Yet here he stood and smiled while Klas Albert appeared to be trying to set the house on fire!

A tall flame burned lustily at the upper end of the brass stand, but Mr. Persson remained calm. He picked up the glass pipe and placed it around the flame, enclosing it. He then placed the porcelain globe on a ring and turned the screw again. The tall flame withdrew a little and stopped smoking. He kept turning the screw until the flame burned evenly inside the pipe.

A clear, warm light spread through the whole kitchen. The flame in the pipe spread its light to the farthest corner.

And now Karl Oskar said in a solemn voice, "Tonight we have a new light in our house—I have bought a kerosene lamp."

He was very much pleased with the surprise he could read in his children's faces. And Klas Albert was even more pleased; he looked as if he had just performed a very difficult magician's trick.

"How clever you are!" exclaimed Marta. "What do you do to make it light up?"

Eagerly Klas Albert showed the girl how the trick worked: The brass stand formed the foot of the lamp. This enlargement held the fluid that burned—it was called the oil chamber. Into the oil he had stuck some twisted yarn, called the wick, and the other end of the wick came up into the glass pipe. The yarn kept burning because it was soaked in oil and was being fed from the oil chamber. By turning the screw he could change the flame, make it strong or weak, any way he wanted it. The glass pipe protected the flame and the porcelain globe softened the light.

"As simple as that!" said Klas Albert, acting as if it were the easiest thing in the world to make a flame come out of the end of a brass stand.

The kerosene lamp would give as much light as ten tallow candles, he explained. Yet the strangest part was that it would burn indefinitely. When the flame grew weak one only had to pour more oil into the oil chamber.

And they were long to remember that autumn evening when Klas Albert brought the new light to their house. The kerosene lamp brought them more satisfaction and pleasure than any other new invention. The nights were dark at every season; between sunset and bedtime a black wall stood outside the windows, and they needed light. They had made their own candles from sheep tallow, they had also used pitch splinters which they fastened to the walls; and in winter the fire on the hearth gave them light. But candles had to last, pitch splinters burned only a short moment, and the fire must be fed constantly. Candles, splinters, and the fire burned out, but the lamp lasted. One had only to refill the oil chamber. It was an eternal light.

Now the evenings were bright in their house and they could stay up longer at their chores. Each night they stole a little time from the dark.

But the new invention could cause a fire and must be used with utmost care. The fluid could catch fire, the oil chamber might explode. They had read in the papers how people had started house fires when lighting their lamps. Because of this, Karl Oskar at first would let no one but himself handle the lamp or carry it while it burned. But after a time he allowed his two oldest children to attend to it. Johan and Marta were almost of age now, and neither of them was careless. By and by Harald was given the same permission; he was as trustworthy as his older brother and sister. But Frank and Ulrika, the two youngest, were strongly forbidden to touch, move, or try to light the new lamp.

Klas Albert came from time to time to check on the lamp and see that it was taken care of. But no accident happened, and the new invention started no fire in their house. The flame from the oil-soaked wick succeeded the daylight and shone cheerfully through the evenings.

Lamp evenings were something new in the settler families.

It was the great moment of the day when Father lit the lamp. Before, the hearth had been the heart and gathering point of the family, now the kerosene lamp became the family's central point around which they gathered. It spread a warm, cozy light, at which the father read the paper, the children their lessons, the boys whittled with their knives, the girls knitted or sewed. In this light they could see to thread the smallest needle, and read the finest print. It saved their eyes and prolonged their evenings.

With the new light—which came to their home in the fall of 1868—the settlers could spend more time at useful occupations.

—2—

Ditto Anno 1868 harvested 234 Bussels Corn, 196 Bussels Wheat and 162 Bussels Potatos, All Heaped Measure.

These were the largest harvest figures Karl Oskar Nilsson had written down in his old almanac. But while he in America harvested his biggest crops, his old home parish in Sweden suffered the greatest crop failure in over a hundred years.

In *Hemlandet*—whose printing office now had been moved to Chicago—he read about the ravaging famine in the old country: The summer had been the driest in memory throughout Småland. No rain had fallen from the moment the seeds were planted until the crops were cut, and there had been no comforting night dew. Barley grew to only five inches and could not be mowed with a scythe but had to be pulled up by the roots. Fields and meadows lay burned black, and brooks and springs had gone dry. People stole grain from each other by cutting the heads from the sheaves out in the fields. And after the summer's severe crop failure, all things edible for man and beast were gathered against the winter: Hazel tops, heather seed, pine needles, white moss were ground together and mixed with the flour for baking. Porridge was cooked from barley chaff, lingon twigs, heather tops, salt, and water; also thistles, dandelion roots, and the leaves from beech and linden trees. Heather was cut for animal fodder and instead of oats, shavings and sawdust were mixed for the cows. The very poorest walked in the fields and picked up the bones that had been spread with the dung the year before; these they crushed and ground and mixed with the flour for bread.

This winter, hunger would be a guest at practically every home in Småland. Each week the bells tolled for people who had starved to death or died from diseases contracted because of hunger.

In issue after issue *Hemlandet* told of the suffering and misery in Småland. Karl Oskar understood how things were at home without difficulty. How many times hadn't he himself left the table hungry! Now remembrance came to him of the great famine in the summer and winter of '48—twenty years ago. Kristina had ground acorns and put them into the bread—his throat had been sore and swollen from the rough food and he had suffered with constipation the whole winter. Begging children had come in droves asking if they could pick up herring heads and other refuse from the scrap pile outside. That was the winter when little Anna had eaten herself to death on barley porridge. After that happened Kristina had changed her mind and promised to go with him to North America.

But this time, it appeared, the homeland had been stricken by a still more severe famine. According to the paper, the suffering grew as the winter progressed. The farmers on the smaller homesteads became paupers. The sheriff in

Linneryd had within two months foreclosed three hundred farms in his district. Many children died at birth because the famished mothers had no milk to give.

The parishes were listed in famine groups, from one to four, according to their need. Karl Oskar read that Ljuder was listed in group two.

Hunger was ravishing his home parish while he sat here with his bins filled to the ceiling. He read about the barley on the Småland fields, too short to be cut, while his crops had grown taller than ever. In the old country they ate bread from white moss, while in his house they ate rich wheat bread with plenty of butter, as much as they wanted. In their old country was famine, in their new overabundance.

Karl Oskar thought again and again of this great difference, and an idea ripened in him.

One winter evening as he was reading *Hemlandet* by the light of the kerosene lamp, a knock was heard on the door. A visitor had come; Klas Albert greeted them heartily, in high spirits. The Center City shopkeeper had been a frequent guest in this house of late although there was no need for him to look after the lamp any more.

Karl Oskar, looking up from the paper, said, "It's bad at home, Klas Albert. They're starving to death this winter."

"I've read it too," said Klas Albert. "Ljuder is now in the second famine group."

"I can't help thinking about it . . . "

"I didn't think you cared for the old country?"

"Not a shit for the useless dogs at the top. But I feel sorry for the poor, good people."

Klas Albert thought they probably had enough food for everyone in the old country, but the Swedes had not yet learned that food supplies could be transported from one end of the country to the other if need be.

"The government won't be bothered to do anything, of course," said Karl Oskar.

What were they doing in Sweden to alleviate hunger? He had seen a piece in *Hemlandet* and he read it to Klas Albert:

"The King, the Queen, and the Princess Lovisa have given the sufferers in Småland 1,000 riksdaler: on King Carl's name day a ball was given at Växjö to help the suffering in the Province, where masked persons representing diverse characters collected money. This brought in 586 riksdaler. Another 140 daler was collected at the Opera Cafe . . . "

Karl Oskar counted in his head: altogether 1,726 riksdaler, almost 500 dollars, really not bad.

Klas Albert laughed. Wasn't it lucky for the hungry people in Småland that the King's name day happened to fall in the middle of the winter, when the famine was at its worst? A royal house was indeed of great help to the people in years of hunger; the bigger the royal family, the more royal name days, the more bread for the starving subjects.

This king was rumored to have sense enough to admit that he was human; no Swedish king before had admitted as much. About King Carl XV it had been written that no false pride prevented him from bending his head and entering the humblest cottage.

"I've thought about something," said Karl Oskar. "I would like to send a load of my wheat to the hungry in Ljuder."

"What a Christian deed!" exclaimed Klas Albert. "Good, white American bread for the hungry!"

"But how can I do it?"

"I'll take care of everything! And I'll pay the freight!"

The businessman from Center City thought and planned quickly. He had connections with a freight office in Stillwater and he was certain they would send the wheat to Sweden. It was sure to get there, especially if they addressed it to the officials in Växjö, with instructions that it was for the sufferers in Ljuder parish.

But Karl Oskar was suspicious about officials in Sweden.

"Suppose they eat the wheat themselves?"

"Oh no! They wouldn't dare! Don't worry, Karl Oskar! You deliver the wheat to me and I'll handle the rest!"

Said and done.

Karl Oskar had thought Klas Albert just happened to drop in this evening, without any special errand. Now it came out that he did indeed have a reason. Tonight all of them were told why the storekeeper of Center City had spent so much time on the road to their house this winter. One of the children in the house knew in advance: This evening Mr. C. A. Persson told Karl Oskar that his oldest daughter, Marta, had promised to become Mrs. Persson. They would be married a week from Saturday.

Klas Albert and Marta had got to know each other when he came to look after the lamp, and he had found many excuses to service that lamp. His real errand had been another all the time: It was for Marta's sake he had come evening after evening.

Klas Albert had come to their house to take away one of the children. The years had fled and Karl Oskar had not realized he had a marriageable daughter in the house.

—3—

KARL OSKAR NILSSON sorted twenty bushels of wheat, of the best he had, to be sent to Sweden. He packed it in strong jute sacks that ought to hold during the long journey to Småland. It made a good load and he drove it with his team to Mr. Persson's store in Center City. This Minnesota wheat would make fine white bread for the hungry people at home.

Why did he give this grain to Sweden? He was not paying a debt with it, he was under no obligation to his native land. There he had wasted the best years of his youth in labor that had only increased his poverty. In Sweden those who governed had so arranged things that it did not pay to work. And he had no close relatives in need. His parents were dead, and hungry no more. And his sister Lydia had written at Christmas that she and hers had all they needed. Nor did he send the grain because he wanted to feel he was a good and helpful person. He did it because he knew what hunger meant. He had seen one of his children die because of hunger. It was in memory of little Anna that he sent this load of wheat.

Klas Albert had surprised him by offering to pay the freight. Why was the storekeeper suddenly so generous, he had wondered. Five minutes later he had been given the answer: Mr. Persson was going to marry Marta; the son-in-law-to-be wanted to be in with his father-in-law.

Karl Oskar Nilsson of Korpamoen would have been greatly honored if the church warden's son, one of the best catches in Ljuder, should have proposed to his daughter. But among the Chisago people men were valued with other measures than in Sweden. The settlers did not ask who the parents of the intended were, they asked only what he himself was good for. Here it was Klas Albert who ought to feel honored in obtaining the daughter of the first settler at Chisago Lake.

Marriages took place quickly in America; a man and a woman might decide one day and go to the pastor the next. People got married on the run, as it were, like making a purchase in a shop while the team waited on the road. Only a week before the wedding Karl Oskar learned that Klas Albert and Marta would be married. They had not asked him if he had anything against it. The girl was of age this spring, the father had no say over her any longer. But the father-in-law wasn't quite satisfied with his son-in-law-to-be. The light-hued storekeeper was capable and industrious, and Marta would be well taken care of as Mrs. Persson. But in her father's eyes Klas Albert followed an occupation he did not think much of. And during the war he had made clever deals when his duty should have called him to war. To Karl Oskar, such a man was not to be trusted fully.

Moreover, he still needed his oldest daughter at home. Ulrika was not yet fifteen; it would not be easy without Marta. Yet Karl Oskar could say nothing: He himself had left his father at fourteen, although he had been much needed in Korpamoen. Now it was his turn to be deserted by his children. No one could change this: The young ones, in order to live, deserted the old ones, to let them die. Thus one generation succeeds another.

But there was something he wanted from Klas Albert in exchange for his daughter.

In the store in Center City he had several times seen a map of Ljuder parish. The year before Klas Albert emigrated he had been a surveyor's helper at home, and when he left he was given a map as a parting gift from his boss, as a reminder of his homeland. Every time Karl Oskar had been in the store he had studied the map of Ljuder; it was on good, thick paper that he beheld his home parish in miniature.

And now that his neighbor in Sweden was to be his son-in-law he said to him, "Klas Albert, if you take my girl from me you ought at least to give me your map of Ljuder!"

Klas Albert thought at first it was a joke, but Karl Oskar insisted he meant it. He wanted the old map in payment for Marta. If this was not worth an even deal he was willing to pay for the map, whatever was asked.

This was a peculiar exchange. But as his future father-in-law was so anxious, Klas Albert did not wish to refuse; he gave him the Ljuder map. But he could not understand why Karl Oskar was so anxious to have the old map. What could he use it for? Why did he value the old parish chart so highly?

But Karl Oskar said nothing more on the subject. He folded the map carefully and put it under his arm.

The boy could not understand why he wanted it, and Karl Oskar did not wish to enlighten him: He would never again see the place where he had been born, but it was some small consolation to have it on a paper, where he could look at it. A paper was better than nothing to the farmer from Korpamoen who must die on another continent.

—4—

AND ONE SATURDAY in March Karl Oskar's Marta became Mrs. C. A. Persson. The first child had flown from the nest.

Karl Oskar felt rather disappointed that his oldest daughter married in such a hurry: Klas Albert and Marta ought to have been engaged for some time, as they would have been in Sweden. If they had delayed the marriage till summer he could have given them a real wedding. He could afford a big party for once. Now he confined himself to inviting a few old neighbors and friends—Jonas Petter and Swedish Anna, Algot and Manda Svensson, Mr. Thorn, the Scottish sheriff, and a few friends he had made while serving on the jury in Center City. One uninvited guest came, Samuel Nöjd. He brought a collar and muff of silver fox for the bride: with these he wanted to indemnify the bride's father for the sheep his dogs had killed many years ago. The old trapper had broken a leg last fall and had been in bed all winter, and during this time he had grown kinder and more mellow. Karl Oskar accepted the gift as payment for the sheep.

Already early in the evening the newly married couple had left for their home in Center City, and Karl Oskar was left behind in the bridal house with his guests. He had brought home a couple of gallons of whiskey and a keg of beer, and the preparation of the food was in the charge of Swedish Anna, assisted by another Swedish woman from Taylors Falls. The dishes were many and well prepared and there was room for all the guests around the table in the big room.

Karl Oskar Nilsson himself sat at the upper end of the table with Jonas Petter, his oldest friend, to the right of him. Soon the men were perspiring and red-faced from whiskey. The clear, friendly light of the kerosene lamp spread its glow over full glasses and abundant dishes and over the faces of sated and happy guests.

Samuel Nöjd sat blinking against the lamp, fingering its oil chamber in curiosity. Jonas Petter warned him that the lamp might explode, he mustn't set the house and the wedding guests on fire.

"That whiskey you're drinking is more liable to catch fire than the oil in the lamp," said the old trapper.

Everyone laughed at this but Nöjd went on: He knew what he was talking about, for he had once had a horrible experience with a German hunter friend, Andreas Notte. The German had drunk about a gallon of Kentucky straight a day for many years. One evening Notte, with many other hunters, was sitting around the campfire eating elk meat and beans and after supper he wanted to smoke a cigar. He put it in his mouth and struck a match. Then it happened: The German caught fire.

The burning match started a fire inside his mouth and flames shot over his face and ignited his hair. He tried to choke the flames with his hands, but they burned too. Notte let out some horrible roars and his fellow-hunters rushed to a nearby brook for water and poured it over him, bucket after bucket. But his innards were burning by then and they couldn't put out the fire inside his body. When at last they quenched the flames, Andreas Notte was dead. Of their good friend there remained only a smoking cadaver which spread an obnoxious stink, like burning dung. Nothing was left of his face. His lips were burnt away and his mouth was only a gaping hole with the tongue left like a well-baked piece of rusk.

The German's body had been saturated with whiskey, his breath was flammable and when he lit the match it caught fire. There had been a long piece about him in the paper under the heading: *Drunkard burned to death through internal combustion.*

Accidents of this kind often happened in his homeland, said the Scot, Mr. Thorn. And this reminded him of something he himself had been involved in many years ago and which had scared many whiskey drinkers. A friend of his, Charlie Burns, also a Scot, had been bitten by a rattler which struck at him and bit him in the right arm. They were hunting beaver in the fall along the Minnesota River and Charlie was climbing over a log and didn't see the critter. The arm swelled up until it was as big as his thigh. Now a person bitten by a rattler was supposed to drink as much cognac or whiskey as he could, at least half a gallon at once. But they had no whiskey or cognac, and Charlie swore and hollered in pain. Then Mr. Thorn made a salve of tobacco, gunpowder, and beaver fat which he rubbed into the swollen limb. But nothing sucks out the rattler poison better than the earth itself, and he dug a hole in the ground for his friend and rolled him into it. For three days Charlie lay with his swollen arm in the ditch. The first day he was delirious, the second day he prayed, the third day the swelling went down and he was able to swear again.

By and by Charlie Burns got well, but his face had changed color: It was greenish, exactly like the belly of the rattler. This was not unusual in such cases, said Mr. Thorn.

Wherever Charlie went after that, his green face caused a hell of a fright. People stared at him wherever he was, and all were sure that he was a drunkard and that his color came from drinking whiskey. One day he met a Methodist preacher who wanted to exhibit him to his congregation as a revolting example of what drinking would do. So Charlie hired himself to the Methodists and was displayed at all the meetings as a warning against drinking. Charlie had always been a sober person never touching whiskey, but now he became known far and wide as the worst drunkard in the world. He got half of the collections and earned good money for many years, working diligently in the field of religion, serving the cause of temperance, and saving many drunkards with his green face. Finally he retired and bought a big house in Chicago—he was still living there in great comfort, Mr. Thorn concluded.

Chicago! cut in Jonas Petter. He had been to that town last winter, and some sight it was! The houses were dirty and black as if tarred. Chicago was a den of iniquity, a home of unnatural vices, filled with sinners of all kinds—murderers, thieves, swindlers, sodomites, whores, and pimps. The women he had met in that town were decked out in plumes and feathers, like peacocks. American women were of course lazy and haughty and didn't want to do anything from morning to night except work on their faces and deck themselves out. And their wicked ideas had spread to some of the Swedish women in America; there were actually Swedish women who now refused to polish the shoes of their men.

He had heard it was predicted that Chicago—world capital of sin—would be destroyed next year. On April 16, 1870, the lakes and rivers round the town would flood it and swallow it up, dirt and all.

"Well, I think they would fish up Chicago again," said Samuel Nöjd. "The Americans are so clever."

The whiskey and the beer had loosened the men's tongues at Karl Oskar Nilsson's party, and even those of few words wanted to talk. But the host himself did not participate much in the talking, he was busy attending to the guests and their needs of food and liquor. He was never very sociable—weeks would go by without callers in his house—and this wedding day was not a day of joy to him. There was now one less in the house and the child he most needed had moved away from him. She had deserted her father to be with the man she liked best, and according to life's order it was the father who suffered the loss, and a loss was nothing to celebrate. But a party must be given by the father when his daughter was married.

"When are you starting on your new house, Karl Oskar?" asked Jonas Petter.

"Never. I won't build any more in my time."

"Well, you've built enough to last. You can rest now."

Jonas Petter had himself raised a new house last summer and he had just sent for a photographer from St. Paul so he could send a picture of it to his relatives in Sweden. This picture was put on leather and could be sent like a postcard to any part of the world, without damage. Mr. Golding, the picture man, had made much money taking pictures of houses to send to the old country. He even had houses he lent to people who had none of their own, so they could stand in front of them to show their relatives.

Jonas Petter regretted he hadn't borrowed a house from Mr. Golding and stood in front of it, instead of his own. It wouldn't have cost a cent more and he could have picked the nicest house in St. Paul and his relatives would never have known the difference.

He was drowned out by Mr. Thorn and Samuel Nöjd, who had gotten into a dispute about the Sioux war. They both seemed to agree the war had been hopeless from the beginning and had only led the Indians to even greater misery than before. But their medicine men had promised easy victory because the whites were fighting the Civil War. Now the savages would have to starve forever while waiting for the money the government owed them. What could the hunter-folk live on with no more hunting grounds, no farms, no animals except dogs, fleas, and lice? When the starved Indians had come to the government supply house in Red Wood and asked for food, the agent had said they could go out and eat grass. The first one they killed on August 18, 1862, was that very agent, Mr. Andrew Myrick, and when his body was found in the debris his mouth was filled with grass.

In this the Sioux showed their understanding of justice; their uprising in 1862 was to get justice, said Samuel Nöjd.

But when he called Governor Ramsey and Colonel Sibley mass murderers Mr. Thorn rose to his feet and grabbed him by the collar. The party was near turning into a brawl; the Scot wanted the trapper to come outside with him so they could shoot at each other like gentlemen.

Karl Oskar told the Scot not to pay any attention to the nonsense Nöjd spewed out, and Jonas Petter stepped between the two quarreling men to calm them: He had a story to tell, well suited for a wedding feast.It was about a farmer and a soldier; he had started to tell this story on many occasions but had always been interrupted. However, he had made up his mind to tell it once before he died, for he was by now the only living person who knew it, and it would be a great loss to science and the culture of the world if it weren't told. He was always glad to tell it, if only someone wanted to listen. He was getting so old now, even he must die, therefore . . .

And the sheriff and the trapper heeded him and sat down again and listened in silence.

—5—

Jonas Petter tells his forbidden story:

Edvard in Hogahult and his wife Brita had been married ten years without having produced an heir. Hogahult was a fine farm, they were well-to-do. If they remained childless, their property would go to Edvard's two younger brothers, who lived dissolute lives and already had thrown away their paternal inheritance in drinking. Neither Edvard nor Brita wanted to leave their fine farm to them and have it ruined. The couple would give anything in the world for a child and heir.

The wife was nearing forty and must hurry if she wanted to bear a child. So the couple at last went to town to see a doctor. They asked him: Why wasn't their marriage blessed with offspring?

The doctor looked over and examined and inspected both Edvard and Brita. Then he gave his verdict: He found no fault with the wife. If it depended on her only they would have had a child each year of the ten they had been married. But the fault lay with her husband: His seed was useless. The seed the farmer sowed in his wife did not sprout.

The farmer of Hogahult was greatly perturbed that he couldn't beget children. He must then die without an heir of his flesh and blood. The brothers would inherit the farm and throw it away on drinking. And it irked him that they already felt sure of the inheritance and were waiting for it. They had for long considered him unable and knew he would not have any offspring.

And Edvard said to his wife Brita: No one ought to let a field lay in fallow because he himself couldn't use it. If one farmer can't sow sprouting seed, the neighbor must do it. If she could have children she must have them. He would hire a man for the work he himself couldn't perform, if she was willing. Personal pride must not stand in the way with him. He himself wanted an heir so badly he had decided to get a man and pay him well; he would in advance make the understanding that he himself would be considered the father. All depended on her, if she was willing.

At first the wife was unwilling. It was against her nature to give herself in that way to a strange man. Instead, she had thought they might adopt a child, some orphan perhaps.

But when Brita of Hogahult had thought over her husband's suggestion for some time, she changed her mind: Rather than raise an unknown child she would prefer to bring up a child she herself had given life to. She asked only one condition: that she herself choose the man who was to make her with child.

To this Edvard agreed.

Some little time passed again and both husband and wife kept their eyes open for young men or fathers who might be able and willing. But they didn't find a one.

Just about that time a new soldier came to the village, and he often came to work in Hogahult. His name was Ferm, he was thirty years of age, well built, and strong as a bull. He had a wife and six children and he had a hard time feeding his large family. They were often without bread in the soldier's cottage. Often the children had to go out and beg for bread before they went to school.

And Brita said to her husband that the soldier was a strong and healthy man, free of all defects—royal soldiers must be first class in all ways. He had so many children already he must surely be able to make one more. And his family was so poor the father would need a little extra. If they were to hire a man for her she would accept Ferm.

When the soldier had worked on their farm Edvard had valued him greatly. He thought him a fine man. He agreed with his wife.

He went to see him and gave him the offer: They needed an heir in Hogahult, they would prefer a male child, but they would be satisfied with only a girl, in which case they might eventually get a son-in-law to take over the farm. The soldier would be well rewarded: If a son were born he would receive forty bushels of rye, if a daughter, twenty, heaped measure. But their agreement must be kept secret, not a word must leak out.

It was a generous offer, at once tempting to soldier Ferm. On his little plot he harvested barely ten bushels a year, which was far too little to keep his family in bread, and he had to work for others many days of the year. Now he would get many times his yearly yield without work! If the wife in Hogahult was shaped the way a woman should be it would be easy work for him to make her with child. And he had never thought that a man would be paid for so pleasant a labor. He himself had had to pay—in more drudgery and labor and worry for each new child he fathered with his wife. Indeed, he was afraid that his ability to beget children would make him a real pauper in the end. This gift would now help him and his family.

The farmer and the soldier were agreed and sealed their agreement with a handshake.

Edvard said to his wife that he would drive to Karlshamn with some logs and stay away as long as she thought would be needed. Exactly how long they couldn't be sure, at first they thought a week, but finally they settled for three days. If this wasn't enough he would have to make another trip to town.

During Edvard's absence the soldier would come to the farm and do day labor.

The farmer drove away, the soldier came. It was shortly before Christmas and the days were short. Nor did Ferm perform any heavy labor these days. But instead of returning home in the evenings, as he used to, he now remained at the farm overnight. His night work was now his real duty. And the soldier did his duty at the farm during the part of the year when the nights are the longest.

For three long nights the farmer remained away from the house.

When Edvard returned from town he was met by his wife, who was satisfied and full of confidence. She said she felt sure the three days he had been away were not lost days. She did not think he would have to drive any more logs to town.

After a few months the Hogahult mistress began to broaden around the waist. She was satisfied, her husband was satisfied.

But in the soldier's cottage Ferm was very worried. He was worrying about his reward, the bushels of rye: Suppose he was so unlucky that it was a girl. Then he would get only twenty bushels. And if he were real unlucky she might have a miscarriage and he wouldn't get a single grain. That would be hell. And all his life he had only had bad luck—couldn't it change for once for a poor village soldier?

And change it did for the soldier in the end: When her days were accomplished the wife in Hogahult bore triplets, three sons.

A triple birth had not taken place in the parish as far back as anyone could remember. But all three boys were well shaped and full of life. The mother was a little weak in her body after her delivery, but she was happy and satisfied in her soul. Her husband was pleased and more than that. He was overwhelmed. One day he had no heir, and the next day three were crying lustily. He was pleased, but he would have been better pleased if the number had been smaller. And as he looked at the three boys in the three cradles he thought what luck he hadn't stayed away a week as they first had figured on; three nights was quite sufficient.

The farmhouse was filled with happiness, and in the soldier's cottage the children's father jumped to the ceiling: forty bushels for each male child! One hundred twenty bushels of rye for bread!

When the farmer of Hogahult paid off his agreement he had to scrape his bins and borrow forty bushels from a neighbor. His wife said Ferm was well worth his pay. Edvard said, as he measured the rye for the soldier, that he had only been talking about one heir, but he had enough rye for three. And no one could accuse Ferm of poor work; he should have his pay. Best of all—Edvard's brothers had taken to their beds at the news of the triplets in Hogahult and they were quite sick.

However much they ate in the soldier's cottage they couldn't consume more than a couple of bushels a month. With three nights' work on the farm the soldier had supplied his family with food for five years.

Ferm did not work any more on his plot. He put it in fallow and lay all day in the cottage and did nothing. He felt well off. Why should he work when he already had bread for wife and children? His bins were so full of rye they spilled over. Why get more grain when he already wallowed in it? Why worry about the future when it was already taken care of?

The soldier's place grew neglected, weeds overran the fields, and the farmers were bitterly jealous of the soldier who pretended and acted like a lord while they had to labor from early to late in the sweat of their brows. And it began to be whispered about in the village: Where had the triplets in Hogahult come from? The couple had been childless for so many years. Where had all the rye in the soldier's cottage come from? They had always been without bread. People added one and two together and the sum they arrived at was very near the truth. And when Ferm was drunk he liked to brag and couldn't prevent words of wisdom, like these, from escaping: It didn't pay to work at day labor if he could find night work, and could sow sprouting seed.

Others completed the half-sung song, and that was how the story about the farmer and the soldier got to be known.

But it didn't hurt anyone. Edvard in Hogahult had got three sons who thrived and grew up to be helpers to him when he was getting old. The triplets were fine youngsters and much joy to their parents, who were greatly honored by them in their old age. Both sides of the partnership had received what they needed and wished, both the farmer family and the soldier family were as happy as people can be in this world. Providence had arranged everything to the best for the people in the two places.

No seed that had been sowed in the fields of Hogahult for a thousand years was so satisfying and sprouted so well as the rye the farmer measured up to the soldier.

So Jonas Petter ended his story at Karl Oskar Nilsson's first wedding party.

XXI

THE BRIDAL CROWN WITH
PRECIOUS STONES

—I—

WITHIN THE SPAN of a few years the Swedish population at Lake Chisago had doubled. Every spring new immigrants arrived, driven from Sweden by pure hunger, victims of the great famine. They came by the thousands from Starvation-Småland, where they had chewed on bread of lichen, chaff, and acorn. Their intestines were ruined, their throats sore and sensitive from famine bread. The new arrivals in the St. Croix Valley were pale as potato sprouts in a cellar in spring, they were gaunt, their flesh gone to the bone. They said themselves they ought to have traveled across the ocean for half fare.

To this peaceful and lush valley there immigrated during these years people who had known intense hunger in their homeland. The Smålanders said they could still hear the echo of tolling funeral bells. They came to a country where good times prevailed and everything was prosperous. There was building and planning, clearing and farming going on. More and more railroads stretched through Minnesota's forests. Pastor Stenius preached against the line being staked out from St. Paul to Taylors Falls, for machines and steam engines turned thoughts to worldly matters and inflicted damage on the settlers' souls. Yet the road was built in its entire length. More and bigger sawmills were built, steam-driven, and machines appeared that could cut the crops twenty times as fast as any scythe, threshing machines were invented that winnowed a bushel a minute. And people were needed to build and transport and work; the immigrants were received with open arms. Here there was still plenty of room.

For ten years now the Homestead Act had been in force, Abraham Lincoln's great gift to the country's farmers, the work of a farmer's son, blessed by all immigrants who came to farm. Anyone who wanted land received 160 acres without paying a cent, the only requirement being that he clear and build on it.

Through that law Old Abe had given homesteads to millions of the homeless. Nothing more important had ever happened to immigrants. The year before Lincoln was murdered he had proclaimed the last Thursday in November as a day of Thanksgiving on which to show the Lord God gratitude for the year's crop. But innumerable immigrants, from all the old countries, turned on this day to Old Abe himself in his grave and thanked him for their fields and their crops. It was, after all, he who had given them the land.

Thus the Starvation-Småland people arrived in the St. Croix Valley at a happy time. Here they immediately found the living they sought. And to their countrymen who had arrived earlier they brought news of the famine and the starvation in the old villages, telling how even the crows had fallen dead from their perches since there was nothing to sustain life in them, how people had died by the hundreds, unable to exist on the chaff porridge spooned out at the church twice a week. But the lords and masters had their usual generous fare during the famine years. The so-called four estates, through constitutional amendment, had been abolished just before the famine—now, so the saying went, there remained only two estates: the well fed and the starving.

When Karl Oskar Nilsson heard of all the misery in Småland he was well pleased that he had sent his home parish a load of wheat.

Hardest to listen to were the stories of children the mothers were unable to feed at their breasts. Many of the babies born in Småland during the famine years left this world immediately. Mothers who had lost their children then became wet nurses in rich homes where they were given food in abundance: Their milk returned to their breasts to feed the upper-class children. Especially sought after were mothers of illegitimate children. The church condemned such women, but the lords liked them.

Ulrika of Västergöhl could remember a similar experience which she had often told to Karl Oskar in great bitterness: At the birth of her second bastard she had been ordered to Kråkesjö to give suck to the lieutenant's newborn son, since his wife was too weak and nervous. She had been offered one riksdaler a month for her milk, and five meals a day of the best food she could eat. But Ulrika had refused the lieutenant's offer: She wanted the milk for her own son. A child without a father ought at least to have a mother's unshared breast. Yet, without sufficient food at home, she had not had milk enough for her baby and after four months it had died.

In Sweden the rich stole even mother's milk from the poor. It was no wonder such great hordes had escaped across the ocean to the New World.

—2—

ULRIKA JACKSON had become a widow last winter. During a preaching journey in severe weather Pastor Jackson had caught a cold which later turned into pneumonia; he died nine days later. The Stillwater Baptist congregation had given their minister a magnificent funeral.

Ulrika had not visited the Nilsson Settlement for several years, nor had Karl Oskar gone to see her in Stillwater. She had been Kristina's intimate friend but he had never counted her among his. Nor did he do much calling. But he heard through rumor that Ulrika of Västergöhl had become a rich widow. A member of the congregation who had died a year before the pastor had willed all his property to Jackson. It consisted of four houses which Ulrika inherited at her husband's death, and Mrs. Henry O. Jackson was now considered well-to-do.

One day in early summer Karl Oskar had an errand to the land office in Stillwater and he dropped in to pay a visit to the Baptist pastor's widow. She had moved from the old home and lived now in one of the inherited houses, a spacious, beautiful building with a lush orchard sloping down to the very edge of the St. Croix River.

Mrs. Henry O. Jackson was delightfully surprised at the visit: "Welcome, Nilsson! It's been a long time!"

"Thought I would call on you."

"I've thought of calling on you many times, Nilsson!"

"Call me Karl Oskar as in the old days. You still speak Swedish, don't you?"

"All right, Karl Oskar!"

Ulrika invited her guest into a room much larger than the living room in the old house. The furniture was new and must have cost much, everything was fine and shiny. Karl Oskar guessed it must look like an upper-class room in Sweden, even though he hadn't seen many of those.

"What can I offer you?"

A young girl in a starched white apron had come into the room and stood waiting at the door for her mistress's order.

"Would you like some cherry wine?"

"I'll try anything you offer, Ulrika."

She gave instructions in English to her maid. The girl went out and returned with a bottle of cherry wine. She poured it into glasses of so elegant a cut they glittered like snow in sunshine.

Karl Oskar drank; the wine had a good although sweet taste.

"So you've hired a maid, I see."

"I have two girls."

"Well, I hear you can afford it. Nice that you're well off."

"Yes, I have plenty of worldly goods," Mrs. Jackson sighed softly, "but I have lost my husband. I'll never get over losing Henry. Now I've only the Lord to comfort me."

Ulrika told him about her husband's sickness and death and her life as a widow. She wanted to do good with the money the Lord had granted her so undeservedly, and with some of it she had started a home for illegitimate children, where they would receive kind treatment. It had cost her a lot and when people asked why she had done it she would reply that she herself had borne four bastards in her homeland, three of whom had died in tender years from undernourishment. But everyone laughed at this and took it for a joke.

"But your American children are getting along well?"

Yes, indeed, the three daughters she had borne to Pastor Jackson had brought her much happiness. They had all married well. But the boy—well, she didn't even want to talk about her son.

Suddenly a flash of anger came over her face.

Karl Oskar asked, "Is something wrong with your boy?"

"He doesn't want to be a priest, the bastard!"

Karl Oskar was well aware of the resolution the unmarried Ulrika of Västergöhl had made at the time of her emigration: She would show the clergy of Ljuder "whom they had stung" when they denied her Communion at the Lord's table. She herself would bear a clergyman.

"Can you imagine that lout, Karl Oskar! He refuses holy orders!"

Red roses bloomed on Ulrika's cheeks as she continued. They had put Henry Jr. in the Baptist seminary, but he ran away. He didn't want to serve as a priest in any church, he didn't even want to go to church or listen to a minister, not even his own father. What could you do with such an obstreperous, snooty child? The boy was so shameless he wouldn't even listen to the Lord's Word. Now he was sixteen, yet he would receive neither baptism nor confirmation, not in any kind of church, be it Baptist, Methodist, or Lutheran. She had borne into this world a hardened heathen.

"Does your son live with you?"

"No, he's away. He travels about."

And Ulrika again sighed deeply. Only with effort could she go on. "My son is an animal trainer."

"What did you say?" Her guest was astonished.

"Yea—Henry Jr. travels with a circus."

Last spring a circus had come to Stillwater, with Arabs, Bedouins, mules, apes, and other monsters, as well as wild bears, lions, and leopards. Junior took a job with the circus, currying horses and shoveling dung after lions and bears for five dollars a week and his keep. He went with the circus when it departed. Last time he wrote he had been in Chicago. He was now almost a fully qualified animal trainer. In a few weeks he would take his animal trainer examination and would graduate, he wrote.

Her only son—carrying on in a circus arena, instead of preaching the Lord's Word from a pulpit! Instead of becoming a priest he was a jester, a fool, at fairs—instead of taming sinful people he was taming wild beasts!

No son born of woman had brought his mother a more cruel sorrow than Henry Jr. She had been denied the birth of a priest.

Karl Oskar looked out over the St. Croix River just as a steamer glided by. It had a high funnel with smoke belching out in gray clouds. The lower deck was piled high with wood—fuel for the engine. In the stern the huge wheel paddled like a river monster that had got caught on a hook. The upper deck was loaded with barrels of flour, for the paddleboat carried a cargo of wheat flour. The settlers of Minnesota were already growing more wheat than they consumed; already they supplied other countries with bread.

"Have some more wine!" And Ulrika filled the glasses. "How are things with you, Karl Oskar?"

"You know. Half of me died with Kristina . . . "

"I reckoned as much . . . "

"In other respects all is well. Except my old leg kicks up at times."

"Your injury? Have you tried Blood-Renewer for it? You can get it at Turner's Drug Store."

She opened a cupboard and took out a bottle: *Sweet's Blood-Renewer heals Scrofula, Aches, Stomach Fever, Chest Fever, Headache, All Female Weakness, and All Sicknesses Caused by Bad Blood.*

Ulrika was convinced that Karl Oskar's pain was caused by impurity in the blood: "The Blood-Renewer helps me when my old legs ache!"

Karl Oskar wondered to himself how old Ulrika of Västergöhl might be by now. She must be over sixty. She had put on a little weight but this did not detract from her appearance; otherwise she looked as always.

And Ulrika wondered if he had reconciled himself with God. But her recollection of his behavior at their last meeting was still in her mind and she didn't ask. She felt he was a little more mellow this time. Perhaps he couldn't endure his own hatred for the Creator. And if he didn't show some humility—God would surely bend him.

—3—

ULRIKA persuaded Karl Oskar to stay for dinner.

They spoke of the old country. Ulrika had never written any letters to Sweden and never received any. She did have relatives at home but they had never wanted to have anything to do with her. Karl Oskar wrote once a year to his sister Lydia and received letters in return, and he gave Ulrika the latest news.

Mrs. Jackson showed him a copy of *Hemlandet* and pointed to a notice. An emigrant from Ljuder had presented a bridal crown to the village church. Who might the donor be? Could it be someone in the St. Croix Valley?

Karl Oskar picked up the paper and read:

"The parish of Ljuder, Småland, has recently received a valuable gift from North America, given by an emigrant from the parish—a beautifully wrought, highly valuable bridal crown of silver, the finest obtainable. The crown, according to the donor's instructions, is to be worn at church weddings but only by brides known for chastity and decent living. This valuable church jewel will be used for the first time this Whitsuntide, when Anna Ottilia Davidsson, an upright and modest virgin, the granddaughter of Per Persson in Åkerby, will be married to Karl Alexander Olofsson from Kärragärde.

"The donor of the crown, now living in North America, wishes to remain anonymous. She was a member of Ljuder parish before her emigration some years ago. The silver crown is in expression of gratitude and appreciation of her native village.

"Honor to each emigrant who remembers his old country and shows his gratitude in this way!"

Karl Oskar folded the paper. "I wonder who it might be?"

"I guessed you," said Ulrika.

Karl Oskar laughed. "No—it must be someone else, someone who is rich."

"Why? The crown needn't be so expensive."

"It's made of silver."

"Silver isn't expensive in America."

Karl Oskar read the notice again. "The giver doesn't want his name known—I wonder why? I wonder how much it cost?"

"How much do you guess?"

"I couldn't try!"

"One guess!"

Now Karl Oskar noticed something sly and mocking in her remarks. A suspicion was born in him and it was confirmed before he had time to say anything more.

"The crown cost nine hundred dollars!"

Karl Oskar started from the chair. "How in all the . . . "

"Yes, nine hundred dollars. Cheap for cash!"

"You, Ulrika! You gave it!"

"Yes, of course!"

Mrs. Henry O. Jackson folded her arms over her ample bosom and enjoyed Karl Oskar's look of surprise. He just sat there and stared at her, utterly astonished. She laughed with great exuberance and it echoed through the house. In this moment, when teasing Karl Oskar, she was again the old Glad One.

"You fooled me, Ulrika."

"I thought you'd guess at once!"

"It didn't enter my head you were so rich you could give away silver crowns!"

"I bought the bridal crown in Chicago last winter. It's covered with precious stones, it glittered so I couldn't take my eyes off it."

"Some gift!" said Karl Oskar. "But why the secrecy?"

"If the people in Ljuder had known who gave it they wouldn't have accepted it."

She was right in this, he thought. Older people at home were sure to remember the parish whore, Ulrika of Västergöhl. But she might have given it under her present name, for no one would have known who Mrs. Jackson was. No one would have guessed by checking the church records that this was "Unmarried Ulrika of Västergöhl, denied the Lord's table for lewd living, excluded from the parish, banished." For the donor was now Mrs. Henry O. Jackson, of Stillwater, Minnesota, North America. And the magnificent bridal crown she had presented to Ljuder church could be worn only by virgins, known for chastity, decency, and unquestionable morals.

"Did you yourself stipulate that only chaste women can wear it?"

"They must have their maidenheads, of course. That very word is on the paper. Sure tough, isn't it?"

Karl Oskar remembered that it was chaste and honorable women, above all, who had looked down on and insulted the parish whore, Ulrika of Västergöhl.

Yet that very kind of woman—fine farm daughters and virgins—would wear her silver crown with the precious stones at their weddings in the village church. Perhaps it was Ulrika's way of taking revenge.

"Why did you donate the crown?"

"I'll tell you, Karl Oskar: The paper is wrong—I'm not grateful to Sweden. That wasn't the reason."

She thought for a few moments, then she added that she was only grateful to Sweden that she had gotten away from that country in order to live the life of a human being in America. At home she had been sold at auction when she was four, and raped by the farmer who bought her when she was fourteen. She had frozen and been hungry, and had been unable to nourish her children at her breast; three of them had died and for this people had spit after her and hated her. Was that treatment something to be grateful for?

Ulrika looked out through the window; her eyes followed the slow stream of the river, as far as they could. They tried to peer into the invisible distance, as it were, as if she wanted to look all the way back to her native country.

But this she must say as well: She had no desire to lie on her deathbed with hatred in her heart for the country where she was born. As the Lord had forgiven her all her sins, so she wished to forgive the people of Sweden. Henry had taught her that a person washed clean in the new baptism forgave his neighbors all their wrongdoings. Now she had donated the bridal crown to show God that she did not carry a grudge against any person in the old country. It had taken many years to get over her bitterness but at last she was reconciled in her heart to the Kingdom of Sweden, which hitherto she had always called a hellhole.

"And yet you were right," said her guest. "Only the upper class lives well in that country."

Mrs. Henry O. Jackson, the well-to-do widow of Stillwater's Baptist minister, leaned back in her chair, still looking out at the stream below her window; the St. Croix flowed in the direction whence she had arrived that day when she landed in Stillwater. She was in deep thought.

"At Whitsuntide my crown will be used for the first time! At a church wedding in Ljuder!"

Then she grew silent; she closed her eyes. Whitsuntide would be here in a few days, in a few days her gift to Sweden would be consecrated. There would be a great ceremony in the church there at home. With her eyes closed she could see people filling the pews, her ears could hear the organ play, the congregation sing, as devout reverence filled the church to the very organ loft.

The singing and the music poured out through the open church windows. Outside the leafy elms swayed, there grew the spring blossoms, fragrant roses, tender lilies. The ground itself was potent with green grass and herbs, and a young and green summer soughed in the elm crowns above the earth.

And inside the church the wedding; the new bridal crown is worn for the first time, shown to the congregation. It is a gift from an unknown donor in the New World. Reverently the young bridal couple moves up the aisle. On the bride's head rises the silver crown with its precious stones glittering like stars and crystals. The couple kneels at the altar, the congregation rises. As the wedding march dies only the soughing in the elms can be heard from outside.

Then the voice of the minister—the ceremony has begun.

All the people in the pews have their eyes on the beautiful crown. *But who is the bride?*

The former Ulrika of Västergöhl sits with eyes closed, in deep thought. She has closed her eyes in order to see. And she sees. She does not see Karl Oskar who is sitting in front of her, or the furniture and knickknacks in her comfortable home in Stillwater, nothing of her surroundings. Under her closed eyelids she sees a bride at the altar in Ljuder church at Whitsuntide. She has recognized her. She has recognized not only the crown, which she herself has bought and held in her hands, she also knows the young bride—her body, her features: It is none other than she herself. It is Ulrika herself who wears the silver crown with the precious stones.

Everyone in the church can see that the bride at the altar is beautiful, her cheeks blooming pink from modesty, her eyes radiating health, happiness. She stands straight and proud, her bosom high under the bridal blouse. She is without a doubt the most attractive girl in the parish, and more beautiful than ever in her white gown. Who could have been more suitable to consecrate the crown? The whole congregation can see the young girl, the virgin, the church bride, a chaste young woman married in her home parish at Whitsuntide— Ulrika as a young bride!

The former parish whore, excluded from church and altar in her home parish, had been the first Swedish bride in the St. Croix Valley. But her innermost, secret dream had been from early years to be a bride in her home church. It was her great desire, for a life different from the one she had lived, and she could never smother it.

Now her dream has come true, in the guise of another woman; she has exacted payment for the life she had been denied. Every time a young bride wears her crown in Ljuder church, Ulrika is indemnified.

For each virgin bride in the home village church is she. Other women have a wedding only once in life, but she will celebrate it many times. Again and again she will be dressed and decked and see herself in the dream she has always nourished in secret. At each church wedding she will be resurrected from her youthful degradation as her head again and again carries the crown with the precious stones.

Mrs. Henry O. Jackson, sitting here in her home in Stillwater, is not young any more. She who with closed eyes views the June wedding in her homeland will soon be a woman of many years. Soon her cheeks will be flabby, the wrinkles spreading, and the legs under her heavy body unsteady. But she can sit and dream in this joyful knowledge: Even after her death she will stand as bride in Ljuder church, year in, year out.

Ulrika of Västergöhl has finally been vindicated in Sweden. She has been turned into the eternal crown-bride.

XXII

THE FARMER AND THE OAK

— I —

STRONG, well-muscled young men were growing up at Lake Chisago's oldest settlement. Four sons had grown into men. Two were as tall as the father, two taller. Any one of them could manage a job requiring a full-grown man. All were broad across the shoulders, strong in limbs, keen and handy. Their growth into manhood was the greatest change that had taken place at this settlement.

Karl Oskar retained a father's authority over his sons; this must remain his as long as they ate his bread and lived in his house. But the older they grew the less he knew about them. He was together with his boys in work, but outside the home they lived their own lives. He was the hermit, seldom away from home, they were lively, often away, associating with other people. And father and sons already used different languages when they spoke with each other. The children more and more discarded their mother tongue for English—when he addressed them in Swedish they would reply in English. This seemed awkward to him and plainly askew. At first he tried to correct them, but by and by he became accustomed to it and after some time it no longer bothered him. There was nothing he could do about it, so perhaps it was better to say nothing. After all, his children were right; he must not hinder them from speaking their country's language. In the settlements hereabouts Swedish was all right, but outside the Chisago Lake district they had little use for their mother tongue. The surer they became in English, the easier would be their success in this country.

Karl Oskar's children were to be saved from the language difficulties he had gone through in America. How hadn't it hindered him! How many humiliations hadn't he endured because he couldn't speak the country's language. At last he managed, but like other Swedes at Chisago Lake he used his own brand of English, strongly mixed with the old language. He would never learn anything else. Lately he more and more forgot the new since he seldom went beyond his farm, and he fell back on Swedish.

He felt that his children, when outsiders were present, were ashamed of their father's way of speaking. The children didn't understand, couldn't understand, how much easier it was for them. All he could do was to pretend he didn't know they were ashamed of their father's expressions.

With the growing children, the new language came into the house and expelled the old. It didn't even spare the name their home had had from the beginning. Karl Oskar's children no longer called their home New Duvemåla. They had given it another name, a name used by people who spoke of the first settlement at Chisago Lake. New Duvemåla was no more, it was gone and would never be revived. Instead it was now called the Nilsson Settlement.

—2—

THE OAK GROVE to the east of the house still stood, covering about twenty acres of fertile land where crops could grow. For ten years Karl Oskar had had his eye on this piece of ground. Then a mild, suitable autumn arrived which was to be the grove's last; the days of the mighty oaks were numbered.

It had taken the farmer a long time to plan his attack on the oaks; this fall the plan was completed, now he had thought it over long enough. He had figured out how to go about it, how to turn this ground into a tilled field: The giant trees would be pulled up by the roots.

Now with the boys he had sufficient help, and Karl Oskar Nilsson and his four sons approached the grove with their team one early morning. Five men and two horses—the combined strength of men and beasts would fell the old oaks.

They began with one of the largest; they dug a ditch around the tree, four feet deep, and cut the roots. They took away the foothold of the oak. This was the trick to conquer it: Deprive it of its hold. They began down at the root; when the ditch was ready two of the boys climbed up the tree with a heavy iron chain, as high as they could get. They fastened it to the trunk and the father joined it to the pull lines from the team.

Human labor had done its part, now it was the turn of the beasts; the horses would fell the tree. But the oak itself would help, its weight would facilitate its fall.

The farmer picked up the reins and urged his strong team forward which he had followed for years after harrow and plow, wagon and timber sled. Today it was hitched to the heaviest load it had ever pulled, a giant oak which for hundreds of years had stood secure on its roots. Now the old one's footing had been undermined.

The horses obeyed their master and started to pull, concentrating all their strength until their backs straightened out and their legs and loins sank. Their hooves took hold of the ground, turf and rocks flew about, the animals tramped, moved their legs, stretched their sinews. The hooves dug into the earth. The pull lines were extended until it seemed as if they would break, the horses crouched as if ready to bolt, their backs straightened out, their hindquarters sank down. But they did not move from the spot; they stood where they were, tramped the same place. They were hitched to a load that remained stationary.

The driver of the team kept urging it on. The horses pulled again, their hooves threw up turf. This was their life's heaviest load.

Now the oak began to tremble from the force pulling in the chains around its trunk. The enormous crown swayed slowly back and forth. The men could see that the oak was beginning to lean. Once it had started to sway, its motion would soon utilize its weight in making it fall.

The team in its place pulled again, the giant trunk was beginning to give, the lines slackened—they were long enough so the tree would not reach the team in its fall.

The farmer and his sons cried out warnings to one another, the calls echoing back and forth:

"Timber!"

"She's coming!"

"Get away!"

The tree was leaning. A sound like an approaching storm was heard in the air—the tree had started to fall! The giant took one last heavy breath as it sank to the ground. In falling the tree had pulled up its own stump. When the branches hit the earth there was a report like a gunshot. Then the great oak lay still. It had left an empty place in the air above.

The giant was felled, the first one. Five men and two horses had gone to work on the grove—oak after oak fell, each pulling up its roots with its fall. The warning calls sounded: Keep away! She's coming! And heavy and big she came, roaring through the air, falling with a thud, her roots in the air, her crown crushed. In the place where the tree had grown, a ditch opened, deep as a grave. Each fallen oak left room for a piece of fallow field.

It was the autumn of the great oak destruction; death ravaged the grove. The owner and his four sons cleared ground—the farmer was using all the human strength that had grown up in his house. This work by the father and his sons would complete the clearing of this farm. In the evenings, tired and pleased, they looked at the row of oaks they had felled, quietly laid down their tools, and went home.

For more than twenty years Karl Oskar had cleared wild land in America, hoed, plowed, cut. Now he had started with the last piece. He was nearing the end. When the oak grove had been cleared and tilled his farm would be completed.

—3—

THE CLEARING went on through the whole autumn. Karl Oskar hoped to be through before snow fell and the ground froze. And the winter was late this year, as if it wanted to aid him in his work.

It was an evening late in November. Only one oak remained, but one of the largest, a giant, almost six feet thick at arm's height. At the time when this tree was a sapling the farmer's parents had not yet come into the world, nor his grandparents. And when he himself saw the shore of Lake Ki-Chi-Saga for the first time, the oak had reached its full years. It had remained in its place while he felled thousands of trees around it. Now its turn had come: the autumnal storms had swayed its crown for the last time.

It was this oak the farmer was to remember.

The first blue approach of twilight appeared in the sky. The farmer's oldest son said it was late, they were tired, and since this last oak was so big and deeply rooted it would be quite a job getting it down. It would be dark before they were through. Couldn't they leave it till tomorrow?

The farmer replied that since only one single oak remained they would fell it too before they went home. Since it was the last one they must not leave it because of approaching evening. With the felling of this tree they could say they had completed their task. Then they could go home and rest, well satisfied.

He spoke with a father's authority over his children and the four sons obeyed him. None of them uttered a word of complaint.

They went to work eagerly, stimulated by the thought that they were to fell the last oak. They dug the ditch around the trunk, two boys climbed up and fastened the chain to the top, the chain was linked to the team. The horses too were eager, as if feeling this must be the last load of growing trees.

The father picked up the reins and laid them around his neck. He urged the team, the horses caught a foothold in the ground and pulled until the harnesses creaked. But he did not keep his eyes on the team, rather, his eyes followed the movements of the oak crown that swayed behind him. He was always watchful, never forgetting to call out: Timber!

But tonight it was the sons who called out to the father:

"She's coming! Get away!"

The giant oak was not so well rooted as they had thought. As soon as the horses pulled it began to rock and lean.

The thud of its fall could be heard almost in the same second as the warning:

"She's coming! Get away!"

In a wink the father saw the tree coming. He always jumped aside in good time—when he heard the sound in the air he always had time to get away. Now he tried to throw himself aside at the same moment he heard it.

It happened within seconds: The oak was supposed to fall to the right of him, he attempted to run to the left—he who couldn't run! He couldn't get his left leg to move fast enough, he stumbled and fell to his knees. He rose again but never reached an upright position; he took no more steps in his flight from the tree. He had the reins around his neck, the horses were restless and pulled him over.

The farmer fell as if his legs had been cut out from under him; over him fell the oak.

It crashed and thundered as its branches broke and splintered. The team came to a stop, the reins coiling behind as they fell from the master's neck. They had pulled their load, the last one in the grove, their labor was completed, and now they rested.

The roar from the fall died down and silence fell over team and tree, until the sons rushed up and called out: Father!

The last oak of the grove had been felled but under it lay the farmer himself. This mighty tree, waiting here for him while the years had run by—it had been waiting for this November evening when they would fall together.

None of the sons had seen their father stumble and be pulled over by the reins. Now he had vanished; he must be under the fallen tree, the lush branches must be hiding him. They grabbed their axes and started to cut through the branch-work—boughs as big as trunks were separated and rolled away in horrible urgency. The sons were hewing their way to their father. Four axes were swinging and with each cut they were nearing him. Soon they could see his clothing; they saw his boots, heels up; they found his hat, brushed from his head. They worked in silence as they cut their way through the enormous oak. The last branch was like a tree in itself, and it lay across their father's back; he was pressed under it. In its fall the giant had seized the farmer with one of its strongest arms and pressed him against the ground. He was a prisoner of the oak.

The four sons cut their father free, liberated him from the mighty tree's grip. They rolled away the heavy limb that pressed his back and stood around him, axes in hand.

He lay on his stomach, his face against the earth. They bent over him. His legs moved a little, his shoulders rose perceptibly. His boot toes scraped against the ground, but his head lay still. But he moved. He was alive.

The sons had been silent as they worked their way toward the father; now they spoke:

"Father! Are you hurt? Can you talk?"

They received not a word in reply, only a deep breath. But when they took him by the shoulders he stirred again. He tried to turn over; slowly, with its own strength, his body turned on its back. Even his head began to move, and the sons saw a face distorted, barely recognizable. It was not cut, no injury was visible, but great puffs of froth showed in the corners of his mouth; his teeth were bared, in a cramp-like bite; his eyebrows were pulled together at the root of his nose, which was poking up at them, enormous, protuberant, like a knot.

"How did it happen? Are you terribly hurt?"

A hissing sound escaped the mouth of the fallen one. He groaned, his teeth clenched so hard it showed in his cheekbones. It was pain that had changed his face.

He felt his back with his hands and groaned again. Then he began slowly to pull up his knees. He could move both arms and legs.

When the sons had first seen him on his stomach, pressed down under the oak, they had not expected him to move again. And as yet they did not know what had happened to him, as yet he said nothing. He rose slowly to his knees, his facial muscles tightening. Again he felt his back, his hands groping about. But his back seemed to be all right; it could not be broken.

The farmer looked about as if in great confusion. He looked at his sons around him, from one to the other, searching for an answer: Was it really true?

Could he still move? Then he must be alive. He was alive, and no one was more surprised than he.

He looked at the fallen oak beside him. One of its heaviest limbs had pressed upon his back, and now when he looked closer he understood why he was alive; he had fallen into a small hollow. Without this slim depression his body would have been crushed.

If he hadn't fallen into that hollow he would never have risen again. If he had happened to fall a foot to the right or a foot to the left he would have remained fallen. If he had taken one step more before he fell he would have been dead.

The farmer said to his sons who stood there apprehensively that he had had a close call. The bough had almost got him. Only a hairsbreadth and they might have had to carry home a corpse this evening.

They stood silent at the thought. Then they asked about his injuries. Did he want them to carry him home?

The father replied that the oak had given him a sound lash across the back and he did not feel well after it. But he thought he could get home on his own legs. If they took the horses and the tools he would try to walk.

Cautiously he attempted to rise from his kneeling position. He wasn't successful; the attempt caused him such intense pain that everything turned black before his eyes and he felt dizzy. When he tried to move one foot he reeled. He sank down on his knees again.

There was nothing to do but accept the sons' offer.

They made a litter for their father from a few branches of the oak they had felled, tying them together with the reins. It was a clumsy, primitive litter, but it would hold for the short distance home. There were four of them and each could carry a corner.

So this evening the farmer was carried home by his sons after his last full working day.

—4—

For a few months Karl Oskar stayed in bed and put plasters on his injured back. A thick blue-black swelling appeared across the small of his back where the oak had hit him. He rubbed the injured part with different kinds of salves for which he sent to the new drugstore in Center City. Some he also mixed himself and with the aid of neighbors. He tried cotton oil and camphor, sheep-fat, pork, unsalted butter. He had leeches put on the swelling—they sat so close, those nasty sucking critters, that they covered his whole back; they drank his blood and swelled up until they were so fat and thick and round they couldn't suck any more and fell off and died. Rows of itching wounds were left from their sharp bites.

The first weeks in bed he was kept awake through the nights by the pain. It felt like a firebrand in his back. But after repeated applications of leeches the swelling went down, the soreness eased, and the pain abated. He thought the critters had sucked out the evil that caused the pain.

When on that November evening he had heard the oak come down on him so suddenly he had had only one thought: I'm dying! He had time to think of nothing else before he felt the pain and lost his breath. The pressure had been so severe that he was unable to get air into his lungs. His next clear thought had been: Has my back been able to take it? Pressed down under the tree he had felt sure his back was broken.

He had not been stricken as severely as he had expected but he suffered intense pain afterward. He had to stay in bed for a long time. Fortunately it was winter and there was no urgency on the farm. He need not worry about the daily chores; his four sons attended to those.

In time Karl Oskar was up on his legs again. But it was spring before he could go back to work. He began with easier chores, but his back was not the same as before: He had to walk with it bent. As soon as he tried to straighten up, the old pain and ache gave him orders: You aren't able! Don't try to lift!

The following autumn Karl Oskar Nilsson and his sons completed the clearing of the oak grove. They stacked the timber, cleared the ground of stumps and roots, and plowed the field; and the father participated all the time in the work. It was his last clearing, he must see it through. Then his farm would be completed.

His injury was healed but his back was not as strong as before the accident. He walked bent over, he couldn't straighten it, and he was unable to lift heavy objects.

It was evident to him that from now on he would be only half a workman; he could participate in the work, but he couldn't do what he had done before, nor would he ever be able to. The last tree he felled had marked him for the rest of his life.

The farmer and the oak had fallen side by side. He rose again, but not fully. One ability had been taken from him: He could never again walk upright on earth.

—5—

A settler's evening prayer:

Well, God, I guess you think you've got me now! But this is not the way to change me. It was a bad blow I got on my back—now I'm stooping. You're the Almighty, nothing happens without your will. You wanted to hurt my back, to make me suffer from it for the rest of my life. Why? I don't think I sinned in cutting down the oaks. I like to clear fields, and people get their daily bread from those fields. Is that why you reward me? What did you do to my father in his days? He fought the stones for twenty-five years and then a stone made a cripple of him. That too you allowed to happen, so you rewarded him. You took Kristina from me, you tricked her to die. How can a person trust a God who acts that way? How can anyone ask me to trust in the Lord after this? You gave me a mind—I've used it to the best of my ability. But if my sense isn't good enough—is this my fault? Why wasn't I given enough sense? I want to tell you, God: I'll never praise you for what you did to Kristina, for what you've done to me. Never. For I do not accept the injustices you allow to happen. I won't budge. I won't submit. I'll always fight against it. Me you cannot coerce. Never will I ask forgiveness. I know I'm a helpless creature before the Almighty. You can do with me what you wish. But never, never will I say it is just. The oak hit me across the back but it didn't change my mind. If the tree had fallen a foot to the right or to the left I would have lost my life. But it would have made no difference, it would not have changed me in the moment of death. You cannot do anything to change my mind. You've bent my body, God, but not my soul. You can kill me, you can rob me of my breath, but you cannot make me say you're just. You can never bend my soul. Never in eternity. Amen.

XXIII

THE LETTER TO SWEDEN

Nilsson Settlement at Chisago Lake
Minnesota
July 30 1875

Beloved Sister Lydia Karlsson,

May you be well is my daily wish, I have not Written since long ago. But if these Lines find you They are from your Brother in North America.

Changes have taken place since I Last wrote. I want to tell you that last year I left my farm to my Oldest Son, you must remember Johan. He was 4 years of age when we left Sweden. Now he has taken over, the Son picks up where the Father leaves off, the other children are still at home except Harald who has gone to St. Paul to work for the railroad and Frank who Sits in the Timber company's offis in Stillwater.

I am not yet old in Years but worn from wear. And I have broken enough land in America. I work a little every day and do what chores I can, if I don't work my bowels won't move. I am in good circumstances and need not worry about Daily Bread. Everything has gone up after the closing of the War. Money situation is now orderly. Our Farm gives plenty of Crops and we sell our Wheat at high Prices.

Glad you like the Portrait of the House. I have had taken a portrait of myself which I enclose. Not much to Look at, the Years show their wrinkles. And our bodies go downhill when we near old Age. Have you started to use Glasses for the eyes? Is your hair graying?

I wonder if Brother and Sister would recognize each other after all the years gone by?

My thoughts often wander to the Place where I was born and where my kind Parents helped me grow up. Sometimes I think I would like to go back for a Visit. But I could not see Father and Mother in Life, only their Tombstones.

It would be burdensome for me to go back to Sweden. I am accustomed to Freedom in all things, you know. There is much difference between the Old and the new country. Here all are equals; here a man and citizen has a vote whether poor or Rich. It would be another order in Sweden if all knew their rights and had free speaking. The Swedes are obedient to law and good people and need not so many proud officials and useless masters to rule them. You have to pay for King and Palaces and Lords who live for entertainment and theatres. The workers feed those who won't work and this is turned-around Order. Sweden needs a new Government which will not bow to the Royal Crown and Mantle. In North America the President is the People's Crown and we need none other.

You write they say at home times are bad in America, that's only talk invented by the Lords to keep people in that Country. And Ministers and Preachers like to keep their sheep together, if they all go to America there won't be many left to shear. I am glad I left home while my blood was youthful, my emigration I have never regretted for a single moment.

We have a heat of 100 degrees here in Minnesota, it is the American counting called Fahrenheit, it nearly burns in bed at night, it is cooler to sleep on the floor.

My memory begins to fail me in many matters but my Childhood is clearer to me as the years fill up, I can see every place in the village and my childhood home. Is the Post with the Rooster that pointed the Compass still standing in the yard? What became of the rosebush to the front of the House? Do you remember when we played hide and seek around that bush?

I send you a draft for ten dollars, you can buy some thing you wish as my gift. Forgive my Poor writing and don't forget to write to your Brother. Whole years run away between our writings. Only we two are left from our old home, we must not stop letters while we still are in Life.

My wish for Health and all Good.

> Written down by
> Your Devoted Brother
> Karl Oskar Nilsson.

E P I L O G U E

I

THE MAP OF LJUDER

CHARLES O. NELSON, a Swedish-born farmer in Minnesota, was lying quietly on his back in his bed in his house at the Nelson Settlement. It was midday, midweek, at the height of the harvest season. In the fields the crops were ripe, or drying in shocks; innumerable farm chores waited to be done. But they no longer waited for him; he stayed inside, in his bed.

In the evening the laborer takes his ax under his arm or his scythe on his shoulder and goes to his home. Charles O. Nelson was the laborer who had gone home from his work forever.

His bed was turned so he could see through the window and look out over his fields. What were the boys doing today? Were they mowing the wheat? Were they busy with the fallow? He could still perform small chores if they asked him. He could mend a harness, sharpen a plane, put a handle in a hoe or hayfork. But they must be chores he could do in a sitting position. He moved slowly, with much difficulty; he could not move without his stick. The old injury to his left leg had turned into a limp, and pains and aches assailed his back. It was because of the ache that he mostly stayed in bed in the old house, the one he himself had built. But when he built it he had not imagined that he would one day occupy it single and alone.

About a hundred yards away a new white main house had been raised, and there lived the new owner of the farm. It was a fine house, with two stories. It was the house he himself had wanted to build. In his mind he had built it many times, figured out how everything must be. He had placed the doors and windows, put on the roof, separated the space into rooms and closets to the smallest detail. And how many times hadn't he described it to his wife: Next time I build . . . !

But it had not been granted him to raise that house. He had wanted to build it for his wife, and he wanted to occupy it with her. But after he had used some of the planks for her coffin he never did anything more about the house. The piled-up timber was used for other purposes, and at last the boys had built the house, and now there it stood. His sons had grown up, they were men in their best years, yet he never called them anything but the boys.

A new generation had completed his plans—it was John and Dan Nelson who had built the house he had planned. He himself was Old Nelson, the old man, in the old house, lying in his bed and looking out through the window at the men working out there.

Nelson Settlement was known as the oldest place at Chisago Lake, and sometimes curious people came to look at it. Some even wanted to see Old Nelson himself, since he had been the first to settle here. But he did not wish to see people he didn't know; he might admit a neighbor or a friend, but he preferred to be left in peace. And he did not want to be in the way of the young people on the farm. He stayed by himself and followed the life at Nelson Settlement, his old claim, through the window.

The day seems longer to one who has left his work, the hours drag without occupation. In the past when he went to bed he used to plan his work for the following day. He lived through the morrow's chores in advance. But this he need do no longer. He knew what he would do tomorrow, and the day after tomorrow, he knew what he would do on all the following days—the same as today. He would lie here in his bed and watch life on the Nelson Settlement.

If time dragged too much for him inside, he tried to follow what was going on outside. He kept track of what the boys were doing, he participated in their chores: How many bushels of corn had they harvested? How many bushels of wheat had they sown? How many gallons did the maples give? What was the price of pork in St. Paul? What did they get for the potatoes they hauled to Center City? All this concerned him as much as before. This he couldn't give up. But whatever the boys replied to his questions he knew what they meant: It was none of the old man's business.

His past had been filled with activity. Every day had been a measure, running over with work. He had lived for his labor, it had been his lust, his worry. In his old age his concern was that he had nothing to worry about any more.

He had lived and worked one day at a time, and thus the days had fled and gathered into one great, heavy pile: old age. And that pile pressed a person down to the ground. A day came when one was no longer useful, when one lived to no one's joy, when one was only in the way here on earth, an annoyance to oneself.

When his good days of work were over, he became awkward, irresolute, stood there fumbling and helpless as if he had dropped something but hadn't noticed how or when he lost it. He was closed out from the present and had nothing to hope for from the future.

This suddenly came over him one day when his life was near its end.

Charles O. Nelson lifted his head from the pillow and looked out. Loud laughter and mirth echoed from the new building—healthy, young exclamations, cries of joy from children's throats. The little ones were playing among the fruit trees that had been planted round the new house.

Old Nelson's grandchildren were playing in their home at the Nelson Settlement. The laborer who had gone home was lying here listening to still another generation. Their laughter and cries and noise disturbed him, yet the sounds were good to hear. They would not have been heard if he hadn't lived.

Yes, those kids playing there were his grandchildren. His oldest son John and his Irish wife had presented him with four, and his daughter-in-law was carrying a fifth. Two of them were so redheaded one could almost fire kindling with their locks. Who could have imagined that he, the farmer from Småland, would become related to Stephen Bolle, the Irish miller at Taylors Falls. The first time John had seen the girl he was still so Swedish that he was called Johan. That was the time they had been caught in the blizzard and almost lost their lives. Johan had thought the girl, thumbing her nose, looked ugly as a troll. She had made faces at him and stuck out her tongue and he had been afraid of her. But later, when he met the miller's wench after she was grown, she didn't make faces at him but probably something much nicer. Anyway, he went almost crazy if he couldn't see her every week. And when she finally moved in as mistress there was nothing left of the sniveling child at the mill.

Dorothy Bolle became young Mrs. Nelson, not half as angry and irritable a woman as her fire-flamed hair would lead one to believe. She had a mind of her own which both old and young Nelson respected, but father-in-law and daughter-in-law got along well as long as they didn't interfere with each other's business. Nor could they understand more than half of what one said to the other, they couldn't meet through words. And people can't fight if they don't understand each other's invective.

Mary—once known in Sweden as Lill-Marta, later as Marta—had borne him three grandchildren with her husband Klas Albert Persson, the storekeeper in Center City. These three were begotten by Swedish parents, Swedish brats all through, yet they weren't half as lively and clever as the four Johan had with his Irishwoman. Nor were they as good-looking, whatever the reason was. Some people said there weren't better traits than Swedish traits in all the world but they might be mistaken. Those half-Irish brats out there made a hell of a stir and noise, as bad as the Indians in the old days when they camped at the lake. If they couldn't get along in the world no one could.

The third son, Dan, was still single; he had stayed on the farm to help his brother and probably would remain there. But Harald had gone into business in Minneapolis and had married a German girl; he had two children. Old Nelson had met the girl a few times but there weren't many words he could exchange with her, for she mixed German with her English and he used Swedish words. But he felt that this daughter-in-law was a kind, quiet, and capable woman. She was fair, and reminded him in some way of his dead wife.

Frank lived in Chicago and had married an American woman. Frank had not yet helped make him a grandfather. But Ulrika had married a Norwegian farmer in Franconia and she had three kids and was probably carrying a fourth, as far as he could judge last time she was home. This Norwegian son-in-law was bull-headed and difficult. He was stubborn as hell, like most Norwegians. He always bragged that it was the Norwegians who had shot Charles XII.

Old Nelson would soon have a full dozen grandchildren if he counted those on the way. And they were begotten and sprung from the four different races. When the parents came to see him he would always lift up the grandchildren and put them on his knee; he wanted to make sure they were healthy and weighed as much as they should. The children were unlike and spoke differently, but this was not to wonder at: a Swedish father, an Irish mother, a Norwegian father, a German mother. What a mixed group of children they were! No one could guess they belonged to the same family. But they did have something in common: the same grandfather. He was the father's father or the mother's father for all of them. Through Charles O. Nelson, the old one in the old house, these human plants were linked together.

When he emigrated his father had reproached him: You drag my family out of the country. Today he understood better than at that time what his father had meant: You take with you also coming generations and decide their fate; you decide for both the living and the unborn. If Nils Jakob's Son now could have seen the great flock of his great-grandchildren at the Nelson Settlement he might have said: Karl Oskar, you have not only dragged my family out of the country, you have also mixed up my descendants with foreign races. In these brats not much is left of my race.

And the Lord only knew what might come of all this mixture of people with different roots from different lands. Would they form a race of their own? But there was no use speculating about this, he himself would soon be gone. At the most for only a few years he would see his grandchildren play around the house. Already a third generation was shooting up from his root, and soon the world would spin its turn without the originator of this family, without the old one in the old house. Nothing would change when he disappeared. People returned to dust every moment and nothing would change when his turn came.

Charles O. Nelson listened, annoyed and pleased, to the hubbub his grandchildren raised down in the yard. Undoubtedly they were up to something, perhaps ruining the new saplings his boys had planted last spring. He was proud of these new plum and cherry trees, he felt responsible for them in some way. They were tender yet could easily be broken; those kids should get a good spanking if they hurt them.

He could hear his son's woman yell at the children; Stephen Bolle's girl had a strong, piercing voice, but he couldn't understand a word she said, she must be talking Irish. She and Johan shouldn't be so soft with the children.

His own children hadn't entirely forgotten their mother tongue. If they wanted to they could speak it. He reproached himself that he could no longer speak his native language well; when some newcomer arrived from Småland he realized how much he had forgotten. How could a man's tongue change so much that he no longer could use words clearly which he had spoken thousands of times?

He looked up at the old creaking clock on the other wall. Only a quarter past two. Still many hours till evening and blessed sleep. But tonight it would be hard to sleep, the ache was coming alive. For a day or two his back would be all right, and then it would start again. The ache sat like an auger in his back, it had its home there, its designated place which it never left. The auger's sharp, steel edge turned steadily, inexorably. It was drilling a hole in his back, but one that it never finished.

Cartilage had grown between the vertebrae, said the doctors in St. Paul and Stillwater. He had once received a blow across his back from the oak he was felling, and in that place the gristle lumps had grown. None of the doctors' many salves, plasters, and liniments had been able to drive out the pain. He had tried all the remedies known, even those of the old country—lying on cat skins and dog skins, rubbing himself with sheep fat and pork bile, or concoctions of flowers and herbs, moss and ferns. Anything neighbors and friends suggested he would try, but nothing really helped. The auger remained in his back and kept on turning, and would keep on turning as long as he lived.

His backache was the final reward for his labor, for the farmer's toil. He drew his pay daily in his old age, the sure reward for the oldster.

Charles O. Nelson moved a little in his bed, made his back more comfortable, turned and twisted a little to escape the auger. It hurt most in the afternoons, by evening it eased a little, and then he would walk about over the farm. This was an old habit, to inspect the Nelson Settlement before he retired for the night. At day's end the old farmer walked to the houses that had been his, saw to it that every door was closed, everything put inside that might suffer from a change in the weather, that the animals were well, that all things— living and dead—were in good keeping. This was a farmer's daily chore, and he had performed it through the years. Now, as he walked about and saw that all was well, he felt he was still the master of the Nelson Settlement.

The evening inspection would take quite a while for old Charles O. Nelson. His limp made him move slowly, he had to lean on his stick each time he moved his left foot. He took one long step with the healthy leg and two short with the injured one. He walked with bent back, he limped; shuffling along he found his way. It was a great effort for him and when he returned to his room he was completely exhausted. But it was his best hour of the day.

Today he was waiting for that hour, and he had an occupation that helped speed the time. He sat up in bed and pulled out a drawer in the table beside him. He picked up a large folded paper and began to unfold it, slowly, methodically, as if in so doing he would cheat the pain.

It was a map of Ljuder parish. It was his home district that was spread before him here on the blanket. Charles O. Nelson always had the map handy, was always eager to look at the thick, heavy paper with a miniature of his home village. Many years ago he had acquired this map from his son-in-law, Mr. C. A. Persson, "in exchange for his daughter" as he called it. He had lost his oldest daughter but he had received instead a map of his home village.

The map of Ljuder during the years had become worn from frequent handling by the old emigrant. It was made of good paper, but he had fingered it so often and turned and opened it, that it was wrinkled and barely held together at the creases. That was why he handled it so carefully.

Here before him he had his whole home parish with well-marked borders, from Lake Laen in the north to Lake Loften in the south. Across this paper his index finger found the markings, followed the roads he once had walked, stopped at places he knew well, familiar names of farms and cottages. Here was the crossroads where he had danced in his youth, the grove where they had celebrated sunrise picnics, wastelands where he had hunted, lakes, rivers, and brooks where he had fished. He followed lines and curves, he stopped at squares and triangles. There was so much to look for, so much to find. And at each place where his finger stopped his memories awakened: This was his childhood and youth.

How many times hadn't his fingers wandered over this map. But he was never through with it. Each day he started his search anew. When he had found everything he was looking for, he began all over again. He had been thumbing and reading the map of Ljuder day in, day out, at night with the help of his oil lamp, when the ache assailed him, when sleep fled his bed, weekdays and holidays, summer and winter, year after year, until the thick paper was worn thin from all the thumbing and was ready to fall apart.

The map of Ljuder, spread over the blanket before him, had the shape of a heart. Somewhere near the center of that heart lay a farm where the old emigrant had taken his first steps on earth.

The old man in the bed was shut out from the present and had nothing to expect from the future. To him remained only the past. Again he found the paths of his childhood. Charles O. Nelson, Swedish-born farmer in Minnesota, was old, lame, and stooped, and moved with difficulty over the ground of his new homeland. But here in his bed he walked freely and unencumbered over the roads of his native village.

MAP

of

Ljuder Parish, executed 1847–49

by

Frans Adolf Lönegren, Official Surveyor

———————————

The map was well drawn and colors had been freely used. Lakes, brooks, fields, meadows, hills, groves, moors, bogs—each had its own color. The lakes' surfaces glittered blue, like large ink spots, while smaller ponds and pools were only specks. Rivers and brooks showed their blue veins across the white skin of the paper. Meadows blossomed in green like fresh spring grass, and tilled fields were as yellow as buttercups in bloom. Hills and wastelands lay black, almost like dirty thumbprints. The pine forest was indicated by narrow black lines, like pine needles, and the deciduous forest with light rings, resembling the crowns of lush trees. In the meadows the surveyor had placed men with scythes, and in the wastelands horses, oxen, cows, and sheep grazed. Moors and bogs were gray stripes across the paper, almost like a splash of mud. Every-thing was there, everything was recognizable to the old one in the bed.

It was a well-illustrated map—he almost smelled the ripe crops, the pungent pine pitch, the sweet birch leaves, fresh milk, sheep wool, bog myrtle, meadow flowers.

The fat, red line across the map was the county road through the parish; vil-lage roads were marked in smaller lines of the same color, even paths, disap-pearing in the wastelands. The borders of farms were marked in red, each place was there, even the bridges, the cornerstones, the rights-of-way. Everything had its proper name in the right place, and the old emigrant found and recog-nized everything; he was again Karl Oskar of Korpamoen, strolling over his na-tive ground.

The timber road through the pine forest, used only in winter, led all the way to Lake Loften. When the birches were just in leaf he had run barefoot on that road to fish in the lake, where the carp played in schools in the shallow bays, their yellow scales glittering in the sun as he pulled them out. From an alder bush he had cut a fork on which he hung the fish through the gills, and he could feel them dangling on his back as he carried them home, proud and whistling. Dried strips of bark in the ruts, from the winter timbering, scratched against his bare feet; some ruts were still moist and cool, sending shivers up his back. But he carried the glittering burden of carp, he was on the right road for a boy in spring; he was walking the barefoot path, the softest, the easiest path in the world.

He took a side road through the dark forest and came to a pool, all in shadow under the tall pines. The pool water was black-brown, the surface mo-tionless. The ground swayed under his feet as he walked along the muddy edge. If you sank down here you would never get up again! He jumped in— the pool was bottomless. He would feel cold and shiver for hours after a swim in the ice-cold water. In that pool he had baited his hook for eel with white worms from the dunghill, and the fat, greenish eels he had pulled out were so old they almost had moss on them. Once he had caught a pike, and he had had to kill it with a stone it was so big—eight pounds it weighed, at least. So well did he remember the pool that he almost felt the chill vapor that always hung over it.

He continued on a road through a clearing to the sheep meadow, but first he had to climb two fences, which he did very easily by placing his hands on the top rail and swinging over it in one leap. It was fun to jump fences and stiles that way, but it was no sport for lame, aching old farmers.

Near the stile was the rabbit run, the finest in the village; he was always sure to get a rabbit there. On clear mornings in the fall, after the first frost-glitter on the grass, he would stand at this stile with his gun, waiting. He could hear the dogs pursuing the rabbit across yellow fields and through the underbrush until the sound echoed against the cliffs. This was the wonderful morning song of the forest, the sound of adventure to the boy, who stood motionless, tense, waiting for the rabbit to come along the fence toward the stile. He held the gun cock with his thumb—in a moment it would happen! The gossamer over bushes and branches glittered in the sun and the ground smelled of healthy autumn frost.

The boy had discovered the rabbit run at the stile by himself. And now the old man sought for it on the map and found it, and many other places that belonged to the time when he moved easily on the earth. His finger on the map was sure to find them.

There was Åkerby Junction, on the county road, where boys and girls met on Saturday evenings and danced under the open sky, and where those not yet men or women fumbled for each other in childish shyness. There were the crossroads, shortcuts, hidden, narrow paths where youth sought its way, and where he once had swung himself over gates and stiles. And of everything he had rediscovered on his village map he could say: Here I was rich and well pleased with my life. Of what use are my poor days now?

Charles O. Nelson adjusted the pillow behind his head. The auger of pain gnawed and dug into his back. An hour of pain had passed while he thumbed the old map. It was not a violent pain he suffered, but it was persistent, it never left him, it stayed where it once had lodged itself. On this he could rely: It would stay with him, for sure, as long as he lived.

But it was no danger to life: He would not die from his backache. Some people took a long time to die. Their strength ebbed but not their life. They kept on dying, day after day, through many years. They became useless, and lived to no one's joy, least of all their own. But they were not allowed to die. They died stubbornly, through the long years, with plenty of time to stroll through old places.

A person ought to die when he becomes useless and not worthwhile any longer.

The old farmer folded the map and put it aside. He looked out through the window, up toward the sky, wondering if the good harvest weather would last.

They had grown fine wheat this year, tall, heavy sheaves, shocked out there as far as his eyes could see. Now if they could only get it in all right.

Sometimes heavy rains fell in Minnesota this time of year. Once it had rained so violently that half his crop washed away.

Now he saw that the sky was cloud-free as far as he could see from this side of the house, and perhaps the dry weather would hold. But everything changed so quickly in America, here no signs were to be relied on. When the sunset was clear in Sweden you could count on fine weather the following day, and when the sun set in a cloudbank you were sure of rain. But that didn't hold true here, perhaps because America was on the other side of the globe.

With his eyes and ears he followed as much as he could of what happened outside. As far as he was able to, the old one took part in the young people's life.

He saw his sons leave the field and go into their house; he raised his head and looked after them. The Irish wench usually had coffee and sandwiches for the boys about this time in the afternoon. But he couldn't see the grandchildren, they had left the garden; now he heard them down at the lake, where they were playing and carrying on.

He tried to keep track of those brats, for some reason; he wanted to know where they were and what they were doing. If he didn't hear their howling or shouts for a while he began to worry.

The auger kept drilling, today his ache didn't give up for a second. Today he certainly received his full pay, his reward for toil and struggle. This was his pay for clearing forty acres of land in America. And much was still due him, many days' pay; he didn't doubt he would be paid in full.

But then again there would be days when he didn't feel it, and those were good days. As yet he could take care of himself, he required no help. He cooked his own food and washed his own dishes and kept his room clean. His daughter-in-law helped him with the laundry and the worst scrubbing, and the grandchildren ran errands if he needed anything. And occasionally an old neighbor dropped in; such changes were good. He didn't do much visiting himself, hardly ever left the Nelson Settlement. It was now several years since he had gone as far as St. Paul. But he remembered well that last time, for he had been with Harald and they had seen a panorama in a tent outside Fort Snelling for twenty-five cents. It was perhaps the most remarkable thing he had seen in all his life.

The panorama was painted on long sheets of sailcloth, ten feet tall, and a man explained what the pictures meant. There was a battlefield of the Civil

War—bloody bodies all cut in pieces, fallen soldiers lying across each other, long rows of corpses piled like firewood. It made him feel as if the war itself was in his throat, he had a nauseating taste of blood as he looked at those pictures.

They had also been shown how the Southern rebels had tortured their prisoners: They pushed the Union flag into the mouth of the Northerners: Men who fought for the Union ought to be made to swallow their flag! If the victims choked or lost consciousness, cold water was poured over them to revive them.

The panorama was remarkable, yet repulsive.

If Old Abe had lived and remained in the presidential chair he would surely have forbidden fools to travel about and show such bloody, cruel pictures. The settlers' own President meant the South and the North to be friends again as soon as the war was over, to live as brothers in the Union. Those who raked up the old dried-up blood from the battlefields and put it on sailcloth to show for money, such people were fostering new hatred. Jesters who made money from spilled blood ought to be flogged thoroughly. They weren't any better than grave robbers. But people did exist who would sell human flesh if they could gain a quarter by it.

There was also another panorama that he liked better: The Mississippi River was shown in its full length on the sailcloth, from the falls at St. Anthony, now called Minneapolis, all the way to the Mexican Gulf. A clever painter had traveled on a raft all the distance to New Orleans and while he floated along he had depicted the beautiful shores on a roll of sailcloth, and here in the panorama tent one could see the great water in all its majesty. Looking at it was exactly like traveling on this river through the heart of America.

The old man would never make that journey in reality, indeed, he might never make any more journeys; not even to St. Paul, if another panorama should come again, it was too difficult for him to move about.

The old settler moved again in his bed, sought a place for his back where the auger might ease its work a little. Sometimes it was better when he stretched out on his back, other times on his left or right side. He never knew in which position he could best escape that torture tool.

But today he could find no escape, no comfortable position. And that was why he picked up the map, to wander those paths he never more would see, to return to the places of his past.

He had once moved from one continent to another. He had once been Karl Oskar Nilsson, at New Duvemåla. How many years ago was that? Now he was the old man at the Nelson Settlement, and only one last move remained for him—from one world to another.

Charles O. Nelson from Ljuder in Sweden would die here in America, he would die on the Nelson Settlement, in this house, in this room, in the bed where he now lay.

Seeking to escape his merciless torturer, his finger moved again over the old map, back and forth, up and down. It found the red county road and stopped at a crossing.

Here a group of people had met one cold April morning—several drivers, with heavy loads, men, women, and children; altogether sixteen of them. Their wagons had been loaded with baskets and bundles, sacks and satchels, like a gypsy pack, as they rolled south to Karlshamn. Those people were to travel a long road, they were leaving their homes for the last time, and he was one among them.

It had frosted over during the night, the ruts were icy and creaked and crunched under the wheels. People looked through the windows at the travelers. He is sitting on the front wagon, looking at this village for the last time. He looks carefully, searching for details, he wants to remember this place and that, for they were part of his childhood and youth; this is a farewell drive.

And now he is back in this village again, the map in his hands comes to life, filled with people and animals; he remembers who lived in each house, the cattle of each field. The mowers swing their scythes, the women their rakes, the hayricks rock on the narrow roads and leave tufts in branches and bushes along the wayside. He can hear the cowbells tinkle from the wastelands, he can hear sounds of busy tools in the houses and outside; scythes singing against grindstones, axes clanging against wood, flails against the barn floor, spinning and spooling wheels in cottages and kitchens.

Then he sees her and he recognizes her at once.

She is seventeen and she is busy at a spindle. She has flaxen hair and kind eyes, rose-hued cheeks, and a few freckles on her nose, like wild strawberries not yet ripe. He has met that girl before and never has been able to keep his eyes off her. She is very shy, she blushes when she turns toward him. He doesn't want to embarrass her but he can't help it! He looks at her again and she turns peony-red.

Now he has found the Klinta fair. Here he had agreed to meet the girl of the spindle. For two springs and one autumn he meets her here.

And where is the road that leads to another village, the road he has tramped so many times, walked so willingly through the nights? A long road, but short to him, shorter each time he walks it, he knows it so well, every curve, every hill, every gate. He walks it with easy feet, he runs when late, in a hurry. He is on his way to a gate before a house in a neighboring village, there she'll be waiting, in a light-blue shawl; she has promised to wait if he's delayed.

He searches for that road on the map, he knows he'll find it, the road to the woman who will be his wife . . .

Nowadays he goes to the cemetery, a few times each year, to visit her. In summer the road is easy; in winter he must stay home.

He had been to visit her a few days ago. Johan had an errand in that direction and he used the opportunity to ride along. The August day had been just right, not too warm; later in the evening it rained.

Before he journeyed to Kristina he washed and dressed with special care. He shaved and combed his hair just right. He put on a clean shirt and his Sunday-best suit, a starched collar. And he shined his boots. It took him a long time to get ready, what with his stiff back and lame leg. But he prepared himself as if he were going to a wedding or some important gathering.

It was barely two miles to the Swedish cemetery, only half an hour with the team.

Charles O. Nelson was usually alone when he visited his wife, and he was alone this time also. He climbed off the wagon outside the cemetery gate; Johan would pick him up after a couple of hours.

It was a calm day. The sun warmed but did not burn. It was shady and cool under the trees in that place set aside for the dead. A new fence had been put up, good-looking, rails stripped of bark glittered clean and white around the home of the dead.

Leaning on the stick in his right hand he limped up to the gate, opened it, and walked inside. Above the entrance a white-painted board had been put up, with an inscription in black:

Blessed are those who here sleep.
Eternal Peace is Death's Gift.

Each time he came to the gate he would stop and read the inscription, as if wishing to assure himself that not a letter had been changed since last time.

The cemetery sloped toward the shore cliffs and below them the sky-blue lake began. On three sides this little peninsula was washed by the lake water. Stately, lush silver maples shaded this last resting place, a joy to the eye on a summer day like this.

Charles O. Nelson, leaning on his stick, slowly shuffled his way along the path between the graves. No other visitor was in sight today. He knew this place well, it was a long time since he had buried his wife here, and he recognized everything. The graves lay in straight rows, some with fresh flowers, others neglected, overgrown with weeds; others again had dry, withered flowers in overturned pitchers or ordinary drinking glasses; on some not even weeds grew.

He had once been among those who selected this place as the burial ground of the Swedish parish. Four of them had gone out a morning in June to choose a plot suitable for the dead. They had come onto this little promontory at the old Indian lake, Ki-Chi-Saga, and had sat down to rest under the silver maples. They did not have to seek any further; their mission was accomplished.

Three of the four now had their graves in this place, three had been lowered into the ground they themselves had chosen as their last resting place. But the fourth was still alive, walking here between the graves. He moved with great effort, he took one long right step and two short left ones. Surely no one moved more slowly over the earth than the fourth man who today visited here.

The first years very few graves had been dug. The immigrants were mostly young people, the greater part of their lives before them. Yet, the very first grave had been opened for a young person, Robert Nilsson, aged twenty-two. But the years ran by, time did its work, the parish members grew old and the hour of death caught up with them. By and by the rows of graves grew longer.

Here lay all those who were older than Karl Oskar at the time of their emigration, and many of his own age group had already moved here. He recognized the mounds. The longest life had been granted to Fina-Kajsa, but she had been old when she arrived in America. Jonas Petter had been almost fifty when they came and had lived to a great age. Only a few years ago had his grave been dug; it was still the last to have been opened for one of his Old Country friends.

The dead had been laid in their coffins, their faces toward the east, toward the rising sun, for it was in the eastern sky that Christ would come on the day of resurrection. Their faces must be turned toward their Redeemer so their eyes could see him at once.

Karl Oskar stopped, resting his left leg as he leaned on the stick, blinking in the sun. Kristina's grave was a few hundred paces from the gate, he would soon be there—about thirty more steps. He could already see the cross he had raised over it. The grave was halfway down the slope under a wide-spreading silver maple.

At a distance of a few paces he stopped and read the words he had carved in the oak cross:

HERE RESTS
KRISTINA JOHANSDOTTER
Wife of Karl Oskar Nilsson
Born at Duvemåla, Sweden 1825
Died in North America 1862
WE MEET AGAIN

On the grave he had planted sweet williams, blue doves, and marigolds, some of the flowers Kristina herself had planted at Korpamoen in Sweden. He tried to keep the grave well attended but weeds were sticking up among the flowers and he bent down to pull them.

The pain cut through his back, and he stiffened at once. He was unable to raise himself. This happened frequently. Slowly, cautiously, he sat down in the grass beside the grave. He must sit a few moments until the pain eased.

Around him the world was silent. A faint sighing in the maple crown above Kristina's grave, like calm, quiet breathing. The blades of grass bent gently in the soft wind, rose as gently again. Down on the lake, below the cliffs, a flock of ducklings played swing on the waves; the eternal motion of the water; the waves broke against the cliffs, were diffused, and glided back into the lake, returned again to wash the same stones. They moved as they had done since the beginning of time.

Not so for a human being; he did not move as easily today as yesterday. To lie in the earth, or crawl over it—which was preferable? When he entered the cemetery gate he had read the words above it, the promise they held out for him, the gift of peace. He wanted so much to believe that this good promise had been fulfilled for all those who were buried here, that it would be fulfilled for him too. This was his wish every day: Afterward no more suffering.

Karl Oskar sat in the grass at his wife's grave, listening to the rustling in the silver maples, to the ceaseless purl of the lake surf. Here was a good, peaceful place. Toil and strife were ended for those having their abode here. Nothing more could happen to them.

Nothing more could happen to Kristina.

While alive she had felt and understood something he could not feel and understand: She believed fully they would meet after death. She spoke of it many times the last spring she was alive. Then everything would be as before between them. But perhaps she had sensed her time would not be long. One night, after they had enjoyed each other, she had said to him: I don't want to be alone in eternity. I pray to God we'll meet afterward. We will meet again. When we can't die any more.

<h2 style="text-align:center">WE MEET AGAIN</h2>

With his own hand he had carved those words in the oak cross. He had put them there because he knew Kristina wanted it. After all, they were her own words. She had said them to him, he had inscribed them as he remembered them. It was Kristina herself who had written over her grave the words of meeting.

She had been so afraid they wouldn't meet afterward that she had been concerned about his eternal salvation.

But how was it after death? What had God prepared? What was His plan for the human beings he had created? No one could answer that question for sure, no one could know for sure about any life except this one. Karl Oskar understood neither the eternal bliss of heaven nor the eternal suffering of hell. His understanding was not sufficient.

But it was good to sit here and read those three words on the cross, Kristina's own words. Then he could also hear them from her mouth. Those, or others with the same meaning. She was not in doubt, or hesitant, when she said: We meet again. She was sure, she was convinced they would meet in a life that had no ending.

Perhaps. Perhaps there was a life afterward where they could be together. Another kind of life, not comprehensible to human understanding; perhaps one must die in order to understand it. He did not know. But neither could he deny it; if he denied it he would also have to be sure.

When we can't die any more. To Kristina eternity was only permanent rest. And she had been so tired the last years of her life; nothing had helped her against that.

Kristina had surrendered herself to God and humbly resigned herself to her fate. But that he had never been able to do, nor would he ever. And it didn't matter. God treated him anyway as he saw fit—and what could he do about it? The Almighty had bent his back, made his body stoop to the earth, filled him with pains and aches, made a lame wretch of him. But why should he resign himself to this and say it suited him? No, he would always make one more try. A human being was indeed helpless, but he need not resign himself to this, he must always try to live as if he could be of some help to himself.

There had been times when he had been close to giving up. That morning on the *Charlotta*, when Kristina . . . But after that they had lived many years together. And during that time a devoted woman with a good heart had shared his days of toil and his nights of rest, all the joys of youth and health. A better lot a couple could not be granted perhaps. Why must he ask for more? Why wasn't he satisfied and resigned to the fact that the joys of life were over and would never return? So terribly difficult was it to reconcile oneself to the fact that life was over.

Where did it now belong, his old, worn-out, useless body? It would arrive at this place, that much was certain. Beside his wife's grave he had reserved enough space for his own resting place; here he would be buried. He was sitting on his own grave. His body would rot and disintegrate beside Kristina's, in the same earth where she had turned to dust. At least this much was sure: *Here* they would both meet. That much he knew: The wide silver maple would shade them both. And then nothing more could happen to him either.

Down at the lake the surf played against the cliffs, sank down, and returned. It had done so as long as this water had existed, and would do so as long as it would exist. And this motion without ending was to him like generations growing up and dying. What was the purpose of this repetition—to come and go, to live and die? Why must this happen? Of what use was it?

Like the fading smoke of a dying fire, so seemed to him his days gone by, the good as well as the bad. His body had stiffened in old age's cold, was withering like the leaves in autumn. Perhaps at last the leaf resigned itself to falling. But it bothered him that he must leave this life without knowing its purpose. In that way it was a disappointment to die.

Karl Oskar sat beside his wife's grave for a couple of hours. When at last he rose to return home it seemed to him the cross on the grave had started to lean a little. He looked closer; indeed, it was leaning. It was almost twenty-five years since he had put it up, and in that time the ground might change and sink a little. No post in the earth would remain exactly in the same position for that length of time.

He took hold of the cross with both hands. It wasn't leaning much, only a few inches, but it looked bad on a grave. After he had straightened it he took a few steps back and looked. As far as his eyes could see, the cross stood straight now. Next time he came to the cemetery he would bring a spade and put some support against it.

A last searching look over the grave, then he turned and walked up the path. He took one long step with his healthy leg and two short with the other; he limped back the same way he had come.

The fourth and last of the men who had selected this place returned to live the life still remaining to him.

Charles O. Nelson, the old farmer in the old house, was in his bed while the slow drip of the seconds and the minutes filled his roomy bowl of pain, his long hour of ache. It was persistent today, the auger. He turned a little, tried another position, first on the right side, then on the left; he lay with his legs pulled up, with his legs stretched out. It was the same however he turned and tried, today it made no difference.

Through his window he looked at the big field of wheat in shocks; beyond, toward the forest, they had planted corn which stood tall and straight. The crops he saw from his window would make many loaves of bread, would feed many hungry people. Those crops would not have grown there if he hadn't lived. Crops would continue to grow out of the earth after he had been buried in it. It was his hands that had changed this piece of ground, and as he thought of all the crops that would be harvested after he was gone, he was well pleased.

But there was little honor in breaking land and tilling fields. Honor was reserved for those who wielded the sword, the gun, or the cannon—not for a man using ax and plow, the implements of peaceful labor. Felling trees and turning turf was for simple folk, but a dirty occupation for lords and masters.

The old man looked out on the farm he had wrested from the wilderness: He had not been able to accomplish fully what he had set out to do. The big main house, the crown of his work, he had not been able to build. He had used some of the lumber for a coffin, and after that he couldn't build anything more. The boys had put up the house instead. His workday had been cut short, he had been carried home by his sons on a litter of oak branches, and they had finished the work. There must be others besides him who had been forced to stop too early.

At the gable near his window grew an apple tree, an Astrakhan tree, which blossomed every spring and bore fruit every fall. It was an old tree now but still youthfully green, a pride to the old house with its laden boughs and abundance of fruit. Now at the end of summer the fruit was ripe; the ground under the tree was covered with big, yellow-white apples, their skin transparently clear.

Fallen Astrakhan apples didn't keep long, he must hurry and gather them. Tomorrow morning he would find a basket and pick them. It was quite remarkable all the fruit that came from that tree, year after year, and now it must be quite old. It was a tree that had grown from a seed from Sweden which blossomed and bore fruit at the Nelson Settlement.

Sweden, the old homeland—well. Perhaps he should have taken one of the new steamers and gone over to see it once more while he still was able to move about. Now it was too late. There was nothing to do about that. Old Charles O. Nelson had to be satisfied with his map of Ljuder.

Here he found all the roads he once had walked. Here ran the county road from Åkerby to the neighboring village of Algutsboda. That road he had walked many times that spring and summer when he had courted Kristina Johansdotter in Duvemåla.

It was a good distance from Korpamoen to Duvemåla, a whole Swedish mile, almost six of the American miles. But he had walked with light steps and never thought of the distance. One spring and summer he had walked that road twice a week: Saturday evening to Duvemåla, Sunday morning back to Korpamoen. His fingers followed the red line across the map. He would never lose his way on that road; he knew it better than any road he had ever walked. There was Sjubonale—the Seven-Farmers village—with an old-fashioned gate made of birch wattles. When he had passed that gate he was almost there, the next farm was Duvemåla. He did not go all the way to the house, he must not be seen by anyone on the farm. He must wait under the huge mountain ash if he should be first. But he knew in advance he never had to wait: In the lingering twilight he could see her light-blue shawl at the garden gate from a long distance.

The old people hadn't gone to bed yet, it was too early to go with her to her room. They walked down the meadow, through a birch grove; at this time of day they never met anyone here. They walked with their arms around each other but they did not say much. What she wanted to know he had already said many times, and what he wanted to know she had said as often. Yet it happened that they repeated it, not to help each other remember, but only because they wanted to hear it again.

Tonight it was light in the Duvemåla meadows; they could see the lilies of the valley under the birches, where the birds still chirped—they were always noisiest right after sunset in May. They walked all the way to the edge of the bog, and then they walked back to the house and now it was silent. They stole in through the kitchen without a sound, she leading him by the hand to her room, now and then stopping to put her fingers on her lips and whispering: Quiet!

Then he lay down on the bed beside her, both with their clothes on: they were engaged and one could sleep with one's fiancée on "promise and honor." But their hands caressed and petted, a girl's fingers stroked the youth's neck, the youth found the girl's braids. Sometimes they trembled as they caressed and their breathing became faster.

They kissed until they were tired and out of breath. But they knew how far their caresses could go, and no further. They must not get closer before the wedding night. She was a virgin and would remain so until they were married. His honor demanded that he leave her intact, and hers that she be left so.

Both had just entered their youth. He would be of age this year, she was eighteen. They wouldn't lose anything by waiting. Everything awaits those who are in the beginning of their youth.

But their caresses were insufficient for their growing desire. Each night they were together in her room they felt less satisfied with it, and at last their caresses grew painful to their aroused bodies. But as they waited expectation also grew, and it was delicious thus slowly to prepare for what would happen later, all that which they had denied themselves.

Her breath flowed hot as it entered his ear and her lips whispered: I wish something . . . That it soon were . . . And that was just what he wished. That it soon were. He replied when his mouth was on hers, she with the heat from hers.

When daylight began to break he remembered the long way home and rose to leave. Then Kristina stretched out her arms toward him: Stay a little longer! Don't go! Just a few minutes more!

He did as she asked him. He returned to her arms, he stayed.

He would stay only a short moment, but it became a long moment. It was daylight outside the window, the sun was up, and he remained. But at last he must go. Nor did she wish him to be there when her parents got up.

But they would not part yet, she would walk a bit of the road with him. Sjubonale gate was their parting spot, farther he could not coax her. Their farewell took time, it was prolonged even though the sun was high in the heavens and people were coming out to attend to their cattle and do the morning chores. Leaning against the gatepost they would kiss and kiss until their breath gave out. It was so when lovers parted.

But at last he was alone again, on the six-mile road home. He hadn't slept a wink, he had been lying awake in a girl's room, in his hands he still retained the warmth of her skin, in his mouth he still had the fragrance of her breath. The clear morning air he inhaled was cool with dew and fresh birch leaves. He did not feel tired; after his walk he could have gone right to his work. He worked six days, and in the evening of the sixth he went to see the girl in the blue shawl who waited for him at her parents' gate. So it was week after week; what had happened this night would happen again and again.

Karl Oskar and Kristina waited and while they waited their expectation increased. They were happy to be alive.

He walked to her in daylight and on dark nights; the seasons changed with the year's turn.

Then a day came when he didn't have to walk the road: The both of them sat together on a spring wagon and drove to the church, followed by other wagons, filled with their wedding guests. They stood together at the altar, arm in arm, a bridal couple. Once during the ceremony he felt her arm tremble. He wondered about it and asked her afterward: Why did your arm tremble at the altar? She replied: I thought—suppose we had to part and couldn't do anything about it—that was the reason. He said that up to now they had had to part every Sunday morning, but it would not be so in the future. From now on they would never part. She was his wife and they were joined for life.

After their marriage they settled in Korpamoen, his parental home, until they emigrated to America to settle a second time. And in that country he had sat beside her bed on an August morning just as the sun rose and listened anxiously for her breathing. And he had prayed to her: Don't die away from me! Stay with me still a little longer!

She had not stayed.

The day was done, the sun had set, and under the vaulted heavens Ki-Chi-Saga's water grew dark.

Charles O. Nelson, the old man in the old house, pushed away the pillows from his aching back, rose slowly, awkwardly, from his bed. It was time for his evening walk over the farm, while there was still enough daylight.

His movements were stiff, he straightened his back with effort, pulled on his pants and socks, found his coat and stick, and shuffled out on the stoop. There stood his wooden shoes waiting for his feet. He bent down and turned them over, emptying out a few pebbles, and knocked the heels against the floorboards before he stuck his feet in them. The smallest grain of sand or dirt irritated the feet of one who walked so poorly. Then he straightened up, looked in all directions, examined the sky.

What kind of weather would they have tomorrow? Back over the pine forest, where the sun had just set, high, thick clouds were towering. The sun had set in clouds tonight, it must mean a change in the weather. And from the clouds pillars of light poked right down into the lake, like spears: The clouds sucked rain. That sign meant rain tomorrow.

And all the fine crop of wheat was still out. For eight days now it had been standing in shocks, and the sun had shone every day; the wheat must be dry by now. He had thought the boys would get it in today, but not a shock had left the field. Instead they had worked on the fallow for the winter rye—there was no hurry with that. The wheat was more urgent. The boys knew what terrible rains they could expect this time of year.

He would go a bit into the field and make sure the sheaves were dry. Then he would tell his boys they must start in the morning, if it didn't rain.

Right above him light, feathery clouds scurried eastward while the sky darkened to the west. To the south, across the lake, the sky glowed like fire; that too meant a change in the weather.

The day silenced its sounds and blew out its light. But as yet twilight lingered over the wide field that sloped toward the lake. Tall and broad rose the shocks with the full sheaves that had grown this year on the oldest farm at Chisago Lake. The last reflected rays played and glittered on the full, heavy heads.

The farmer was out for his night watch, to see that all was well. He shuffled down the steps of the stoop, leaned on his stick. The wooden shoes clanged against the boards. He must be careful and not step too heavily on his lame leg. With some difficulty he reached the ground; now it would be easier. He took one long step with his good leg, dragging the other a little until he got going.

Thus limping and shuffling Charles O. Nelson began his evening walk over the Nelson Settlement.

II

THE LAST LETTER HOME

Chisago Lake Settlement
Center City Minnesota
December 20 1890

Missis Lydia Karlsson
Åkerby in Ljuder Parish
Sweden

Being an old neighbor to your Brother Charles he has on several occasions asked me to write to his Sister in Sweden and let her know when he died. No one else could do this for the reason that your Brother's children have forgotten Swedish and write English and this might cause trouble for his relatives to read. Therefore I promised to write.

Speaking for his Children I wish to advise you that your Brother Charles O. Nelson came to the end of his life the 7th of this month in the Evening. At half past eight he was up and took his supper and washed Himself. Then he went to bed and at eleven o'clock his soul was liberated. He went to sleep peacefully, no one expected his time to be so near.

Your Brother's Birthday was October 31. His life lasted 67 years, one month, and seven days. He had lived on this place since Anno 1850. Exactly 40 years ago he came from Sverige and we have been neighbors since Anno 1872.

Your Brother was brought to his last resting place the 15th of December. Many were gathered, 6 children, 4 Sons and 2 Daughters and Sons-in-law and daughters-in-law and Grandchildren and Neighbors were also there. The Funeral text was David Psalm 15, the verse that speaks of "He that walketh uprightly, and worketh righteousness, and speaketh the truth in his heart, he shall never be moved in Eternity."

Nelson is regretted and missed much because he was a Man of Order and Just. He had much concern for Children and Grandchildren. He has also fulfilled his obligations rightly and with good sense and no one can step forth and blame him. I visited with him the evening before he left. He had told me many times he was ready to Die.

With those lines I have fulfilled my Promise to my neighbor while He was in Life that I would write and notify His Sister. Your Brother often spoke of you. I send the letter to the Address he gave me and would be grateful if you will let me know that it reaches you.

I apologize that my writing is so poor and disjointed. I am full of years and my hands tremble so it is hard to write. I am the oldest of 10 brothers and Sisters. All except me have forded the River Jordan, 3 rest in Swedish ground, 6 in America's. I was the oldest and now I have been left to the last. I will be 80 next March if the Lord lets me live that long. I am ready when He wants to call me home to Him.

Your Brother Nelson's family who are close blood relations to you all send their heartfelt greetings to you. I am an unknown Stranger in North America writing these Lines to you, I reach you my hand in Friendship and Wish you Well.

Over my Old Native Land I call down at last Lord God's Blessing and Eternal Peace.

    With Respect
    Axel J. Andersson.